NOT BY FORCE BUT BY GOOD WILL

Enjoy your escape into the 4th Century!

Hannah Bonsey Suthers

NOT BY FORCE BUT BY GOOD WILL

The Odyssey of a Runaway Slave At the Time of Constantine the Great

A Novel by

Hannah Bonsey Suthers

Library of Congress Control Number:		2005911428
ISBN 10:	Hardcover	1-4257-0632-0
	Softcover	1-4257-0631-2
ISBN 13:	Hardcover	978-1-4257-0632-6
	Softcover	978-1-4257-0631-9

This book was printed in the United States of America.

To order additional copies of this book, contact:
Xlibris Corporation
1-888-795-4274
www.Xlibris.com
Orders@Xlibris.com
30102

To my Latin Teacher
Miss Grace Crockett
who ignited my interest in
Roman history
Maui, Hawaii

PERMISSIONS

Brief excerpts, Jeremiah 15:16, 15:18, 15:19-20, from J. M. Powis Smith and Edgar J. Goodspeed trs., 1939, *The Complete Bible, An American Translation*, are used with permission of The University of Chicago Press.

Other Biblical passages are used with permission of Division of Christian Education of the National Council of Churches of Christ in the United States of America, 1971, *Revised Standard Version of the Bible*.

A brief fragment of Archilochus, from *Greek Lyrics*, tr. by Richmond Alexander Lattimore, 1949, is used by permission of The University of Chicago Press.

"The Blast of Love", "Ungiven Love", "Shall I?", from *Sappho and the Greek Lyric Poets*, tr. by Willis Barnstone, Copyright © 1962, 1967, 1988 by Willis Barnstone, are used by permission of Schocken Books, a division of Random House, Inc.

THE STORY BEHIND THE NOVEL

The novel *Not by Force but by Good Will* represents nearly a lifetime of recreational research and imaginary reconstruction of personal lives in an ancient Roman farm household. The writing began on Maui, when my high school Latin teacher, Grace Crockett, ignited my interest in Roman life and history.

In contrast to Julius Caesar's wars to build an empire, we were fighting the Second World War, the War for Freedom. As I was learning how the Roman republic degenerated into a military empire, the Territory of Hawaii was under wartime Martial Law, under which my schoolteacher parents were given the choice to sell our seven acre subsistence farm at a loss, or house six officers. We housed the officers.

While in the high school American History class I learned about our Civil War to prevent secession of the Southern States, and to emancipate slaves, in the Latin class I learned that about two-thirds of the Roman Empire were slaves, and that the idea that slavery was wrong had scarcely been born.

Attending confirmation classes and reading the Bible on my own, I was shocked to read that early Christian slaves in the Roman world were told to serve the master as the Lord. (1 Cor 7:20-22; Eph 6:5-8; Col 3:22-23). How could they possibly do it? The theme for a novel was born.

Coping first with war, then with the social isolation of being the only *haole* in a high school of nearly a thousand, and of having to work before and after school and weekends on the farm, instead of keeping a teenage diary I started the novel. To write from experience I set the novel in the countryside where three-fourths of the free Roman population lived.

I placed the novel during the reign of Constantine the Great. My purpose was not to deal with the heroics of martyred Christians; rather to deal with the quiet heroics and the holy in daily life, a theme neglected in novels on the Roman Empire. I would breathe life into the grass roots.

At the second writing during the 'sixties, I was a young mother of three with an undergraduate degree in religion from Oberlin College and with audited graduate level theology courses. The novel provided creative use of lonely evenings as a young missionary wife at home with babies.

In subsequent rewrites the novel became a way of working through the heartbreak of a lost marriage, and a reprieve from the stressful responsibility as a working head of household with young children. Eventually writing became a celebration and affirmation of life as a survivor, an act of devotion and thanksgiving. As I progressed through the stages of my life, I could be in the heads of the characters at those respective stages. I could not abandon these creations of the imagination; their voices deserved hearing.

The fascinating objective persisted, to explore in imagination how the slave in the ancient Roman empire could accept physical slavery in the name of Christ, a concept that is unacceptable today. That such a transformation did happen is implied in the letter of Paul the Apostle to Philemon (Philem 1:15). Slaves, realizing their worth as God's children, freedmen in Christ and affirmed as persons, fulfilled their commission as living sacrifices in thanksgiving, involving themselves in the work of God in their world, even when there was not so much as a whisper of hope for freedom. Not unlike them, modern man continues to experience slavery, whether physical slavery, or spiritual slavery in the potentially suffocating demands of the industrial, corporate, or professional world.

Hannah Bonsey Suthers
Thanksgiving, 2005

ACKNOWLEDGEMENTS

Major resources in a large bibliography for this novel are gratefully acknowledged: Initially, in the late 1940s, I devoured the Roman collection at Baldwin High School and Wailuku Public Library on Maui: Reginald Haynes Barrow, 1928, *Slavery in the Roman Empire*; George Willis Botsford, 1902, *A History of Rome for High Schools and Academies*; William Stearns Davis, 1913, *Readings in Ancient History, Rome and the West*; Edward Gibbon, 1909, *The Decline and Fall of the Roman Empire*, Vol. 1-3; Fairfax Harrison, 1913, *Roman Farm Management, the Treatises of Cato and Varro*; Harold Whetstone Johnston,1903, *The Private Life of the Romans*; Henry Stuart Jones, 1912, *Companion to Roman History*.

I am indebted to Michigan State University that granted townspersons use of the libraries. There in the 1950s and 1960s I accessed the Bohn's Classical Library, Bohn's Ecclesiastical Library, The Columbia University Records of Civilization, The Loeb Classical Library, and others. In translation were: Aristotle, *On The Generation of Animals*; Aurelius, *Letters*; Cato, *On Farming*; Columella, *On Agriculture*; Epictetus, *Enchiridion*; Hippolytus, Bishop of Rome, *Apostolic Tradition*; Lucretius, *On the Nature of the Universe*; Ovid, *The Love Books*; Eusebius Pamphili, Bishop of Caesarea, *Ecclesiastical History*, and *The Life of the Blessed Emperor Constantine*; Plato, *The Republic*, and *Timaeus*; Pliny, *Natural History*; Plutarch, *On Love, the Family and the Good Life*; Seneca, *Letters to Lucilius*; Theodoretus, Bishop of Cyrrhus, *A History of the Church from 322 AD to 427 AD*; Virgil, *Georgics*; Vitruvius, *On Architecture*; Xenophon, *On Horsemanship*, and *The Oeconomicus*.

Early Christian liturgy came to life in the mid 1960s through the lectures of Massey Hamilton Shepherd, Jr., and his books, 1953, *At All Times and in All Places*, and 1960, *The Paschal Liturgy and The Apocalypse*; Dom Gregory Dix, 1945, *The Shape of the Liturgy*; William Delbert Maxwell, 1949, *An*

Outline of Christian Worship, its Development and Forms; Cyril Charles Richardson, tr. and ed., 1953, *Early Christian Fathers*, including *The Didache*.

Other resources, many at Princeton University, were Jakob Christoph Burckhardt, tr. 1949, *The Age of Constantine the Great*; Roth Clausing, 1925, *The Roman Colonate, the Theories of its Origin*; William Reginald Halliday, 1927, *Greek and Roman Folklore*; Edith Hamilton, 1932, *The Roman Way to Western Civilization*; Mary F. Hedlund and H. H. Rowley trs. and eds., 1958, *Atlas of the Early Christian World*; Otto Kiefer, 1935, *Sexual Life in Ancient Rome*; Walton Brooks McDaniel, 1924, *Conception, Birth and Infancy in Ancient Rome and Modern Italy*.

In the 1970s and later, new books provided more detail: John R. Clarke with Michael Larvey, 2003, *Roman Sex, 100 BC-AD 250*; Michael Grant, 1994, *Constantine the Great*; Michael Grant with Antonia Mulas, 1982, *Eros in Pompeii*; Luisa Franchi dell'Orto, 1982, *Ancient Rome, Life and Art*; Sarah B. Pomeroy, 1975, *Goddesses, Whores, Wives and Slaves: Women in Classical Antiquity*; Michael Simkins, 1979, *The Roman Army from Hadrian to Constantine*; Carol Tavis and Carole Offir, 1977, *The Longest War: Sex differences in Perspective*; K. D. White, 1970, *Roman Farming*, and 1975, *Farm Equipment of the Roman World*; Paul Veyne, ed., Arthur Goldhammer, tr., 1987, *A History of Private Life: I. From Pagan Rome to Byzantium.*

Dates of the events during the reign of Constantine vary according to the sources. As Michael Grant, 1993, commented in the Preface to his *Constantine the Great*, 'Hundreds of attempts have been made to reconstruct them; here, in this [his] book, is another endeavour to walk over the same treacherous quicksands.' Such a walk is not attempted in the novel; I tried to follow the sequence of events.

My gratitude goes to Derwent A. Suthers for tending our children while I audited graduate school summer classes, and for reading and commenting on the 'sixties version of the novel, and to the late Edward J. Humphries for reading and commenting on the 'eighties version. Many thanks to my brother John Bonsey for designing the cover, and for proofreading the manuscript.

THE PRINCIPAL CHARACTERS

Lucan, runaway army slave, Thessalonian
Quintus, freeman, master of market farm Good Will, Roman
Marcellus, knight, landlord of Good Will, Roman
Marcipor, personal slave of Marcellus, Roman
Titus, notable, Magistrate of Puteoli, Roman
Aulus, Fulvia, Quintus's parents, warehouse owners, Roman
Olipor, slave of Aulus and overseer of Good Will, Greek
Dorothea, freedwoman, head housekeeper, Olipor's wife, Greek
Gaius, homebred slave, their youngest of four sons, foreman
Kaeso, rescued slave, cook's helper, kitchen gardener, Gaul
Postumus, orphaned slave, head cook, kitchen gardener, Roman
Cara, rescued slave, housekeeper, Postumus's wife, Roman
Paulo, rescued slave, Cara's bastard son, vinedresser, Roman
Alexis, homebred slave, Cara and Postumus's son, vinedresser
Gregor, homebred slave, their middle son, night watchman
Letitia, homebred slave, their daughter, maid
Servius, homebred slave serving the third generation, Roman
Mamercus, rescued slave, stable manager, gardener, Arab
Baltus, rescued slave, plowman and farm hand, Baltic
Manius, rescued slave, plowman and farm hand, African
Sextus, rescued slave, farm hand, Iberian
Megas, battle trophy, boiler fire and wood tender, Slavic

NOT BY FORCE
BUT BY
GOOD WILL

PART I

ABBA, FATHER

As for me, your word is my joy and delight;
For I bear your name, O Lord, God of Hosts.

Jeremiah 15:16

CHAPTER I

Roman Campania, Holy Week, A.D. 321
Rescued into slavery

"Sisters Three, take me!" Lucan gasped. The relentless ascension of the highway from the seaport Puteoli took his breath. Torture and slow death closed in with that brute of a slaver in pursuit. He sea legs rebelled. His guts hurt from the scourge that seized his bowels while he stowed away in the cabbage bin of a merchant galley from Thessalonica.

The Fates only mocked him in the slaver's sickening grin.

Lucan turned onto Via Solfatara that followed mercifully along the contour of the hillsides and ran parallel to the Legerius farm wall. The slaver gained on him. His time was at hand.

As the slaver cast chains at Lucan, the Fates answered with a rumbling crescendo from behind. The slaver broke stride to look. Two noblemen in racing chariots with spans of four mettlesome horses turned at the intersection and bore down on them. The slaver stepped off the road immediately. Lucan stepped deliberately into their path.

"Way! Way!" The Magistrate's bays swerved to avoid him.

"Haa! Haa!" The knight's blacks lunged past them all and sent Lucan sprawling against the farm wall.

"Should've killed me!" Lucan gestured obscenely.

The chariots stopped and wheeled about. Damn if they weren't coming back to get him! At the sight of a gate self-preservation took over. Lucan flung himself against the gate and attacked the latch. It held.

"For the gods' sakes open!" he shouted up at the gatehouse. *Non vi sed voluntate*, the inscription overhead read, not by force but by good will. With desperate self control he turned the latch. The gate gave way, unlocked and unguarded.

Lucan burst into the beautiful formal garden of the Good Will farm villa. He dove for cover in the stately cypress bordering the driveway. All hell stormed that gate behind him. The span of blacks tore wildly in from the highway and the chariot careened toward the stable court. The slaver's voice bellowed after. Lucan glanced wildly about, mustered a final burst of energy and sprinted across the clipped grass, broad jumped the stream and plunged into a maze of richly growing boxwood.

An urgent voice made him run all the more frantically. "Here! This way!"

He heard the owner of the voice crash through the shrubs in hot pursuit. The chase was as brief as it was wild. Lucan tore blindly through the bushes, flushing panicked sparrows who betrayed his whereabouts. He twisted, turned, zigzagged through the maze, anything to throw off his pursuer. He ran on all fours when he fell. He dove head first through the thickets. The force of his hands against a wall flung him to the ground. Everything was against him. Panting, he met the inquiring stare of a young Greek slave like himself.

"You've come to the right place," the other said, then with fingers to mouth whistled an urgent code.

"Damn traitor, you!" Lucan bounded up, and nearly collapsed except that the other, equally quick, seized his wrists and pinned his arms behind his back.

"I'm trying to help, you fool! Now will you come with me or do I have to," the other increased the pressure on Lucan's arms, "force you?"

"*Ad malem crucem*, I'll come!" Lucan leaned heavily and groaned.

Quintus, the young master of the villa, heard the whistle from his library, kicked over his stool, ran downstairs through the villa, and out the atrium door.

"Hey! Hey! What's going on here! You can't come breaking in like that; this is a private farm, a peaceful household!"

"Are ya tellin' me?" The slaver roared back from the driveway. "You c'n tell that runaway!"

"What runaway!"

"That young Greek what busted through your gate just before them horses."

"What horses?" Quintus's blue eyes twinkled.

"Dammit, boy, time's a wasting! Go get your domine!"

"Here, in person!" Quintus smiled. "Now why the intrusion?"

"Well!" the slaver jeered. He cocked his head at the barefoot farmer in the brown wool tunic and smirked. "They grow em younger every year."

"Where's your respect!" Quintus chided good-naturedly. "Farming is considered the noblest profession!"

"Yeah? Tell me about it!" the slaver drawled and looked him over closely.

"Say, you like to eat, don't you? Cabbage? The finest of vegetables? How about tender shoots of Pompeian cabbage? Or the incredibly crisp and sweet leaves of the Sabine? Ah! The giant heads of Tritian cabbage. And leek? Tender and delicate?"

"Yeah, yeah, but . . ."

"See, I grow them for you. And cucumber? Yes? How about an early variety. That's what I'm working on now! And olives for your salads. Pork sausage from my herd, charcoal brazed, on the Street of Booths, with hot mulled wine from my vines. Doesn't that just make your mouth water?"

"Well now, sir, I apologize." The slaver wondered how much this fool of a farmer with a smiling voice could be taken for and changed his tact. Perhaps he could dump the runaway onto him. For a price, of course. "Couldn't do without your sort, actually."

"Nor without my household of humble friends. Now, about that young Greek."

"I could sell ya a sturdy helper," the slaver hedged.

"I could use another farm hand." Quintus inadvertently handed over his bargaining power.

"Him has the stamina of a camel, though. Stowaway for weeks on the ship with near nothin' to eat."

"Easy keeper, then?"

"Camel's disposition too," the slaver held back strategically. "Beyond me why anyone'd want to handle him."

"I've had that kind before. Loyal when you win them over." Quintus was talking himself into a sale.

"They say him's dangerous. Incorrigible!"

"Nonsense," Quintus was effectively suckered in.

"Ya should see him first. If ya'd permit—well I'll be damned!" the slaver gawked.

The Greek foreman of Good Will appeared out of the bushes and led the runaway by the wrist.

"Release him, Gaius," Quintus ordered his slave.

"Please sir . . ."

"Yes I know, Gaius."

"Hang on now't you got him!" the slaver protested.

"He will stand." Quintus nodded at the fugitive.

"As you say, sir." Gaius released his hold on Lucan.

The fugitive clenched his fists and stood with downcast eyes.

Quintus was shocked at the stinking rags, the matted hair, the shackle and whip scars. "By the gods, you are badly handled. Did you really just come off the ship? Who would treat you so?"

Lucan could not answer for that would be direct accusation forbidden by law. He would be punished anyway for not answering, and he trembled at the dilemma.

The slaver stepped up threateningly and Quintus restrained him.

"Don't you know that you can appeal to the Magistrate for resale?" Quintus pleaded with the runaway, and the slave glowered at him. "Who is your domine, anyway?" He now put the question in answerable form.

"A Roman dog," Lucan snarled.

"Ah! I see you have no love for the canine," Quintus quipped.

The slaver clouted Lucan with the handcuffs. The slave gasped and collapsed. On his way down his hands clutched at the thigh of the young Roman and with several weeks' growth of fingernails raked him to the ankle. Quintus flinched in pain. Their gazes met and another shock bolted through Quintus. Those light brown eyes were incredibly alive.

The slaver grabbed at the fugitive.

"Let him be!" Quintus ordered sharply, and the slaver deferred to his superior.

"What will happen to him?" Quintus asked.

"Interrogation under torture, and what's left sold for compost."

Quintus winced. The hands clasping his ankles had tightened painfully. He looked down into those eyes again.

"I'll buy him," he declared. "Now. As is. Gaius, go get the purse."

"Actually I ain't no trader," the slaver tactically withdrew, "my specialty is to recover runaways."

"Then I'll appeal to the Magistrate on his behalf!"

The wretched one looked up again, panic in his eyes.

The slaver, not wanting a public scandal for a mere stowaway, quickly retracted. He had heard rumors about the House of Good Will, how a runaway could crash its gates and emerge a freedman. "I'll make a deal with ya," he said.

When the transaction was completed, and the slaver gone, Quintus bent down over Lucan. "You can let go of me now," he said gently. "Come, you need rest and food." Quintus helped Lucan to his feet and ordered Gaius to take him into the villa. "Only liquids at first, Gaius. And give him a bath!"

"I say there, Quintus!" a voice called from the atrium door. The knight, Quintus's landlord, came out into the garden.

"Marcellus! Greetings! What's with the purple stripe today?" Quintus commented on the silk tunic with the knight's narrow purple stripe running from shoulder to hem.

"The races. I'll get recognized if it's the last thing I do!" Marcellus gloated. He would piece the news out gradually, like the tease that he was. "I settled my blacks in your stalls." They clasped each other's forearms in greeting. "I'll stable your slave girl too, if you don't watch out!"

"Letitia?"

"Haven't you noticed her lately, budding out all over?"

"Of course!"

"Has she had to skip work yet, for regular reasons?"

"Down, boy!"

"Don't worry, but don't neglect her!"

"I won't! Will you be staying a while?"

"Home after supper. Say! The blues won again, Beans! You should have been at the races! What a finish! We had a pile up of chariots coming down the last bend. And the winner barely made it by a nose! It was obvious from the judges' stand but the people weren't convinced and they rioted. Had to get the soldiers in to cut them back to order. You should have been there, Beans, why don't you go! Good place to womanize, you know, find yourself a nice wife."

"I would, except that I need all my time feeling out my responsibilities here."

"Did your father really put you in full charge?"

"Don't laugh! I'm going to be the best farmer Campania has ever seen!" Quintus boasted.

"And your brothers?"

"Stuck in the army for some time yet. And I'm not about to enlist," he assured. The edge to his voice revealed his resentment of the Emperor Constantine's conscription that had pulled away all three of his brothers and their menservants. "So I'll be your tenant for a good while, Marcellus."

"Well good, friend! Say, want to breed fine horses?"

"Me? I prefer girls," Quintus could not resist it.

"Oh, you've opened her up, then? Let me try her some time."

Speechless at being caught in his empty brag talk, Quintus shook his head and smiled.

"She's exclusive property, then?"

"That's right, Marcellus."

"Just checking."

"Furthermore, I'm working on an early variety of cucumber. More money in that than in horses. Takes less capital."

"Oh you and your vegetables! I had to tell you, Beans, that Titus was disappointed when his colors lost Sunday. And to top it off, I just now won the span of magnificent bays out of the Magistrate's hands!"

"Titus's bays?" Quintus looked at his friend in disbelief.

"Yes! I beat them with my blacks! On the highway! I came upon him on the way home and challenged him. You should have seen me! Now here we were like this," he gestured intently with his hands. "I would have been lengths ahead except . . ." Marcellus stared at Gaius who approached with the runaway in his hold. "This is the rubbish that handicapped my blacks! Good catch, Gaius! Titus will have fun with him! New fishpond, you know."

He drew himself up threateningly before Lucan. "If you had fouled my horses—if you had caused me to lose my blacks—you don't want to know what I would have done to you!" He made a slashing gesture.

Lucan stared speechlessly.

"Insubordinate! Looking at me like that! I'll bash your face in!"

Lucan fouled his loincloth in terror. He stepped back quickly and appealed with his eyes to the young farmer who was simultaneously thanking heaven alive that he didn't have to appeal to Titus the Magistrate on this unfortunate's behalf.

"What is it, Gaius, you have your orders." Quintus urgently wanted the two slaves out of sight.

"The garden gate is locked, sir. I have to go around front and in by the stable court."

"Very well, Gaius. By the looks of him, you'd better go in the front door and shortcut through the villa before he collapses. Quickly! Go!"

"He may break loose in the house, sir," Gaius protested.

"He will behave!" Quintus asserted, and noticed that the fugitive gave him a quick look of surprise.

"Yes, sir." Gaius led the wretched Lucan to the atrium door.

"Now," said Marcellus with mock gravity, "what I came to ask, lend me some money, friend?"

"You were just looking at my cash." Quintus felt a tingle of satisfaction that his emergency fund was out of Marcellus's reach.

"What!"

Quintus chuckled nervously. "He came bursting through the gate and bolted into the maze."

"I know. I drove in behind him."

"Did you see the slaver come charging through the gate after him? Ha! I had to laugh. He was bellowing like an angry bull. He stopped short when he saw me, and asked for my domine."

"So you sent him packing."

"Well, not in the way you would have."

"Meaning?"

"I ransomed the runaway first."

"You what?" Marcellus should have known. Quintus had not an unkind bone in him. "How much did you pay for him?"

"Too much, I guess," Quintus hedged.

"Come on now, Beans, tell me."

"A talent, Marcellus," Quintus confessed.

"A talent! Ye Gods!" the knight gestured in exasperation. "Keep that up, and you'll go bankrupt with a fine staff of fugitives!"

"How would I know what they cost; you paid ten thousand for Marcipor!" Quintus countered defensively.

"Well, certainly, for Marcipor. But you could have gotten a bargain while you were at it, like ten good farmhands, sold off the ship today. And then something to boot for taking that carcass off the slaver's hands. Now why on earth?"

"Something about him appealed to me." Quintus blushed under his landlord's hot gaze. If Olipor his steward could buy certain fugitives that appeared at the gate, with standing permission from his father, why couldn't he?

"Can you find the slaver again?"

"He is to bring me the sale papers," Quintus admitted.

"Well, you must return the boy," Marcellus insisted.

"Marcellus, I can't." Quintus could be annoyingly stubborn.

"What do you think this farm is! Some sort of rescue mission? You are acting like that Christian Church in Puteoli."

"As a matter of fact . . ." Quintus began, but Marcellus interrupted.

"And this is tax year too," Marcellus sputtered. "Now what are you going to do with him?"

"Take him on for my boy, I guess," Quintus said lamely.

"Beans, you're crazy."

"I trust that my talent will be well invested, Marcellus."

"By the looks of him your talent is about to be buried," Marcellus retorted. "Ah well, *caveat emptor*, buyer beware. As long as you present me with my full half of the crops and meet your taxes. And you think you can trust that mongrel to be your personal slave, when the well-bred Gaius was raised and trained for you?"

"It's a challenge, Marcellus, I'd enjoy it. As a matter of fact," Quintus confided, "I've always wondered what would happen if one of these badly treated ragamuffins were given a good break. Here's the perfect chance to find out. It seems to me that even the worst sort can be restored to humanity when treated as a person, not as a thing."

"Zeus! How naive can you be! As though you had something worth while there, like a prize colt!"

"A hardy, gritty colt with a penchant for survival. He can tell the home-bred how well off they really are. Don't worry. I'll prove my skill on him. If I take on the well-bred Gaius I will learn nothing about managing slave labor. My success as a farmer depends on the help, you know. It's like you and your horses, Marcellus. A well-trained span will take their colors through the race to victory even without a driver, like those famous horses of Corax. What then have you learned? But a team like your blacks that has to be won over and disciplined by your mastery, now that develops your horsemanship. That is manhood."

"Thank you for your insight, friend," Marcellus beamed.

"Then please understand my position. In this household we regard slaves as valuable human beings."

"Ha!" Marcellus teased. "You and your idealism!" Then he added mischievously, "Bet you don't succeed!"

"Bet I do!" Quintus took him on. "I rescued him, you know. He'll roll at my feet, he'll be so grateful."

"Grateful, my foot! You be kind to him and he'll take advantage of you, he will! He'll walk all over you!"

"I believe in the inherent goodness of man, Marcellus," Quintus answered in quiet heat.

"Poppycock!" Marcellus ejaculated. "Ah well, I suppose it takes a good man to have faith in the goodness of others," he teased, and playfully punched his friend. "You'll find out soon enough that only the whip will tame an unruly slave. That is, if you have the guts to use a whip."

"I'll use a whip," Quintus declared with sudden inspiration. "He shall be my whip! If the homebred steps out of line this fugitive off the ship shall replace him so fast he won't know what hit him."

"You mean Gaius?"

"Precisely."

"What balls!" Marcellus breathed and regarded his friend in new light. "I didn't know you had it in you. We'll put the fugitive to test sometime. Our bet, you know. If he fails, he's mine. If he is faithful, I'll reimburse you his purchase price. Agreed?"

"Agreed."

They boxed playfully for a while, then sprinted panting and laughing up the hills past the orchards, into the woods, and to the unfailing stream and favorite swimming hole.

* * *

Gaius strode rapidly into the little upstairs library and stood before his master's desk for permission to speak. Quintus was up late, studying Varro's authoritative treatise on farm management. Marcellus had left after an early supper, in order to get home before dark to his villa several miles away toward Puteoli.

Quintus studied Gaius's sensitive face for a moment, then he leaned back in his chair. "What is it, Gaius?" he gave his foreman permission to speak.

Gaius tried in vain to hide his excitement. "Domine, forgive me for disturbing you after supper. I took care of the boy as you ordered. His name is Lucan. I put him to bed in the sickroom."

"Good."

"He fell asleep right away."

"Are you interrupting me to tell me this? Come to the point, boy," Quintus helped him. He had seen the excitement in Gaius's face.

"Domine, he is having a nightmare or something."

"Didn't you try to wake him?"

"He won't awaken, sir. He cried out all the more and slugged me. He is trying to talk. He's virtually hallucinating! Please come."

"Thank you, Gaius."

Quintus rose immediately, ran downstairs and led the way rapidly to the sickroom in the servants' hall just off the kitchen. The household slaves stood at the doorways of their rooms on the opposite side of the hall. Many of the agricultural slaves had left their straw mattresses in the servants' hall and were gathered about the door of the sickroom. They stepped back to admit him. "Go back to your beds," Quintus ordered quietly. They sheepishly withdrew.

When Quintus entered the sickroom, Olipor his overseer rose.

"What, Olipor!" exclaimed Quintus. "Is the entire household roused? Keep them at their beds," he ordered sternly.

"I will, sir."

Quintus nodded approval at Letitia, the young slave girl who was sponging Lucan's forehead. "Be careful of him," he spoke into her ear, and she blushed. He gently put his hand on Lucan's forehead. It was quite hot.

"Did you catch any of his words, Olipor?" Quintus sat at the foot of the couch.

The elderly slave hesitated, then he answered. "I could understand some, sir. He spoke in Greek. 'Pater! Hurry home! The Romans are trying to subdue Meter and the girls! They overpower us!'"

Quintus's brow puckered thoughtfully.

Olipor's words entered into Lucan's subconsciousness, and brought up the dream again. Lucan tossed and struggled as he re-lived the tragedy of seven years ago.

In the dream, Lucan and his father run home from nearby fields. They hear screams. Five soldiers are fighting his mother, brother, and two sisters. The leftovers of what was to be the family supper lie on the table. The soldiers are drunk with wine. Lucan and his father fall upon the soldiers.

Soon with a broken voice Lucan cried "Pater!" And with horror, "Brother! Pater, no!" Then he cried urgently, "Meter! Lucia! Lysistra! Run! They overpower me! Pater!"

Letitia left the room. Her imagination worked vividly. Olipor and Gaius each had a pained look on their faces. Quintus still held his thoughtful frown.

Lucan sat up struggling with the covers. "You brutes dare to use them! You dare to use them! Oh that damn rope! That damned rope!" Then Lucan let out such a heart-tearing scream that Gaius seized him by the shoulders and tried again to wake him. Lucan wrenched himself free and tossed over on his stomach. He buried his head in his arms and attempted to choke back the grief that racked his body.

Lucan's sleep became peaceful again. Quintus waited a few minutes longer, then left for his room. The slaves in the hall were sitting up on their mats. Quintus empathized with their concern. "He's sleeping peacefully now. Don't you worry."

It seemed to Quintus that as soon as he fell into a good sleep, commotion aroused him again. He stumbled groggily downstairs. According to the water clock in the kitchen, a few hours had passed. He slipped into the servants' hall and sickroom. Some of the slaves still slept.

Lucan was tossing again, mumbling. "Do not beat me," he cried out repeatedly and most piteously, "I only asked for my supper. Hunger! Hunger!" he moaned. Then he sat up, fully awake. His innards hurt, badly, though not from hunger. He paled. "What kind of new torture is this!" he choked out feebly and twisted back onto his stomach again, nauseated.

Olipor got the basin to Lucan in time, but Lucan in his anxiety to get the basin closer knocked it and its contents to the floor. "I'm sorry!" he gasped. "I'm very sorry!"

"Now don't you worry," Quintus soothed and supported him by the shoulders until the retching passed. Lucan soiled his loincloth as well. It stank.

It stank so much that those adjacent to the door mumbled about moving Lucan to the stables, until Quintus scolded them for their insensitivity. He singled out Gaius who stood by anxiously.

"What did you give him to eat?" Quintus demanded to know.

"Why, he came to table, sir! He ate like an animal."

"You fed him solids? With a fever like that? You'll kill him, Gaius, you'll kill him! He came off the ship with a scourge. Does he not still have blood in his stool? No wine either, not even myrtle wine to settle his stomach! Don't you think I know anything? Didn't anyone here tell you?"

Gaius fidgeted, then confessed. "Dorothea told me, sir."

"And you didn't listen to your mother again," Quintus rebuked him firmly. "You're going to owe me a full pouch, Gaius, if he's dead tomorrow."

"Yes, sir, I'm sorry, sir," Gaius answered resentfully.

"Go to bed, Gaius."

Wasn't the domine going a bit overboard? Gaius wished that he hadn't even seen the fugitive. His first mistake was not to let him slip quietly to the back woods to die in hiding. His second mistake was in fetching the money. All of it. He should have drawn a small amount from the pouch. Only he thought his domine wanted to make a display of power with the full pouch. Or he should have brought a tablet for a promissory note. It never crossed his mind that the domine would spend all of it. The whole pouch. His father will have it out with him for not consulting him first, even though he was obeying orders!

Now his mistake with the food was the last straw. He should have listened to his mother. At times like this he couldn't seem to do right by his domine. He was four years his master's senior and there was a vast difference in mental set between seventeen and twenty-one. His head was on a different plane. And he was supposed to be his master's right hand man. He drifted back to sleep with unhappy thoughts on his mind.

Quintus intercepted Olipor returning from a storeroom with an armful of clean rags, and sent him back to bed with orders to call him every time Lucan had a nightmare. He wanted to impress upon the indisposed slave, upon the entire household for that matter, that the master was at your side in your hour of need.

"Here, you need help," Quintus strode into the sickroom and declared his intentions to Letitia.

"Thank you, sir," Letitia took the rags from him. "Let me do it, please, sir." Their eyes met.

"I take care of my household," Quintus said firmly.

"You are most kind, sir. Sometimes it would be even more considerate not to help with every detail."

"Do you think I'm squeamish, or something?"

"It's not that, sir. Please," she continued with an out, "the kettle of water is on the stove. It's heavy for me. Would you please bring it up to a comfortable temperature and carry it in here for me?"

"Certainly." He left a little stiffly.

Lucan had been watching them anxiously as they discussed his care over him from opposite sides of the bed. As soon as Letitia managed to get Quintus out of the room, Lucan mustered the strength to beg her not to let the Roman touch him. The effort nearly nauseated him again.

Her intuition was absolutely on the mark. She wet a cloth with cool water and sponged his face and neck. Then she started undoing his soiled clothing.

Quintus brooded at the stove. He was anxious to get command over Letitia, not take orders from her. Would she take him seriously, her former playmate before he went to the Eternal City to live with his parents and go to school? Actually as playmates she had been the dominant one! Now he had to take command, treat her with authority, with no familiarity and especially without partiality. Would she notice? Of course. Would she be hurt? He had to risk it. There was no other way.

Quintus returned with the warm water and poured off a basin and set it on the bedside stand. When he reached for a rag she gently took his hand and frowned and shook her head and mouthed that Lucan would be too embarrassed. Quintus yielded and proceeded to sponge the sick boy's burning forehead with cool water. He lifted the slave's head for a sip of water and suggested that he at least rinse out his mouth. Lucan complied, then turned his face away. Quintus understood that he was not wanted. He was determined, however, to have the last word.

"Give him a sip frequently, Letitia, as long as he is awake. You may fetch yourself a pallet in here. I'll unlock the storeroom for you. I shall be on call to spell you, and you are certainly to call me every time . . ."

Letitia interrupted him with a finger to his lips and he gave up and went back upstairs.

Just before daybreak, Olipor bent over Quintus's bed and woke him. Lucan was talking in his sleep again. Quintus was groggy, but he bounded up; this was exciting. He and Olipor listened alertly for the occasional sentences.

"You have no claim over me! I am rightfully a free man!"

The dream comes into clear focus now. Lucan is at his father's farm again. Only this time he is alone, and he is in a one-room shack that he assembled himself from the ruins of the farmhouse and barn that the soldiers had burned to the ground. He sits eating a meager supper scrounged from the vegetable fields. A Roman soldier darkens the doorway. Lucan bounds up and grabs his hunting knife. The soldier is all over at once, at all sides, and floating overhead. Swords thrust themselves at him. Lucan's dream-limbs won't move. The scene spins. He screams. The dream room comes into focus again, and all the swords press upon his throat. He is captive again, taken away in chains.

The scene changes to fields, woods, streams of the German frontier. Lucan is trying to run. Trees and foliage reach out their arms and clutch at him. Wavelets in the stream become huge barriers. Lucan scrambles under a leaf. A giant finger uncovers him. He looks up. The form of his second master fills the sky. The master's distorted hound drools bucket-size drops upon him. The dog's panting becomes bellows puffing on a huge forge. An enormous glowing branding iron comes at Lucan.

He screamed again and fought the restraining bedcovers.

"Do not brand me!" he panted hoarsely. "I'm freeborn! I'm not incorrigible! Flog! Starve! But not brand! Not brand! Not brand . . ."

Lucan struggled off the bed. Quintus caught his fall, and with a yelp Lucan bounded over the bed to the other side. The brown eyes glittered yellow like a frightened animal. He pleaded piteously to be permitted to sleep on the floor.

"A couch has some kind of terror for him," Quintus commented to Olipor in private.

"He may have been forced to be a lover," Olipor speculated.

"Olipor, he's entire, isn't he?"

"Why, yes! But there is a scar on his groin, an ugly, jagged red welt of a scar."

Lucan slept that entire day and night. Toward daybreak he roused the entire household with the same heart rendering scream and again choked back grievous sobs. Quintus hurried to the bedside. When Olipor tried to wake Lucan, the boy flailed his arms all the more.

Dreaming, Lucan relives his arrival at Puteoli. He sneaks off the merchant ship and scavenges the marketplace for edible refuse. Lucan sees a slaver come after him and weaves among the booths of produce. He looks over his shoulder at the oncoming slaver and collides with a white haired slave who forces him to his knees. "Let me go! *Ad malem crucem* let me go!" The elder bends over to his ear. "By the sign of the blessed cross, save yourself! Go to the Basilica, second street left. Draw a cross upon the ground." Lucan is biting the elder's wrist. The slaver catches up with him and reaches out for him. Lucan quickly draws a cross upon the ground, whereupon he is magically borne up into a paradise and is reviewing his life before a Judge. A pair of scales hang by the Judge, upon which the frayed yarn of his nightmarish youth is weighed against the golden childhood thread that the Three Fates had spun for him earlier. The Judge mercifully waves him on and he is taken to a glowing room to rest from his long perilous journey. He hears singing unlike anything he had heard before.

> "Hallelujah! I love the Lord, because he has heard my
> voice and my supplications.
> Because he has inclined his ear to me, therefore will I
> call on him as long as I live."

The assembled household in the kitchen sang the Wednesday Station commemorating their Lord's betrayal.

In his dream Lucan sees an illuminated youthful god and his cohorts bend over him in greeting. The god speaks to him kindly.

As Lucan tried to focus on the young Roman and the elder with a halo of silver hair, the singing continued.

> "The snares of death encompassed me;
> the pangs of Sheol laid hold on me;
> I suffered distress and anguish.
> Then called I upon the name of the Lord:
> O Lord, I beseech thee, save my life!"

Lucan sat up suddenly. "They come for me! They come for me!" he cried. "Please let me go with them! I want release!" He tried to reach for the elder who was leaving the room. "Lord, please take me with you!"

Quintus wrapped his arm compassionately around him and grasped for something reassuring to say. "You are in the House of Good Will now. No one will harm you here."

"No!" Lucan tried to free himself. He broke into anxious sweat and panted. "No! I don't want this house! I don't want this life! They were taking me with them! You mustn't stop them! Don't make them go away without me. Lord, take me with you!" He reached toward the door.

"Lucan!" Quintus called firmly.

"I am here, Lord!"

"Lucan, you are hallucinating. You are now in your Domine's house," Quintus declared.

"Not dreaming . . . they came for me . . ." The wretched fugitive leaned heavily and pressed his face into his benefactor's shoulder and trembled uncontrollably.

"O Lord, I am thy servant . . . Thou has loosed my bonds."

So the singing went. Only he was not freed from his bonds, and his Domine's house was on earth. He was still a slave, worse than death. Bitter tears filled his eyes.

"Everything will be all right, Lucan," Quintus assured him over and over, and stroked him and rocked him like a compassionate parent. "Live, Lucan! Live! Get well! Live for your Lord!"

"Live for my Lord?" Lucan stared in a stupor at the Roman youth. The return from the beatific vision was brutal.

Olipor came in with a bowl of warm broth and handed it to Quintus.

"Here, drink your broth," Quintus ordered gently, "and go back to sleep."

Sustained by uncompromising training, Lucan remembered his manners through the grievous disappointment. "Thank you, sir." He drank the broth. "I am sorry to disturb you, sir," he apologized. His eyes followed Quintus out of the room. "Roman dog," he whispered brokenly, "Why didn't you let me die! They came for me! Why didn't you let me go! Slavery, worse than death!" He buried his face in the bedclothes and wept, while the singing continued.

"I will offer to thee the sacrifice of thanksgiving
and call on the name of the Lord."

CHAPTER II

One of Us

Saturday, the fourth day after Lucan's arrival, dawned another beautiful spring day. The sky was studded with cloud puffs, a cool sweet breeze blew steadily from the orchards and forest on the hills behind the villa. The cheerful melody of thrushes floated down with the breeze. Sunlight flooded the sickroom and the adjoining rooms.

Lucan stole into the kitchen. Hunger seized his stomach, twisted it in the middle, and pinched it in the sides. He felt light-headed. He dropped down on a bench and watched Postumus the cook and his helpers prepare the noon dinner.

"Hello, here's the boy." Postumus noticed him. "Here's a cup. Go dip yourself some milk out of the pan in the pantry. All you want. And get yourself some bread and cheese, and raisins and olives too. Dinner at noon on the farm, you know."

"That's what I needed," Lucan thanked Postumus contentedly when he had satiated his hunger. He had secretly helped himself to the ham also. And why not? If you are not given your due, does not justice allow you to take it?

"What can I do now?"

"What can you do! It's early. Go back to bed; get your strength back," Postumus answered. "Or is you ready to get up after half a week in bed? Walk about outside and see where you is. A beautiful farm. We call it Good Will." Postumus spoke with pride. "Here meet some of the family. Cara, my wife, a true friend." Then Postumus pointed to a Gaul, fortyish like himself, descending from the kitchen loft. "Kaeso, my helper. He also waits table, and helps me with the kitchen garden. Perhaps you will help me too."

"Who's that!" Kaeso suddenly noticed Lucan. "*Ai!*" he stumbled on the stairs and the earthenware crock of cheeses tumbled out of his arms, clipped each step with a thud, and finally smashed on the floor. The thick grape juice, used as a preservative, splattered across the floor.

"Don't just stand there gawking, boy, help me clean up!" Kaeso snapped.

"You all right down there?" a warm, masculine voice hailed them from upstairs.

"Yes, Domine!" Kaeso shouted back, then looked at the mess and stroked his beard pensively.

Lucan stared in amazement. "Domine?" he uttered.

"And here comes Gaius," Postumus went on as he casually helped with the mess. "Him's in charge of the market garden. Him's Olipor's son and will succeed him someday."

"We have met before," Lucan murmured through his teeth.

"Don't take it so hard, Lucan," Gaius laughed. "Do you like farm work? You and I may work together." Turning to Kaeso, Gaius teased, "Good work, Kaeso!" and proceeded to help clean up.

A strapping, sweating, deep voiced Slav with a load of wood came in through the kitchen and stacked his load in the boiler room.

"Here's Megas," Postumus introduced him. "Big, ain't he! He chops wood and keeps the boiler fire."

"Ho young man," Megas boomed. "Me you will help? To be sure, you will some more meat on you for this job have to get!"

Then Megas noticed the accident. "What the matter is?" he exclaimed in his native tongue.

"Only a cheese pot," Lucan answered, clutching at the use of Megas's own language as a basis for fellowship.

"So you Slavic speak?" Megas wheeled excitedly on Lucan.

"Only a little," Lucan answered, enthusiastic at what seemed a good response.

"Where else but at the Slavic Danube you could learn? So I have your kind for my capture to thank! On you King Rausimod's death I avenge!" Megas towered over Lucan and seized his throat.

"No! Not I!" Lucan choked in terror.

"Never mind him, Megas," Postumus came to the rescue. "You go on out." He put his arm around the big Slav's waist and eased him toward the door.

Lucan, painfully squelched, let out a sob.

"Listen boy," Postumus said to him when he returned, "if you values your neck any, don't remind Megas at all about his homeland. Today is an anniversary of their defeat and his enslavement. He gets ugly on days like this. He ain't 'one of us', you know."

"I understand," Lucan said though Postumus's last remark puzzled him. What did he mean, 'one of us'?

"So you have been at the frontier?" Gaius asked as he continued to wipe up the spill.

"For something like seven years," Lucan almost boasted.

Gaius whistled. "Tell us about it?"

"No! You really don't want to hear about it," Lucan added uneasily.

"Yes I do!" Gaius persisted, and rested on his haunches. "My three brothers are there, with Quintus's three brothers. Quintus has to serve his term and soon he and I . . ."

"I hope not," Lucan interrupted, feeling very uncomfortable.

"Is it true what they say about the allotted King of the Saturnalia at the camp festival?"

"I don't want to think about it," Lucan shuddered.

"Unfortunate man! Then we don't want Quintus up there".

"No." Lucan needed urgently to change the subject. He asked about another thing that puzzled him. Each slave asked him if he were going to help with his particular work. "Who is domine here, anyway?" he asked.

Postumus pointed upstairs. "That young sprout, Quintus Lottius Legerius, is our domine."

"Him?" Lucan was scandalized. "He is the domine? Quintus?"

"Why not? Who did you think he was?" Gaius asked.

"A freedman! Or someone's fifth wheel, after his mother's liberty child. The foreman."

"Oh him's the fifth bean all right, in the Legerius pod, a rare nut indeed," Postumus said, and they dissolved in laughter.

"And I am the foreman," Gaius stood up.

"And if I wear a clean tunic can I be a foreman too?" Lucan quipped and Gaius punched him on the shoulder.

"Quintus is a market gardener," Gaius continued to explain. "We supply the resort villas on the shores of Puteoli. Aulus Lottius Legerius, his father, is a merchant in Rome. Owns a huge warehouse." Gaius spoke with pride.

"I'll tell you what," Postumus gossiped. "Quintus is in charge here while his parents and sister is in the city. His three older brothers is, as Gaius say, at the frontier. It's the first time Quintus has full charge. Him's trying to prove to his father he can manage. Scholar into farmer." Postumus chuckled. "The young domine is upstairs in his library now, having a conference with Olipor. Olipor is the overseer, also Aulus's personal slave. *Auli-puer*. Aulus's boy, you know. Him has a real name too. You'd better mind him. His family is born into the household." Postumus punched Gaius playfully on the arm and added, "privileged. Olipor's sons serve Aulus's sons."

"And the young domine?" Lucan prompted, listening for attitudes.

Gaius chuckled. "The young domine? Sometimes it's funny. You assessed him right. The young domine spent his holidays here on the farm during his early school years, so he thinks he knows how to farm. But he's been at school in Rome for several years, and has lost the touch. So he orders untimely things like selling storage crops when they could be kept and sold for a higher price later. And planting beans too early so that they rot in the ground from the rain before they can sprout. Or ordering the rainy-day maintenance and cleaning jobs done on good days so that come the rainy days we are out of work. And assigning on workdays jobs that could be done on holidays. Yes, he really thinks he knows what he is doing, and you can't tell him much. Dad is sometimes really hard-put to straighten out his orders tactfully. And to keep each task on schedule so that everything else won't be late. Dad is not supposed to think that he knows more than his domine." With this Postumus and Kaeso roared with laughter.

"But we obey him." Gaius firmly defended the young master.

"Ah yes, listen to him talking; that's Gaius for you," Postumus teased. "Olipor's son, you know, someday will serve the young domine personally. And go on to being overseer. Gaius has to obey; he has a position at stake." And when he noticed by the widening of Lucan's eyes that he had exposed his sarcasm, Postumus added quickly, "We do obey him, Lucan."

The slaves jested and returned to their work. Lucan strolled out the door into the kitchen garden. Before him lay the vegetable seed nurseries. The beds obviously needed weeding. One side of a bed was already started. The hand tool lay on the ground where Postumus had left it. Lucan dropped to his knees and his nimble fingers swiftly began on the weeds still wet with dew. What kind of place is this, he wondered. What I've seen of it is beautiful. What does Postumus mean by 'some of the family'? The slaves aren't related. Postumus and Cara are married. They are Roman. Gaius is Greek like me. Kaeso is a Gaul, and Megas a Slav with a Greek nickname. A powerful man too. Is he a Legerius battle trophy? I don't want to meet him alone at night. 'He isn't one of us yet.' What does Postumus mean? Am I going to become 'one of them'? Wonder what my work will be. I'd better see the young Roman and get orders from him before these fellows try to boss me around. What kind of fellow is the domine? They seem to like him well enough. Roman dog; why did he have to take possession of me anyway? He could have let me die.

Then Lucan became quieted by the soothing powers of mother earth. Time flew past. Lucan forgot his troubles, his uncertainty, his fear. In thought he was at home on his father's farm again, doing close work on his hands and knees with his father and brother. They often discussed philosophy and life while doing tedious work together. Lucan cherished those times.

'We are children of the earth,' he seemed to hear his father say, 'and to earth we must return. While we live, we must play well the game with Fortune. We Greeks were once rulers of the world, until Fortune consented to leave our perch and spread her wings over Rome so now we are subject to Rome. Our crops, our livelihood, are subject to the whims of nature. However we must not let Fate get the better of us; we must use reason to make the most of whatever Fate brings us; use reason to seek the good for ourselves and those around us. We must strive for harmony with the order of the universe.

And precisely how was he to do this in the clutches of disharmony and cruel injustice? How? How? Why did this all happen!

A bee buzzing around his head brought him out of his reflections. He paused and observed what he had done. He was doing a good job. He sorted out the weeds with nimble fingers, pulled them up carefully by the roots and threw them in a pile to be gathered into a compost heap. The seedlings made a pretty contrast against the black, weeded earth.

The sun that had been overcast for the past few minutes came out from behind the cloud. Immediately Lucan saw the shadow beside him. He had been thinking so hard about his father's farm that he did not hear anyone approach, nor did he feel eyes on him. He froze for a moment. He slowly wound his fingers around a weed, and then he suddenly whirled about. He looked at the other's feet. There was something terribly familiar about those feet. His gaze moved up to the hands, those powerful hands. Lucan's eyes sought the other's face and widened in alarm. He was about to speak, but he held his tongue. Maybe the terrible other doesn't remember! Lucan's gaze fell to those hands again, those powerful hands that recently held him with a vice-like grip in the Street of Booths in Puteoli while the slaver came for him.

The other put his hand out to Lucan's shoulder. Lucan cringed. The hand rested on his shoulder as a caress, not as the grip that he expected. Lucan stood up and closed his eyes momentarily as a wave of blackness and ear ringing passed over him.

"So they sent you here," the other spoke kindly. He remembered.

"I have you to thank," Lucan admitted sullenly, and looked the terrible other in the eye.

"I am Olipor the overseer, Lucan. I am to advise you and put you to work on the farm. And my first advice to you, Lucan, is this: if you behave yourself and work hard, you will be well treated. If you do not behave yourself, and do not work hard," Olipor broke off. This kind of talk would not impress Lucan's sort.

Yes, yes, I already know, Lucan was thinking. You do not have to tell me, Olipor. Floggings, Starvation. Shackles. The stocks. Perhaps the trestle. Does this villa have a dungeon? Where is the dungeon? And worst of all, a crucifixion. My buddy Petros was crucified at the front. For stealing. He was not scourged half to death first. Horrible how he took three days to die. I almost got nailed on a cross too. For driving off the carrion crows attacking his eyes. A mercy to a dying friend. 'Hey you there! What you trying to do! Prolong his life? Are you 'one of them'? *Ad malem crucem*, want to die too?' Perhaps not this new domine. 'Are you all right down there?'

Olipor was looking at Lucan's scarred wrists and ankles. He paused a moment longer to assure Lucan's full attention. He knew now how he would finish his sentence. He knew how he must handle Lucan's sort. He must come out with the unexpected to reach him. And it was essential that he arrest Lucan with a deep impression that he would not forget.

"As our Lord lives, Lucan, if you do not behave yourself, and do not work hard, you will still be well treated!"

Lucan looked up suddenly and spat on the ground.

Olipor ignored it. Perhaps he had failed. Perhaps not. "Your domine wishes to see you now, in the library upstairs. Do you know how to have audience with your domine?"

"Yes, I know what to do before a Roman dog," Lucan muttered.

"Take care!" Olipor warned sharply.

"Yes, sir," Lucan said in mock intimidation.

"I will see you at the noon rest hour," Olipor continued quietly, "and we will talk about your work assignment. Have you been about the villa?"

"No, sir"

"Then acquaint yourself with it after you have seen the domine."

"I will, sir." Lucan did not go directly in. First he sought out the slaves' privy located over one of the manure pits. He urinated in a vat in which the precious liquid was being collected as fertilizer for the vines. He took subversive pleasure in aiming at the flies about the rank brink. Romans, he called them. Relieved, he ambled toward the villa. He went to the stable court and entered the servants' hall from there. As he passed the sickroom, that curtain opened suddenly. War nerves took over. He shrank reflexively against the wall and crouched, ready to strike. His heart pounded. The slave girl, humming a pretty tune, came out of the room with duster and broom in hand. Unexpectedly seeing Lucan, she recoiled.

"Oh!" she exclaimed. "You frightened me!" She met his wild-eyed stare and noticed the beads of sweat form on his face as he lowered his hands.

"Lysistra? Lysistra!" Lucan slowly straightened and stared intensely. His breathing came in little gasps as he reached towards her. "Are you really here? Did they do it to you too?"

"Letitia," she said, and froze at his glazed-over stare. "Lucan, I am Letitia," she emphasized slowly. "I took care of you while you were in bed. Don't you remember?"

He wiped the sweat out of his eyes with the back of his hand and his eyes focused again.

"Yes, I remember." To find out that the bright angel of mercy was only a girl was more than he could bear. Yet he owed her his thanks, and she did remind him of his younger sister. He flushed deeply.

"May I call you sister? I had little sisters once. Lysistra, and my baby sister was Lucia."

"Why of course!" Letitia was acutely aware of what his words meant. She felt hesitant to inquire about the sisters and her eyes misted as she groped for an out. She regarded him with an interest that was more than sisterly. "Look at me, Lucan, I'm not so little, am I," she suggested gently. She pulled in her abdomen and lifted her chest to accentuate her spring buds. She was wearing her first bandeau now, and she was proud of it.

Gaius entered the hallway. "Letitia my love," he sang, a habit that annoyed her. As highest-ranking slave of the younger generation he was entitled to her, Letitia, joy, the only young female among them, as his bride. It was only a matter of time now before he would possess her.

Lucan was embarrassed. "Gaius," he asked quickly, "where would I find my domine?"

"Come, I'll show you," Gaius replied. "Letitia, you're needed in the kitchen, dear," he lilted again. Letitia smiled in resignation and went her way. Gaius sighed happily and followed behind. He led Lucan through the kitchen, through a hall to the colonnade that surrounded the open courtyard or peristyle of the house. He stopped at a flight of stairs.

"His library is the first to the right." Gaius pointed up. "I wish you luck," he added with a twinkle in his eye, upon seeing Lucan's nervousness. Gaius returned to the kitchen.

Lucan surveyed the peristyle with its central fishpond and fountain, flowers blooming brightly in pots, the clipped box, and grass. Then he took a final deep breath and went up to the indicated room. The door was closed. Quintus must be busy at his desk, as they said, with the farm accounts. Lucan hesitated a moment, then deciding not to disturb Quintus, started down the stairs again.

Sharp ears inside the room heard the footsteps, soft as they were, come to the door, stop, then turn back. Quintus came out to see who it was. Lucan, hearing the door open behind him, hurried down the stairs and broke into a run to the kitchen. Breathless and half laughing at his panic, he found Gaius.

"What! Back already?," exclaimed Gaius. "You didn't see him?"

"I-I—the door was closed!" Lucan blushed.

"He won't eat you up," laughed Gaius. "He is a reasonable domine. Go on back!"

Lucan made another attempt to report to his master. This time the door was open. He paused. His domine would be busy at the desk. He would walk up to the desk, salute, and wait for permission to speak. His domine would ask questions and he would answer. Indirectly, of course: 'the domine', or at best, 'my domine'. A slave never addresses his master directly. However a domine usually addresses his slave directly: 'you'. By a simple underhanded turn of thought a slave could easily see that indeed the domine was a thing, a 'the', whereas he the slave was the person, a 'you'. The proud Roman is really a blind deceived fool, Lucan thought. And if this one wants me to call him 'my domine' he will have to earn it. Why didn't he let me die!

When he stepped into the room, their eyes met. Lucan stopped short; Quintus's steady gaze froze him, though the blue eyes were friendly. He could not move, nor could he lower his gaze. He forgot all protocol. Him! This—boy—in a common laborer's garb—is my master! Beware! Underdogs make the worst masters! He felt the master's eyes searching his, sizing him up, reading whatever they could. Destructive fear banished all Lucan's thoughts.

Quintus had no difficulty analyzing what he saw in Lucan's face. Fear predominated. Something else showed in the head set, though. Defiance? Indomitable spirit? Quintus scrutinized Lucan. Clean tunic, good. Handsome enough. Some day a beard will hide those scars on his face. Dark hair, he needs a haircut. Get rid of those pederast's-slave locks behind the neck. The shadow of his brow dilates his pupils, makes him look wild. Strong, but thin. Good food will . . . I like him. For some reason I like him. If he proves himself I may promote him as my personal slave instead of Gaius. That would show Marcellus! He's not as young as I thought, closer to my age. A lot of tension written on that face. He's embarrassed now. Look at him blush.

Lucan felt uneasy. He was doing the forbidden to look his master in the eye. He looked down. His face glistened. His jaw quivered. What sort of Roman is this? he asked himself. Praise of a domine from his slaves is something to be regarded, and Gaius said he is a reasonable domine. He's younger than all of them. He seems kind. But what when he's angry? They're all the same . . . they're all the same . . .

Quintus finally spoke, gently, experimentally, in educated Greek. "Lucan," he said, "come here, tell me your background."

Tell him how I was free, and then unjustly enslaved? Describe to this mere puppy the crimes of his countrymen? Nothing doing! Lucan bit his lip and looked up defiantly.

Quintus took Lucan's defiance for what it was. He knew from the nightmares that Lucan spoke Greek. Apparently Lucan did not realize that he knew. Quintus was not certain whether he could win Lucan with warm casualness, or whether he had to terrify him into no nonsense with clipped formality. How can I best reach him? He probably knows nothing except brutality, he probably thinks kindness a weakness and won't respect it. I don't want him to think me some sort of malleable putty. Well, I guess there's no use trying to push him or rush him. I must wait until he responds. 'The Roman conquers by sitting down.' The old Roman proverb was not without meaning in his own life. He would lay siege with kindness and patience. Quintus changed the subject to help Lucan save face.

"How old are you, Lucan?" he asked, changing his language also, back to the Latin.

Lucan put on his stupid look. 'If you misbehave, you will still be well treated,' Olipor said of the master. Try him! Expose him!

Quintus was somewhat flustered. So he's giving me the silent treatment. He took up his scroll and his eyes followed the lines as he thought over his next step. Suddenly he looked at the slave again.

"Have you figured it out yet, Lucan?"

"Sir?" Lucan uttered off guard. Had the Roman read his thoughts?

Ah, mark a score for Quintus, I got him to speak. "How long have you been walking this old earth?"

"Too long!" Lucan shot back.

"You will never have reason to speak of life in this household in that tone I promise you," Quintus said earnestly.

"Thank you, sir," Lucan answered without gratitude.

"I was asking your age, please, Lucan."

Oh, so now he's begging me! Lucan impudently proceeded to calculate out loud back to his last celebrated birthday, his tenth. "The battle at the Slavic Danube in which King Rausimod fell, let's see," he hesitated.

"That was two years ago," Quintus prompted patiently.

Lucan looked up at the ceiling. "Then it couldn't have been longer than three years? five years? before that, when Licinius lost Thessalonica to Constantine."

"On which side were you?" Quintus interrupted to throw Lucan out of his nonsense, not a tactful question, considering that it was civil war.

"At the side of a Roman dog," Lucan retorted bitterly.

"I remember your scorn for the canine," Quintus smiled at the slave's obstinate pun and shook his head. "Have you forgotten all your manners, Lucan?" he asked seriously. "Or have you never learned them? Is bullying the only language you will understand? If you want bullying, Lucan, you are at the wrong address. If you will listen only to harshness, you had better leave right now through the very gate you stormed, and find harshness for yourself somewhere else."

Lucan stared, then his eyes narrowed as he detected the trap. If he stayed, that action would be equivalent to pledging his obedience. If he called the bluff, the Roman dog would seize him and flog him for attempting escape.

"I am serious, Lucan," Quintus reassured him upon seeing the slave's hesitation. "And on your way out read the inscription over that gate."

Try him! Expose his pretext of kindness! Lucan did not know how to respond to this sort of treatment. He was prepared only to fight, with all his heart, soul, and mind. Yet this Roman was not provoking him to fight. This Roman was instead, well, Lucan was not willing to admit that Quintus was getting past his defenses. To save face, he turned and went out of the room. He re-entered immediately, smartly, and greeted his master with a military salute.

"Ah!" Quintus exclaimed. "The inscription?"

"*Non vi sed voluntate*," not by force but by good will. Lucan looked down at the floor. His hands quivered. Now he had by no means surrendered. This was only a truce, a temporary yielding until he could back off and brood and come up with a new defense.

"Your name?" Quintus began again, with a twinkle in his eye.

"If it pleases my master, Lucan Oikonomikos, sir."

"You are still Lucan. Lucan Oikonomikos Legerius, slave of Quintus."

"My master is kind," Lucan bowed. He had permission to keep his basic identity.

"How old are you, Lucan? Do you know?"

"My master's slave—"

"Leave off your formality," Quintus interrupted. "This is a farm, not a patrician's resort."

"I am seventeen, sir," Lucan answered straightforwardly.

Quintus did not betray his delight. Lucan looked younger on the couch in the sick ward. He was old enough to be a peer; Quintus had recently turned seventeen and had been admitted into manhood on his birthday.

"You look well rested," Quintus commented.

"Yes, sir!" Lucan was well rested for the first time since disaster came to his home.

"Do you feel as well?"

Almost well enough to thank you for rescuing me, sir, Lucan thought, however he was not ready to admit that yet. "My master's slave . . ." Lucan stumbled to a stop and started again. "I do, sir," he admitted.

"That is good. Then you may start work. Only a little at a time. You have been ill. And you are thin!"

"Yes, sir." Lucan glowered. He wasn't thin before taken into slavery.

"Tell me, how did you survive that sea voyage? You had to eat and drink something!"

"Cabbage, sir."

"Cabbage!" Quintus laughed delightedly. "What a coincidence! Living proof of the virtues of Halmyridian cabbage. I grow it on contract for the ships. Keeps green and fresh on a long voyage, doesn't it?"

Lucan swallowed back the nausea in his throat with concentrated effort.

"Cabbage, the great heal-all. Rotting cabbage is rather awful, isn't it?" Quintus grimaced at the irony. He could see that Lucan told the truth. "Well, you don't have to eat cabbage here; there are many other vegetables. And eggs, fruit, cheese, even meat once in a while, and of course grain and beans, and oh yes! Beans and grain! As for wine, well, have lots of milk. All you want. It will help put flesh on your bones."

"Thank you, sir." How about all that food! Lucan looked up amazed. For the past seven years he had nothing much more than cheap coarse grain with stomach searing vinegar as an excuse for wine. That was all he as a slave expected to have for the rest of his life. I have already helped myself to the meat, master, he thought.

"What is your work, Lucan?"

Lucan's eyes narrowed.

"You know, your training. Your talents."

Lucan looked away.

"Don't you know?"

Lucan did not want his talent raped.

"You said you were at the side of a Roman," Quintus hesitated for emphasis, "soldier. Were you his body servant?"

"Yes, sir," Lucan admitted sullenly.

"And you are afraid I will assign you the same?"

The resentment nearly boiled in Lucan's eyes.

"No need to be so conceited, Lucan," Quintus dressed him down dryly. "Olipor will assign you duties on the farm. However I wish to see you privately every day. Olipor will advise you when to report. Do you understand everything?"

"Yes, sir," Lucan breathed. Now why all this personal attention? he asked himself suspiciously.

"Also you will sleep in the hall with the other slaves. Gaius will help you get settled tonight. You may go now."

Lucan lingered a brief moment and squirmed uneasily as he searched Quintus's face. What kind of Roman are you? he thought. I escape into your villa and you don't turn me over to certain death; you buy me instead and tend me in your sick ward. You assign me excellent food, not the lot of the lowly. You don't beat me for forgetting my manners. Your slaves are not fearful. They are good-natured. They speak of themselves as a family. I don't understand. Lucan saw an aurora of light framing the young Roman, like the illuminated god. He blinked and realized that it was only that his eyes had filled. Yes, the young Roman had gotten past his defenses, and that annoyed him.

Lucan snapped back to reality. He was supposed to be leaving now, not standing and staring. The master will be angry. This kindness may be only conditional. Don't think you can win me by it, master. I am planning how I can have my way with you!

Quintus had seen the wonder that had passed over Lucan's face and he cherished that sign. That spark of response would have much to do with his own success or failure with the slave. "You may go now," he repeated to give the slave an out.

"Yes, sir. Thank you, sir." Lucan saluted smartly, then backed toward the open door. He backed into the doorjamb instead and, flustered, turned and bolted out.

"Lucan!" The sharp summons stopped him in his tracks and pulled him back into the awful presence.

"No-o-o, no, Lucan," Quintus's blue eyes sparkled with amusement, "when you leave, turn around and walk out like a man. Diocletian's eastern innovations have not penetrated this household, nor will they. Look, I'm out of ink. Get me some, would you please, quickly? There's a big pot of it in . . ."

That was all that Lucan heard. Destructive fear banished the instructions. Quintus held out the empty ink pot. Lucan, afraid to ask his master to repeat, took it and set out to find the ink himself. He shunned the idea of asking another slave. He found the ink by himself although in the process he had to search almost the entire house. He paused in the colonnade at the bottom of the steps. At his end of the peristyle lay the baths and summer dining room with frescoed walls depicting the *memento mori*, skeletons dining on succulent dishes and lush fruit. Eat, drink, and be merry, for tomorrow we die. At the opposite end was the senior master's office in the alcove that divided the private peristyle from the entrance court, the atrium. On the west side of the peristyle would be the bedrooms; no need to look there. Remaining to be searched were the easterly side of the peristyle, the alcove and adjacent rooms at that end, and the rooms about the atrium. On the easterly side, next to the stairway where he stood, was the winter dining room. It was still in use these nippy spring days. This room was delightful. Ferns hung in baskets from the ceiling. A middle-aged woman reached up to water them. The walls were frescoed with bright rural landscapes. The floor was mosaic. Three dining couches curved around a carved round dining table. A carved sideboard stood against the wall.

The next room entranced Lucan momentarily. A library. Cabinets around the walls and in the center held a copious collection of scrolls. How easily he could get absorbed in them and forget his time! There were busts of authors and Minerva, and a story in mosaic on the floor. He would like the task of cleaning and dusting this room. This nostalgic reminder of his childhood ambition, to be a scholar, filled him with longing. Suddenly he was a child again, at his books, his father bending over him to help. "You are a Lucan," his father would say, for his name was a poet's name, and a derivative of the word light. And the father with his hands laid gently on the boy's shoulders would add, "You shall be a light to the feet of men so that they shall not stumble." At this recollection tears stung Lucan's eyes. He was still only a slave, he reminded himself bitterly. He hurried on. The room next to the alcove was locked. A storeroom, he surmised.

He went into the alcove. Ink would be found in this office if anywhere. Here were the household and farm accounts, records, documents, and the strongbox. From here the lord of the house could watch the comings and goings in both household courts, or he could curtain off the sides of the alcove for privacy. Here the lord's dominion was concentrated. Still no ink. Tingling from the awesome atmosphere, Lucan tiptoed out into the atrium.

This court was roofed, and the roof sloped down to an open skylight in the center so that rain water was collected in the center pool of the atrium and piped to a cistern. Various colors of marble veneer fashioned the patterned walls. The rich mosaic floor was dazzling under the sunbeams from the skylight.

In the transverse wings of the atrium Lucan saw busts of ancestors, and statues of household and rural deities. Lucan looked into the rooms, two conversation rooms, a cloakroom, and a wool-working room.

He entered the other room next to the alcove. This was a reading and writing room, and hurrah! Here was the ink. Lucan then realized how much time he had taken. As he stepped into the colonnade again he looked fearfully across the peristyle up to the balcony where he could see the young master's door. Oh miserable slavery! He broke out into a fresh sweat as he ran along the colonnade to the stairway.

Meanwhile Quintus waited and waited and waited for Lucan to come with the ink. He was irritated and ready to get some for himself when Lucan finally returned. "Where have you been! What took you so long!" he demanded.

"P-please, sir, I-I lost my way."

"Lost!" Quintus exclaimed. He searched Lucan's face to see if the slave was in earnest. "What do you think this place is, a labyrinth or something?

Lucan was speechless.

"You do know what I'm talking about?" Quintus pried.

"Yes, sir, the Knossos palace."

"And you learned that growing up in an army tent?"

"No, sir, I grew up in a one-room cottage."

"I see, overwhelmed by grandeur. You haven't seen your old master's villa?"

"My old landlord?" Lucan's face closed in resentment.

"What did you do, go from room to room?"

"I did, sir,"

"I see. And your direction of search took you to the study last?"

"Yes, sir. After the alcove."

"What you're trying to tell me is that my instructions went in one ear and out the other, and you were too damned scared to ask me to repeat. Right? It's about time you learned that a Roman can be human too."

"Y-yes, sir." Lucan's look said, how did you know?

"And you had better learn the layout of this villa!"

Seeing that the water used with the ink needed changing, Lucan shakily refilled it with fresh water. "May I go, sir?" he asked timidly.

"Yes, Lucan, thank you," Quintus answered, acknowledging the act of initiative.

Lucan toured the villa again, with keen interest. He had better learn it. Besides, once he assumed a normal routine, he may not have opportunity to enter the family section of the villa at all. This was only a modest farm home, but by Hestia! Compared with his childhood farm hut this was really something! He peeked into the master bedroom and gawked at the pair of frescoes of the reluctant bride and the passionate bride. His father would love these, he thought. He found the family bath suite off the peristyle and adjacent to the slaves' baths off the kitchen. There in the family bath suite was a water closet. Indoor plumbing! The kitchen had running water as well. Underfoot he felt the central heating by means of hot air circulating between the double tiles of the floor. The mosaic floors, and the statuary were copies of the finest works of art.

Lucan could see that the Romans had a particular genius for providing so much material comfort and beauty for a large number of people at one time. He had heard that the eternal city really was a sight to behold. Out of his great curiosity he took the nerve to ask the background of this modest rural villa. The family ancestors had built it on a do-it-yourself basis. The builders had architects draw up the plans, probably according to rules laid by Vitruvius, and this accounted for the harmony of the layout, the solid foundations and the pleasing proportions of the rooms.

Lucan returned to the kitchen when the water clock indicated noon and found to his surprise only three places set, and the others assembled in the servants' hall. Letitia explained that the others, being Christians, were keeping a fast during the days in which the Bridegroom is taken away, the Friday and Saturday before the Resurrection Day, whatever that meant. "You will be eating with the young domine and Megas."

Zeus! Not if he could help it! "Are you going to serve us and wait table while you fast, Letitia? That's awkward! I'll wait on them. You go on."

"Why, thank you, Lucan."

Lucan served his master first, then Megas, and then stood at attention near the table.

"Aren't you eating?" Quintus queried.

"After you, sir."

"Nonsense! Here! Sit down!" Quintus put his plate in Lucan's place. "Get me a plate now, and bring the whole kettle on so nobody has to jump up and down."

"Very well, sir." Lucan obeyed. Seated, he waited for his master's lead. Megas waited politely for his domine to begin.

"Eat!" Quintus commanded good-naturedly.

Lucan fell to. Megas followed, and finally Quintus. What Lucan could not know yet was that Quintus was not being suspicious; he was being a solicitous husbandman. They relaxed, and Quintus engaged Megas in conversation about his newest observations of wildlife while he was out after wood. Megas related watching an active fox den beneath a fallen tree, which he asked permission to spare, and told of an encounter between a boar and the vixen. Quintus was fascinated and asked for more details. Lucan listened attentively and spooned into a second plate of stew.

Letitia's big brother Alexis, a vinedresser and self appointed guardian of his maturing sister, upbraided her afterwards for allowing Lucan to wait table.

"He could have poisoned the domine!"

"How? Where would he have gotten it?"

"He could have picked mushrooms, dummy, murder and suicide in the same dish."

"What for?" She was in tears.

"How do you know he wouldn't? He ain't branded for nothing; he's incorrigible. You have to watch that kind. He wasn't sent here, you know, he crashed the gate."

"He was so sent here, Olipor said!" He's gentle. I've taken care of him, you know."

"If you don't watch out, he'll take care of you! You had better put his straw pallet in the middle of the servants' hall where we can keep an eye on him."

Lucan was listening in the shadows of the corridor. He stepped into the kitchen. "Please don't scold her. I was only trying to be helpful. I am sorry to upset you." With out waiting for an answer, he continued back to the servants' hall.

They were talking about him there, too.

"A talent? A whole a talent?" Old Servius was incredulous.

"That's right," Mamercus the Arab stable manager's voice was terse with disappointment.

"A fine filly for you, Mamercus," Paulo, Alexis's half brother quipped sarcastically.

"Here, Mamercus, here comes your filly now," Baltus the plowman cracked, indicating the approaching Lucan with his chin and his black assistant Manius leered out of a tongueless mouth. They all laughed.

"Walk down and trot back and show us your points, filly," Sextus, the sixth acquisition, a lusty Iberian, ordered.

Lucan dropped down quickly on an empty pallet, not near the warmth of the smoke room, nor the comfort of the kitchen, but right in the middle where all could watch his comings and goings. He did not intend to become the rest hour entertainment, or worse, the object of satiric gratification.

"See here, Mamercus, your filly can't even stand properly," Paulo, also a vinedresser, put in. "Do we have to cross-tie him?"

"The entire bag of money? All of it? Some bag!" Baltus made another bid for laughs and Manius leered loyally.

"Drop it, will you?" Mamercus said. "You wouldn't want to be in his place, would you?"

They were talking over him. Lucan got up and headed for the exit to the stable court.

"All right, all right, little round mortar, no harm done," Kaiso called after him.

"So let's not get sore about it, don't you agree?" Alexis said.

Lucan kept going right on out.

"Someone had better go after him," Alexis said.

Lucan broke into a run across the stable court. A chestnut horse neighed at him in passing and the weanling lambs bleated expectantly as he ran by the milking shed into the storehouse. He ducked into the sun-heated olive oil press and extraction rooms, found them too revealing, tried crouching behind an amphora in the olive oil storeroom, shuddered, went out to the center aisle again and tried the fruit and root storerooms. Locked. The swallows in nests glued to beams sounded alarm. The wagon room at the outside entrance was too easy to search, and there was hardly any straw left. He went out onto the threshing floor where a breeze chilled his sweaty body. The vegetable fields out there wouldn't conceal anyone. Back inside on the cool side of the storehouse he felt that the wine presses and fermentation court were sparse of cover. He dashed back into the center aisle yet another time amidst now frantic cries of swooping swallows and climbed a ladder to the granaries on the second floor.

He climbed into a bin of grain. He could flounder under, if necessary. He wiggled in a little to see. Then he realized that nobody was pursuing him. He breathed deeply, sighed, and moved to get out, and discovered that the grain could be as treacherous as quicksand. With a yelp he made a spread eagle, then like a viper rising to strike he reared up suddenly, clasped the edge of the bin, and pulled himself out. What an itchy mess of grain and weevils and sweat all over him! He would certainly get a scolding for stirring up the weevils. The infested grain could easily have been skimmed off the surface, that is, before he went swimming through it. Lucan shucked off his tunic and loincloth and shook out the grain.

Swallow warnings activated the alarm in his stomach. Someone was down there.

"Lucan? Are you up there? It's Olipor."

"I'm here, sir."

"I'm coming up."

"Y-yes, sir." Lucan wiggled into his clothes again and walked out to a window in the aisle by the time Olipor reached the top. There was no telltale trail of grain, Lucan noticed with relief.

Olipor stood beside him. He did not let on if he thought it unusual that Lucan be found in the loft. "Gorgeous view, eh?"

"Beautiful, sir."

"Recognize the crops?"

"Most of them, sir. It's been a while."

"How long?"

"About seven years."

"It will all come back to you fast." Olipor took Lucan on a verbal tour of the vegetable and grain fields, alfalfa meadows, fallow fields being grazed by sheep before the spring plowing, fruit and olive orchards and vineyard, as they casually moved from window to window. They could see the others, including the young master, giving the vineyard its monthly spading.

"That's the Domine's library that you see across the courtyard."

"Can he see everything from there?" Lucan asked uneasily.

"Yes he can."

They talked about Lucan's work assignment, and agreed that Lucan would try each of the various tasks to see which best fitted his abilities and interests. Of course Olipor would have tried him out like this anyway; that was good management. He shrewdly knew that he could solicit Lucan's cooperation more readily if Lucan felt that he had a part in the decision.

"Then it's the kitchen garden for a few days until you get your strength back. Come on down with me now and I'll issue you your clothing."

Lucan hesitated, obviously agitated. Try him! "I need to help winnow the southeast bin of grain, sir. Soon."

"Yes I know it has weevils. They go down only a hand's breadth, you may have noticed, unless we try to cool the grain by winnowing. Then the infestation would be scattered throughout."

"I'm afraid they're scattered deeply, sir." His stomach hurt at the confession.

"Why, did you dig down deep?"

"I-I nearly drowned in it, sir."

"How did you manage that!" Olipor then noticed the telltale dust in Lucan's hair.

Agony twisted Lucan's face. "I-I Mamercus's filly. I'm not a pederast's darling, sir!"

Olipor comprehended. "Lucan, no one will touch you here! They were talking about a mate for the Arabian stallion down there. The young domine has virtually promised Mamercus a filly whenever he has the cash."

"That talent for me, sir? A whole talent?"

"Don't you value your life?"

"I didn't then. I wanted release from the calamities of life."

"You had better start valuing your life now that he has redeemed you at such a price."

"I value it, Olipor, I value it." His eyes brimmed. "So much that I want to buy my life back. He has put such a price on my head that I shall never earn my freedom!"

"Don't let that concern you."

"How can you say that?"

"Many of us have volunteered our bondage here, an island of refuge in a sea of crassness, brutality, injustice. You shall find out."

"He won't sell me, then, when I'm restored?"

"Hardly. Get well in peace." They regarded each other silently.

"I'm ready to go down, now, sir," Lucan acquiesced finally.

The fiery chestnut horse stuck his head over the stall door again, and stretching forth his neck, gave two inquisitive nickers. Lucan went up and took a look. The Arabian stallion. "Holy Apollo!" he exclaimed softly. "Have I got to ride you!" The horse arched his neck and shoved his muzzle into Lucan's breast and sniffed.

Lucan caught up to Olipor and followed him to the storeroom near the servants' quarters where he was given a cloak, a pair of stout leather half boots, and a blanket, all to last a year. "And though one usually has to earn it, here is a second tunic, to change into before interviews with the domine."

Lucan nodded. The others will appreciate this special treatment, he thought apprehensively, especially after his wisecrack to Gaius in the kitchen. He put his bundle of acquisitions at the head of his pallet and proceeded to explore the kitchen area enclosed by the bakery, boiler room and slaves' baths at one end, and pantry and utensil storerooms at the other. He paid particular attention to the tool room where there was a place for everything, carefully outlined in charcoal on the wall, so that one would lose no time in finding the various farm implements. Finally he sneaked a slice of cheese and a handful of raisins from the pantry and returned to the job of weeding the seed nurseries.

At the evening chore time Lucan lingered about the stables and sought ways to make himself useful feeding the pigs and lambs. He ached in anticipation of the horses. So dazzled was he by the fiery Arab that he scarcely noticed the meritorious black gelding, and the quality cart mules. Mamercus finally acknowledged his volunteer helper with music from heaven.

"Do you ride?"

"Yes, please!"

"Then choose."

"Thank you!" Lucan selected the finest halter and bridle in the tack room. Only the best for the best! He took up a fistful of grain. He hung the bridle on the hitching post and went for his prize. Mamercus said nothing. Baltus and his mute helper Manius loitered outside their ox stalls to watch. Gaius came in to help exercise horses, gave Mamercus a startled look, and shrugged. Mamercus returned a smug smile. Baltus winked. The young upstart will learn the hard way. The others slowly filed into the stable court from the servants' hall to watch. Lucan let the stallion sniff him over thoroughly, then haltered him with ease.

The stallion came out rearing. Lucan slipped a hand under his neck in a caress, and speaking soothingly, hung on until he came down. Then he nimbly braced his forearm on the horse's neck between the front of the steed's shoulder and the halter shank, leaned in and kept his feet out at an angle to avoid the flinty hooves. With this firm leverage on the horse he wheeled and turned with him, soothing him unceasingly with his voice, until the stallion relaxed his neck and responded. At the hitching post Lucan correctly secured the lead line around the animal's neck before slipping off the halter. The horse wasn't going to permit the bridle until he got a sniff of that fistful of grain. Ears forward, neck arched, head lowered, the horse ate up the bit with the grain, and he was bridled. A murmur sounded among the observers.

Lucan stood and waited until Mamercus and Gaius were ready, each ponying a mule. Lucan led the dancing stallion alongside the mounting block. The observers were laying their bets among themselves. With a slow but steady movement Lucan stepped onto the mounting block and slipped up. They applauded.

The horse stepped forward and Lucan checked him with a flick of the wrist. Then he sat there, hands light, legs relaxed. The horse bent his neck around and muzzled him on the foot. The others laughed. Lucan fell in behind the other riders.

"He is like fire," he said to Mamercus.

"That's his name! Ignis!" Mamercus replied.

They jogged briskly along the farm roads bordered with elms, leading to the fruit and olive orchards, vineyards and fields. At the stone wall separating the cultivated lands from the meadows and woods, Gaius said, "I'll take you to those woods sometime." They admired the commanding view of the country rolling down to the sea and ending in cliffs and beaches.

"This is God's country," Gaius gestured widely, "what made Virgil and Pliny lyrical! Roman Campania!"

Almost back to the villa, Lucan spoke up tremulously. "May I?" He pointed back from where they came.

"Go ahead," Mamercus said.

Lucan turned the stallion about. With a whoop he had him at breakneck gallop back to the wall. They watched him turn the horse on his hocks, stop, and stand. He legged him into full gallop again, and reined in for a stop about half way back. The horse shook his head and refused. Lucan clamped his legs down and doubled the horse back. The surprised horse grunted and scrambled for his balance and stood trembling. Lucan turned him toward home again, put him into a gallop, and signaled for the halt. Ignis obeyed. Lucan walked him up to the others.

"Holy Pegasus, Lucan!" Gaius reproached him.

Lucan scarcely noticed. He was somewhere in heaven. Then his scanning eyes took in the upstairs library windows and he flinched and followed the others wordlessly back to the stables and helped rub down and feed the horses.

They joined the other young men in the baths. They scraped the dirt and sweat off one another, soaked in the hot bath, and scraped again. Then they plunged in the cold bath. Lucan watched with uneasy fascination as the solicitous massaging erupted into masculine horseplay, benign, however, compared to that in the army camps. He hung back and got dressed. He did not want anybody tweaking his groin. They seized him and threw him in.

"Try your extra tunic, Lucan!" They laughed and jeered at him.

When Quintus ran in to see what the ruckus was about, they laughingly pulled him in with them too, clothes and all. Olipor checked on the uproar. "I—got wet," Quintus declared with great dignity, and they all laughed and splashed at Olipor who walked out together with the young domine.

"Relax, Lucan," Quintus commented in passing to Lucan who was regarding them all with wide-eyed astonishment.

There was much joviality at supper about the possible contents of the soup as they ravenously partook of it. Quintus's good humor did not last long that evening, however. Back upstairs again he worked at his accounts in preparation for calculating taxes. He couldn't seem to be able to calculate the areas of the various commercial croplands and calculate the proportion of tax for each parcel in units of the *iugerum* and come up with a figure that agreed reasonably with Gaius's calculations. And damned if he was going to ask Gaius for help! He was also angry at himself for paying so much for that disreputable refugee last week in a moment of rash magnanimity. How could he possibly show responsibility and maturity and leadership that way! And why did Gaius, his apprentice overseer, bring him the whole damn purse for the slaver to see! Oh curses! He castigated himself soundly. Overwhelmed with a feeling of inadequacy, he ran his fingers through his hair, scratched his head, and tried to concentrate again. And why did he have to get so damn sleepy! He propped up his chin on the heel of his hand. He was in no good mood when someone shuffled softly before his desk to get his attention.

"What! are you doing up here?" he demanded sharply without looking up. "No one disturbs me up here in the evening."

"I'm sorry, sir," Lucan hastened to back out. This Roman isn't to be trusted! At one moment he is your new friend and the next he is jumping down your throat and barking at your liver! I'd do best to stay clear of him!

"Oh, it's you!" Quintus was surprised. "Come back here!" he coaxed.

Thoroughly scared, Lucan obeyed. He only wanted to report that he accomplished his master's bidding of this morning. He knew the layout of the villa. Of the whole estate, in fact. He also felt obligated to thank this young man for rescuing him. Now look at what he got himself into. He resented the Roman that he should be afraid of him.

"Did someone send you up here?"

"N-no, sir, I-I . . ."

"And you didn't report to anyone when you left the servant's hall?" Quintus was annoyed. Where was Gaius's head? This fugitive could be dangerous!

"N-no sir, I-I didn't tell anyone." Lucan suddenly realized that he should have.

"Did you come and go freely about your former master?"

"Why yes, sir, of necessity at the frontier in a campaign tent."

"And I suppose as far as the guards were concerned you didn't exist," Quintus quipped sarcastically.

"They knew me, sir."

"In more ways than one, I daresay," Quintus commented dryly and Lucan flinched. Quintus deduced that he was an officer's boy at one time. And he seemed willing to talk now. "At ease, Lucan," he sighed.

"Thank you, sir." Lucan remained wary.

"I suppose it's no secret anymore down there what I am doing up here." Quintus indicated his scrolls and tablets.

"It's admirable, sir."

"Indeed!" Quintus looked up suddenly and searched Lucan's face. He didn't think he could take it having this slave make fun of him also.

Lucan was thinking to himself that it seemed he couldn't do anything right tonight.

Quintus glanced at the window. "I watched you take my stallion out this afternoon."

"You did, sir?" Lucan tensed for trouble.

"Nobody, but nobody, rides my horse."

"I-I d-didn't know!" Lucan blanched. Surely Mamercus knew that!

"Do you always act first and ask later?"

"Not at all, sir."

"Who put you up?"

Lucan knew better than to name names. "They asked me if I wanted to help and told me to choose, sir."

"So you chose the best animal in the stable." Was there a trace of a smile on the master's face?

"Yes, sir, the best."

"And just what were you doing with him?

"Some cavalry exercises, sir. You see, Xenophon . . ." he stopped. He shouldn't presume to instruct the master.

"Holy Castor and Pollux! You were a knight's boy?"

"Oh, no, sir, I learned from the grooms, sir. When my master didn't need me I used to help at the cavalry tents, sir."

"I have to admit I admire excellence. You may continue exercising him. But don't let my landlord catch you with the horses. He's the knight. He'd confiscate you."

Lucan shuddered. "I won't sir. Thank you, sir!"

"Now, Lucan, you haven't explained why you came up here."

Lucan couldn't explain that he was curiously drawn to this young Roman with the smiling voice who had rescued him at more than nominal cost to himself. "To-to a-apologize for my s-shortcoming this morning. I know the villa now, sir."

"Really! So that if I needed to sharpen my quill?"

"The pen knife is on the desk in the alcove of the atrium, sir."

"Is that where I left it!" Quintus snickered. I'll have to be more careful, he thought.

"Shall I fetch it, sir?"

"No, but you may go. I need to get back to work."

Seeing that the ink water needed changing again, Lucan attended to it. He checked the oil in the reading lamp, and lit the night-light. He found the nightshirt in the clothes chest and laid it at the foot of the bed. He lifted the mattress swag. No urinal? The master must use the water closet downstairs. He turned down the bed, then it suddenly occurred to him that the master may think he was hinting to join him there. He threw the Roman a quick glance and felt certain that it had crossed the Roman's mind also. He had to explain himself fast and get out. He hadn't said thank you yet. He couldn't just blurt it out, he needed a way of easing into it. A whole talent for me? Why?

Quintus was annoyed at his dallying. He didn't want anyone controlling him, telling him when to go to bed under the pretext of waiting on him.

"Lucan, whatever are you doing?"

"Please, sir, I—You look tired, sir," he dodged.

"Why, Lucan?" Quintus insisted.

"I-I am t-trying to say th-thank you, sir, for rescuing me, at such a great c-cost to yourself."

"A great cost?"

"A t-talent, sir?" Lucan blurted out. "Not a d-decimal error?"

A decimal error? The wiseass Greek proofread his work upside down? Lucan can compute? Quintus found the decimal error, worked intently on the wax tablets for a few moments, then put the stylus down and sighed. He looked at the slave waiting very uncomfortably before him. He was about to pun sarcastically about talent when something from his own past struck a different response. This slave, he realized, was making an offering in the only way he could. The crushed flowers. Remember the crushed flowers, he said to himself, alluding to his early childhood when he came running up to his mother offering her precious lilies that she had hand bred and had been cultivating and watching for weeks. She had accepted them graciously, and then she had burst into tears. Now he was at the other end of things. Is this how God feels about burnt offerings of his beautiful creatures?

"Now, Lucan, about that talent. I don't want to hear those words again. Not from anyone." His voice was rather firm.

"Yes, sir. No, sir. No more, sir." Lucan's voice thickened. "Only that I shall never be able to repay you, sir."

"You need only to be useful, Oikonomikos," Quintus replied in a softened tone. "That shall be thanks enough."

"Yes, sir, I shall, sir," Lucan replied without relief or gratitude.

Quintus realized he had said the wrong thing to the slave. On the farm Lucan would have no opportunity to buy himself back and they both knew it. He should never have implied that the slave's place on the farm was so hopeless. How could he then inspire incentive in him to work? He had made another strategic error in slave management. He really needed the help of Olipor the overseer more than he was willing to admit. Those who knew him when he would put his boots on the wrong feet he let Olipor handle; that way he wouldn't upset their harmony. This one he would cut his teeth on. But it's a damned if you do, damned if you don't. He had to ease over his blunder somehow. Yet the fact that Lucan even bothered to come upstairs to see him was a point in his favor. Yes, score a point for Quintus.

"Thank you for coming up, Lucan," the smile returned to his voice and face.

"Good night, sir." Lucan left quickly before his frustration became too evident.

* * *

When he returned to the kitchen Lucan found out what Postumus meant by 'one of us'. The slaves, instead of going to bed, were assembled in the kitchen and, with scripture readings and psalms and prayer, began the Paschal Vigil which would last until cockcrow the next morning, Resurrection Day. Though the Emperor Constantine had only this year declared Sunday an official holiday in the cities, the farm slaves had to work as usual and could not go down to their parent church in Puteoli even for this great festival. Bishop Nicodemus at Puteoli sent up a visiting bishop to baptize and celebrate. With him came Marcellus's slave Marcipor who would be initiated into the faith.

Lucan, unable to sleep through their fervor, finally joined them in the early morning. At the joyous singing of a psalm, he realized that this is where the singing came from that he heard in his dream about paradise and the golden god.

> "The stone which the builders rejected,
> has become the chief cornerstone.
> This is the Lord's doing,
> and it is marvelous in our eyes.
> This is the day which the Lord has made;
> let us rejoice and be glad in it . . .
> O give thanks to the Lord, for he is good;
> for his steadfast love endures for ever!"

They flowed into the singing of Holy Scripture pertinent to Easter.

> "Christ being raised from the dead will never die again;
> death no longer has dominion over him.
> The death he died, he died to sin, once for all,
> but the life he lives, he lives to God.
> Likewise look upon yourselves as dead to sin,
> and alive to God in Christ Jesus."

From Gaius's reading and the bishop's preaching Lucan heard the remarkable story of how wicked men put to death Jesus their Domine God Incarnate who went about doing good, and healing and teaching. Their Lord, to whom love was more important than even the strictest religious observances, than even his own life, taught that the Kingdom of God was here now within us inasmuch as we step out of our selfishness and live lovingly with those around us. Christ, God Incarnate, died for his cause. On the third day Christ rose from the dead, and came among his disciples on various occasions during forty days and broke bread with them and reassured them and forgave them their unfaithfulness. He commanded his followers to preach repentance and forgiveness of sins in his name among all nations, to the uttermost part of the world. He returned to the Father, and sent the promise of the Father, God's Holy Spirit, upon us. "And remember, he said that he is with us always, even to the end of the world."

"... Christ has been raised from the dead,
    the first fruits of those who have fallen asleep.
For as by a man came death,
    by a man has come also the resurrection of the dead.
For as in Adam all die,
    so also in Christ shall all be made alive."

At cockcrow the baptismal party, leaving the others in silent prayer, took up torches and singing a psalm they processed around the outside of the buildings to the stream in their master's garden. Lucan slipped out and followed. He looked up and noticed that the young master, also unable to sleep, stood watching from an upstairs window.

"As a deer longs for the water brook,
    so longs my soul for thee, O God ..."

At the stream Marcipor renounced any allegiance to Satan and was anointed with the oil of exorcism. Then he stripped himself of the old garb and stepped into the stream with the bishop who questioned his belief and baptized him three times in the Name of the Father, the Son, and the Holy Spirit. Marcipor emerged a new-born Christian from the flowing water. Anointed with the sign of the cross, the new lamb put on snow white new clothes, the new life. Then the enlightened new lamb processed singing with his sponsors back into the kitchen where they would celebrate the Eucharist.

". . . I went with the throng, and led them in procession
to the house of God,
with glad shouts and songs of thanksgiving, a multitude
keeping festival . . .
The Lord is my shepherd, I shall lack nothing."

In the presence of all the bishop confirmed the baptism with the laying on of hands. They all exchanged the kiss of peace. At this point Lucan, the only unbaptized person among them, was dismissed. He drifted into the servants' hall which was unoccupied except for Megas, and the big Slav slept. Fearing that Megas might awaken and take this opportunity to undo him, Lucan sat down next to the kitchen door.

They proceeded to break bread with their Risen Lord. The table was decked with a white linen cloth and the scrolls of scripture, and a chalice and plate to receive the offerings of bread and wine from the faithful. The bishop, Olipor, and Gaius took their places behind the dining table, facing the standing household.

Lucan tried to listen to the prayers. He must have dosed off, for the next thing he knew, Marcipor had stumbled upon him. He rose to his feet.

"Excuse me! Lucan, I am Marcipor," the young man introduced himself as they strolled to the stables where Marcipor started to tack up his horse. "You met my domine when you first came here, didn't you? Marcellus, your Domine's landlord. The knight."

"I'm not sure whom I met on that day," Lucan grimaced.

"Marcellus claims that you are lucky to be alive. You can thank God that you have come into this household."

"Is slavery something to be thankful about, Marcipor?" Lucan returned.

"Haven't you noticed?" Marcipor asked. "It's so obvious!"

"Noticed what?"

"The love these people have for each other."

Lucan did not answer right away. In his short time at Good Will he already sensed an undercurrent, and one never knows when an undercurrent becomes treacherous. "Yes, I have noticed," he commented dryly and rubbed his bruised throat.

"I heard about that. I mean they are like a family," Marcipor explained, "one family in God. And the young domine is a strong sympathizer," he confided. "Sometimes it is hard to tell whether Quintus is acting out of his humanitarian Stoicism, or whether he is trying to practice the Christian ethic apart from the faith. I myself have just become one of them. I have been an initiate."

"I know, I watched," Lucan said. "What does this baptism, as you call it, do for you?"

"I became God's son more than in the general sense that he made us all. A special relationship has begun between God and me. Perhaps you shall . . ."

"Oh no," Lucan declared, "not I! The gods have betrayed me! I am not going to give any god allegiance again! Especially not a god who sacrifices his own son. I still have nightmares about a treacherous father. Will this god be as treacherous to his adopted sons? That makes me ill!"

"Get acquainted with the Christ before you reject him, Lucan. Ask any of these people what great thing they know," Marcipor urged. "Through him who does not distinguish between male and female, slave and free, they have new human dignity and in gratitude they have dedicated their service to him to the death and life after death."

"How do they serve a god they can't see?"

"They show their love for him by loving those around them. And they serve the young domine as though they were serving their Lord."

"Oh no, Marcipor. Whoa! Ask me what grave thing I know!"

"Lucan, we mean it in all seriousness!"

"Sincerity doesn't necessarily commend a belief," Lucan retorted. "I have known men who sincerely believe, in the worst!"

"I dare say you have," Marcipor thoughtfully regarded Lucan's scars. "Believe me, Lucan, as I came to know the Christ, my life was transformed. I have been a slave for only a little over three years. My father, God rest his soul, was a state official brought to ruin by tax quotas. Marcellus's step-father bought me. Shortly after, I met the household here. When Marcellus comes up to see Quintus, I visit with the household. That is how I came to know the Christ. I came to realize that slavery was not brought down upon me by some capricious god, rather, our Heavenly Father helps me through it. Certainly in body I am at the mercy of Marcellus, but in Christ I am free!"

Marcipor led the horse out of the stall and turned to Lucan full face.

"Lucan, there is nothing our masters can do to our lives, our bodies, that will destroy our souls! You and I will probably never be free from slavery, but in Christ, who does not distinguish between slave and free, we become freedmen, persons of worth. We can take personal responsibility for our lives and our small part of the world."

"Are you in your right mind?" Lucan cocked his head.

Marcipor laughed. "Yes, Lucan, I assure you that. Furthermore, I am an educated man. Well, this is too much for you at one time, I can see. And I must hurry home. I have to get back before my domine wakes and calls for me and I am found out. I'd get a hundred lashes at least, or lose my head at the worst. You see, I am away without leave."

"How do you manage that?"

"My domine dismisses me at night when the chamberlain goes on duty," Marcipor explained.

"Oh. Does my domine know that you have been coming?"

"Yes." Marcipor mounted the horse. "But he won't tell Marcellus on me. He promised."

"And you trust the Roman?" Lucan asked incredulously.

"Certainly!" Marcipor exclaimed and rode out into the dawn.

Lucan watched Marcipor go and pondered him. Marcipor risks his neck to come here, and he has been doing this for some time. He comes from a good family. And he hasn't been a slave as long as I have. An intelligent educated man, and he finds wretched slavery transformed! And he trusts my domine! Lucan was arrested by the evidence that in Marcipor there was no guile.

The others emerged from the servants' hall on their way to work, happy, excited.

"Christ is risen!" they greeted one another joyfully.

"The Lord is risen indeed!"

CHAPTER III

The Courage to Respond

After Olipor marched the men singing to work, he joined the young domine in the stable court. Mamercus the Arabian stable manager brought them the horses and the two rode out for the daily inspection of the farm.

"Is that Lucan working alone in the cucumbers?"

"Yes, sir. He is setting out the manure baskets of seedlings, sir, the ones we started in December."

"Let's go to him first. He didn't come up to the library this morning for his interview."

"He said he knew what he should be doing this morning without being told." Olipor hesitated to say more.

"Don't tell me he's getting that way too! Olipor?"

The elderly overseer did not look at his young domine. "He informed me that the spring equinox is long past now, and we damn well had better set out the baskets before the seedlings run to stems."

"At least he's interested." Quintus's voice was lowered. It was no secret to him that his slaves crinkled their crow's feet at him. "Dammit, Olipor, the mornings have been too snappy for the seedlings. And if you the overseer do not respect my word, how do you expect the others to obey me?"

A point excellently made. Olipor nodded. He was glad that Quintus had steel in him.

Lucan looked up when the long shadow of a horse moved across his work.

"Good morning, Lucan, I missed seeing you this morning. How are you?"

Lucan glared at his master. He rose to his feet and his vision blackened from the change of posture. His thoughts escaped into words. "What do you mean, 'How are you?' Why do you ask! You don't care!" He turned away trembling and broke into anxious sweat.

"What! Lucan!" Quintus dismounted and put his hand on his slave. "I wouldn't bother asking if I didn't care, Lucan. You know that."

"Like Baltus cares for his oxen!" Lucan moved away from his master's touch.

"You have to help us become friends."

"P-please go a-away." Lucan choked back his bitterness. There was no way he could disclose the grief that the others were giving him about the special attention being shown him. Why, just this morning Gaius the foreman told him that since he was apparently fit for work, he need not waste the master's time going up for an interview, and to get his butt out to work.

"Very well, Lucan, we will have words about this later." Quintus returned to the stallion. Ignis, sensing his master's tension, nervously moved away just as Quintus was about to bound up. Quintus tightened the reins and the testy animal proceeded to back up.

"Dammit, Lucan, why won't this horse stand for me!"

Lucan came over immediately, put his hand lightly over his master's rein hand, deftly tightened the far rein and loosened the near rein. "Try it now, sir." He bent over so his master could use him as a mounting stool after the Persian manner.

"No, Lucan, back off. I will neither degrade you nor humiliate myself." Quintus sprang again, and the fiery horse, obeying the rein pressure, leaned slightly toward him. Quintus was up. The horse moved on. Quintus turned and gave a long look at Lucan who boldly met his gaze.

He wasn't going to degrade me, Lucan reflected.

When they were out of earshot Quintus spoke to Olipor.

"See what I mean, I'm getting absolutely nowhere with him? At best he manages to give me cool disregard. Why, he's virtually insubordinate! You've seen it, Olipor."

"He was working himself up for some punishment, sir," Olipor said.

"I refuse to give him a concrete reason for hating me!" Quintus declared. "We cannot learn to get along together until we honestly admit our feelings."

"You are right, Domine. And a real relationship comes at the price of much pain. See at what cost God reunited man with Himself!"

"Now let's not get into that!"

"Domine, I pray that you come through."

"I could have hit him, Olipor."

Quintus stopped at the next field and waited for Baltus the head plowman and his small, white Campanian oxen to end a furrow. The Baltic pushed the yoke forward on the oxen to allow their necks to cool off. He palmed the sweat off his perpetually sunburned face, flicked his hand and adjusted the conical cap on his red hair. He followed the domine's glance from himself onto the field. The black light loam sent up a delicious aroma. The surface was smooth. Quintus complimented him on it, and commented to Olipor that the field was ready to be planted. Evidently Quintus was not going to give the soil any more than eye inspection. That would be a mistake in management.

"See, I have maked up for lost time," Baltus said. He was impudently rubbing it in that April was here and Quintus had ordered the plowing late.

Olipor, behind Quintus's back held up three fingers. Baltus gestured inconspicuously with two fingers. The field had been plowed only twice. "Does the domine intend to let the plowman test the soil?" Olipor hinted.

Quintus swung his horse against the border of elms and snapped a stick. The stallion, thinking the stick intended for him, danced. "Hold still, damn you, Ignis! Stand!" Quintus fumbled for his knife and cut the tough bark. He dismounted and thrust the stick horizontally through the soil. It bored across the furrows readily. He thrust it through another spot. A clod resisted the stick and he blushed. Again he made the test. He struck another clod. He wheeled upon Baltus. "You lazy deceptive clod-hopper, you, get busy and plow this field again! And I want the furrows so close that I can't tell one from the other!"

Olipor winked from behind the young master's back and Baltus bowed to hide his laughter. Quintus adjusted the reins as Lucan showed him, mounted and rode away. He was learning.

Baltus, more terrifying than cruel, set the yoke back in place and shouted a fierce command at his oxen who respectfully wheeled about and leaned to their task.

Further on, Quintus glanced back over his shoulder at his plowman. He saw that Baltus had stopped his assistant Manius, the African muted by Roman cruelty, and they stood idle. Quintus turned his horse and looked at them. Baltus is telling on me, I suppose, he thought with a twinge of resentment. The teamsters noticed that they were being watched so they signaled to their oxen and got busy again.

Quintus and Olipor rode to the vineyard and examined the budding vines. The vineyard looked neat for the slaves had finished spading it recently and they left the soil evenly broken up and level. The vinedresser and orchard keeper Alexis, oldest son of Postumus and Cara, Letitia's brother, saw to that. He was now grafting fruit trees. Paulo his older half-brother and assistant worked with him. Quintus did not yet fathom the intricacies of the delicate operation, and the condescending manner in which Alexis explains would annoy him today.

"You go on down to Alexis," Quintus said to Olipor. "I'm going to see Megas for a few minutes first, then I'll join you." Quintus turned his horse up toward the woods where he heard the ringing of the big Slav's ax.

"Megas, your heart is heavy these days, I can tell. What is troubling you, Megas?" Quintus dismounted, sat on a log and invited the Slav's confidences.

Megas wiped his sweaty face with his forearm. "Nothing, sir, only about my family I am thinking."

"Your family, Megas? Ah, yes, I am very sorry." Quintus was embarrassed. He might have known that this would be the complaint. Megas was a prisoner of war, brought back from the German front by the older Legerius brothers. Quintus sat in silence and wished to heaven that he had more tact. "Pretty, isn't it?" he commented on a singing Mistle Thrush. He finally rose and sympathized, "Take it easy, Megas," and rode down to the orchard.

On the way back to the stable court Olipor explained to Quintus what trees Alexis and Paulo were grafting, the choice of method and why. Then Quintus detoured to the cucumber patch.

Uh oh, here it comes. Lucan finished packing the soil around the basket of cucumbers he just set in. He deliberately popped a pesky cutworm between his fingers, and carefully covered an exposed earthworm. Then he looked up.

"You are almost done, aren't you," Quintus observed.

Lucan didn't trust himself to answer, and if he didn't look down pretty soon, the domine would notice that his jaw quivered.

"When you are through, you may go into the sickroom and take a good mid-morning nap," the domine said firmly. "All right, boy? Nothing's wrong with you that sleep won't cure."

Lucan squinted up at his master. The trustful naiveté struck him as a burning judgment that ignited his bitterness. You don't know how I feel about you. Furthermore, the discrepancy between how I am and how I ought to be is more than a matter of mere sleep. Lucan bent all the more determinedly to his work.

Back in the stable court Quintus commented to Olipor about Lucan. "He's as stubborn as a jackass, but he'll work himself to death like a spirited horse."

They joined Gaius and old 'Ya a know when in the a olden days when a man ran this a farm' Servius and lusty, gap-toothed Sextus the Iberian in the fields. Working in pairs, they set out cabbage plants that had been started in the nursery beds next to the kitchen. One man dug the holes and filled the soil in around the plants. The other wrapped the root of each cabbage plant with three bands of seaweed to promote tenderness and a good green color when cooked, set the plant, and poured water into the planting hole. Sextus the odd man and the strongest hauled the seed flats, seaweed and water.

With no conversation from Olipor to distract him, Quintus wandered in thought back to Megas the Slav. It must be awfully hard being separated from one's family. Perhaps Megas blames me for it. And it may gall him that I try to be on friendly terms with him. Shall I just let things go as they are, or shall I try to get him to talk about it? What if I can't help him. Would it be better in that case if I did not make him face his grief? Shall I give it a try? Will I be letting myself into an obligation, having heard, that I do not want to meet? Well, I intend to hear that silent Lucan out, why not Megas too? I may as well have a try with him.

When Megas came down to the villa mid-morning to tend fires for the noon dinner, Quintus followed him in. He detained him in the servants' hall. "What about your family, Megas?"

The towering Slav fidgeted, then spoke. "Sir, my littlest son seven years old last week was. The child I have not seen three will be."

Quintus was moved. "Can your family still be found, Megas?"

"Domine, I am sure. Unless . . . No, the front in that far yet has not moved." Megas was silent a moment. Then he asked fiercely, "What this to you is? You to torment me with my burden are trying?"

"No, Megas, no. I thought perhaps we could send for them."

"For them send?" Megas was incredulous. "Them down here as slaves bring?"

"Oh, Megas, I am trying to help you. I'm sorry if I blunder." They looked at each other in silence, then Megas turned away and went to the boiler room. From behind the woodpile he drew out a bundle. He opened out his native blouse and trousers and looked longingly at a lock of golden hair sewn to the inside of his blouse where it would lie over his heart. He shook his head sadly and put them back in hiding.

Quintus, feeling as though he had done nothing but put his foot in his mouth all morning, walked through the villa and out the front door to the formal garden. He hesitated on the front driveway and watched Mamercus the stable manager top-dress the commercial cut-flower beds. The Arab spoke to him in soft accents about the sheep now grazing in the upper meadow with Cerberus the sheepdog watching, the pigs foraging in the woods, and about his favorite, the Arabian stallion Ignis, that Quintus rode on inspection. If only the domine could exchange Niger the gelding for a nice little Arabian filly.

"It would be nice, Mamercus. But I'd have to pay a talent or so on the exchange."

The Arab was silent.

Yes, I know, Quintus thought. You are saying to yourself that I spent that talent on Lucan. Quintus wandered across the formal lawn from flowering shrubs to the shade of plane trees and nut trees and observed the dash of hyacinths around the tree bases. Mamercus has a fine sense of design, he thought. Or is it the night watchman's idea? Young Gregor will be up and working out here this afternoon, and he should scythe this grass.

The sound of horses' hooves at the gatehouse brought him running. "Marcellus! Come walk with me. It's nearly dinner time. I just came in from the fields. Marcipor, tell Postumus that your domine and I will have dinner in the dining room." Marcipor bowed and led the horses to the stable court. Quintus liked him. The highborn slave had what it takes for getting along with Marcellus.

"Don't you always?" Marcellus asked. They took the paved walk along the side of the villa bordered with a foundation planting of roses and evergreens.

"Always what?"

"Eat in the dining room," Marcellus said.

"I have my supper served there in the evening if I am particularly tired. Usually I have my meals in the kitchen with my household."

"You eat with your slaves?" Marcellus was scandalized.

"Well, why not? This is a farm, Marcellus, not a resort. I work with my slaves, I eat the same loaf, vegetables, salad, meat, and drink the same wine; why should I bother them to serve me apart from them?"

"You're telling me you feed your slaves meat?"

"Well certainly! We chase a chicken through the stew now and then. And can you imagine how long it would take one person to eat a whole ham?" Quintus confronted Marcellus on the bridge that spanned the canal outlet from under the house. "Don't you give them meat?"

"No! And my menial laborers get coarse rations. It is more economical. Try it; you have to bring me in a good profit. This is tax year!" Marcellus's outburst contrasted with the cool water that flowed quietly, having spent its force in the household water works.

"It boosts their morale to feed them well, Marcellus." Their gaze went naturally up to the woods from where the stream coursed and, held in check by irrigation gates, by cultivated rushes for baskets and by willow scions for tying vines, ran between the orchard and kitchen garden before it descended under the house.

"Morale?" Marcellus frowned at his friend. Choosing not to continue to the back gate, they followed the meandering stream across the formal garden.

"They find their tedious work easier to take," Quintus explained. "They are more willing. Their labor really could be thankless drudgery."

"But slaves' feelings don't count!" Marcellus insisted.

"In my house they do. That is why I sit at table with them, and when I want to commend one of them for good labor, I invite him to sit at the place of honor next to me." They sat on marble benches under willow trees. "And I sport with them. And give them personal responsibilities. And work at their sides. To me they are persons, Marcellus."

The knight lost patience. "You work at their sides because you get twice as much labor out of them by being there! If you looked at yourself honestly you would admit it."

"Marcellus, you don't understand!" The element of truth in his friend's words stung. They got up and continued along the paved stream bank.

"More than you think I do, Beans. Well, anyway, I am glad you are changing your dinner habits today," Marcellus smiled at his farmer friend.

"Someday I'm not going to change for you, Marcellus," Quintus declared, "and you are going to like it. You actually shun the slaves as though they were your enemies." They avoided the maze by crossing another bridge and taking the path down to the lily pond. "It is a savage pride which quotes the proverb, 'So many slaves so many foes. They are no foes to us until we make them so. Slaves, do I say? Rather men. Slaves? No, but comrades. Slaves? Say rather humble friends. No, slaves if you like, but fellow slaves with you, who own one arbiter of destiny, fate. Is not a slave of the same stuff as you, his lord? Does he not enjoy the same sun, breathe the same air, die, even as you do? Let your slave worship rather than dread you. Is it too little for a domine, which is enough for God? For love casts out fear.'"

"Eloquent, my educated tenant farmer, eloquent. Where did that useless speech come from?"

"My vainglorious knight," Quintus teased, "those were the words of Seneca the great Stoic. Haven't you read him?"

"My education is in my purse," Marcellus boasted sensitively. He picked up a pebble and skipped it across the pond. A mallard drake in the water quacked and swam out of the way. "And I suppose," he aimed at another duck, "that Lucan worships rather than dreads you?"

Quintus threw at a duck himself and admitted Lucan's stubborn refusal to be companionable.

"I would whip him until he talked if he were mine." Marcellus skipped another stone. "Why, you have already lost ground with him. If you want obedience in other things, you had better bear down on this matter!"

"No, no, Marcellus," Quintus explained patiently, "you don't court willingness with a whip. Farm slaves are not to be driven like animals; they are to be treated courteously like your prize slaves—like people! Look at it this way. If my father tries to force something upon me, I rebel. If I am not compelled, I am willing. If I were told, 'You will do this', I would be inclined to tell someone where to go. If I were asked, 'Want to do this?' I could not refuse. I don't know why. Personal integrity, I suppose. You see, that is why in our villa I put no force over the slaves' heads. They may or may not work as they wish."

"What do you do if they refuse?" Marcellus challenged.

"The thing is, they don't refuse."

"You dreamer, what if they do?" Marcellus persisted.

"The whip is strong, Marcellus, but you shall see that the power of patience is even greater."

"Except when it comes to getting Lucan to talk," Marcellus reminded his friend. They took the walk across the lawn toward the villa.

"Some day he will tell me . . . everything!" Quintus declared with conviction.

"Bet?" Marcellus teased.

"Bet!" Quintus resounded. He was determined to go about his purpose in the seemingly trivial encounters with his slave in everyday life.

* * *

When the sun began to pierce, Olipor strode with irritation to the cucumber field. "Lucan, you must be tired! Didn't Domine tell you that you should go in mid-morning and rest?"

"So?" Lucan admitted sullenly.

"Well hang it all, boy, why don't you obey! Do we have to lock you in the sickroom to get you to take your rest? You are not up to strength yet. You will wear yourself to ruin in another month's time at this rate. The work will wait! But your health will not! You pick up your tool right now and go lie down!"

"As though I weren't going in!" Tool over shoulder and head high, Lucan outdistanced Olipor. He stopped outside the kitchen door where pot cheese was in the making. The earthenware vessels of ewes' milk hung in a row. Pepperwort leaves curdled the milk and the whey dripped through a hole in the bottom of each vessel to pans below. Soon the curds would be seasoned with herbs, and the vessels covered and sealed for storage. Lucan took a long drought of the cool whey. When he looked up he saw Dorothea, Olipor's wife, standing there with hands on hips.

"The domine sent me in to rest, really he did." Lucan did not expect the head housekeeper to believe him.

"Come on in and sit down, boy," she said kindly enough.

As soon as Olipor came in, Postumus sputtered from the charcoal range. "What's the domine going to tell me to do next, breathe?"

"Don't let the young domine offend you, Postumus," Olipor appeased.

"He infuriates me!" Postumus gestured emphatically. "This morning him asks me if I was going to water the seedlings. Coming back from the fields him asks me if I was going to start dinner."

"He's only making conversation," Olipor attempted.

"Well, plague take it, if him can't do any better than that with a fellow man."

Olipor shrugged. "That's life, Postumus. Looking through a dim glass. Whereas in the next life, *viemus coram*, we see face to face, both God and man."

"We'll find out what sons of bitches him must really think we are," Postumus interrupted sourly.

"And vice versa, perhaps," Olipor suggested gently.

Postumus grunted and attacked the vegetables on the chopping block.

"Then we can either make peace forever, or draw up the veils forever," Olipor said.

"Well him could start making peace with me right now if him would stop checking on me. Don't him see I know my routine work and can do it? We can handle our special responsibilities; why else was we placed on the farm!" He stumbled to an embarrassed silence. Olipor had been placed here for an altogether different and painful reason. A Greek was usually not assigned to manual labor unless for disciplinary reasons. Olipor had cause to be bitter too, only Olipor was not. "Why don't him go back to school," Postumus mumbled, "or at least quit checking on me merely because I happen to work nearest the house."

"I'll drop him a hint as best I can." Olipor said and went out again to work before Postumus should go on to say more things he would regret.

"He did that to me too, Letitia complained. He came by when I was scrubbing the bathroom tile and he said if I go at it so zealously, I'll take the mortar off with the mold."

"Yes, of course, you scrub away the mortar and water can leak through and rot the wall," Postumus instructed his daughter peevishly.

"Now you tell me!" she pouted.

"I suppose you was going to tell us you took out chunks?" Postumus pressed her.

"I'm sorry, Letitia, I should have thought to tell you," Dorothea the housekeeper said.

"You're supposed to know these things, dummy, you're an assistant housekeeper now, aren't you?" Gaius cut in.

"I'm not talking to you!"

"That's some way to impress the young domine," Gaius jibed.

"Ma?" Letitia ran over to Cara. Tears stood in her eyes.

"Now don't worry, dear, Gregor will fix it," Cara put her arms around her daughter.

"Only don't wake him up early, he needs his rest!" Postumus looked out for their youngest.

"I won't!"

"We need him wide awake on night watch. I'm telling you that now, Letitia, do you understand?" Gaius browbeat her.

"Gaius, I'm sure she understands," Dorothea placated her son.

Letitia stuck her tongue out at him from the safety of her mother's arms.

"Besides, I probably have to buy the supplies on the next market day," Gaius sputtered.

"Why? Haven't you kept them in stock?" Dorothea queried her son pointedly.

"Mortar doesn't keep, you know, goes damp and hard."

"Watch your tone when you speak to your mother," Dorothea warned.

Gaius snorted and glanced at Lucan who was taking this all in with his aloof and cynical silence.

At noon when the household assembled in the kitchen for dinner, Baltus related to the other slaves how the young domine judged the plowed ground ready for planting, without even testing the ground.

"I teased him for being late with the plowing, I did, I said, 'See, I have maked up for lost time.'"

The slaves laughed. Lucan looked on, dumbfounded at their daring. Postumus noticing his amazement nudged him and said, "Never you fear, we tease him only because we loves him, and him knows it."

The words did not convey the intended reassurance since Lucan had experienced only teasing that sprang from hatred and malice. And Lucan already found out that nobody, but nobody, could gossip as Postumus could. Here Lucan detected the barb, their subconscious desire to get even with the one who imposed frustrations upon them. Only these slaves were too civilized to express their undesirable feelings openly. Lucan was no less astonished at the household.

"Just wait an' lemme finish," Baltus was saying. "Olipor asks if the domine was gonna to let the plowman test the soil. So the young domine has to get off his horse right then 'n there and make the test. Well, you know, Manius and I plows the field only twice. Naturally there is clods. The young domine yells at me. He really does! 'You lazy de-' something or other, 'clod-hopper, you, get busy and plow this field again!'" Baltus waited for the guffaws to subside. "And I says to me, what's eating the young domine up! And all to once Olipor there kinda winks, you know, from behind the Domine's back. So I says to myself, oh I see, something else is bothering. And I hollers at my oxen and gets aworking. I has to stop Manius and tell him. Can't wait. Is too funny. Then Domine turns and looks at us. Well, you can see daggers! He wants the furrows so close he can't tell one from the other!"

Megas shook his head compassionately. "Just a scholar he is, no farmer."

"You have to admit he's learning," Gaius said. "He studies the ancients on agriculture until late at night while we are all sleeping."

"Oh yeah?" Postumus corrected him. "Only until Olipor goes up, all sleepy, and offers help. After two or three nights of it the domine has to go to bed so poor Olipor will go to sleep. That's how Olipor rules over the domine."

"That's enough, Postumus, serve the dinner," Olipor stopped him quietly.

Postumus chuckled. "Him's going to find out one of these days that his elders, who have been awfully dumb since he was fourteen, will be smart, all to a sudden." And he and Cara, and Olipor and Dorothea, who had raised their own boys, had a special laugh.

"Now we don't want him to farm in such high style that he can't meet his expenses," Olipor cautioned. His comment was met with deep silence. Quintus and Marcellus stood in the kitchen hall.

"Listen to that," Marcellus said into Quintus's ear, "and you think you know how to manage slaves!"

"I need your help in learning, boys," Quintus said out loud. "Baltus here, is the best plowman in Campania. Ask anyone!"

Baltus staked his masculinity on his handling of the oxen in much the same way that Marcellus staked his on his span of four. "Thank you sir, any time, sir," he grinned, "much obliged."

Marcellus was shocked.

"Haven't you heard Baltus cut up before, Marcellus?" Quintus asked. "He really is a clown!" Privately Quintus added, "You have to allow them to release their grudges somehow, Marcellus, and teasing is certainly better than a knife at the throat."

The slaves apprehensively cleared the tables of the salgamas, the herb sprouts and stalks and buds, that the women were pickling. They moved the earthenware vessels off the benches so that they could sit down. The odor from the big vats of brine and vinegar sharply permeated the air. 'Vinigger,' Cara called it.

"Your ventilation is bad in here," Marcellus screwed up his nose.

"Yes, it stinks." Quintus was just as glad that he would not be eating in the kitchen with his seventeen slaves that noon.

* * *

In the evening after supper, Quintus sat alone in his upstairs library and read. Baltus came up and shuffled awkwardly before the young master.

Quintus looked up, anticipating Lucan. "Baltus! What are you doing here!"

"Domine, you is angry with your plowman?" Baltus asked.

Now just what does Baltus mean, coming up here uninvited and asking if I am angry! Quintus's eyes narrowed. He wanted to say, Baltus I could chew your hide off. He sprang up and their eyes met. He said instead, "Must you, Baltus, must you in front of everyone?"

"Domine, your plowman doesn't know the young knight was with you when he, er, tells the story in the kitchen. Please, your plowman apologizes."

So that is it! Baltus is not sorry that he had poked fun at his domine's expense. He is only sorry that Marcellus heard. I, the young domine, am an object for humor. That is assumed to be natural. That adds spice to the slaves' lives. It's that this fun making isn't supposed to be for any other than slaves' ears. And I caught Baltus outright. Quintus forced himself to speak kindly.

"Don't lose any sleep over it, Baltus. Go to bed." He smiled at his slave.

The plowman grinned sheepishly, bowed gratefully, and left with a spring in his stride.

"Damn!" Quintus ejaculated. "All right, I'm a fool for their sake." Nevertheless through his indignation he sensed that his plowman was wholeheartedly behind him. Why else would Baltus bother to come up to my private rooms and apologize? Quintus chuckled. He bolstered his confidence with the advice he learned from the farmer's manual that one could talk more familiarly with country slaves than with town slaves. And jest with them. And let them jest. This lightens their unending toil and makes tasks more palatable. And it encourages a feeling of good will towards the master, Quintus added. Anyway, that was his thesis. He hoped that he was right. It was his nature to be friendly to his slaves.

Marcellus treats his slaves as tools to bolster his vanity, Quintus thought. His slaves pussyfoot about his villa, and speak only when spoken to, and even then, in fear of disapproval. Well, perhaps that is exaggerating. Quintus could not say that Marcellus was cruel, well, not exactly. Marcellus does not beat his slaves; his slaves are too valuable for such abuse. His Marcipor alone, for example, cost some ten talents. And one does not abuse a valuable piece of property. Marcellus is politely mannered toward his slaves. He does not shout at them. He does not even raise his voice in anger. No, Marcellus's cruelty, in the eyes of the sensitive Quintus, is of a different sort. A sort so subtle that advanced civilization does not even recognize its cruelty. "If you praise a slave he will get lazy. Keep him on his toes; never let him know how he stands with you." Marcellus's whip is unacceptance, his cat 'o nine tails perfectionism. And the flesh-tearing knucklebones knotted onto the lashes are Marcellus's refusal to communicate. Marcellus is brutal to your very selfhood. Marcellus also has nightmares that a slave is holding a dagger at his throat.

Olipor had commented on Marcellus once, from scripture. "You know how those who rule the heathen lord it over them and their great men tyrannize over them. But our Lord says it must not be so among us. Whoever wants to be great among us must be our servant, and whoever wants to hold the first place among us must be our slave. We must act according to the example our Lord gave us by his life." On the surface these words had annoyed Quintus; imagine being his slaves' servant! Deep down inside, these words impressed him. What impressed him more was that Olipor the overseer lived by them.

Quintus entertained the thought that he had an unusual household of slaves. They were noisy, yes, but orderly, diligent, and loyal. They did not plot and scheme to get out of as much work as possible; they took their work seriously. Their reverent industry was a joy to their master. It was as though there were some benignant deity watching over the household. Didn't Epictetus the slave philosopher, write about how 'man should endure all things with noble calmness, confident that a benevolent Providence is ruling everything for an ultimate good end'?

The household of Good Will claimed that the benevolent Providence was knowable and furthermore they know him personally in Jesus Christ! Quintus was stabbed with a sense of wonder whenever he thought about it. He wanted to know if really there were a living God among them. He longed to meet this God. He had his moments when he wondered if his search for the Supreme Being must end with the realization that this God had been with him all the while, seeking him, only that he had never acknowledged his presence.

Well, I suppose if I would be the great master I should go down and see how Lucan is. Quintus found Lucan on his straw bed. The slave was drawn up tight with arms around legs and head on knees. He jumped when Quintus spoke.

"What's the matter, boy?"

Lucan's scalp tingled. The choking tight sensation came over him, and he remained silent.

"Will you tell me, boy?" Quintus urged. He tried to invade Lucan's eyes, but the slave avoided him. Lucan breathed a quivering sign. Quintus ran his hand over the boy's neck and arms and found his muscles tense and hard. Lucan withdrew from the touch, indignant that the master dare encroach upon his personal territory.

"You worked furiously and acted moody all day. Are you trying to get something off your mind? Look at me, Lucan."

Lucan glowered at him.

"What is it?"

No answer.

Quintus tried to relax him with massage but the slave growled and moved aside, his fists clenched tightly.

"Don't worry about it. I'll get you something." Quintus left quietly and returned shortly with a cup.

"Here Lucan, take this."

Lucan only stared.

"It's fine wine. To help you relax. Call it golden juice of mercy. Sometimes a body needs it. Will you take it?" Quintus extended his arm. "And it's more than just like Baltus caring for his oxen," he said firmly.

Lucan reached for the cup, lost his balance, and to his horror knocked the cup down with a resounding clang. Quintus glared at him. I didn't do it on purpose! Lucan wanted to say, but his tongue wouldn't move, nor was anyone else awake to witness for him.

"Come with me," Quintus snapped, "and bring the cup."

Lucan dared not disobey. He followed. Quintus led him to the kitchen sink, picked up a rag and turned and held it out to him. Their eyes met.

"Here, clean up with this," Quintus said in cool heat.

Lucan reached for the rag, his eyes never leaving his master's face.

Quintus could see his jaw quiver. "The cup," he said, "give it to me."

Lucan handed it over. Their hands touched, momentarily.

"I will refill it for you," Quintus said quietly. "Come up and see me tomorrow morning. Perhaps you will have your tongue back—by the Gods sit down before you fall down! I never thought anyone could be that afraid of me!"

Lucan collapsed on a bench and trembled uncontrollably. He did not take his eyes off his master.

Quintus sat next to him on the bench and waited for him to get ahold of himself.

"Now! We can talk in here. Out with it, boy, if you know what's good for you."

"I'm a m-man!" Lucan could not believe he actually said it.

"Very well, man! Then you can speak to me like a man, with no more of your servile insolence, or you shall bear the consequences like a man." He would upgrade the slave's behavior, virtually at the slave's own request.

The master's firmness sent a shiver down Lucan's spine. He held up the rag. "I-I didn't do that on p-purpose."

"Never said you did."

"P-please f-forgive this m-morning," Lucan apologized obediently.

"What was the matter with you this morning!"

"S-slavery."

"So you're taking it out on me. Is that fair?"

"Is s-slavery f-fair?"

The slave's audacity startled Quintus. "That depends."

"I-I am f-freeborn."

"I am looking into your circumstances, Lucan. That will take time and money. I've already spent my reserve on you, if you know what I mean."

Lucan's eyes widened with astonishment and comprehension. "Th-thank you, sir!"

"Now what specifically upset you?"

"The cu-cuc-cumbers."

"What about them?"

"N-needed to go out. Y-you wouldn't let. G-going to stem. Y-you would be a-angry."

"Oh I see. Damned if you do, damned if you don't. Consult me about it! I don't like you going over my head like that. Supposing everyone did. We'd have chaos!"

"I-I'm s-sorry, sir," Lucan said tentatively.

"But what, Lucan?"

Lucan was about to reveal the chaos between himself and Gaius, but changed his mind. "Im-p-portant p-p-project," he covered.

"You'd better believe it's important, Lucan. Those aren't just cucumbers, you know."

"I kn-know."

"Those are my Legerius Early. I hand bred them myself. I don't want them to get too cold at night."

"I c-covered them, sir, this e-evening."

"With what?"

"B-baskets."

"Wiseacre. You're entirely right, though. And you have been on a farm before," he pried.

"My family, sir." It was too painful to elaborate upon.

"If a farm were dropped on your shoulders, think you could manage it?"

"It would take more than the old Roman virtue of diligent work, sir."

"Oh, so you recognize something good about the Roman?" Quintus couldn't resist.

Lucan flushed hotly at being caught admiring his master's hard work habits. "C-contrary to the ancients it takes intelligence and learning, as well as common sense and diligence."

"That's exactly what I'm trying to show them."

"Y-you are working very hard at it, sir."

Quintus appreciated the commendation in his voice. "It's the only way; read the authorities and listen to the men here. You've heard them discussing the farm, haven't you?"

Lucan became wary. Either way he answered, he could let himself in for trouble. Oh, no, sir; then what is he trying to hide? Yes, sir; then what did they say?

Quintus sensed his hesitation. "Never mind, I know they make fun of me, Lucan. You'll get used to it."

"No, I won't sir. They don't understand that we have to contend with exhausted soil." Lucan's swift answer surprised them both. And he had said 'we'.

"What? Say that out loud? You have it exactly! And I've been trying to get it through Gaius's head. Thank you, Lucan!"

Their eyes met but Lucan had thrown up the barrier again.

Quintus got up and Lucan quickly rose to his feet.

"Let's get some sleep, now," Quintus said. "I'll get your wine."

"Yes, sir. Th-thank you, sir."

"And I don't want any more of that horseshit about my not caring."

"No more, sir." Lucan looked down in embarrassment, and stood there in awe until Quintus filled the goblet from the locked cabinet and gave it back to his hand, as setting it down on the table would deprive it of its efficacy. Lucan drank the cup down. Then he went to clean up the spilled wine.

* * *

Olipor lay awake next to his wife in bed. "He is aggravating Dorothea, I have forgotten how aggravating they can be. None of the others came quite so bitter."

"Aggravating, Olipor, but not hopeless."

"By what I know of his type, he's really incorrigible."

"Incorrigible if left to himself, yes," Dorothea conceded. "But not impossible if, God helping, we could give what he needs, and God helping, he could respond."

"I told him once that I would teach him how to behave," Olipor said.

"What do you mean?" Dorothea asked anxiously.

"Didn't you hear it? The bickering in the tool room this morning?"

"I heard it. It was simply awful. What are you going to do about it?" Dorothea asked suddenly.

"Woman, why must you ask me such questions?" Olipor scolded affectionately. She giggled, and they lay together in silence.

"What am I going to do?" Olipor pondered. "He has me baffled."

"You have been firm with him, haven't you, Olipor?"

"I have seen to it that he does what he is supposed to do, when he is supposed to do it. That is more than the young domine does for the most part."

"What does the young domine do?" Dorothea asked.

"Quintus merely suggests that Lucan does something, or does it in a certain way, and then walks off without even waiting to see if his word is carried out. He doesn't follow up his orders!"

"So?"

"So I must come along and do the unpleasant for him," Olipor muttered.

"The unpleasant?" Dorothea suppressed a smile. Olipor was getting the flip side of what he used to deliver as the favorite parent who let the other parent, herself, do all the disciplining.

"That is putting it mildly," Olipor complained. "Lucan gets downright nasty. He rebels, and I usually have to send him on his way with hot words. Then he acts highly insulted, as though . . ."

"As though what, Olipor?" Dorothea urged.

"As though he were going to obey all along," Olipor hesitated.

"If only you gave him the chance, Olipor?" Dorothea suggested.

"If only I gave him the chance," Olipor finished his sentence with sudden insight.

"Remember when our sons were Lucan's age?" Dorothea ruminated.

"Gaius is not like Lucan!" Olipor exclaimed.

"Gaius is a very mild boy. And remember, Gaius is twenty-one now, four years older than even the young domine. Four years older than Lucan! Those few years make a lot of difference!"

"Well, Postumus's son Gregor is only fifteen, and very reasonable."

"You don't have much personal contact with Gregor," Dorothea reminded him. "You are not around Gregor when he is having his moments. He night watches while you sleep, and sleeps during most of your working day. Remember twenty years back when Felix was fifteen?"

"Well, hardly, Dorothea."

"And five years after that, Leonidas was fifteen. And two years after that, Artemas was fifteen. Remember Leonidas at that age? You couldn't tell him anything! Or make him do anything! Only let him feel that the decision was his own, then you could guide him easily."

Olipor remembered with a sheepish laugh. "Frankly, I was relieved when Leonidas left home with Aulus's second son! At thirty he is still like a lion!"

"Well, we still have to show him that we realize he is grown up," Dorothea said.

"I suppose that I have to show Lucan the same thing," Olipor mused. "I must not force myself upon him. The young domine has more wisdom than I have credited to him."

"The young can usually understand the young," Dorothea said.

"And the old understand the old." Olipor kissed his wife tenderly on the mouth. "But Dorothea, I haven't got the patience anymore! I am an old man of fifty now, no longer thirty!"

"I know it's hard. But patience is the only way. Lucan needs it desperately. He has had some rough jolts from life, you know."

"There is more to it than rough jolts, Dorothea, and you know it. Basically, much more. The trouble with him is that he cannot think beyond himself. Even if he did know how to act he would cling stubbornly to his way. Yes, I'm afraid so. His yoke will be difficult and his burden heavy as long as he clings to himself. And if I predict rightly, his patience will only support his stubbornness. Yet must not this rebellion end somewhere? Sometime in his life a man must learn the freedom that comes through mature obedience and responsibility. He must really grow up! Not try to assert his adulthood with his immature rebellion and self-seeking, but really grow up!"

"Even at fifty a man has his moments of rebellion against obedience," Dorothea reminded him gently. "Even rebellion against God's command."

"Hush, woman, you are not supposed to say things like that to me," Olipor teased, and kissed her again. Then he rolled over onto his back and meditated out loud with measured words.

"I can tell you now what I mean by teaching Lucan how to behave. Lucan says that fate brought him here, and that the young domine is the despised instrument of Fate. I said to that rebellious pagan that God put him here, and that the young domine is the bearer of God's mercy! God has indeed seen the plight of his child and has heard his cry under his oppressors. God knows his sorrows, and has come down to rescue him.

"How would I like him to behave? I would like to see Lucan stop fighting the world, Dorothea. To accept life, instead, to embrace the world! Now I do not mean that he should become so accommodating to life that he goes along with everything. I would like to see him unconformed enough to seek the new life. To do this he must realize that evil is a real part of this fallen world, along with the good. Then he can work creatively in the face of evil, instead of burning himself out in bitterness against evil! I'd like to see him live creatively by giving himself to the Lord, by serving the young domine as though he were the Lord. God help him! And me too!"

"Amen," Dorothea whispered. With one accord they drew together as though marital chastity were a Christian heresy. They proceeded at the leisurely pace of old lovers, incredibly delicious, the like of which the young knew not. They used every manner available to them to orchestrate their passion, some ways which in younger days they were too prudish to engage, so that when he was finally able to plunge home she was already so high off the ground to meet him that they were swept together in the spiraling thermal to the clouds.

* * *

Lucan still lay sleeping the next morning when the slaves were gathered in the kitchen eating breakfast. Dorothea knelt beside him, stroked his hair and patted his neck gently. He smiled in his sleep and playfully turned his back. Dorothea tickled him in the ribs.

"Meter!" Lucan laughed in Greek, and squirmed.

"Yes, boy, I am your mother," Dorothea said in her usual Latin.

Lucan sat up immediately, and blinked at Dorothea, bewildered. Then he bounded to his feet and glared down at her as though he were about to strike her. "Do not get fresh with me!" he threatened vehemently.

Dorothea sank weakly back on her heels. Olipor's words of last night came to her with new impact. 'I must not force myself upon him.' O God, she prayed, what to do with this?

"Lucan," she said, steadying her voice with effort, "Lucan, I am sorry you lost your mother, your family, very sorry. I know you loved them dearly. Yet your family isn't altogether lost, Lucan."

He breathed sharply.

"Lucan, the beans are up now aren't they? They grow in the springtime, then come summer you pull the plants for the compost pit and thresh out the seeds to sow into new life. Do you think that our Reaper does not save the seeds of our selves to plant into new life?"

Lucan turned his back and his voice wavered. "My brother and sisters were but tender shoots."

"Do you think that the Vinedresser doesn't know how to graft the tender shoots onto the Living Vine?" Dorothea got up and stood behind him. She continued softly. "And as for you, dear, you will find mothers and fathers, brothers and sisters, given back to you a hundredfold if you will be sensitive to the needs of others and respond. Our Lord promised us this. We can be concerned about others because first he is concerned about us. Now I know what you are thinking, however in your angry battle against the universe you may receive another shock; that some people in this rotten world are still kind and concerned. You may not want to respond for fear of getting hurt again. Nonetheless you must take the courage to respond so that you may live. Yes, Lucan, courage; not weakness, courage."

Lucan said nothing. However she could tell that he was still listening.

"Please, Lucan" Dorothea pleaded, "I understand! Come now and get some breakfast. You are late, but I will serve you."

Lucan ate cheese and olives and raisins in silence and watched Dorothea darkly as she moved about the charcoal range and fried him some bacon and hotcakes. She felt awkward under his steady gaze, though she was given the grace, thank God, to remain outgoing toward him.

"Do you think this would be a good day to weed out the newest seedling rows?" Dorothea finally asked. "It looks as though it is going to be overcast today. So the sun won't parch the seedlings, will it, when the weeding loosens the roots? It may even rain tonight. Go and see what you think about it, Lucan, would you? You don't have to report to Olipor; he knows that you are about your work."

Still without a word, Lucan rose from the table and went out to work. In the vegetable field, his feelings unleashed themselves into thoughts. So she dares to presume that she can understand me! She hasn't the slightest inkling of what suffering and struggle are all about! Take the people around me as my mothers and fathers, and brothers and sisters! Why should I care for others! She can harbor this saintly thought only because she has not been tried by fire! She dares to think that she cares for me, and that I will let her. And that it takes courage to respond! Ha! Not what my Stoic teachers would say! She can go ahead and call herself my mother if she wishes! Lucan channeled his bitterness through his work with the tiny weeds and seedlings.

Yet something about Dorothea stood out in his mind. He had hurt her, which was easy to see. But she had not come back at him coldly. Instead, she had taken the pains to talk with him. 'We must take the courage to respond, so that we may live. We can be concerned about others because first our Lord is concerned about us! Please, Lucan, I understand!' He felt that by her actions, perhaps she meant it. She had remained gentle even though he had been harsh with her. She had sent him out to work with a good breakfast in his tummy, even though he had deliberately overslept. 'Please, Lucan, I understand.' Lucan was suddenly ashamed. Something stirring in his deep memories told him that there was such a thing as love. He himself had known it, in the golden days, in the golden days . . . Back then he knew love not as a weakness to be scorned; indeed he knew it as the very nurture of life. The will to live, to become what he was meant to be, hungrily demanded that nurture again. He must open himself to love; he must take the courage to respond. 'Please, Lucan, I understand . . .'

CHAPTER IV

A Price on His Head

On the eve of Ascension, Bishop Nicodemus sent up two officiators who arrived at the villa about suppertime. They were Presbyter Vincentius from Rome who supervised the churches in The Marketplace, Capua, Puteoli, "and all points south," as Vincentius humorously put it himself, and Deacon Leander from Alexandria, Egypt. "And Marcipor will be joining us himself before dawn tomorrow."

Quintus entertained them at supper, "Please, in the kitchen as usual with your household." One guest sat at his right, the other at his left. The travelers related to the household the latest news. One piece of news was grave. Rumor had it that the Emperor was to tighten the tax laws. Too many farmers had deserted their land in desperation, and those bound to the land by debt were running away. Even merchants, who had been given a heavier share of the tax burden, were deserting their trades. The inevitable was at the door.

"Would you like to trade places with me, Domine, to avoid financial straits?" Gaius asked innocently, and the unsuspecting remark gave Olipor a painful jolt from his own past.

"You are most generous, Gaius," Quintus answered so wistfully that the household rippled with laughter. Only Olipor and Dorothea had reason to think it not so funny.

"More better you run away while you still have the chance," Baltus teased.

"They'll get your family for it!" Lucan muttered bitterly, whereupon the master stared at him with astonishment. That ejaculation revealed more about his past than three months of attempted conversation and work together. Does Lucan really know the truth about his family?

"Have you heard the latest about the Arian controversy?" Presbyter Vincentius at Quintus's right leaned forward and asked Olipor.

"No. What?"

"Arius called for support, you know, after he was deposed," Presbyter Vincentius related. "Bishop Eusebius of Nicomedia called a Council there at the capitol, and sent out letters to the bishops in which he supported Arius!"

"He did? So he is Arianizing?" Olipor became excited.

"Probably more on a friendship basis than on doctrine," Deacon Leander on Quintus's left put in.

"But Bishop Eusebius is a favorite of the Emperor," Olipor observed. "He can . . . ! The episcopate at Alexandria must be hot on the defensive!"

"They are!" Leander confirmed. "And Deacon Athanasius is drawing up a justification of their action to be circulated to the bishops at large."

"Who ever thought the argument would take these proportions," Olipor commented.

"What is this all about, anyway!" Quintus who had been listening with puzzled silence broke in finally.

"I'm sorry, Quintus!" Olipor's sudden familiarity caused a blush to rise in Quintus's cheeks. Then Olipor addressed his master as an equal. The other slaves who had been conversing among themselves hushed to silence.

"Quintus, we have a quarrel in the church. Yes, I know, no sooner do we gain outward peace from the persecutions, than our inward quarrels are made public. It is regrettable, I'll admit. And there are those who are impatient with us. Well, it seems, with the new influx of pagan converts, that we have to struggle once again for the understandings that have already been firmly laid."

"That which is clear teaching to us in the West apparently is not as clear in the East," Presbyter Vincentus interposed. "We are talking about the relationship between Jesus Christ and God the Father."

"Jesus Christ," Quintus thought aloud, "yes, the Son of God. Isn't the Son a mediator between the world and a far off and inaccessible God the Father?"

"Well," Vincentius said, "that is the Platonic view, not the Biblical one. In Scripture you don't hear as much about man's search for God. It is the other way around. We don't have to search for God because he has first come to us."

"God is not far off and inaccessible," Deacon Leander elaborated, "Jesus Christ the Son is God Incarnate."

"Wait a minute, God come down to us?" Quintus asked.

"Yes, sir," Leander explained, "God focused himself in Jesus Christ so that we may know him. Our Lord said that who ever has seen him has seen the Father."

"Now let me get this straight," Quintus frowned. "You say that the supreme Deity, the first self-existent Cause of the universe, a spiritual entity, bridged the chasm between men and his mysterious self and lived among us?"

"Why not Domine," Letitia put in. "You yourself dine with us."

Quintus started to criticize his own motives, then quickly stopped in embarrassed silence.

"Jesus Christ is a manifestation of God in the flesh, Quintus," Olipor said.

"But God is such an extremely vast entity," Quintus objected. "How could the infinite confine himself to being a mere man? He is too far off," he broke off with a shrug of mystification.

"This is precisely what Arius is trying to explain in a manner which those of us with a pagan outlook can grasp," Olipor pointed out.

"Well, what does Arius say?"

Presbyter Vincentius answered. "Arius wants above all to maintain the isolation and spirituality of God the Father. To him the Father created the Son. One of his creatures. Therefore the Son did not exist once, so the Son is not eternal."

"Well, what of it?" Quintus wondered.

"Arius goes on to argue that the Son is one of God's creatures like all of us. We all are sons of God because God created us. The Son isn't God Incarnate according to Arius. The Son is a lesser being with limitations. Nor is he really human either. He is more than human, and as Son of God he is to be worshipped."

"Included in the God bundle," Balthus quipped, "like the fasces of a lictor."

The household sniggered.

"That is not such an innovation on your faith, is it?" Quintus asked.

"On the Biblical faith, yes, although many do not see how. If the interpretations of our teachings were more precise, Arius's error would be more obvious." The presbyter was emphatic.

"Why is Arius so intent on maintaining the simplicity of God?" Quintus asked.

"Quintus," Olipor answered, "it is to keep men with a heathen background from slipping back into polytheism as they interpret their varied experiences of God. In trying to insist on the singularity of God, Arius does away with the divinity of Jesus Christ. But don't you see, Christ is the Divine come down to us. Quintus, supposing we slaves should define away your authority over us as the embodiment of our senior domine's lordship?" It was a daring analogy.

Quintus chortled uneasily and searched Lucan's inscrutable face. He had some harsh news for Lucan about authority, on parchment in his tunic, Lucan's sale papers and ownership history, that Deacon Leander delivered in the afternoon. He did not know how he was going to break it to Lucan.

Deacon Leander noticed how Lucan squirmed and kept glancing at his master as though wanting permission to speak.

"What is it, man, want to say something?" the deacon pressed him.

Lucan looked down and blushed. He was put on the spot. They waited. He finally spoke, slowly.

"Well," he reflected, "how can this Christ be a *Savior* if, as Arius would have it, he isn't God? How can he be *your* Savior if he wasn't, as Arius says, really man? You say he overcame sin and rose from the dead. Certainly a god can do this. Now unless a man could overcome sin, and unless a man was victorious over death, the promise of these victories would mean nothing to you. As you say,

> "For as by a man came death, by a man has come also
> the resurrection of the dead.
> For as in Adam all die, so also in Christ of God
> shall all be made alive.

Arius would make a mockery of this, sir."

"Excellent, young man!" the Presbyter lauded him.

"Say, with a mind like that, you could help us!" Deacon Leander beamed. "Lend him to me, will you, Quintus?"

"You wouldn't want him with the weight that's hanging over his head," Quintus warned. He could hear Lucan draw breath.

"We can help," Leander said. "When you're ready, just send him to me."

"Brother . . ." Presbyter Vincentius checked his deacon.

"Thank you, sir, I shall remember," Lucan uttered swiftly, reflexively. He looked intensely at Leander, then at his master, and shuddered. Not only had he shown up his master; he was nearly exposed himself. And he had no right to reply to the Deacon's offer. He was triply on the spot. He glowered at Olipor.

Olipor returned a look of pity. Dear boy, he thought, if you could understand yourself with the same keen intelligence that you displayed on the theological question, if you could understand, you could begin to fathom what your life needs.

Quintus graciously resumed conversation. "So why should a religious controversy be so disruptive to the Empire?" He stepped off the sore spot of the status of his slave directly onto the sore spot of the Arian Controversy.

"Politics, sir," Leander became embarrassed for the church. "You see, should The Way become a state religion . . ." Leander regarded the overwhelming majority of slaves around the table and searched for delicate words.

"It poses a conflict in obedience to authority," Vincentius jumped in bluntly, then floundered in his own insensitivity.

"That's right," Lucan muttered into his cup. "If Christ weren't truly God, then why should slaves, two-thirds of the Roman Empire, have to obey those set in authority over them as coming from God?"

It was not his intention to be heard, but in the gap of conversation while the disciples of The Way fished for words, there it was. His comment was met with shocked silence. Not even Balthus dared to quip.

"You're quite right," Quintus replied good-naturedly enough. "I can understand that. But what you need to understand is that anyone here who would challenge the authority set over him," he lifted the scroll tucked in his tunic and narrowed his eyes at Lucan, "that someone would be wise to realize that he is quite mistaken."

It was a cruel blow. Quintus saw the comprehension, the shock, and the glistening eyes. The truth about Lucan's status was too awful to disclose in detail. Here the slave played right into his hands the opportunity to get the message across. Quintus wondered how much Lucan knew, and if it were still too traumatic for words. He regarded Lucan with profound sadness while the slave sipped from his cup and choked.

"You know," Olipor quickly attempted to ease the tension, "logic does not solve everything."

"Arius himself forgets this," the Presbyter took up. "We have to insist always that Jesus the Christ was both truly God and truly man. Otherwise, no hope."

"That is why your faith is so incomprehensible to me," Lucan interjected, and Olipor stared him down.

"Granted, Lucan, the nature of the Divine is much beyond our comprehension," Deacon Leander acknowledged kindly. "Our Lord himself said that no man knows the Father but the Son. We can well obey the injunction not to seek what is too difficult for us, nor to investigate what is beyond our power."

"What happened to Arius, anyway?" Quintus seemed not to care that his slave displayed a mind sharper than his own.

"Yes, getting back to Arius," Deacon Leander laughed nervously. "He was the Presbyter in charge of the church Baucalis, in the See of Alexandria when this all began some four years ago. Same See I come from. He preached a sermon in which he described the Son as a creature inferior to the Father. He used a verse in Proverbs as his text. 'The Lord formed me as the first of his works.'"

"Wait, I'll get it!" Gaius jumped up. Then he checked himself. "Excuse me, Domine, may I?"

"Yes, please do." With this permission, Gaius hurried off to fetch the scroll.

"Well," Leander continued, "our Bishop reprimanded Arius for being careless, then, by God, he found out that Arius was dead serious! Bishop

Alexander tried to persuade him out of his position, but he wouldn't yield. Here, Gaius, it is in the eighth chapter, verse twenty-two."

Gaius read:

> "The Lord created me at the beginning of his work,
> the first of his acts of old.
> Ages ago I was set up,
> at the first, before the beginning of the earth.
> When there were no depths was I brought forth—"

"Arius argues from that last line too," Leander broke in.

"Let me see that," Quintus reached for the scroll. He skimmed around the referred passage to put it back in context. "Hm. Wisdom speaking. I suppose Arius takes Wisdom to be the Son. Wait a minute!

> "Wisdom has built her house,
> she has set up her—

Say, hasn't Arius gotten his he's and she's a little mixed up?"

The household guffawed uproariously. Lucan laughed too, for the first time in this household, with tears of mirth so it seemed, but Quintus, watching him closely, knew better.

"I suppose Arius quoted scripture out of context?" Quintus suggested to the clergy. "You can prove most anything by quoting out of context," he shook his head.

"Perhaps also that God doesn't even exist," Lucan lipped under his breath and grimaced at the warning look from Olipor.

"Actually, it's only a matter of Hebrew grammar," Presbyter Vincentius explained. "Wisdom is a feminine word. So is war. Wisdom is interpreted here as a personification of the Christ."

"Arius has backed up his position with much scripture and has refused to yield," Deacon Leander continued. "So Bishop Alexander called a Synod of the bishops of Egypt and Libya. Arius was deposed and excommunicated. Now Arius has enlisted support and Bishop Eusebius of Nicomedia has circulated a letter on his behalf. So I suppose the bishops of Nicomedia and Alexandria will fight it out."

"With the help of all of you," Quintus commented, and they all laughed.

"Well, you know, there's some professional jealously involved too," the Deacon added. "Arius had expected to be made Bishop of Alexandria himself."

The Presbyter nudged him from behind. "We will overlook that just now, brother," he said quietly.

"This has been an enlightening evening!" Again Quintus disregarded the comment. He rose, and the others with him.

"Will you hear the Living Word with us, Quintus?" Olipor asked.

"Why, yes! If I may."

"I'll wake you when it's time to get up for worship, and we will also tell you when you must leave." Then Olipor was suddenly aware that he was talking in this way not to his equal, but to his domine. He dismissed himself quickly to hide a smile.

* * *

They all got up again before cockcrow, and it was only a matter of minutes before the table was pulled out and covered with white linen. They heard hurried hoofbeats in the stable court, and Marcipor ran breathlessly in.

"I'm not late? Good morning, sir," he saluted Quintus.

"He's joining us?" Marcipor asked Lucan as they drifted to the men's side of the room.

"Last night they got to talking, so Olipor invited him," Lucan snickered.

"Talking about what?"

"About a bunch of nonsense," Lucan chuckled. "They act as a family, just as you say, even towards the domine, in the name of, as I have said, incredible folly!"

"Is your mind limited to that judgment?" Marcipor punched Lucan playfully and laughed back.

"Not at all! I dared to open my mouth just once last night," Lucan confided with a chuckle, "and it seems that I made the statement of the evening. I showed up the young domine. Then I couldn't stop! If Olipor's looks could kill . . . I'll tell you about it, if I survive to tell, that is. And Marcipor, I learned something bitter about myself."

"What is it?" Marcipor urged. But Olipor had already begun reading from the Acts of the Apostles.

> "'. . . you shall be my witnesses in Jerusalem, and in all Judea and Samaria and to the end of the earth.' And when he had said this, he was lifted up, and a cloud took him out of their sight. And while they were gazing into heaven as he went, behold, two men in white robes stood by them and said, 'Men of Galilee, why do you stand looking into heaven? This Jesus

who was taken up from you into heaven will come in the same way as you saw him go into heaven.'"

Then the Presbyter began expounding the scripture. "Dearly beloved, the Ascension tells us that Christ is King!"

* * *

After breakfast that morning Quintus saw the travelers on their way. As they started out, Marcellus and a sleepy eyed Marcipor arrived, equipped for hunting.

"Who are they?" Marcellus asked about the travelers.

"A Presbyter from Rome and a Deacon from Alexandria," Quintus answered. "They are traveling to Rome."

"Christians! I suppose you sat at table with them." Marcellus sounded disgusted.

"I did," Quintus answered with a grin, and held open the atrium door for his friend.

"Don't you know about the Christian sect?" Marcellus asked disdainfully when they were inside.

"My household worships the Christ, Marcellus, didn't you know that?" Quintus enjoyed shocking his noble friend with his question.

"They do?" Marcellus responded.

"They call him Domine, Lord, just as they do me. Sometimes when they go about uttering Domine this, and Domine that, I don't really know which one they are addressing, as though they are not quite sure either. As though they confuse me with their Lord or consider us synonymously. Almost as though I were the Domine God."

"Do they really venerate you, Beans?" Marcellus was all ears.

"Well, they have a teaching of theirs, 'Slaves, obey your lords as you would your Lord. Serve your master as though he were your Lord.' Olipor is always saying that. And they also have a teaching that goes, 'Everyone must obey the authorities that are over him, for no authority can exist without the permission of God . . . so that anyone who resists the authorities sets himself in opposition to what God has ordained.' You see, Marcellus, there is nothing subversive about them at all. And you know, it is a strange feeling to be regarded in that way, as though, well, I feel that I ought to . . ."

"Play God to them, Beans? Are you foolish enough to think that you must enslave yourself to their notions about you?"

"You put it rather odiously, Marcellus, when after all, it is a responsibility. There are two sides implied even in Seneca's advice, to let your slaves worship you rather than fear you."

"And how long has this been going on?" Marcellus wanted to know.

"This Christianity? In our household? Father found out about our slaves during the civil war between Constantine and Maxentius."

"That long ago?"

"At least. Father had asked Olipor to gather together the household to offer sacrifices in behalf of Constantine that he should deliver Rome."

"The traitor," Marcellus groused. "My father was killed in that battle at the Milvian Bridge, on Maxentius's force; no family bloodbaths after, kindness of Constantine. Well, go on."

"Olipor had said that he and the other slaves could not make sacrifices to the gods since they found their God. Olipor begged Father not to ask it of them, and not to be angry."

"Why the nerve!" Marcellus remarked. "And your father never reported them to the police?"

"Well, Father says that a slave has a hard enough time with someone else owning his body and dictating his life, without trying to possess his mind too. Father says that you cannot completely possess the best of them anyway, and I agree. So you see, Father let them gather and worship in their own way from the start."

"Are you serious, Beans, or could you be teasing?"

"Certainly I'm serious! I can remember myself the year after when the news of Constantine's Charter of Religious Freedom in the West reached Good Will. That was before I went off to school, some eight years ago. The slaves spent the night in thanksgiving, and I remember Olipor wept in gratitude to my father for guarding his tongue during the previous scourge."

"So your father actually let them do it." Marcellus could not believe it.

"Yes, really, Marcellus. And this little bit of freedom does wonders. Boosts their morale. They *want* to serve us. As a matter of fact, the harmony among the slaves had remarkably improved after they became Christians. Father had asked Olipor how this harmony came about. Olipor answered, 'It is not my work, sir, but the work of my Domine.' Or something like that. Anyway, Father thought Olipor was referring to him. Later Father found out that Olipor really meant the Domine Jesus Christ."

"Well, these Christians have not been suppressed without good reason, you know," Marcellus reminded his friend. "What about that plot in Diocletian's court to overthrow the state? Even before that they were expelled from the army because they wouldn't venerate the sacred standards. Why, their disregard for the public welfare is indolent! If many became Christians, who would do the administrative duties of the state, and who would fight back the barbarians from swarming over the frontier?"

"Now wait a minute!" Quintus countered. "Maybe they were accused of conspiracy, and maybe falsely so. Anyway, that was a ready excuse for a hell of a bitter persecution against the only decent and orderly group in the empire."

"Whew! See where your prejudice is showing!" Marcellus interjected.

"Listen here, Marcellus, do you challenge what the Emperor Constantine has done? Constantine has Christ's monogram on his battle standard, you know. And the soldiers, his army, mind you, who are fighting back the barbarians, and who delivered Rome from Maxentius, carry Christ's monogram inscribed on their shields."

"Ugh! The Rho superimposed over the Chi makes me think of a man on a cross," Marcellus grimaced. "I don't like it."

"The enemy doesn't either," Quintus said.

"It's just superstition," Marcellus decided. "Besides, Constantine is just using the Christians in his propaganda against Licinius in the East. Can't you see through that? Christians are loyal to Constantine, so Licinius persecutes them as traitors. If the Christians call upon Constantine for protection, well, that will give Constantine a tidy excuse for taking up arms against Licinius and uniting the empire once again!"

"Marcellus, what I am trying to say is that Christian soldiers fight under him. He is their protector and leader. This is no shirking of military duty on the part of the Christians!"

"Well, why not be their protector! The Christians can't be crushed out, so why not win this well-organized natural resource with their spiritual influence over to his side? In fact, I wouldn't be too surprised if he put 'go to church' posters in every marketplace. Don't deceive yourself, Beans. Constantine is not going to give himself over to any one party; he is too shrewd for that; he has himself and his rule to maintain. He may revere Christ because of his war victories, but he also reveres Mithras. And he is, after all, Pontifex Maximus of the state religion."

"Maybe," Quintus was not quite convinced that Constantine was only being a superstitious and calculating politician.

"Maybe!" Marcellus challenged the remark. "See here." He drew a handful of coins out of his wallet. "The Victories. And here, Mars. This one, Jupiter. And the Genius Populi Romani. The old gods. And here, Mithras, the sun god himself. The Emperor's 'unconquerable companion.'"

"Granted, yet the Emperor decreed that Jesus's birthday be celebrated on December twenty-fifth, near the winter solstice, in place of Mithras's birthday."

What are you trying to tell me, anyway?"

"Just that the Emperor's patronage started me thinking," Quintus admitted.

"Patronage, Beans, granted. That is as far as it goes, I assure you. Is his use of Christianity really that shocking to you, Beans? When you come right down to it, the Emperor is not behaving any differently than you, my friend, only on a larger scale. You yourself tolerate Christianity because it makes better slaves. As you have pointed out to me from scripture, a Christian must obey the authorities over him and serve his domine as he would his Lord. And you can't tell me you are having Lucan instructed in the faith for any reason other than making a better servant out of him. A better servant according to you, that is. As for me, if anyone in my household became a Christian, I'd cut his throat!"

Marcellus's analysis cut Quintus. He was in truth manipulating the faith much in the same way the Emperor was. He never thought of it in that way before.

"If that is how you feel about the faith, Marcellus, you had better run off to Licinius in the East. As for me, I have been to worship a few times." Quintus smiled and added in a more friendly tone, "I sat in on them this morning and nearly got taken by it."

"You did? Tell me about it! Does their worship really move you?" Marcellus was all ears again.

"Almost moves me. And it is true that I have instructed Olipor to make a Christian out of Lucan."

"Yes?" Marcellus was surprised that Quintus would admit it.

"Lucan is resisting. Blind fools, he says, just letting yourselves be hoodwinked into serving these Roman dogs."

"He said that to *you*?" Marcellus was astonished.

"No, no, to-to Gaius." Quintus almost slipped; Lucan had said this to Marcipor who must keep his faith a secret from Marcellus. "Gaius keeps me posted on his confidences."

"I certainly would not tolerate that," Marcellus said indignantly.

"Olipor says you can't force The Way on anyone. You can only spade the soil, so to speak, then let the Lord work his will. Darn funny thing about it is that Lucan has expressed to Gaius a longing for a God like theirs."

"Yes, slaves must have their gods. Then I suppose he will not be a Christian just out of obstinacy to you."

"Or something like that," Quintus agreed. "He does attend all their worship, though. You know, I can't help admiring his pluck. And by the way, we know that he is educated, too."

"How's that?"

"Of course Lucan will not tell anything about himself, but last night he came out with some beautiful logic. And Gaius overheard him talking in his sleep. Lucan sleeps next to Gaius, you know. Gaius says Lucan was quoting Lucretius. At length. In Greek."

"Really?"

"'If there is a God, he did not create this chaotic world,' *et cetera*."

Marcellus chuckled. "Sounds like him. Lucan, I mean. Arrogant."

"He's a thinker, Marcellus. I'd like to get him to talk with me. It would be interesting."

"You and your fraternal ideas with your slaves!" Marcellus chided. "Let's go hunting!" He was through listening.

Quintus was not through talking. "Not merely fraternal ideas," he insisted, "but the truth. We can't treat our slaves as property or things. We deteriorate if we do."

"You deteriorate if you get too intimate! I warn you, Beans, not to get too intimate with them. You will lose discipline. If they get to know you too well, they may find that you are not admirable enough to obey."

"Dammit," Quintus ejaculated, "do I have to be perfect before anyone will respond to my kindness? I don't think I will lose discipline, Marcellus. I may lose the discipline that holds one to a rigid obedience to a code; I may lose the whip-over-the-head discipline. But this old discipline will be replaced with a new law, a law that springs from respect for me even though I may not be 'admirable enough to obey,' a law that springs from, well, gratitude, love."

"Gratitude and love for what?" Marcellus asked.

"For being just who I am. I am just as much their servant as they are mine. Fellow men, all dear to God."

"Love and service! Come, come, now, Beans, phew!" Because of times like this Marcellus came to call Quintus Beans; not only because his last name stemmed from the same root, not only because legumes were a major crop, but also because Quintus was taken to expounding his idealism, and then he sounded to the worldly Marcellus like certain results of the ingested product. "Seems to me that you are more than 'nearly' carried away with this Christian stuff. You are undermined by it! You are really determined to break down all barriers between you and your slaves! Go ahead. The bet will prove."

Quintus turned away, hurt.

"Now I didn't mean to hurt you," Marcellus appeased. "I know only too well that you are right. Idealistically, that is. Only to be right is not enough. You also have to be successful. Your truth has to be practicable. And in order to be successful, you will have to follow the world. If you don't, you will suffer for it. Including your slave girl. Have you opened her yet?"

"Come on, let us go hunting," Quintus avoided the last question.

They hunted and fowled with nets most of the morning, and when they returned to the villa, Quintus presented each of his slaves a fat partridge for dinner.

* * *

Lucan did not stop eating when he heard the footsteps. You are going to get punished anyway, he thought, so you may as well eat as much as you can. The footsteps stopped in the pantry doorway. Lucan deliberately cut another large bit of ham and stuffed it into his mouth. Then he turned. It was the young domine himself. Lucan could not be more obviously caught.

"Well, well, well!" Quintus exclaimed, somewhat embarrassed at being caught at his own afternoon practice. Lucan chewed defiantly and watched the Roman. So what are you going to do? he thought.

"Any bread in here?" Quintus sauntered past him and looked around. Lucan did not offer to move. Quintus went across to the bakery and got a loaf. He took the butcher knife from Lucan's hand and cut a wedge out of the loaf, salted it, and covered it with a slice of cheese and some green-olive relish. "Have some!" Quintus motioned toward the loaf. Lucan who had finished his mouthful regarded his master rancorously and scarcely breathed.

"Come on, Lucan, let's go upstairs," Quintus requested, and led the way briskly. Lucan cursed under his breath and followed directly. If you do not behave, you will still be well treated. Stealing. He could hardly have done worse. Try him, Lucan, try him to his limit. Upstairs Lucan stood before his master and wore his blank expression. However he kept glancing past the domine to the chariot whip on the wall.

"Yes, there's dust on it," Quintus said suddenly. Lucan met his eyes in astonishment. Quintus sighed and shook his head. "You can't seem to avoid trouble, Lucan, can you. Sometimes I can understand why you have been beaten. Sneaking in like that, not telling Olipor where you were going, of course. I saw your beautiful maneuvers—never thought you would get past Postumus. What were you at the front, a spy?"

Quintus noticed that Lucan had paled and that his teeth were clenched.

"Why did you do it?"

"I was hungry, sir." Lucan started to tremble.

"That's all right, that's all right! I'm a growing boy too. Gaius said he was near twenty before he no longer needed the snacks. I assume this isn't the first time?"

Lucan lowered his gaze then looked up quickly a few times, appraising Quintus's face. "Not the first time, sir."

"The point of the matter is, why didn't you ask? You don't have to steal in this house to meet your needs."

Lucan did not answer. The defiant look returned to his eyes.

"You must understand that if everybody just helped themselves the menus would be sabotaged and the inventory put to confusion. Or did you expect to be punished for asking?"

Lucan stared with horror into the past. Dunkings. Whippings. Starvation. Atrocities on the bed. Always with shackles. The hurt animal look glittered in his eyes.

"Don't you have any more faith in me than that?"

His master's words snapped him back to the present. He studied the Roman in amazement.

"Now listen, Lucan, I want you to go back to the orchard. First you must stop off at the pantry and finish your snack. And while you are at it, cut me a slice of ham too, and bring it up on a wedge of bread. With a cup of milk too, please. My afternoon snack was, ah, interrupted." Quintus marveled at how Lucan could look him straight in the face even when he expected the worst, though Quintus thought he detected a quiver in the lower jaw as the slave turned to go.

Lucan brought up the snack too soon to have eaten more himself. He regarded his master with awe. He lingered ever so slightly before turning to go. Quintus could have simply dismissed him. Instead he inquired delicately, "What is it, Lucan?"

Don't tell him! Never! Try him! Try him!

Quintus waited for an answer. He studied his slave steadily until Lucan wished that he could shrink out of existence. "Go ahead and finish your snack, Lucan, and come in and get one whenever you are hungry."

"I'm not hungry, sir." It was the truth; Lucan's stomach was in knots.

"No, I suppose not, when you expected to have the living daylights beaten out of you." Quintus put his fist against the hollow of Lucan's stomach and shoved gently. "But you will be. Now go."

"Thank you, sir!" There, he got it out. Lucan left quickly, choking with emotion and cursing the moisture that blurred his eyes. Damn Roman. Damn Roman. He gets inside my skin. So if I do not behave I will still be well treated? Try him, Lucan, try him to his limit! Don't take any snacks. In fact, skimp at meals, and see what he can do about it!

Lucan's self-imposed hunger strike did not last long. The gnawing hunger in the midst of plenty overtook him, and when he saw that the young domine was going to do exactly nothing, he ate heartily again. Next out of defiance he snacked freely, ravenously, whenever he had chance to go by the pantry. Unseen, of course. He decided that he would gorge himself to obesity. He soon found out, considering his underweight and the hard work he was doing, that this maneuver was virtually impossible. Finally he dropped his foolishness and limited his snacking within reason. The abundant food in addition to his diligent work was doing his lean, growing body good.

Lucan could tell, even from out in the fields, when fresh bread was coming out of the oven. He left his hoe in the beans and wandered into the bakery. "Oh Letitia, that bread smells awfully good. Give me a hunk, I'm starving!"

"Who else but Lucan," she teased. "You keep watch over the bakery like a vulture over a new lamb. Who do you think you are, stealing snacks, anyway?"

"I'm not stealing," he said earnestly as he walked across the hall to the pantry and helped himself to olives and raisins. "The young domine told me to get something to eat whenever I am hungry."

"A likely story, hollowlegs." Letitia began slicing a loaf.

"Honest! You ask him! Olipor knows." He wiped the milk ring off his mouth and returned to the bakery and put a wedge of cheese next to the hot loaves. "Say, how about slicing and salting a whole loaf for me to take out to the boys?"

"What boys," she said shrewdly, "Lucan, and Lucan, and, oh yes, Lucan?"

"O come on," he urged, "someone is coming in the stable court. I must make myself scarce, with the loaf of course."

Letitia handed him the prepared loaf. She had tucked pieces of cheese between the wedges of hot bread.

"That's the girl," he said, hiding the hot loaf in his tunic, "nothing like bread hot from the oven. Bye now, we shall love you forever!"

"I wish you really meant that," she called after him wistfully.

Quintus and Marcellus walked in just as Lucan left.

"Here come two hungry mouths," Letitia greeted them. She was the only one who spoke openly to the young master, a carryover from the early childhood sweetheart days before he was sent off to school, and he lapped it up.

"Um-m-m!" Quintus deliberately reached through the curves of her waist to get a loaf, and she drew breath in pleasure.

Marcellus pinched her buttock and teased her. "Turn the other cheek, Letitia, that's what Christians are supposed to do, you know."

The crass pun annoyed her. The teaching means that you don't seek revenge, she reflected to herself, replacing 'an eye for an eye.'

"You men are all alike," she scolded out loud. "What will it be? A raisin loaf? With honey? And wine? In the dining room?"

"We will bask in the domesticity of the kitchen," Quintus replied eloquently. He was acutely aware of the charms of his early maturing female slave. He tore open the loaf with his hands. "Somebody else has been at it, I see," he said, reaching for the knife and cheese.

"A certain hollowlegs who claims to have your permission," Letitia replied.

"Well, he has," Quintus confirmed.

"To eat five meals a day?" Letitia wanted to be certain that Lucan was not getting himself into trouble. She was ready to plead his cause.

Quintus lifted his eyebrow in surprise. "Don't refuse him. We do not want to starve him into being a thief. That is common sense, don't you think so, Letitia?"

"I think you're wise, Quintus." Letitia smiled directly into his eyes.

"I'm glad you agree," he regarded her gratefully.

Marcellus did not approve. "And what did he do to deserve this indulgence?"

"He is hungry, Marcellus, that's all," Quintus said.

"He will pay you back, I presume," Marcellus said.

"He doesn't have to earn it." Quintus became defensive.

"God's sun and rain fall impartially both on the worthy and the unworthy," Letitia put in, "and he scatters his love as lavishly as a sower broadcasts his seed, knowing well that not all of it will last to bear fruit, so who are we to be partial?"

"Well said, Letitia," Quintus affirmed and smiled at her.

"You are spoiling him, Beans," Marcellus offered his opinion.

"I think not," Quintus countered.

"And if he overindulges?" Marcellus asked.

Quintus lost patience. "Look, Marcellus, he busts his balls out there working for me."

"He has balls?"

"Zeus, you're in some mettle today!"

"Dammit, I've had a bad morning. I lost a substantial bet, went to ease my frustrations on my favorite kneading trough and she was with another client, came home to my flute girl and she's having her monthly. Couldn't even find a round mortar to knead in. So I came up here."

"None of your kind of trough or mortar here, Marcellus."

"Letitia! How would you like me to scatter my love and broadcast my seed on you?" Marcellus looked about. But Letitia was nowhere to be seen.

After Marcellus had left, Quintus summoned her to his office in the alcove and scolded her for her behavior.

"That was singularly rude on your part to disappear like that. What kind of hostess were you! How do you think I felt!"

She hung her head. She couldn't even apologize.

"What do you have to say for yourself, Letitia?"

"Domine, I was so scared! I'm sorry!" Her voice quavered.

"Scared? Of what! You may tell Quintus."

"Of-of Marcellus! I-I didn't think that I would be allowed to refuse."

"No, I suppose ordinarily you wouldn't," he replied seriously.

She gasped. Of course it was true. She was a slave. She had no right to personal feelings or to her own body.

"Furthermore, Letitia, you may call me by name in private, but never, no, never, in public!"

She could not even look at him. A tear started down her cheek. He got up from his desk and went over to her. She hid her face in the hollow of his shoulder and tried unsuccessfully to stifle her sobs.

"Sweetheart! Come, come now!" He enfolded her protectively in his arms and pressed his face into her neck. "This is Good Will! No one can touch you without my permission, and I do not intend to allow Marcellus, or anyone!"

"Not even Gaius?" she asked into his tunic.

"Not even Gaius," he affirmed. "Not until you tell me you are ready." He could feel her body relax in his arms. He cupped a hand under her chin and lifted her face so that she looked at him again.

"Now as for refusing Marcellus or anyone else, there are ways of turning a man down that still makes him feel good about himself. Make that a part of your charm, Letitia. I depend on you to hostess for me."

"I'll try," she promised.

He kissed the tears from her eyes, and nibbled her neck. "Letitia, you should be aware of something else. This isn't the first time that Marcellus has been asking about you. I have led him to believe that you were, well, exclusive property. Mine. To say that you belonged to Gaius would mean nothing to him."

"Do I have to be property, Quinnie?" She asked it so sadly that he felt sorry for her, and didn't mind the old familiar use of his proper name.

"Yes, I'm afraid that's the way it is. For your protection," he answered seriously. "I'm sorry, Letitia."

She loved him for his sensitivity.

He lightly caressed her temple, lifted her face and kissed her very gently on the lips. She could feel that his whole body responded to that closeness. She pulled away slightly. He caught her breasts in his hands, her tender spring buds.

"Do I have the right to refuse you, Quintus?" she asked shyly.

"I give you that right, Letitia," he pledged solemnly. He noticed how girlishly self-contained and unresponsive she was. He brushed her another kiss and whispered into her ear. "I'll tell you a secret about yourself, Letitia. Someday you are going to want it. When you are ready, you will want it very, very much."

"Never!" She replied so vehemently that he chuckled. Her body was budding into womanhood, but her mind was yet a girl's. He wondered if her mother had told her horror stories from the brothel to discourage her from exploring, or if the men in the servants' hall were making passes at her, frightening or repelling her. He would have to do something to protect her from being pinned down by the men; talk to Gaius, her brothers, or something.

He sent her on her way with a pat on the other cheek. Watching her go, he recalled when she had first flown to his arms for protection. The bigger boys were making her undress under duress for examination. The little boy Quintus on his pony had heard her cries, had come at a gallop and lit into the big boys with his riding crop. 'Punty whip' he called it. Olipor intercepted the riderless pony in the kitchen garden, heard the screams and came running.

"He can't hit us, we're bigger, tell us that's so, Dad."

"When we are big they will have to call me 'Sir', is that not so?" Quintus defended himself tearfully. "Olipor, tell them it's so!"

"Yes, Quintus, it is as you say," Olipor had replied sternly. "Postumus's sons and my sons will grow up to call you sir. That does not, however, give you the liberty to use a whip on them, ever!"

Quintus had stood in silent humiliation before them. Olipor had herded the triumphant bigger boys back to the servants' hall. So engrossed were they all in the slave-master dynamics that they had forgotten about Letitia. Quintus noticed her curled up under a shrub. He drew himself up and glared at her.

"See what you caused?" he had accused her scathingly.

She had burst into tears, desolate, afraid of him now that he had been humiliated in her presence. He remembered swallowing his hurt and pride, kneeling down under the bush next to her, drawing her out, dressing her and comforting her. Having seen the horror on the face of his beloved playmate, he grew up unable to buy into the cultural practice of exploiting slaves for sexual pleasure. He would always feel protective of her.

Letitia did not regard herself as girlish and unresponsive, especially around Lucan. She reflected upon her growing awareness that she was indeed property, that indeed as a female she was but a pawn to male politics and pleasure. Her parents had not forewarned her at their quiet and loving celebration of her puberty. Now there was absolutely nothing she could do about the horny studs except to refuse to grow up.

CHAPTER V

Give Him Your Heart

Quintus lay sleepless in bed. He felt alone, very much alone, even in a houseful of slaves, especially so because they were gathered together in the kitchen and he was not included. They were keeping the Vigil on the eve of Pentecost, the final and important feast of the Paschal celebrations. Their singing between the scripture lessons was filled with the spirit, and at times a solo voice rose above the others.

> "When thou sendest forth thy Spirit, they are created;
> and thou renewest the face of the ground."

Quintus's bedroom was above the kitchen and he lay relaxed on his back and basked in the rising and falling flow of music. A few times the music nearly lulled him to sleep, then the quiet of the readings between psalms aroused him again.

> "Behold, how good and pleasant it is,
> when brethren dwell together in unity!"

Quintus longed to join the slaves. He wanted to walk in as though he belonged and sit among them, shoulder to shoulder, in the warmly companionable group.

> "It is like the precious oil upon the head,
> running down upon the beard . . ."

He knew of course that he could not. Were he to try, the slaves would stop singing and rise as soon as they saw him. He could bid them sit again, and continue their singing, but it would not be the same.

"It is like the dew . . . on the mountains of Zion!"

He was not a member of their body. If he would be just, he must mind his own business, he supposed.

"For there the Lord has commanded the blessing,
life for evermore."

Would I find life forevermore through them? On the other hand, Platonic justice demands that each class carries out its diverse and specialized duty, that each class minds its own business and does not interfere in the affairs of the other classes. Live and let live. Look out for your interests and everybody else's will be taken care of too. This is the justice which is the crown of the classical virtues of wisdom, courage, and temperance. This justice is the harmonious and unified function of society.

Or is it? Look at the harmony in my household. And these Christian slaves with their outgoing concern are not disposed to minding their own business. They are all involved in the affairs of each. They seem like a living body; when one part is affected in any way they all feel it. Nor do they exclude me from their solicitude. Is this apparent concern with the affairs of one another really a new kind of justice tempered with love?

Getting right down to it, Quintus knew that though he would be just in the Platonic sense, he found himself trying to be companionable, associating with his slaves and inquiring into their state of affairs. He meant to be concerned. Was he being merely a busybody and hence unjust? Marcellus had pointed out that he was indeed using his slaves' religion on them in the same way that the Emperor was using Christianity in state affairs. That kind of relationship would not do.

So Quintus realized sadly that his loneliness was the price he must pay for being the master. He felt a nostalgic longing for the boyhood days when to his child mind there were no slave and free. There were instead the happy playmates, especially Letitia, and the doting grownups. Then as boyhood changed to manhood he had to put away the open-mindedness of childhood and acknowledge the barriers, artificial though they seemed at first. The day he was admitted into manhood the barriers were drawn entirely up and fixed forever. To the once doting grownups he was now "the young domine." To his former playmates, including Letitia, he was now "sir." He imagined that soon he would sink into adult conformity and the change even between himself and Letitia would no longer bother him. The childhood truths would be lost forever, never to be recaptured. They would be replaced with this classical justice. Or would they? Olipor once quoted something about being as a child to enter the kingdom.

> "You have gone up on high,
> You have led captivity captive."

They could sing that one with such fervor, such joyful expectation of final release from slavery. Or do they mean spiritual freedom from slavery here and now, and where does it put me? Quintus thought gloomily. He questioned the segregation that Platonic justice imposed upon him. No contact meant no love. And he longed for someone with whom he could share his deepest feelings. He felt that he could be satisfied if he could break down the barriers between himself and Lucan. At least with that one slave. Then perhaps he would go on from there.

And I'm making progress too, Quintus recalled with a chuckle. The rascal, recording six dozen eggs when he brought in only five dozen. He looked rather worried when I questioned him. "Tell it to me straight, Lucan. You must know by now that I won't punish you for speaking out."

"I broke a dozen, sir," Lucan had confessed boldly.

"After you recorded the six?"

"No, sir, it was before I brought them in. The hens laid the eggs just the same even though I didn't bring them in."

"What are you trying to tell me?"

Lucan stammered. "I did not wish to discredit the hens for my-my carelessness."

"And I suppose you ate the eggs shell and all, to hide the evidence?" Quintus remembered the level look he gave the slave.

"Not quite, sir." Lucan had answered in a small voice. "I'm not that hungry anymore, thanks to your generosity," he added boldly.

Quintus smiled. "Let me guess what happened. You failed to take the precautions against the great red rooster. We don't call him Acribus, devouring, for nothing, you know. Unless you display a stout stick, he rushes at you and claws your face. Is that not so?"

"Yes, sir, that's what happened."

"You're a farm boy, why didn't you think of it? Didn't anyone tell you?"

"Gaius told me, sir, but . . . but . . ."

"What?"

"I thought he was trying to make me look foolish. Anyway way I didn't want to expose myself to the rooster twice. I filled the egg basket too full. Acribus attacked. I'm sorry, sir. The hens gobbled up the broken eggs, shell and all, sir. I hope that the hens don't get ideas and raid their own nests."

"So you are telling me that you mastered my stallion at first try, but you can't handle that strutting feather duster?" Quintus smirked. A puff of laughter escaped Lucan's nostrils and suddenly they were both laughing out loud. Thinking about it Quintus didn't feel quite as lonely.

And wouldn't my victory come easier if Lucan were to latch on to this new kind of justice? How close is Lucan to embracing the faith? I shall see Olipor about that, Quintus decided.

". . . Be still then," sang the voices from the kitchen,

"and know that I am God . . ."

Then Quintus rolled over and fell asleep.

* * *

Lucan and Gaius loitered in the kitchen during the rest hour the next day while Letitia did her sweeping.

"Well, is he or isn't he!" Lucan demanded.

"Must we get into that again?" Gaius protested.

Letitia stopped sweeping and leaned on her broom. "Is who, what, Lucan?"

"Is Jesus Christ the One God Incarnate, or is he merely another deity among many? I really want to know, Gaius; I'm not trying to quibble with words."

"Well?" Gaius resigned himself to discussion.

"According to that letter from Alexandria the Son created the universe and is our god in that sense; except that he is subordinate to the Father—one of the Father's creatures like us. So there you are! If Christ isn't God, I don't have to obey him!" Lucan was emphatic.

"Now wait a minute," Gaius corrected him, "that is precisely what the Church is contesting! Hear the guidance of the Holy Spirit as spoken through the church!"

"The Church is speaking splits and schisms, arguments and stubborn egotism," Lucan put it cynically.

"You have been listening only to the spirit of the world that divides and destroys," Gaius said. "Waywardly man . . ."

"There you go again," Lucan interrupted.

"What?" Gaius took him on.

"Talking about waywardly man. You Christians are always harping on sin."

"Well?"

"You cannot feed me that. Man is not weak. Man is strong! Magnificent! In God's image!"

"You can still say that after all that's happened to you!" Gaius said. "When I speak of sin I do not mean it merely as some outer force to which man yields in human frailty."

"The first victory of the devil is to persuade man that the devil does not exist," Letitia commented.

"Now let me finish!" Gaius silenced her. "I am speaking also of sin as human strength. Self-centered strength. Man is incredibly strong and persistent in the pursuit of his own way. Often man is clever enough to escape the consequences of his determined marathon. Others suffer in his stead. The world crucifies Christ constantly. And God in consideration of man's free will may not reach that man in his lifetime. Sometimes man must be broken down by the consequences of his own folly to utter despair before he will even consider thinking about God."

"Like a spinning wheel off center," Letitia contributed again. "The off-centered wheel wobbles and squeaks 'Me! Me! Me!' And unless the Spinner stops the wheel and sets it on the true Center, the wheel bursts into flames and destroys itself from its own friction."

Lucan grinned appreciatively.

"No," Gaius picked up. "Man slips off center from his true responsibility."

"That's what Letitia just said," Lucan muttered irritably, and noticed her smile.

"Your responsibility," Gaius pushed on, "your true responsibility to Christ, my friend, is to serve the young domine as though he were your Lord! You can find great joy in it!"

"I am already doing my best here," Lucan declared.

"You have given your domine excellent work, Lucan, there's no denying that. But you have not given him the only thing that he asks of you."

"And that is?" Lucan challenged.

"Your heart, Lucan," Letitia answered before Gaius.

"What!" Lucan protested. "Do you fall for that, Letitia? Let the domine control you completely? Determine who you are? In the name of this—Christ? Can you think of nothing better?"

"No stopping short, Lucan," Gaius said.

"You can exhort me until you are blue in the face, but that won't give me the will or the power to do it," Lucan protested.

Gaius jumped at the insight. "This is precisely what I mean about sin and evasion of responsibility, Lucan."

"Now just a minute, Gaius. Can't you stop that theologizing and talk about real life for a change?"

"God is the greatest reality," Gaius said.

"Gaius," Letitia broke in, "I think we need to hear Lucan. Perhaps we are so steeped in the message that we cannot see the people and their circumstances."

"Hey!" Gaius jutted his chin at her. "Who's asking you!"

She made a face at him and glanced quickly at Lucan.

"Look, Gaius," Lucan argued, "how do you think that you can claim merit out of abstinence from pursuits which fortune has already put out of your reach? How can you claim any outstanding love when you haven't been dragged through hell and back by your fellow man?" He rubbed his scarred wrists.

Letitia waited eagerly for Gaius's response. She loved to hear them debate. They were matching their powers of the mind. She loved words, not only the manner in which words were put together, but the ideas, the contexts of the words.

To Gaius the discussion was accelerating to verbal warfare. He thought for a moment before he found his rebuttal.

"A wise man Pittakos said that it is difficult to be a good man. Simonides commented that not only is it difficult to be excellent—only a god could do that—but it is impossible for a man *not* to go bad when he has more bad luck than he can handle."

Lucan did not respond right away.

"Except that with Christ all things are possible," Letitia tried to bring them back. "Christ takes the pain away so we are free to serve him, to live a life of thanksgiving."

"Don't try to keep up with us, please," Gaius chided her.

Then and there she vowed to learn how to read, so that she could follow the great debates that preoccupied the men in her life. She noticed that Lucan was also annoyed by Gaius's rudeness to her.

Lucan took up from the venerable philosopher-slave. "Epictetus said, 'Don't show me your theorems. Show me the acts which come from their digestion. Sheep don't vomit up their grass to show to the shepherd how much they have eaten. Rather, when they have internally digested the pasture they externally produce wool and milk.'"

Letitia gave him a grateful look.

"Have my acts failed you, Lucan?" Gaius asked in a conciliatory tone. "Paul says that by grace we have been saved through faith. This is not our own doing, it is the gift of God, not because of any works that we can boast of."

"Faith? Have faith under my circumstances? Faith in what, I ask you!"

"Faith in our Lord's forgiveness," Gaius reiterated, "so that we can get on with life."

"What are your circumstances, Lucan," Letitia asked.

"I'll tell you where I'm at. I lost my family, violently, at the hands of the domine's kind. I'm hurting! And you talk to me about faith in forgiveness? I was spared. Who knows why? Perhaps I feel guilty about it. Perhaps I cannot give myself to the Roman. And you call that sin? That really makes me bitter."

"I'm so sorry, Lucan," Letitia looked deeply into his eyes "I know we can't always choose how we feel, but we can choose what we do about it."

"If your guilt and bitterness keep you apart from God, then they are indeed sin, yes, they most certainly are," Gaius affirmed. "Nevertheless we Christians try unceasingly to fulfill God's command, not thinking that we can ever succeed on our own, instead giving thanks that he forgives us even though we fail."

"Forgiveness for failing impossible demands; that makes me sick!" Lucan said.

"I feel that way sometimes," Letitia said.

"God's love does not depend on our worthiness," Gaius replied thoughtfully. "You know, you and Arius need the same thing. You need less quibbling with words whether or not Christ is God, and more personal relationship with Christ himself, God Incarnate."

Lucan shrugged and held his tongue and looked at Letitia. Here was someone with a glimmer of understanding, a kindred soul.

Olipor came to the door. "So you fellows are still at it."

"The Arian controversy, Dad. I'm trying to show Lucan that . . ."

"Yes I know. Let us not have the controversy break open this household; you know what our Lord said about a house divided against itself. Come on, fellows, we transplant leek this afternoon."

Letitia lingered at the door and watched them go. A shiver of excitement over the debate shook her shoulders. She was thinking that she must get Lucan to talk out his sorrows with her, and that perhaps he would teach her to read. There was so much she could be thinking about as she did her housework. While she worked with wool she could spin thoughts and weave meditations, tossing the thoughts into the warp like the shuttle feeding the weft. And she could beat the thoughts into tight logic the way she beat the threads into firm fabric.

Then she experienced the first of what was to be a series of surprises in her life. She who had been keeping herself so pure in mind and body for Gaius, while at the same time resisting him and all those who would disturb her peace, suddenly realized that she had found a soul mate in Lucan.

* * *

Lucan went directly to the field before the others had time to gather and march out of the villa. His head ached from the discussion. He looked longingly at the forest. Only a stretch of meadow lay between him and the forest. Lucan felt that he had the time. He resisted no longer. He thrust his trowel into the ground, and like a wolf slinking away to hide, he trotted off to the woods. A quail whirred from under his feet and he jumped aside then ran wildly as though for his life, or perhaps from it.

In the woods he slowed and drank in the enchanting beauty. He noticed every detail with intense pleasure, the fantastic patterns of shadow on the undergrowth, the mixed flock of foraging tits moving among the trees. He stumbled on a long serpentine tree trunk and fell on his knees and stayed there motionless. He lifted his eyes to the lofty volcanic ridge rising majestically above the forest. He knelt there, his eyes lifted, arms and palms outstretched in spontaneous supplication. Where can the meaning of life be found? Is the God of Jesus Christ really God? Am I indeed dependent upon God for my very being? Am I really enslaved by selfish revolt? Can I accept the Christ as my Lord and obey him? Do I dare to take the challenge? Fear crept over him. He felt small, humble, insignificant, in the presence of the trees that have stood and will yet stand many times his life span. Here—yes, here! In the beauty of nature, he sensed a purpose, a meaning, a deity. He silently, desperately begged mercy of the lofty ridges, the trees, wind, grass, birds, all things around him, that they do not persecute him, crush him, or tell where he was hiding, rather that they give him a glimpse of their mystery, their source and their purpose. He was afraid to stay, he was afraid to go back.

The serenity of the surroundings soothed his feverish mind. It seemed to tell him to have faith that all would be well. Faith in what? He didn't know. Just—have—faith. Half an hour later he rose to go back. He was no longer desperate and afraid, but refreshed in body and soul. The enchanting peace and quiet of the place for the moment banished all of his fear and doubt. This was a place of refuge, this is where he would always come when he was disturbed and distressed. Yet deep inside himself he felt that he could not really in this place come to know fully the God that he longed to know.

With a last look he soberly made his way back to the field. He paused at the edge of the forest. What excuse shall I give for running off to the woods? For being late? A chill came to his stomach as he noticed that he must go past his master to get to his trowel. His fears had been banished only momentarily. Taking a deep breath and feeling very conspicuous, he trotted back to the field. As he walked by the master, Quintus looked up. Their eyes met. Lucan stopped.

"I also go up there to be alone," Quintus said warmly. Lucan swallowed and his eyes wavered. Your heart, Lucan. You have not given him the only thing that he asks of you. Roman dog! As though you can buy my devotion with kindness! Lucan walked away abruptly and began transplanting a flat of leeks. He wondered at his master's kindness.

Not speaking, slave? Quintus thought. You are stubborn, Lucan, but I am patient. And I have plans for you.

CHAPTER VI

A Very Spiritual Task

The mid-June sun beating down during the noon hour was subtle in its effect. It felt good on Lucan when he first went out, but soon he felt light-headed. Merciful Apollo! This heat is good only for drying fodder! He was making a little fern and wildflower niche in the maze for his own hideaway.

"Come in out of the heat before you faint, Lucan," Olipor interrupted that project.

"I won't get sunstroke," he replied.

"Why are you out here?"

"I get bored, sir."

"Keep this up and you'll get yourself into trouble."

"I'm not doing anything wrong!"

"Lucan, I'm not consulting you. I'm telling you!"

Lucan tisked irritably and rejoined the others at rest in the servants' hall. He hated his rest hour now. His strength had responded fully to the three months of five meals a day. He had fifteen pounds of new muscles. He did not feel the need to sleep during the rest period. At the idleness his mind turned to moody thoughts, thoughts that he did not want. The conversation among the others seemed to him idle talk, and small talk was not one of his talents. The others did not make any particular effort anyway to include him in the chitchat and jesting. It seemed to him that no one listened to what he had to say, nor made any effort to help him with what it was he tried to put into words, the universal experiences and longings felt far before the capacity to articulate them. So for the most part Lucan sat in silence, or lay on his straw bed and brooded. Oh yes, he sat among the others from time to time and laughed with them, and felt as though he had a good time, then his feelings afterwards seemed to indicate that again, he wasted his time, that this was all emptiness.

Olipor was right about the sunstroke. But gods alive! He had to be doing something! If only it were not too hot to sing, he thought, and we had some musical instrument to play. By Minerva! I must be doing something! Lucan remembered the manuscripts in the library, and his scholarly ambition. He slipped out and the others, intent on their talking, did not notice, only they did notice and they were saying among themselves that Lucan was somewhat of a snob.

Lucan stole into the library. Luck would have it, Letitia had left a dusting cloth there. A good alibi. Tingling with anticipation, he browsed through the scrolls for one to read. He finally chose Plato and became engrossed in exploration of the mysterious nature of the supreme Deity. Plato's human mind could not conceive of how the first self-existent Cause of the universe, a Being who was in essence a unity, could permit the infinite variety and diversity of ideas that formed the model of the intellectual world. The physical world was patterned after the perfect model of ideas. Neither could Plato conceive how an incorporeal Being could mold the physical world out of the rude and independent chaos. There must be three original principles, three gods, mysteriously united. Plato imagined the One as the First Cause. He imagined the reason or word of the One to be a subordinate Demiurge who created the world. Then there was the Spirit of the universe. The second, the Demiurge, was seen as the more accessible Son of an Eternal Father. Sounds like Arius, Lucan thought.

Lucan chewed with relish upon this delicious meaty discourse. He was enjoying himself. The Gospel of John, he recalled, that Olipor has read many a time, that Gospel speaks to those of the Platonic frame of mind. However John makes an opposite affirmation from Plato, emphatically, clearly. God's Word, or Son, was not a subordinate being but Very God of Very God. In the beginning was the Word, and the Word was with God, and the Word was God. God's Word was made flesh in Jesus of Nazareth who was crucified. That crucifixion was a scandal, if you ask me, Lucan thought. And he rose again. His followers say they saw him! It doesn't make sense. God himself in the flesh, crucified! To give us a free handout of pardon and life—just for the asking. Nothing to earn, no way to make up for our past, really an outright gift. And this gift cost him the cross. The recipients are so grateful that they lead others to this free dish. Here we work our brains out groping for the Supreme Being, and it turns out he was in our very midst! Really, now, would a Supreme Being, an Eternal King, allow . . .

Lucan was of course completely unaware of the hot wasps stirring in the servants' hall. Quintus, unable to stay awake at his books during the rest period, had come wandering downstairs looking for him.

"What do you mean he's not here, Olipor! Hasn't anyone kept track of him?"

"He does that, Domine, I'm sorry. I've spoken to him about it many times. He protests that he has not done anything wrong; he has never left the property, not even when foraging for berries. And he returns reasonably on time for the afternoon work. Now I can't argue with that, can I, sir?"

"Well I can! Again you're not backing me up, Olipor! He is never around when I want him! That is tantamount to absence without leave! A hundred lashes isn't it? I'm going after him!" Quintus went off in a huff, saw a crop on the wall of the toolroom in passing, snatched it up, turned and almost collided with Letitia.

"No!" she said urgently.

"What do you mean, no."

She met his angry eyes. "It's all right, Domine," she appeased. "He's in the library. I gave him standing permission."

"By what authority?" Quintus could be intimidating.

"Assistant housekeeper, Domine." She held her ground. "By the authority that goes with responsibility."

"Indeed!"

"Please, Quintus." She reached for the crop and took it from his hand. She wasn't accustomed to crossing his will like this, and she was terrified.

This wasn't the first time his young female slave kept him from doing something rash. "Why don't you tell me these things!" he scolded. "There's more reading to be done upstairs now than I can nod through in a year!" He walked past her and strode to the peristyle and turned left for the library.

She watched him speechlessly then smiling to herself returned to her cubicle.

Suddenly Lucan realized that the footsteps he heard were in this very room with him! He was caught outright. He raised the scroll a little higher in front of his face and tried to think what to do. The dust cloth lay untouched on the cabinet. Who was in the library? Did he see him behind the scroll? For one awful moment Lucan tried to determine from behind the parchment if the intruder were even in the room still. Then he heard a throat being cleared and gave up. He lowered the scroll.

Between the peristyle and the library Quintus decided not to be angry, if he could help it, that is. "Well," he drawled. He stood with his hands on his hips. "You almost got yourself into a lot of trouble disappearing like that, telling no one."

Lucan stood. "I-I've been dusting books—helping Letitia." Beads of sweat stood out on his face.

"Never mind the alibi. What are you reading?" Quintus released the rolls of the scroll from Lucan's white-knuckled grip. "Plato, nonetheless!"

Lucan declined comment. "I'm terribly sorry to inconvenience you, sir. If I had thought anyone would want me I'd . . ."

"You'd what, Lucan?"

"Tell someone where to find me."

"You should. Always. You should at all times be available to me. We've had words about that before. What kind of slave are you, anyway?" Quintus chided and regarded him quizzically. The slave wasn't as much afraid of using the library without permission as he was of being caught away from his post without permission. That's the army for you. "And what makes you think nobody would want you?"

Lucan dropped to his knees so that his master could not see how much they were shaking.

Now what is this? Quintus thought. It seems that as time goes by he becomes less defiant and more afraid. He is not an easy one to handle. I cannot scold him when he is down, now, can I? Have I found out something he didn't want me to know?

"Lucan, why wouldn't you tell me you were educated?"

Lucan's voice would not work. He averted his eyes.

"Did you not want to trust me with it?"

"N-no, sir, not that." Lucan tried to dodge the exposé. "It's, I'm not educated. Not like you, sir," he added with a touch of awe.

"You're sitting here reading Plato and you tell me . . ."

"I've never been to school like you, sir."

"Who taught you, then?"

"My father. Evenings, around the lamp. He would sit between my brother and myself and read aloud and point to the words with his finger so that we could follow. Meter sat opposite us and did handwork by the same lamplight and listened. My sisters bedded down on their pallet against the wall. I promised Lucia that when she was big enough to stay awake I'd teach her to read. Sometimes we'd take turns reading aloud with Pater and he would fade out on me and I'd be on my own, and my father would put his arm around me and . . . ," he came to a stop and his eyes glistened at the memory of his father's words.

"And?" Quintus prompted softly.

Try him! "He would say to me, 'Lucan, light. You shall be a light to the feet of men so that they shall not stumble.'" There, he confessed it. He could not be accused of hiding anything further. His submission was complete. What would the domine do with it?

Quintus stared in astonishment. The slave had revealed a touching picture of intimate family life and personal aspiration.

Lucan took his master's hand. "Please, sir, you don't mind? S-some of the scrolls need m-mending. May I do that for you?"

Quintus was not prepared for this request. Was Lucan trying to bargain out of punishment, or insinuate himself into having his way? The audacity of him sneaking into the master's prize possessions without permission, then implying that they were not in the best condition!

"I'll think about it," he answered stiffly.

"Have I been too forward, sir?"

"Yes, you have." Now why am I handling him this way when I want to draw him out? Quintus drew breath deeply and started over.

"Lucan, you are the only one who takes my book learning seriously. I don't want you to think that I haven't noticed."

"I am happy if it pleases you, sir," Lucan replied subserviently. An uneasy foreboding pinched his stomach.

Quintus was relieved to have Lucan practically hand him the opening to his next move. "It pleases me if you stand to take orders!"

"At your service, sir." Lucan got to his feet apprehensively.

"Humble friend, supposing you were to move upstairs and attend me? Perhaps you would advance your learning, listening to me reading the manuals."

"If you wish it, sir." Lucan was not thrilled at the prospects of education at the price of intimacy.

"Yes, I request it!" Quintus was expecting more of a reaction, a glimmer of excitement. His generosity was not even acknowledged. "Do you understand?" He could not help being irritated.

"Yes, sir, I am to attend you upstairs," Lucan answered quickly.

"And sleep on a couch. And get your hair cropped like a decent Roman servant."

"As you say, sir."

"And get that worried look off your face," Quintus barked. Then what at first seemed an irrelevant thought struck him. He remembered one of Lucan's worst nightmares the first night he spent in the villa. 'Do not brand me! Flog! Starve! But not brand . . .' Quintus realized that he had never seen a brand on Lucan, even while they worked stripped to their loincloths in the fields. Quintus moved close to Lucan, and with his hand lifted the rich dark hair off Lucan's sweaty neck, first on one side, then the other. There it was, at the hair line behind Lucan's ear. It was meant to be on the forehead, the letter FUG for fugitive. Because of Lucan's violent struggling the iron had slipped and left an ugly blur on his neck like a cross. Not all the world's pigeon dung mixed in vinegar could fade that mark.

"Is this something else you didn't want me to know about?"

Lucan evaded him in mortification.

Quintus put his hand on the slave's shoulder and spoke gently. "Get your hair cut, Lucan. Those nape locks make you look like a sex slave. Get rid of them. You will look more like an educated man. Never mind the brand. Look, Lucan, here." He got out a silver coin and pressed it into Lucan's hand. "You may go to market with Gaius tomorrow, and go to a barber. I hope that someday you will not be ashamed to wear that cross upon your neck!"

Thus Lucan became Quintus's personal servant, the Quintipor. Quintus had decided not to wait for Aulus to visit and perhaps give consent, rather, to appoint Lucan now and train him so that he could make a good showing when Aulus did come.

That afternoon Lucan harvested late beans with a vengeance on the plants for his new and loathsome appointment. To serve devotedly, as Olipor does, is one thing; it has grace and beauty to it. To be ordered to serve against your will is another thing; it is downright degrading both to master and slave, especially the slave.

When Quintus announced his plan to Olipor, the old slave took it with composure. Alone in his room with the curtain shut, Olipor clutched at his breast with intense disappointment. Oh Lord, he grieved, why does Quintus want Lucan to serve him, and not my son? Why? I have failed Gaius, that he is not the chosen one! All these years of carefully nurturing him to be the Quintipor and I have failed. They sat together on my knee for stories. I accompanied them to and from school, and tutored them in their Greek. They grew up together, for each other, and diligently have I schooled Gaius in the affairs of the villa. Yet I have failed! The homebred is turned down, denied his privilege. I have failed, Olipor wept bitterly, prostrate on his couch.

I can still act! Olipor rose up from his grief with this new thought. I can see to it that Lucan falls into disfavor in the young Domine's eyes. I shall put Lucan to test, and we shall see that he isn't nearly as composed or competent as my son. Lord! he prayed with determination. Then Olipor hid his face in his hands and sank back on his bed again.

"Lord," he whispered miserably. "I cannot do that. That is not your will. In your parable, did not the lord of the harvest give the same wage to those hired late afternoon as to those who toiled in the vineyard through the early morning and the heat of the day? A generous day's wage. And are we gentile Christians not late-afternoon workers for God compared with the Jews? Our Lord is gracious and we are humbly thankful.

"Who are we then to begrudge our young domine's generosity toward Lucan? I must help my son," his thoughts faltered painfully, "I . . . must . . . help Gaius to welcome the newcomer . . . and to rejoice that the domine extends the same generosity towards him . . . as towards us the home raised. I must . . . help . . . Lucan fill his new position, and I must help Gaius . . . prepare for another life . . . accept his already high position as head market gardener . . . without expecting more.

"Oh Lord, Lord, how can this be!" His thoughts rushed him again. "What will become of my Gaius! My son! My happy son! Disillusioned! Turned down! Not wanted!

"By Jesus!" A new thought presented itself. "This can be divine providence indeed. Why hadn't I thought of it sooner! The House of Ophelus shall rise up again! My youngest son, the only son who could possibly marry, is clearly free to do so now. My son, or perhaps even my grandson, shall come into his rightful heritage again!

"Jesus Christ," he prayed again, "I cannot go thinking this way. Forgive me, help me! Give me strength! I need more strength than I have! Without you I can only rebel. Lord do not fail me with the strength to do your will! O thank God! O thank God for the victory through Jesus Christ!" Thus the loyal elderly slave struggled with himself and prepared to comply with his young domine's wishes. The struggle was by no means over. The very sight of Lucan grieved him. Almost as often as he saw Lucan or thought about him, Olipor would pray for strength that he yield not to the temptation to act unlovingly.

* * *

At chore time Lucan took a thorough bath and begrudgingly admitted to himself that he enjoyed it. Then he found Olipor and submitted to him for a haircut. Lucan was afraid of how Olipor would feel about Gaius's position going to him. He was in no mood to face the older slaves' disapproval.

During the haircut Olipor instructed Lucan in the new appointment. "You are to help your domine dress in the morning. And shave him."

"*Ad crucem* I'll cut his throat," Lucan muttered spitefully.

Olipor ignored the remark. "And serve him breakfast in the dining room."

Lucan cursed. This meant that he would have to eat on the run as he made trips to and from the kitchen, if he were to eat at all. He was always ravenous in the morning.

Olipor continued during Lucan's cursing. "Right after breakfast you are to saddle the horses and accompany the domine on the tour of inspection of the farm. After that you stand in waiting while the domine attends to business. If you keep your ears open you will learn much about the farm management from my daily report. You will work on the farm as usual the rest of the morning, and afternoons, unless, of course, your domine orders you otherwise. At chore time you will help your domine with his bath."

"Come in tired and desirous of rest, only to dress up and wait on my domine! How do you like that! I'll scrape him raw."

"And you will not refuse him if he offers to rub you down."

Lucan seized the edges of the stool and sat upright. "The domine assist me? If he touches me I'll . . . !"

"Hold still! I cannot do a good job when you wiggle. You will allow him to massage you. And you will serve his supper in the dining room unless he asks to eat with the household. Then when you have cleared away the dishes you go upstairs to him in the library and stand in waiting until he is ready for you to help him to bed. In short, you are to take care of him."

"I thought I was to do intellectual work," Lucan grumbled.

"That will come, when you have proven yourself."

"And how do I do that?"

"Make him feel comfortable in your presence."

Lucan snorted.

"Your position is a highly responsible one, Lucan, and requires a sensitivity to your domine's needs. You have one of the most spiritual tasks on earth."

"Spiritual!" Lucan choked.

"Service can be degrading," Olipor continued the lecture. "It can also be an art. It can even become an act of devotion, of love. You are too intelligent not to know that, Lucan."

"Love—" Lucan was visibly disturbed.

"What is it, Lucan?"

"Olipor, will he ask me to—I'll kill him! I'll kill myself!"

"To do what, Lucan?" When Lucan did not answer, Olipor thought a moment. "To be his femmenella, Lucan, is that it?"

"A lofty position indeed," Lucan mocked. "A most spiritual task. O my God." He clenched his fists when Olipor cut short the hair that hid the brand.

Olipor continued. "You will have leather sandals to wear indoors, and you have a second tunic to put on evenings after the daily bath. You must keep yourself clean for the domine. Hear? No more skipping baths."

Lucan let loose with a volley of curses. "As though I have to be instructed like a barbarian on how to be civilized!"

"You have kept yourself like a barbarian," Olipor said evenly.

"Dammit, Olipor, that was just part of my offensive to repulse the domine from me. It didn't work. Besides, I did not want to wash away my vitality with daily baths."

"Feel better now?" Olipor asked when the stream of curses ended.

"NO!"

Olipor was about to burst out with his own feelings about Lucan's appointment and give the young fellow a piece of his mind. Instead he caught himself with a shrug and said "All right." It would be better to listen to the boy than to exhort him.

"I hate his guts." Lucan experimented.

"You are not the only one in this household who sometimes feels that way about him," Olipor said. "But not many of us would accept freedom from this household if it were given us."

"You wouldn't!" Lucan was utterly astonished. "Why, Olipor, why?"

"Lucan, I am an old man with not many years left. Do you think that I could go out on my own and support my family on a day-to-day basis? Do you think that many of the others could? Who would care for us when we got ill, or injured? How could we earn our day's keep then? What about the rainy season? How would we find food and shelter?

"Most of you are skilled, Olipor."

"Certainly. But see us try to break into the free world and see what happens. We'd be lower than slaves. We'd virtually sell ourselves into another slavery in attempt to establish ourselves. And then one night in the street we find a knife in our back because the freeborn laborers don't relish the economic competition from freedmen. From slave to senator—those days are long gone by."

"Have you no courage of conviction?" Lucan scorned.

"I am simply saying that freedom isn't as simple as you propose, especially when there is no freedom from need. Furthermore, my conviction is that I can serve my Domine God best in the position where I find myself. And scripture advises us to remain in the station of life where we were when converted, and bring new life to it."

"Well, you are all fools. And why doesn't Quintus have Gaius serve him, since Gaius seems to be so devoted? He can well leave me in the fields."

"Among the vegetables, where you do not have to dedicate yourself entirely to him? Is that it, Lucan?"

Lucan shot Olipor a startled look and Olipor continued. "How do I know, Lucan? A person of your intelligence is restless until he uses his endowments. God has planned it that way to encourage our faithful stewardship. God also makes us restless until we discover how he wants us to use our talents. And his way may not always be the same as ours. A person like you is content to serve beneath his capacity only because he is trying to evade his full responsibility. Not so?"

Lucan was silent. That was precisely it. 'You are a Lucan and you shall be a light to the feet of men so that they shall not stumble.' Is this how I am to answer my calling, Lucan asked himself bitterly, as a Quintipor?

"My son does covet your position," Olipor continued. "Now that you have it, you must serve well. I do not want the odious task of administering punishments."

"I am not impressed, Olipor." Lucan was really saying, I don't know how to react toward your uncalled-for tolerance of me, Olipor. You act as though you like me! You knock the props out from under me.

"Now Lucan, we've had quite enough," Olipor answered the defiant remark, meaning that Lucan need not carry on beyond the purpose of his hot words.

Olipor said 'we.' Lucan whirled around and faced the door. "Was the young domine listening?"

"And if he were?" Olipor said coolly.

"He would have an opportunity to demonstrate how patient he really is," Lucan murmured and blushed.

"Yes he would, Lucan," Olipor said firmly. He brushed the loose hair off Lucan's neck. He took some perfumed oil from a flask and rubbed it in his palms, then on Lucan's hair. Olipor was granted a discretionary fund for little luxuries like this, or for pretty buttons for the women's sleeves, and similar items to help cheer the lot of the slaves. Lucan's hair shone with life. Olipor picked up a hand mirror and held it before Lucan. "Now there's a dandy," Olipor said with a smile.

"Watch your language, old man," Lucan snapped back. Then he looked at his neat reflection. He beamed. The storm was over, for the time being. "Here, Olipor," he said and he drew the silver coin out of his tunic and put it into Olipor's hand.

"What is this?"

"The domine gave it to me and said I could go to the barber in town if I wished." The coin was enough for more than one haircut.

"You keep it," Olipor said, and he put the denarius in Lucan's palm and with his two hands closed the boy's fingers gently around it. "Get something you want with it."

"Now, Olipor." Lucan's tone implied that he could not be bought by anyone.

"I know you will serve him well," Olipor concluded. Olipor was thankful that he did not jump down Lucan's throat for blowing off steam, as disapproval would only have driven Lucan deeper into rebellion.

Lucan wondered what Gaius's reaction would be to losing his anticipated appointment to him. He found out after supper.

Gaius held out his hand in congratulations.

"You're not ready to run me through for it, Gaius?"

"No, Lucan, I don't mind. You're only a body servant. As I pointed out to Dad, I am head market gardener with potential of being promoted to overseer. As Dad clearly pointed out to me I can marry now, whereas a personal slave cannot. Actually I'm glad you're the Quintipor! The house of Ophelus shall rise again, you shall see."

"The what?"

"Oh, I get carried away. Dad's way of saying better times are coming. You see, I can build up my savings much more quickly as head market gardener. From selling surplus crops and culls. The young domine will not tip a personal slave, you know."

Lucan was suddenly envious. "What will you do with your savings?"

"Buy my freedom, I suppose." Gaius was flippant.

"How long would that take?" Lucan was reacting as Gaius intended.

"Before I am old and bent," Gaius said lightly. "But Dad says that that is a worldly pursuit I need not bother about."

"What do you mean!" Lucan was eaten with exasperation.

"A Christian slave need not try to buy his freedom because he is already a freedman in Christ. Christ has already ransomed me from my real bondage."

"You are really hoodwinked," Lucan replied.

"And you're only a bodyservant," Gaius mocked.

"Well, maybe I'll just become the best damn bodyservant that this place has ever seen!"

"You do that," Gaius replied.

* * *

Quintus had the farm journal before him, but he was not thinking of farm management. He wanted to go to bed, and it occurred to him that he did not know how to be waited on. Olipor had been attending him nightly, but he never let Olipor touch him. He would undress himself and hand Olipor the clothing to fold or take to the laundry. Supposing Lucan really does know how to attend a man? Quintus wanted this to be an act of submission on the part of the slave, not an exposé of his own ignorance. What should he do? Where was it in the literature that he read of the bedtime ritual? He must get Lucan out of the room and go look through the scrolls.

"Lucan, some fresh water, please, and a bit of wine." The wine was in a locked cabinet. That would take time. Only Olipor had the key, and Olipor would be asleep by now.

Lucan was only too happy to be relieved of standing at attention at the doorway. As soon as he stepped out Quintus ran to the cabinet and began scanning. Not Columella. Was it Varro? Scrofa? The Sasernas? Stolo? Maybe it wasn't an agricultural writer at all! He had read it when he was in school. Cicero? Cato? Pliny? No, no—it sounds like Seneca. Where was it!

Lucan came back too soon. Quintus had to bluff it. He sat down on his couch and accepted the wine. He had no way of knowing that had he remembered the author he wouldn't have found the scroll anyway. Lucan had already slipped it out of the cabinet to review it himself.

When Quintus finished the wine, Lucan proceeded with the undressing. He knelt before his master to unlace his sandals and felt as though he were doing an act of surrender in spite of himself. He drew his master's foot onto his lap to undo the sandal, and massaged the thong marks on the calf and ankle.

Quintus sighed gratefully. He decided that he was going to like this kind of service. And look at the rebellious slave, will you, on his knees!

The sandals finished, Lucan rose and looked at his master expectantly. Quintus did not respond. The clod really doesn't know how to be served, Lucan thought. Now how will I get him onto his feet to remove the tunic? The cincture should be loosened by reaching from behind, with the master standing. Oh plague take it, let's not embarrass him.

Quintus was sensitive to Lucan's hesitation.

"Lucan, would you teach me what to do?"

"You stand to be undressed, sir," Lucan said stiffly.

"Thank you." Quintus stood up.

I'll teach you, Lucan thought bitterly. The master had gotten past his defenses again. He reached from behind to undo the tie to the master's tunic. The tunic came off easily enough. Lucan folded it and laid it down. He reached for the night shirt, but Quintus sat down again.

"Lucan, scratch my back? Up and down! Now between the shoulder blades. Yes, right there—oh! Oh!"

Lucan began to feel uneasy. He feared the inevitable that would follow. He got the nightshirt on, and knelt before his master again to do the loincloth. Quintus did not know to lift his hips one at a time. Lucan had to clue him. Would the master think he was being suggestive? Lucan put his hand under his master's thigh to lift upward while pulling the cloth with the other hand. Quintus chuckled and squirmed ticklishly, of all things. Lucan apologized swiftly and negotiated the other side. When he slipped off the loincloth, there was the object of his fear, erected in its full glory. If Quintus had stood for the removal of the loincloth that powerful organ would have been level with Lucan's mouth. Memories of the inevitable request overcame him, and he suppressed a retch.

Quintus seemed not to notice. "Nice piece of equipment, don't you think so?"

"Y-Yes, sir," Lucan answered, nearly faint with dread.

"I enjoyed that, Lucan, all of me did. You have a wonderful touch. Would you like me to scratch your back?"

"No!" Lucan got up quickly. "I mean no thank you, sir. Please, may I go to bed, sir?"

Quintus dismissed him to bed. He fidgeted with chores until he thought his master wasn't watching, then he tried to slip into bed without undressing.

Quintus caught him. "Aren't you going to undress yourself?"

"Aren't you going to fetter me to my bed?" Lucan retorted.

"What? You've been fettered to the bed?" Quintus chortled and rose up on his elbow. "I wouldn't wonder, the way you flit about. Now clothes off for you, before I come and undress you myself. And the night lamp stays on."

How did this young master manage to be so naive! Lucan undressed sullenly under the close watch of his master, and folded his clothes neatly into a pile by his bed.

"By Hercules, you're beautiful, Lucan," Quintus murmured.

"Thanks to your generosity with the food, sir," Lucan returned the compliment coolly. He was in fact upset. Before his master could signal that he should come to his bed, he slipped under the covers. Part of the nightmarish past visited him again, his desperate escape efforts from his second master who fettered him to his bed so there could be only a limited resistance against the perverted ones who fought for the use of his then boyish body. Lucan fingered a stolen dagger that he had ready under his pillow in case his new master Quintus offered any advances on his body. Stupid Roman, he thought, so I'm being funny? So I'm beautiful? Just you try. Just you try . . .

"Lucan!"

Lucan nearly jumped out of his skin and Quintus sniggered.

"Am I really supposed to tie you to your bed? Do you think that I anticipate your running away, or cutting my throat?"

Lucan answered with the pain of the past in his voice.

"I have never before been allowed to sleep in the presence of my domine without first being fettered and locked to my bed."

"Well, congratulations!" Quintus teased magnanimously. "You are now out of the dangerous category!"

"Well, you're not," Lucan muttered inaudibly, turned his back to his master and clutched the stolen dagger under his pillow.

"Lucan!"

"Sir?" Lucan's voice trembled.

"I have no intentions of using your body. That's a promise!"

"Why—the idea!" Lucan turned and stared and did not betray his relief.

Quintus wondered what Lucan's life story would reveal. I may be a damn fool yet, he thought, but I am determined to prove my theory to Marcellus. Lucan shall be the real fruit of my efforts. He lay stiff and self-conscious until he could tell by Lucan's breathing that the slave was asleep. Quintus woke that night every time Lucan stirred, and waited anxiously for Lucan's return when the slave went out to the privy.

The next morning Lucan was somewhat unnerved to wake up and find his master already at work at his desk. He dressed rapidly and stood apologetically before him. The master asked him for a shave. With trembling hands, he made preparations to obey.

"It's a pleasure to be pampered, Lucan," Quintus sighed. "Besides, think of the time that you are saving me for my studies by taking care of the daily chores for me." He stared at the bright reflections the knife made on the ceiling. Lucan gingerly began the shaving. The knife was very sharp. As Lucan cut the whiskers on his master's throat, Quintus giggled ticklishly. Lucan stopped for just a moment, with the blade against his master's throat. Quintus met Lucan's eyes, which were enormous. A fearful reaction upon seeing the look on Lucan's face would have been suicidal. But Quintus did not start against the keen blade. He smiled and said "Go on, Lucan," and closed his eyes and abandoned himself to his slave. He was afraid.

With icy hands and tremulous breath, Lucan finished the job. He felt greatly relieved. He was trusted. He felt freed to behave half decently.

During the next several nights after he cleared away his master's supper dishes, Lucan reported to his master at his upstairs library. There he stood at attention while Quintus wrote, or read loud enough for him to hear.

Quintus felt a bit mean making Lucan just stand there after long workdays of reaping and threshing barley, especially when Lucan leaned against the doorframe and almost went to sleep while still appearing to be at attention. The struggle to keep awake was awful, Quintus could see that. Also the sense of wasted time. Quintus caught Lucan's longing looks at the scrolls. But tough Roman discipline was not for nothing, nor was the lesson to submit one's feelings and desires to duty.

Lucan however felt strongly that this was all vanity. He regarded the long hours of standing with indignation. What a waste of time! Life is too short. Think of the reading I could be doing! Or the sleeping! After a few nights Lucan did fall asleep as he stood upright with his back against the doorframe.

Quintus watched him for a few minutes and wondered if Lucan's legs would buckle under him. Then Quintus had a mischievous idea. He picked up the cork stopper from his ink bottle, aimed, and threw. It struck Lucan lightly on the temple. Lucan started and looked at his master who concentrated at his books. He turned his face away and drew a heavy breath of travail. Quintus gave Lucan a sidelong glance. Lucan lifted an eyebrow and stole a look at his master out of the corner of his eye. A roguish smile curled the corners of Quintus's mouth.

"Lucan, go to bed before you fall over."

"I'm sorry sir, I'm all right."

"Do I have to put you down?"

"No, sir. You're not angry with me, sir?" Lucan asked anxiously.

"Why should I be? You're overtired; you go to bed. That's all there is to it."

"Yes, sir." There was tentativeness in his voice.

"Why? What did you expect? A flogging or something? Answer me, Lucan."

"Forgive me, sir. My other masters—"

"I am not your other masters!"

There he did it again, gotten past his defenses. Reached him with the unexpected. Lucan picked up the cork and carried it to his master's desk and deposited it there.

"Thank you, sir." Then the remarkable happened. He smiled at his master for the very first time. Suddenly he saw the humor in the situation. He could not help himself. His body shook with silent laughter, silent except for spasms of air rushing out his nostrils. He blushed. At last Lucan was learning to relax.

Quintus chuckled. Perhaps also, he hoped, Lucan may learn not to take himself so very seriously.

Lucan fell asleep before he pulled the covers over himself. A sigh escaped his throat each time he exhaled.

"Lucan. Lucan?" Quintus called, thinking Lucan was having another nightmare.

Lucan woke with a jump. "I am sorry, sir," he said wearily.

"Lucan, you are overtired."

"That is nothing, sir," Lucan mumbled. He did not want to be disturbed. He drifted into sleep again.

"Lucan!"

"Sirrr?"

"You didn't even pull the covers over you."

Lucan made a feeble grasp at the covers. His fingers hardly touched them when they relaxed. He was asleep again. Quintus rose, walked to the bed, gently put the relaxed arm under and drew the covers over Lucan's shoulders.

In the morning Quintus noticed that Lucan woke in exactly the same position in which he fell asleep. A sign of fatigue. Quintus assigned Lucan indoor tasks for the day. He was not one to deny others the occasional relief that he took himself. So Lucan helped the women preserve pears and plums. They packed the fresh fruit in earthenware vessels, covered the fruit with raisin wine, and plastered on the covers. Lucan despised this woman's work for the teasing it would bring him. But Letitia prettily humored him and even got him to admit that he used to help his mother quite a bit packing fruit and was well acquainted with the glowing satisfaction of preserving these bright jewels against winter scarcity.

"Only please limit your sampling to windfalls, Lucan."

That night Quintus told Olipor to send Lucan right upstairs and to have someone else clear the dishes.

"Is there trouble, sir?" Olipor inquired.

"No, Olipor."

As soon as Lucan came upstairs, Quintus ordered him to bed. Lucan protested in all seriousness that then he could not attend to his master's comfort. Quintus gave him a level look. Although Lucan had been serious all day, Quintus thought now that he could detect a twinkle in the slave's eye.

"Must I put you to bed?" Quintus threatened, rising from his desk in mock sternness.

"No, sir," Lucan sang, and flashed his bright smile again.

Quintus congratulated himself joyfully. He was making progress. He was going to show Marcellus yet. He should have let well enough alone. Instead, he followed the tired slave over to his bed and offered him a massage.

"No thank you, sir, really," Lucan answered swiftly with alarm in his voice.

"Nonsense!" Quintus helped Lucan remove his clothes, and when the slave resisted, he slapped him on the buttocks. "Dammit, slave, you are going to let me be caring for you too."

What's he going to do next, Lucan thought, come ramming up my rear? Quintus slapped him again, and he lay face down and submitted with a groan. He buried his face in his pillow and waited for that painful abuse that he had to endure from his other masters. He fingered the dagger under the pillow. But Quintus meant precisely a massage, and only a massage. The master's hands sought out the knotted muscles in his shoulders and kneaded them soft. Then those hands, which by now were feeling quite wonderful, ran up and down his spine, and he throbbed secretly in his groin. Then the master's hands reached under his abdomen and pulled upward toward the small of his back in a luxurious movement of massage.

Zounds! He's lifting me up to plunge in! Lucan reflexively clutched his pillow and braced for the intolerable pain. Quintus repeated the motion and Lucan spun defensively on his back.

"For Priapus's sake, the pomade!" he uttered.

"The what!"

At the startled look on Quintus's face he realized his mistake and that he also completely exposed his secret. He was mortified.

Quintus's eyes crinkled with humor. "You see? You rise to the occasion too, don't you. Just remember that, when it's my turn, so you don't have to panic." Quintus chuckled and to Lucan's immense relief ambled back to his books.

Lucan regarded his master with wonderment. So it was acceptable to be normal, so to speak, and nothing debasing would happen to him. This Roman really wasn't going to debauch him.

CHAPTER VII

With Whom Can I be At One?

Blistering heat ushered in July, relentlessly augmented one's fatigue and accentuated Quintus's loneliness. They were harvesting wheat now, intensely racing against a brewing storm. The oncoming storm would break and spend itself and leave the world fresh and clear, and then his depression would also lift. He worked hard all day and felt a real sense of camaraderie in the smoothly running teamwork. They cut the stalks half way down with sickles and for now stacked the piles in the wagon shed. The wheat would be dried repeatedly in the sun and threshed when opportunity offered. The straw would be used for bedding. The stubble and leaves left intact in the field would be grazed by the sheep who would in return manure the land. The field would be plowed after a month, ample rain permitting, and sown to vetch for fodder.

Even though he was more tired than usual that night, Quintus ate supper with his slaves in the kitchen. The noisy jesting helped to hide the emptiness inside him. He lingered in the kitchen after supper too, instead of going right upstairs to his library and his books.

However the slaves were not used to their master's prolonged presence in the kitchen. While they would ordinarily have lounged there themselves, they one by one began to make excuses and take their leave. Mamercus the Arab departed anxiously to check the newborn piglets, which would bring a huge profit as suckling-pigs at market when they began to put on weight. Olipor had to check the barn doors and windows against the oncoming storm. Gaius guessed he would go along with his father. Gregor had to leave for his guard duty at the gatehouse. "And Alexis, would you help me to carry out the tools that I am to sharpen?" Gregor's was the only real excuse of the whole bunch, Quintus felt. Old Servius begged fatigue and went to bed. No stories about the "old a times" from him tonight. The three women modestly withdrew. And so on, until only Postumus and Kaeso were left finishing up the pots and pans. Quintus lounged on the bench and listened in on their sparse comments as they industriously scrubbed the pots with sand.

Lucan stood tensely nearby. He knew what was happening. He wondered if his master knew. He watched him intently with wide eyes. Soon Postumus and Kaeso took their leave, and only Lucan and Quintus were left. Quintus seemed not to notice. Nonetheless Lucan felt that the Roman must know. Lucan felt almost pity for his master, especially after the manner in which the young Roman sighed and rose and went upstairs and engrossed himself in his scrolls. Those books can be a barrier to human communication, Lucan thought. The master hides behind his books.

Lucan took his post standing at attention near the door. He cursed the barrier between them. His brow furrowed deeply.

Quintus noticed. "Why so serious, Lucan?" he asked gloomily.

"Sorry sir, I—it's nothing, sir."

"Come on, man, no slavish answers tonight, please."

"I-I was thinking about the kitchen, sir."

"So was I. What about it, Lucan?"

Lucan hesitated, then came out with it directly. "How everybody excused themselves and left you alone, sir."

"And you? Aren't you somebody? I say, do you exist?"

"Why, yes, sir, by your kindness, sir."

"How are you sure?"

Lucan thought a moment. "Well, I feel, and see, and hear, and smell, and think . . ."

"How are you sure that the senses are not only deception?"

"If what I have sensed in my lifetime is only deception and not real—and you're certainly more than a figment of my imagination, sir—I wouldn't have done all that to myself."

Now what does he mean by that. Quintus sparred with a quote from Epictetus, the revered Stoic who was himself a slave acquainted with torture.

"'Men are not disturbed by the things which happen, but by their opinions about things. The ill-instructed man blames others for his own bad condition.'" Then he wished he hadn't said this for he had invited his slave to speak, and didn't mean to squelch him.

"Pardon me, sir, I struck a nerve." Lucan's dutiful apology boldly contained a barb.

"Ah, maybe I'm human too," Quintus quipped.

"And I suppose, sir, that you are going to add that 'the partially instructed man blames himself, but the well instructed man blames neither another nor his own opinions but accepts the condition.'"

"Lucan, come here!"

"I've overstepped my bounds, sir. Please forgive me." Lucan approached and studied Quintus's face.

"I'm inviting you over your boundaries. Here." Quintus indicated a stool. "Sit down."

They were silent for a moment.

"Do you ever get a chance to talk, downstairs?"

"Yes, sir."

"Were you ever lonely, Lucan? I mean down there?"

"Terribly lonely, sir." Lucan shuddered from the depths of his being.

The tone of Lucan's answer tore Quintus. "I mean, just think, Lucan." Quintus spoke rapidly now. "Here you and I live closely together. No one is closer to me than you. And yet—we are worlds apart. Why, Lucan, days go by and I hardly know that you exist! I take you for granted. I see you attend me, we converse, but I am not really aware of you, I don't know the real you. We live only parallel to each other, not with each other. Then I suddenly notice you and ask myself, who are you and what are you doing here? Do you feel that way, Lucan?"

"Yes, sir, I do wonder what I'm doing here," Lucan answered sharply, then shuddered at his boldness.

"You're serving me, that's what," Quintus matched the sharpness.

"My apologies, sir!" Lucan caught himself. Then he admitted pensively, "I am lonely, sir, in the midst of the family. It is hell."

"Does one have to accept loneliness, as Epictetus says?"

"Loneliness eats at the very soul," Lucan replied. "Who can live with that? Who wants to?"

"What do they say about that downstairs?"

"That Christ transforms all things and nothing can separate us from God's love."

"So?"

"So in response we should become involved in the living body of Christ of which we are the members."

"Down there they teach involvement with each other's lives, not detachment?"

"Yes, sir, reaching out with love."

"Not like the Stoics!"

"Completely different, sir."

"Will you become one of them?"

"I don't know, sir, I'm not very religious."

"You do attend."

"I like the togetherness."

"What else have you learned down there?"

"'That God so loved the world that he sent his only son, so that no one who believes in him should be lost, but that they should all have eternal life.'"

"And?" Quintus prompted.

"'If I have no love I am but a clashing cymbal.'" Then Lucan was overcome with embarrassment for he had been resisting more than learning down there.

Quintus came to the rescue. "Would you like to read something?" He gestured toward the cabinet. "Or proofread my copywork for me?"

"I will proofread, sir," Lucan offered tactfully.

"Thanks," Quintus said self-consciously, and handed Lucan his newly made copy of Columella's second book on agriculture.

Lucan hid behind the opened scroll. He did not notice at first that the scroll was upside-down. Quintus was enjoying his slave's spunk, but he was sensitive enough not to laugh. Lucan casually uprighted the scroll. But neither of them could relax. Suddenly Quintus could take it no longer. He chuckled. Lucan looked up.

"Upside-down," Quintus said, "that takes talent."

"Oh, don't you do it that way?" Lucan quipped. "It's a trick of the trade, truly." Puffs of laughter escaped his nostrils and they laughed together.

"If you could learn some of this stuff and brief me on it, I'd be most grateful." Quintus sighed. "There are so many details."

"Certainly, sir."

"Confidentially, I'd like to know how Gaius calculates the amount of seed needed to plant fields of various shapes, and the number of vegetable seedlings needed to set out in a field. Sometimes I feel that he tries to overdo it, or skimp on it, to his own benefit. As though it's me against them, Lucan. How can I confide in Olipor when he is one of them? You are an outsider. You could be a real ally."

"I will help you, sir," Lucan pledged and his scalp prickled. He knew exactly what the master was asking of him; to serve as a go-between with Gaius, no, more than that. To serve as a check, yes, even a whip. He knew that it was only a matter of time before he would be in big trouble.

"Actually I would like to try a new way of keeping the books," Quintus continued. "It will take a lot of time to set up but I think it will pay. I want to account for each product separately and charge for tools, materials and labor for each. It means renting tools and labor from ourselves, so to speak. Do you follow me, Lucan?"

"Yes, sir."

"Gaius doesn't agree. He thinks it's picayune. He says, 'Isn't plowing—plowing—whether it's done for cereal or vegetables?' He thinks I'm wasting my time, and he persists in keeping the records the old way while I must do the new, up here late at night like this."

"Would you like—?" Lucan remembered his master's decimal error, then dared to finish his offer, "help with the computing?"

"I would like help copying Columella's books on agriculture!"

"I can do that for you, sir," Lucan offered.

"You approve of my idea, then? Don't be afraid to say no.

"I am familiar with your idea sir. My father did a similar thing."

"He did?" Quintus tried to penetrate through the mist in Lucan's eyes.

"That's how I learned to compute. For the ledger. He always knew what percent of income came from each area of production, and how well our labor was paying off, and where our labor could be put to better profit. He was always talking about that to my brother and myself and how one could—" Lucan caught himself warming to the memory.

"Go on, Lucan."

"Pater studied the authorities on how to improve the land. He'd get into shouting discussions with the landlord about how one could be more innovative in rotating crops and green manuring instead of letting so much land lie fallow. One doesn't have to be so rigid in assigning specific crops to specific soils, he would say."

"Is that also what your father did?" Quintus hesitated and made a stirring gesture with his hand. "Innovate a little?"

"Innovate a lot, sir! He used intelligence over common sense," Lucan elaborated, then realized that he may have slurred his master's intelligence.

"Then we can show them, Lucan!"

"Very well, sir," Lucan retreated into formality, lowered his eyes from his master's intent gaze and returned to his scroll. But his mind did not follow the words.

Quintus could see that the windows to Lucan's mind had closed, and the conversation was over at the slave's will, not the master's. That annoyed him. He observed the slave's far away look changing back to that inexplicable hurt and resentment. He realized that Lucan's father, like himself, studied the authorities to learn how to farm in the first place, and that the so-called innovations could have been acts of ignorance. Don't you know who your father really was, Lucan, or are you unwilling to admit it? Has it never occurred to you that you may be named after your procreator and not after certain aspirations for you? Don't you know what can happen to you if you really are Oikonomikos's son? As it is, perhaps you can realize those aspirations.

They remained silent, in the pain of isolation from each other.

The thunderstorm arrived later in the night. Quintus wistfully got out of bed and walked softly over to Lucan's bed and looked down upon him. Lucan slept peacefully through the thunderclaps, on his back, with his face up. The lightening lit his relaxed countenance.

Lucan, Lucan, Quintus thought with longing, how badly I wish to take you in as a lost brother, and you will not. Can you sleep so peacefully at a time like this? Look at the sweet smile curling your lips. What lost happiness do you cherish now in your dreams? What agonies do you suppress?

Lucan opened his eyes and looked up at the dark form bending tenderly over him. "Pa?" he called softly, his voice resonant with joy and affection. Then he bounded out of bed and tensed for attack.

"Lucan! It is I!" Quintus cried and seized his slave's hands.

Lucan shrieked in terror and wrested himself free. With another flash of lightening, he saw that it was only Quintus and fell face down on the bed again.

"Oh sir," he said in the small voice of complete dejection, "Please sir, do not do that again! I thought you were . . . you were . . ."

"Tell me, Lucan, tell me!" Quintus urged.

"I can't! I don't know what it is!" He lay with his face buried in his arms, his body rigidly restraining the choking grief that racked his being.

Quintus sat on the bed and proceeded to massage Lucan's shoulders and neck in attempt to calm him. With a squeal of anguish Lucan twisted and crashed his elbow into the domine's chin. Quintus gasped and sprawled. Without a word he got up and rubbed his chin and went back to bed. Nor did Lucan apologize; he lay tense and clutched the stolen dagger under his pillow. If only he could meet the demon called memory face to face and recall why there was so much pain! Then he could grapple with it.

The next morning Lucan hesitated in the servants' hall on his way out to the fields. Quintus had just dismissed him, and the young master was now hearing Olipor's daily report. Nobody was about. Postumus and Kaeso were in the kitchen garden. The women were outdoors drying apples, pears, and figs for relish.

With whom can we be at one? Tingling apprehensively, Lucan stole into Olipor's room. The object of his search was not to be seen. Lucan looked in the locker. There on the shelf!

Lucan took down a scroll of the Living Word and opened it. It was Paul's letter to the Romans. He started reading. Some of the paragraphs were familiar. Some stood out as though for the first time

> But God shows his love for us in that while we were yet sinners Christ died for us.

You are the prisoner of your own selfish revolt, Gaius had said. Now our Lord can help you escape your prison.

Lucan heard footsteps. Fear prickled his skin. I will be punished! Why did I do this anyway! He deliberately studied the scroll before him.

Olipor had come downstairs from his conference with Quintus, and went to his room to change into a work tunic. At the door he turned and hurried on as though changing his mind. He went to the kitchen, found Dorothea, and whispered that she must not go into their room during the entire morning.

> For all who are led by the Spirit of God are sons of God. For you did not receive the spirit of slavery to fall back into fear, but you have received the spirit of sonship. When we cry "Abba! Father!" it is the Spirit himself bearing witness with our spirit that we are children of God . . .

Yet I am afraid. The footsteps were gone. Lucan relaxed. If we are children of the same Father, I need not be afraid.

Lucan, are you ever lonely?

Terribly lonely, sir. Lonely in the midst of a family. It is hell.

Adopted into the family of God . . . Father, my Father! Would it be so!

> Likewise the Spirit helps us in our weakness; for we do not know how to pray as we ought, but the Spirit intercedes for us with sighs too deep for words.

Yes, I know those agonizing longings too deep for words, Lucan acknowledged to himself.

> What then shall we say to this? If God is for us, who is against us? He who did not spare his own Son but gave him up for us all—will he not also give us all things with him?

> Who shall bring any charge against God's elect? Is it God who justifies; who is to condemn? Is it Christ Jesus, who died, yes, who was raised from the dead, who is at the right hand of God, who indeed intercedes for us?
>
> Who shall separate us from the love of Christ? Shall tribulation, or distress, or persecution, or famine, or nakedness, or peril, or sword?
>
> No, in all these things we are more than conquerors through him who loved us.
>
> For I am sure that neither death, nor life, nor angels, nor principalities, nor things present, nor things to come, nor powers, or height, nor depth, nor anything else in all creation, will be able to separate us from the love of God in Christ Jesus our Lord.

Those words penetrated Lucan. *Nothing* can separate us from the love of God! Here is he with whom we can be at one! Regardless! I can be at one with him. My Domine can be at one with him. If we are both adopted into the family of God then he and I . . .

Does this mean I must forgive the Roman for keeping me in slavery? Can this mean that I must be reconciled to *Quintus*? At one with *him*? With the Roman dog? This is beyond me! But . . . but . . .

> I appeal to you therefore, brethren, by the mercies of God, to present your bodies as a living sacrifice, holy and acceptable to God, which is your spiritual worship. Do not be conformed to this world but be transformed by the renewal of your mind, that you may prove what is the will of God, what is good and acceptable and perfect.

With his aid you can realize potentialities beyond what you thought possible, Gaius had said. You can serve Quintus as though you were serving our Lord. And take great joy in it! And find freedom in being a slave! This is a great challenge! Do you dare to take it?

With whom can we be at one?

I would tell you, sir, if I knew.

Once knowing the mercies of God, I must give myself to Him. I must make peace with—and love—yes, even my domine.

Can *I* know this God?

But God the Father sacrificed his only Son. Will he sacrifice his adopted son?

"Well!" a voice drawled. It was Quintus. "So you are 'dusting' books again. Olipor told me that I would find you here."

"I . . . is it time . . . I shall go out with you now, sir." Lucan rose to his feet and hoped that the young master would not scold.

"No, Lucan, I am coming in. The others will be in any minute now."

Lucan's gaze shot up, startled. "Dinner time already, sir? I'm sorry, I have gotten . . . quite absorbed."

"Yes, so I see." Quintus noticed the far-away look on Lucan's face. "Is it really that absorbing, Lucan? What are you reading?"

"A personal letter from Paul the Apostle of Christ to the Romans, sir. To-to you!" he glowed. "It is really provocative!"

"Really!" Quintus searched his face expectantly.

"It relates to our conversation last night. That's why I forgot the time, sir. Please forgive me. I'll make it up."

"Never mind. And when you come upstairs after dinner-ah-bring me that scroll, will you?"

* * *

Marcellus's reaction to Quintus's account of the philosophical evening was the usual worldly-wise teasing. That a slave is a person, and is therefore of great value, and that companionship with your slave is to be desired, why the idea!

"But these poor slaves are so much under the mercy of our whim, Marcellus," Quintus pleaded his point.

"Why of course!" Marcellus exclaimed. "That's what slavery means."

"That's using them, Marcellus, like things." Quintus objected. Quintus knew how his father would have sympathized with him. 'It's hard enough to be a slave without being mistreated.' Once when Quintus had parroted that comment to Marcellus, Marcellus had guffawed and had said, 'Is it hard enough for the domestic dog to be a dog, without collar and chain?'

Likewise again Marcellus teased Quintus mercilessly. "If my slave got companionable with me, and tried to manipulate me the way I do, for example, my mother and step father, I'd whip the hide off of him. No, Quintus, I wouldn't give a slave even a toenail hold toward familiarity."

"Marcellus, you think only of yourself." Quintus disgustedly closed the topic. "If you weren't my landlord, you wouldn't be my friend."

That night while Lucan prepared his master for bed, Quintus recalled this conversation with Marcellus. Jupiter! He thought. I guess I'm using a slave too.

Damn! Can't win! Quintus, you are selfish too, he went on rebuking himself. You mostly want to win a bet, though you do consider Lucan in the process.

Lucan was uneasy with his master's contemplative silence. After they had both gotten into bed, Quintus broke the silence.

"Lucan?" he called from his bed.

"Sir?" Lucan sat up in his bed.

Quintus raised himself on his elbow. "When Marcipor comes with Marcellus on a visit, does Marcipor complain?"

Lucan became wary. Spying on Marcipor? He didn't answer.

"Not even just a little bit?" Quintus coaxed. "Come on, tell me. I've challenged Marcellus that he isn't the world's best master. I want to know if I'm right.

Lucan panicked. His answer either way could only lead to trouble. The silence was awkward.

"Well?" Quintus became suspicious.

"Sir I—he—a slave doesn't have an opinion," Lucan hedged.

"Now, Lucan," Quintus was determined. "Come here."

Lucan reluctantly went to his master's bedside and stood before his sitting master. Lucan reviewed in his mind the conversations with Marcipor. Marcipor complaining about Marcellus? Oh, no, the conversations had been quite the opposite; Lucan pouring forth his bitterness about slavery, about being chosen as the Quintipor, and about his contempt for his master.

"You will be a slave the rest of your days," the silent Marcipor had spoken at last. "You cannot possibly be anything but a slave. Now face facts." Marcipor's voice had become sharp. "You take yourself too seriously. Stop your self-pity and make the most of what you have. What you have! Think of what you have, Lucan! I'd thank God if I had a human being like your master to serve. I'd gladly lose my life to find it in what you have. You just don't know when you are blessed!"

Marcipor's words had annoyed Lucan. Lucan had expected sympathy.

And then Gaius had chimed in, "He's entirely right, Lucan."

"Maybe my rescue was a gift of God as you say, but does that mean that I will therefore like it?" Lucan had muttered.

"No, that is true," Marcipor had reflected. "We do not necessarily like God's gifts just because they come from God. We are called to give thanks for all things, but we don't. See what we do with God's greatest gifts to us. Take the gift of life itself. We deny the source of our being, and carry on as though our life were really ours. Take the gift of freedom. See how we abuse it and let our egotism become a barrier between ourselves and our true Freedom. And daily we deny and crucify our Lord, God's greatest gift of love. We are too damn proud . . ."

"What has this got to do with being a slave!" Lucan had grumbled defensively.

"Lucan," Marcipor had answered, "Taking care of another person is one of the most spiritual tasks in the world!"

Then Lucan had sullenly held his tongue. Same thing Olipor had said. I can't confide in them again, he had thought. They just don't understand. Besides Gaius is envious; he was supposed to have been the Quintipor.

Now, suddenly, at Quintus's direct question Lucan realized that it was he who hadn't understood himself. He couldn't possibly tell Quintus about these conversations. He'd rather vanish.

Quintus thought Lucan really had something to hide that he must know. He would lean on him a bit to get it out.

"Sit down, Lucan," he said gently and patted the bed next to him.

Lucan sat, and shivered in fear of the inevitable dagger hidden in a master's gentleness.

"Answer me, Lucan?"

"Marcipor doesn't complain."

"What does he talk about?"

"Jesus the Christ, sir."

"And?"

"Freedom."

"Freedom? What does he want with freedom? Why, without Marcellus, Marcipor would be nothing. No family, no status, no home. Go out and compete with the freeborn and find a knife in his back. Why, he'd have to latch himself onto a patron, and isn't that another kind of slavery? By the gods, you slaves don't know when you have it good. Why that doubtful look, Lucan?"

"Do you really believe all that, sir?"

"Do you?"

"No, sir."

"I'm not so sure that I do either, Lucan. But that's the way it is." Quintus felt that he was really coming to an understanding with Lucan. "You may go back to bed."

Lucan was pierced with the separation between them.

With whom can we be at one? He asked himself with renewed pain.

If there were someone to whom I could pour forth my mind, without having to censor thoughts, and weigh words . . . someone who would understand and really care . . .

* * *

The next time Marcipor was up to worship, Quintus managed to take him aside.

"Marcipor, I wish that you would talk with Lucan," he said candidly.

"Certainly, sir! About—what?"

"Let him tell you, Marcipor, you can get it better from him."

"You mean, sir, about his bitterness?"

"Yes, Marcipor." Quintus feigned knowledge to draw Marcipor out.

"He has been troubled with it no small amount. I know that it must be trying for you, sir. I'm confident that he will come through. Please, your patience has been a blessing to all of us. May you be steadfast in that virtue, sir."

"Thanks, Marcipor." Quintus left with a smile of satisfaction. So this is what Lucan could not tell me the other night. The scamp. Marcipor hasn't been complaining to him at all. It is the other way around! So, 'A slave doesn't have an opinion,' Lucan? Ha! Your domine has brains too. And your domine will have to use his brains if he is to overcome your bitterness and win the bet!

CHAPTER VIII

A merciful kind of justice

Lucan awoke suddenly in the dark. He sensed danger. His eyes widened, his nostrils expanded, his lips parted, and he listened intently. There was a man in the room! Terror gripped him as though he were at the front where the enemy stole in the Roman camp and slit the throats of only one of the eight men in each tent while they slept. Lucan slid silently out of bed onto the floor. He did not have time to steal over to the wall and take down a sword for his master. The intruder was at Quintus's bed, now bending over. Lucan seized the dagger from under his pillow and grounded him with a flying leap.

"To arms, Domine!" he cried, and slashed open the intruder's heavy cloak.

The man checked him with an authoritarian tone. "Off, slave!"

"Pater!" Quintus bounded out of bed, very much awake.

"*Christe! Deus!* It's Aulus!" Lucan cried, too scared to even help the senior domine to his feet.

"Welcome home!" Quintus laughed with relief.

"So the young domine of this household sleeps with both eyes shut and trusts himself to a watchman who sleeps at his post and a cutthroat who sleeps with two eyes open and a dagger in his hand. And the entire household in the servants' hall snores away while I walk clear through the whole house. No one challenges me except this boy who slits your throat first, then finds out who you are!"

Aulus turned upon Lucan. "What in Hades are you doing up here! You may call the senior domine of this house your lord, but never by his first name!"

"My lord, I beg your pardon, for both my mistakes!" Lucan's insides seized. He recovered his wits enough to help Aulus remove his traveling mantle, and took his felt hat. "Did-did I hurt you, my lord?"

"Didn't you intend to?" Aulus snapped. "And tell me, what are you doing with that blade?"

"I procured it, my lord," Lucan hedged hastily. "Domine, please," he appealed to Quintus.

"I gave him money, Pater," Quintus, wondering himself, rose to the defense.

"Why?" Aulus was curt.

"My duty is to take care of my domine," Lucan answered for him, quickly and somewhat stiffly. Aulus accepted the explanation. Quintus stood there in dumb silence. Lucan's only thought now was to vanish, fast. He did not want to subject his master to the humiliation of being interrogated in his presence. He bore the whip scars from that lesson learned long ago, the hard way. He lit a lamp.

"Shall I summon Olipor, my lord?" he asked Aulus.

"No! No," Aulus answered first sharply then wearily, "do not wake Olipor. Let him sleep. Let them all sleep."

"If you please, my lord," Lucan volunteered, "I shall see if your rooms are ready for you."

"They had better be!" Aulus snapped. Then an annoying thought came to him. Is this young slave trying to build on the circumstances? To his own advantage? I shall find out.

"Very well, Lucan, you may attend me." Aulus said out loud.

Aulus sat down on Quintus's bed and pulled his mute son down beside him. Lucan took up the hat and mantle and left. With no unnecessary ceremony, Aulus noticed.

"Pater," Quintus pouted, "why did you have to come unannounced in the night like this?"

"I assumed that my son wished his second wagon returned before the vintage," Aulus said.

"I beg your pardon, sir. It's only I was going to have a nice surprise for you, and you surprised me instead."

"I was surprised," Aulus said rubbing his chest where Lucan had attacked him, "very surprised."

"I was training Lucan so that I could impress you with him." Quintus squirmed. Perhaps he shouldn't have admitted his motive.

"And get my consent to keep him?"

"Yes, sir." Quintus couldn't seem to keep anything from his father. He went on to tell his father of the bet with Marcellus, and his own efforts to prove his principles, of Lucan's resistance, and of his own triumphant moments. "I like him, Pater."

The account took Aulus back to his youth when he wooed the loyalty of his own personal slave, Olipor. He will learn, Aulus thought of his idealistic son, after a few hard knocks he will catch a glimmer of reality. The experience will be good for him.

"I will sound Lucan out myself, then give you my answer tomorrow," he said.

"Thank you, sir."

"Now listen to me, son. I have come back with some drastic news. The Emperor passed a new edict that directly impacts us. I have been expecting it. I rode to Good Will as soon as I found out. The man who works the land must pay the taxes, no matter who owns the land! Furthermore, you are now bound to the land, son, and your children after you."

"Pater! I am a free man! I am not held to the land by any debt! I paid my rent!"

"Legally you are still a free-tenant, son. In terms of the colonate, though, you have been made a serf. You may not desert your land or you will be punished as severely as a runaway slave. You cannot sell any slaves off the land either. They are also serfs now. I am also bound to my trade. Mercury, Holy Patron, help me! I cannot run away from the increased taxes put on the merchants. Nor can I help you much. I do not know what will happen to your brothers; we will have to find out when they come home on furlough."

"Why Pater!" Quintus exclaimed when the news sank in, "I am not much better off than my slave!"

"No, you are not, son. You are all serfs."

"The slaves may as well be freedmen! How am I going to keep control over them?"

"You are still their master, Quintus."

"Are you going to tell Olipor?" Quintus asked.

"It will make no difference with his loyalty."

"I am afraid it will with Lucan's. I don't want him to know."

"That should not make a difference with your authority over him," Aulus asserted. "Be honest with him."

"Pater, how am I going to win him over? Do I have to pound my authority into him? How did you get Olipor's loyalty? Did you have to whip him?"

Aulus did not answer right away. Then he admitted regretfully, "I flogged him. Just once. Until he begged me to stop. I never even had to raise my voice after that."

"So the flogging did it, Pater?" Quintus searched his father's face. "Is Marcellus right?"

"Perhaps, son. Perhaps not. Sometimes I feel that the flogging was entirely unnecessary. I don't really know."

"Why do you think it was unnecessary, if I may ask?"

"Olipor's faith exhorted him into wholehearted service. 'Serve your domine as though you were serving your Lord.'"

"Is that why you never turned the Christian slaves over to the law, Pater?"

"Son, the Christians have something that will outlast many laws. I could not presume to destroy their spirit, not that I would want to. It cannot be done."

"Then why haven't you become a Christian, Pater?"

"Because it is a slave's religion. And I will not be a slave of Christ. Or anybody."

"A slave's religion, Pater? The Emperor . . ."

"The Emperor is a slave of 'necessity'. I am not a slave." Aulus affirmed. "Not a slave." He hesitated. "That is, until the new law was issued. Now I am a slave to the state. This will be the ruin of Rome yet, my son. We no longer see the opportunities for individual advancement that we saw in the generations before. Nowadays a man can no longer rise from slavery into the senate! Now the farmers' sons remain farmers, merchants beget merchants, craftsmen stay in their crafts, the bakers' sons must bake. The decurion's son must bleed to death in the decurionate since he cannot bleed the people enough to meet the taxes, and the deficit must come from his own means. The sap of our vitality is being drawn out. With opportunities gone, we Roman people will lose our nerve. See if we don't. Military strength is not enough. And that is all we have now. Military strength that has relaxed its discipline and that has filled its ranks by arming the conquered! Our society is effeminate with luxury. Our great philosophers and artisans are men of the past. Today we are sterile. Today we only imitate at best."

"Pater, you are terribly pessimistic!"

"I do not mean to discourage you with my hopelessness. You must still try to live your best. Take over the villa and give it your all. Do not let it run down and deteriorate. Whatever you do, do not let your own household rot! This is the least, perhaps the most, you can do for yourself and the state."

Quintus nodded, and Aulus continued.

"The state is desperate, I am sure of it. The land must be cultivated in order to raise revenue. Also to feed the metropolis. Revenue and food from the provinces are already slacking off. You may be called upon to cultivate the deserted neighboring land, son. We cannot afford to lose land altogether to unhealthy marsh. You must not exploit the soil of Good Will to ruin; you must build it up. Well, son, we can talk more later. Let's get some sleep now. I must return to the city the day after tomorrow." They embraced, and Aulus went downstairs.

Quintus fell back into bed and thought over his new status. What if Pater is right, that this will be the ruin of Rome? What if Rome is overrun? By the barbarians? I am not willing for this to happen! What if our civilization is destroyed? What a great loss it will be! An appalling loss! Our knowledge! Our art! Our scientific and medical research! Our ingenious law! Our engineering advancements! Everything we take for granted right down to our indoor plumbing, sewers, and central heating! Will as many people ever have as much comfort again, or as much beauty around them, when all the technical skills are lost and mankind must start from barbaric scratch again? How many centuries will it take to regain all this? Think how long mankind already took to achieve even this!

It is Olipor's private opinion, Quintus recalled, that the world and Rome will be no more before these things come to pass. The Second Coming of Christ, he called it. But Christians have been waiting for centuries for that second coming. Anyway Olipor says that Rome will fade away no matter what we do, so while we are yet here, let us attend to that which lasts into eternity.

What is that which lasts into eternity, Olipor? Is the way I treat my slave, for example, more important in the light of eternity than all the wisdom contained in the scrolls in our libraries, than all pride and glory of fulfilled ambition? Now Marcellus says that we must uphold the social distinctions to prevent deterioration. Well, Marcellus could be wrong. So could Olipor, for that matter. Or perhaps I shall end up the fool though I don't think so.

With this, Quintus fell asleep.

* * *

Lucan deliberated whether he should walk right out through that gate past the sleeping watchman while he could, to escape possible death for having attacked the senior domine. However, Aulus sounded reasonable enough, and Quintus had covered for him. Try him! Lucan continued quietly and swiftly through the darkness to Aulus's rooms. He went directly to the lamp and lit it. He was good at finding his way about in the dark. To his relief he found the bedchamber ready for occupancy. He tried to surmise what Olipor would do for Aulus. He pulled back the bed covers, looked through the wardrobe until he found a nightgown, and laid it out.

Now for some refreshment, he thought. He lit another lamp and went to the kitchen. On the way he lit the lamp in the hall. No one stirred in the servants' quarters. Silently he prepared a tray. Let's see, bread and cheese, a slice of ham, relish. Fruit would be nice. Milk, no, wine. Where is the wine? Oh yes. Damn, the wine cellar is locked. Olipor has the key. Shall I wake him? Or serve the slaves' wine?

The thought of Olipor now struck Lucan hard. What am I to do, he thought in dismay. What can I do? The senior master's wishes come first. He will be angry with me if I don't obey. And Olipor, he will skin me alive if I don't wake him. He will think that I am trying to climb, if I attend Aulus myself. Aulus will think I am trying to impress him by serving him myself. Or he will skin me alive for waking Olipor? I'm in for misunderstandings either way. Can't I just pretend that Olipor woke by himself? And saw my light? Or something? Wretched slavery!

By the time Aulus came downstairs to his rooms, Lucan had returned with the tray and was pouring water into a washbasin. Aulus was not in the habit of crossing the line and engaging a slave in conversation. However he wanted to sound out this fellow he met so abruptly upstairs. Now would be a most interesting opportunity. He sat down before the tray and fell to.

Lucan picked up the wine flask and goblet. "Please, my lord," he apologized, "This is the servants' wine. The best is in the locked cupboard. Shall I dilute it more than the usual, say, one to ten?"

Aulus nodded, and Lucan poured the water into the goblet. The lord of the villa took a sip, then a drought. He put the goblet down and purposely sighed with satisfaction. He looked up at the slave who watched him nervously.

"The servants' wine is not good enough, Lucan?" Aulus put it to him pointedly.

Lucan shifted his weight. "The b-best is in the l-locked c-cupboard, my lord."

"And you would not wake Olipor for the key."

"I almost d-did, my lord," Lucan admitted, and proceeded to refill the goblet. "But I-I thought I had better obey."

"Yes you had. Here, dilute it only one to three. The servants' wine of Good Will is, as usual, rather good. Have some yourself." Aulus unlocked the bedroom cabinet and removed his own drinking cup.

Lucan breathed and obeyed.

"Olipor will be very angry with you for not calling him." Aulus watched closely for Lucan's reaction.

"Yes I know, my lord," Lucan answered softly.

This boy speaks quite openly, Aulus thought. "Lucan," he asked suddenly, "why do you want to serve the young domine?"

"He rescued me, my lord," Lucan answered swiftly.

"Now tell me the truth, Lucan," Aulus coaxed, "no flowery or dutiful reasons."

"I am sentenced to live and serve him, my lord."

"Is that bad, Lucan? Talk to me!"

"Slavery." Lucan shook his head and said what came to his mind. "I despise slavery. Slavery is unclean, rank. It stinks of man's alienation with himself and with others. It reeks of sin, not only as a particular manifestation of sin but as a symbol of man's ensnarement by his underlying capacity towards evil." Oh damn that wine!

"And the best way to overcome it, my boy, is not to expend yourself in barren bitterness, but to confront it squarely. Slaves do earn their freedom, you know. And even if they don't, there is the one liberating doorway through which every one must pass."

"I will not take my life, my lord."

"Quite right. You belong to your domine."

"To the Domine of all," Lucan uttered unexpectedly. "Nor will I wait passively for that doorway." His eyes fired. Double damn that wine!

"So! You are a Christian?"

It was out, wrested from him, when he scarcely knew it of himself. Lucan did not answer. The wine burned in his stomach.

"And what does the faith say about slavery?" Aulus knew only too well.

Refusing to be humiliated, Lucan continued to take slavery in its deepest meaning. His eyes narrowed and he faced Aulus directly.

"'Put on the whole armor of God that you may be able to stand against the wiles of the devil . . .'"

Aulus was no fool. "And with this armor of God you cut down your oppressor?" He was feeling out any love on Lucan's part for Quintus.

Lucan was trapped, for an answer either way could refer both to sin as that 'slavery unto death', or to Quintus and immediate slavery, and Aulus was sure to take him to task. He called for a truce with a disarming smile, and averted his eyes.

"I have my back to care for, you know, my lord."

Aulus would not let him off. "Is that why you are doing such a creditable job at it?" His comment could be taken either as commendation or sarcasm. He looked up expectantly from the tray to see Lucan's reaction.

"Resistance is inappropriate in this household," Lucan sighed.

"Until the right time comes?" Aulus seemed understanding.

"The way I'm treated here, the right time will never come," Lucan muttered gloomily. He wondered when Aulus was going to pounce.

"What do you mean?" Aulus asked.

"I am provided no overt cause to resist or rebel."

"But?" Aulus prompted.

"But kindness is not enough," Lucan blurted.

"What else would you have?" Aulus remained kind.

Lucan was amazed. His eyes roved across the courtyard to the library. Represented there were the Idealists, Sophists, Epicurians, Stoics. This man is a philosopher, Lucan realized. Perhaps he agrees with Seneca the Elder that you should make sure that those to whom you come nearest be the happier by your presence. Well, it's worth the chance; I've already lost my hide by knifing him.

"What else would you have?" Aulus repeated.

"Justice," Lucan whispered.

"Justice, Lucan? Is it unjust for the ruling classes to take their due?" Aulus was openly enjoying himself.

"There ought not to be slavery, my lord," Lucan warmed to the subject. "Under God all men are equal. Therefore the distinctions that civil law make are arbitrary, aren't they?"

"The serving classes and the free are interdependent, you know," Aulus said.

"Even so, my lord, people must not be used as though they were things, or means, even to a worthy end!"

"You would be free?" Aulus asked directly.

"My lord, no one is at heart a slave."

"Yes, I know," Aulus replied sympathetically. "Yet we are all in fact slaves. Slaves to each other, and slaves together to the state. Do you think that I am not a slave to the imperial economy? Do you think that I, the free man, am independent, while you the slave are the only one in bondage? No, my young thinker, think again. A group of fine slaves work this farm and my warehouse. The products I market are transported by ships. These ships are conveyed if not by the wind, by galleys, manned with slaves. See, Lucan, I am dependent upon your kind. Still I don't hate any of you for it. We are dependent upon each other. None of us can escape it. And I use my freedom to see to it that all of you have the necessities of life; I do my part so that you may carry out your role in society. Is this not enough justice for you? Justice, Lucan, what is justice to you?"

Aulus took another bite of food and leaned back on his elbow and chewed leisurely as he watched the slave. He expected Lucan to answer submissively with the classical Platonic concept of justice, and to bow down in humility because of the obvious implications. Then he was prepared to press the obvious home in a tidy little lesson. Justice: specialization, differentiation of function with unity and harmony of all.

Lucan did answer in humility, however it was not the answer that Aulus expected. "Justice, my lord? Loving-kindness, sir. Tender mercy. Responsibility toward the oppressed, to lift them up out of their oppression! Restoration to liberty! That is more than merely taking your due as the ruling class; more than minding your business and expecting what is good for you to be good for everyone."

Aulus chortled in amazement. "And what sort of justice is this, Lucan?"

"The justice of the New Covenant, my lord. God . . ."

"Yes, yes, only a god could perform this sort of justice." Aulus rejected the idea as being beyond the realm of human life.

"Also he who would be just, my lord," Lucan persisted quietly.

"Lucan, you dreamer, not even a god could accomplish such justice without great cost to himself," Aulus rejoined dismissively.

This is what God Incarnate in Jesus Christ accomplished, Lucan reflected, and answered thoughtfully. "Indeed it is costly, my lord. It seems that this God—out of his love for his people—puts aside the retaliatory aspect of justice . . . and suffers the pain of our rebellion . . . and forgives, and makes the first move to reunite us with himself, and . . . and . . ."

"And?" Aulus drawled.

"Expects us to do the same." Lucan really let himself in deep with that.

"Ah!" Aulus sat up. "Supposing this god's people did not want this—merciful—sort of justice." He took a pointed lead.

"They would be a stiff-necked people, my lord."

"Yes?" Aulus prompted with interest.

"Bent on their own ways, they would refuse, revolt," Lucan said.

Aulus did not respond right away. He was still going to drive a lesson home. He had Lucan cornered where he could do it by using the slave's own words. He thought about how to proceed. "What would this god do to his stiff-necked people?" he asked.

"I suppose he would become righteously indignant. He would wrathfully allow his people to take the responsibility and consequences of their folly." Lucan gasped. He saw that he could be talking of his own relationship with Quintus. He hoped that Aulus didn't notice.

Of course Aulus did notice. He chose this moment to close in for the kill. "Do you know the game of soldiers?" he asked.

"Yes, my lord." Lucan's apprehension became molten lava in the stomach.

Aulus was surprised; what was this boy's background! Army brat! "Well," he said, "I have you surrounded."

"Yes I know, my Lord," Lucan answered breathlessly. Aulus's lesson was well taken.

"Now, Lucan, supposing this God's people did earnestly want this merciful sort of justice, but some of their fellow men withheld it from them? Would they revolt?"

This question was the intended deathblow. Of course they would revolt! Lucan's scalp prickled. The philosophical discourse was now a personal query and he knew it. He had better surrender, now.

"Answer me, Lucan."

Lucan resumed his subservient voice. "My lord, scripture advises us to 'never mind if we were slaves when we were called and cannot earn our freedom, but rather to make the most of our present station, serving in singleness of heart, as to Christ.'"

"And will you attend to this calling?" Aulus lifted his eyebrows.

Lucan understood the Gospel intellectually, but not with his heart. He answered honestly. "I submit myself to the irresistible challenge to look within myself and make the most of my life."

"Lucan, why do you risk telling me these things?"

Lucan perceived that he was safe. "I thought that I had no more to lose, after my regrettable mistake upstairs, and that I may as well entertain my lord in the process."

Aulus laughed. "Well done, my boy. Do you talk like this with my son?"

"When he invites me, sir."

Aulus nodded approval. He saw the potential in Lucan as a catalyst of Quintus's maturation. "Now back to bed with you. Wait. First, here." He rose and filled Lucan's goblet with fragrant wine from the bedroom cabinet, emptied a small vial into it, and offered the cup to him. With a touch of warmth in his voice he added, "You look as though you can use it."

Lucan hesitated. The wine would feed the fire in his stomach. How could he explain? You had better take it, his head warned. But does it have poison hemlock in it? Is he offering a merciful way out? Drink it, or tomorrow you may wish you had.

"Or does my son's Thessalonian cutthroat accept libations only from his master's hand?"

"My senior domine accepted supper from me. I will accept whatever it pleases my senior domine to give me." Lucan took the cup.

"Drink it down, Lucan, and get up to bed before it hits you."

"You are very considerate, my lord." Lucan bowed, and drank.

* * *

Hearing footsteps in his sleep, Quintus dreamed that Lucan was approaching him to knife him. He woke up with a start. He really needed to confront his delinquent slave. He covered for him, but really! To possess a concealed weapon! What did that slave think he was doing, attacking his father like that! To arms, Domine. What a strange thing to say when there were no weapons to be had; only a dusty chariot whip on the wall, and his beloved pony crop. Punty whip he used to call it. Mars Almighty! That slave was out of his head! He had to demand an accounting even if his father had already done so. Damn! Just when he thought he was making progress! He was both shocked and disappointed. What would he say so as not to cause a setback? He really should do it now. Quintus sat up.

Lucan dutifully came over and stood before him.

"Well? How did it go?" Quintus indicated a place on the bed next to him.

"Very well." Lucan sat down. "So well that he gave me a goblet of strong wine to sleep on. It's gone to my head."

"What did you do for him?"

"I brought him a cold supper and wine. He started asking me a lot of questions. I answered them. From the heart."

"You would, Lucan. What sort of questions?"

"About why I wanted to serve you."

"Ha!" Quintus chortled sarcastically. "Did you tell him the truth?"

"I did. What did I have to lose, already doomed for attacking him? I got quite philosophical. He loved it."

"I can imagine."

"So instead of cutting my throat he gave me this potion in strong wine to relax by," Lucan concluded lightheartedly.

"So that if I were to cut your throat right now, you'd be too happy to notice."

"No, no, don't cut my throat, I've made us a conquest!" Lucan boasted boldly.

"Oh, so you think you're safe? Pater's like that. You can't decapitate a rooster when he's got his head curled up off the block. When he's relaxed and rests his head on the block, wop! The ax falls."

"I'm not relaxed anymore," Lucan said, bending slightly in the middle.

"Goddam, Lucan, what were you doing with that blade, anyway! Where did you get it?"

"The toolroom, sir. I . . . helped with the inventory." Lucan whispered.

"And I covered for you. Is Marcellus right? Trust a slave and you find a dagger at your throat? Answer me, Lucan, why!"

"For defense, sir, you see, at the front the enemy . . ."

"You are no longer at the front, Lucan. And who is the enemy?"

"Please, sir, my duty."

"Duty! Plague take it!" Quintus said with sudden insight. "You got that thing to use on me, didn't you! If I touched you."

Lucan cowed face down on the bed and shivered. Quintus whipped him up to a sitting position again.

"Didn't you, Lucan! And don't you lie to me, man!"

"Y-you have s-said it, s-sir." Lucan fell prostrate again, buried his face in the bedcovers and began to tremble violently. A sob escaped his throat.

"Lucan, Lucan, your distrust will be the ruin of us both!" Quintus sank down and buried his face in his pillow and moaned.

"Oh . . . merciful . . . God!" Lucan clutched his master across the shoulders. "Domine, I don't need it, Domine. Here, let me get it."

"Stay where you are!" Quintus ordered sharply.

"I'll put it back where I got it tomorrow, please, sir."

"You do that! And have Gaius enter it on the inventory," he added, wondering why Gaius had not reported it missing from the inventory in the first place.

"Don't take it personally, Domine, I was reacting to the past . . . I . . . I . . . oh Domine!"

"A blade in the breast if I touched you. What could be more personal?"

"Domine, I wouldn't hurt you, Domine," Lucan pleaded and moved closer against him.

"You already are hurting me. I may not be able to keep you as my Quintipor," Quintus grieved. "Pater, after all, has the final say. And I have to face The Man myself tomorrow, without strong wine."

"Perhaps now you want to use that blade on me," Lucan lamented and pressed his face contritely into his master's shoulder.

With a cry of anguish Quintus spun around. "You fool, Lucan, you dear little fool!" He seized Lucan's arms impulsively. "How I care for you! How you defy me!"

To receive affection from a master was completely unexpected. To respond was almost more than Lucan could handle. He knew only to offer his body, and that was not what his master was seeking.

"I don't defy your caring, Domine."

"Worse than that. You don't even acknowledge it."

"Domine, my Domine. I . . . do. Please . . . forgive . . . Believe me! Domine . . . Domine . . ." Lucan's voice trailed off into a moan.

"Lucan, what is it!"

"Nothing, Domine, it's only the wine. It will pass . . ."

"What about the wine!" Quintus straightened up in alarm. Pater wouldn't?

"Too strong. Hurts. Always . . . does."

"Your legs! Are your legs going numb?"

"Weak in the knees, Domine. Too much always does that. Sorry . . ." Lucan gave way to pain and grief.

Quintus drew the slave's backside up against his breast and enfolded him in his arms and thigh as though to shield him from the Furies. He is calling me Domine, Quintus thought to himself. He is calling me Domine for the first time. And is it too late? Quintus could cry. He pressed his face into Lucan's neck, and his hot tears fell where the brand lay.

Lucan clutched his master's warm hand to his middle, against the raging pain. His master's encompassing warmth was comforting and he felt his whole body responding. He drifted off with the Apostle's admonition burning in his mind to 'be obedient to those who are your earthly masters, with fear and trembling, in singleness of heart, as to Christ.'

* * *

Gregor the young night watchman entered his parents' room about half an hour before rising time and awakened them. "Mater!" he called. "Pa?"

Cara stirred, then sat right up. "Postumus! Wake up! Gregor, what is it! You are so upset!"

"Oh Ma, I am undone!" Gregor moaned. He threw himself on the bed beside his mother.

"What is it, son," Postumus said. "Tell us!"

"I had a terrible nightmare." Gregor rubbed his forehead. "Yes, I fell asleep at my post. I must have slept all night. I didn't get any of the winnowing baskets mended. I didn't inspect the villa once! I dreamed that Aulus was making a fast trip home, and that I was to meet him at the last outpost with our horses, and ride the last part of the journey with him. Well, he came, and I wasn't prepared to meet him. I ran to the stable to saddle our two horses when I saw him coming, but he didn't wait. He leapt on a post horse and rode away. I tried to catch up. I couldn't. I got to our gate just after he shut it and locked it. I called to him. 'Domine! Domine! It is I! Please open the gate for me!' He didn't. I knew he was still there for I could hear his horse's hooves on the pavement. I begged him to open to me, and he answered harshly, 'I tell you, I do not know you!' Oh Ma, it was terrible. Then a robber rode swiftly upon me with his sword uplifted. My horse threw me, and both horses reared and neighed and plunged away. Darkness came all about me, and the dream left me, and I did not awake until just now.

"But here is the worst! I woke with the smell of fresh dung heavy in my nostrils. In the entranceway lay some fresh dung! I ran to the stables and found Aulus's mule in the stall! The second wagon is in the stable court! He's home! He came in the night! He unlocked the gate, led his mule and wagon through, locked the gate again, and I was asleep. I did not even stir! Caught outright! And Cerberus didn't bark! Oh, Mater!"

Olipor emerged and walked down the hall. Gregor called to him when he passed their door. "Olipor! Olipor!"

Olipor came to the door.

"Did you hear him come?"

"Who, Gregor, the Bishop? I didn't hear anyone."

"No, sir, Aulus. Aulus is home. I slept on my watch," Gregor confessed freely. "I only now woke up."

"Lord have mercy on us," Olipor said soberly and hurried to his master's bedroom door. He heard no sign of life within. Olipor waited at the door in agony. What will happen to us? he worried. Gregor has been warned before. Will he be flogged and discharged—sold at the market place? There was a time when he would have been put to death as an example. Olipor shuddered. Aulus had the capacity for dealing out punishment with exacting justice. Olipor had been witness to that. True, it has been many a year since Aulus has shown anything but firm kindness. A kindness that you would rather die for than betray. Yet Olipor never forgot the wrathful side of Aulus.

What shall I say to him, Olipor wondered. As Olipor fidgeted in the colonnade at his master's door, some words of his Lord came to mind. Blessed are those slaves whom their domine finds on the watch when he comes. I tell you, he will gird himself and have them sit at table, and he will go around and serve them. Whether he comes late at night or early in the morning and finds them on the watch, blessed are they. As for us, Gregor and I, we are the sort who will be put with the hypocrites, to weep and grind our teeth. Will the domine force me into retirement and with a writ of manumission expel me from my comfortable home? Will he acknowledge me if I knock, or will he say, "I do not know you?"

Olipor heard a stir inside. Lord, tell me what to do, he prayed, and tapped softly with his foot. "Domine?" he called with a lump in his throat, "It is Olipor."

"What is it, Olipor?" Aulus drawled pleasantly from inside the room.

"I would help you, sir," Olipor answered.

"I'm getting along very well alone," came the cheerful answer.

"Domine, please," Olipor pleaded urgently.

"You slaves will not let us alone. What is it, Olipor?"

"Domine, please let me come in . . ."

"In the night when I needed you, you were nowhere to be seen; and now that I don't need you, you clamor at the door. Even so, I'm not stopping you from coming in, Olipor." Aulus's voice had that terrible gentleness.

Olipor swallowed and entered the room.

"Good morning, Olipor," Aulus greeted him. He had just finished dressing.

"Domine, you had no one to wait on you," Olipor lamented.

"I am not helpless, Olipor. In fact I got along rather famously last night though I didn't have the hot supper that you would have prepared me." The crows feet at his eyes deepened slightly.

"Domine, you used the slaves' wine," Olipor observed.

"Because the overseer was snoring on the key to the household wine," Aulus chided.

"Why didn't you wake me?" Olipor asked.

"I ordered Lucan to wake no one. He did right well by himself."

"Lucan?!"

"He nearly killed me last night. *He* woke up while *you* slept. He thrust a dagger at my breast when I bent over my son's bed. My mantle saved me. I thought that the household had already heard about the colonate and had mutinied."

"Aulus, please!" Olipor cried out in pain.

Aulus laughed. "We will let Lucan serve Quintus, Olipor."

"As you say, Domine." Olipor drooped. So that's where the ax would fall. Gaius.

"No, Olipor," Aulus reassured him, "It isn't because of your neglect last night. It's simply that it would do Quintus a lot of good to try and win that boy. Fulvia and I decided this before I came. Lucan's behavior last night did confirm the decision, though. Olipor, you have done well in providing sons for my three older sons. How fortunate you have been in having sons! My Quintus is different, Olipor. He needs a challenge to help him mature. He is too much of a dreamer and needs a shaking before he faces the world. Are you with me, Olipor?"

"Yes, my Lord," Olipor pledged faithfully, but not without pain.

"You are a true servant, Olipor," Aulus praised him. Then he added seriously, "You will have to whip Gregor. Tonight so that his sore back will keep him awake. Well, now I'm ready for breakfast. With Quintus, if he's about."

Olipor bowed and went perturbed to the kitchen where the household slaves worked with careful industry. He knew he could not bring himself to whip Gregor. When Lucan came into the kitchen for his master's shaving water, Olipor released his feelings in anger. "You wretched mongrel," he seized Lucan tightly at the neck of his tunic. "You did not wake me!"

Lucan looked at Olipor in dumb terror.

"Do you know what Aulus did to me?" Olipor asked fiercely.

"No sir," Lucan gasped.

"He forgave me! Do you know what that means?" Olipor tightened his grip.

Lucan shook his head.

"It means that I cannot give you the throttling that I am itching to give you!" Olipor released Lucan suddenly, and proceeded to prepare a breakfast tray for two.

Lucan staggered and stood panting. Olipor had it in bad for him. However, he recalled, had not his own domine smiled at him this very morning?

* * *

Gregor had an appointment with Olipor, in the saddle room, after supper. There was no question whatsoever what this appointment was about. Gregor paced the saddle room floor miserably. Nor would his shame end here. Sometime during the course of the evening, Aulus himself would either send for him or come to the gate house on his evening walk to see him. This interview would be a painful review of the whole incident, and a final plea for pardon from Gregor. If he didn't know before what humiliation was, he would know after this. Gregor's stomach was in knots. He fidgeted with the saddles and harnesses.

Olipor finally came into the saddle room. He silently took a riding crop off the wall and regarded Gregor soberly. Gregor knew what to do. He dejectedly took off his tunic and knelt in trepidation before Olipor. He held out his hands to be tied to a beam. He wondered how many lashes it would be, and wished that Olipor would get over with it.

Orders were orders. Nevertheless Olipor suddenly turned his back on Gregor. He struck grievously at the wall with the whip, and hung the whip back on the hook. Then he seized Gregor's hands, drew the frightened boy up to his feet, and embraced him. Olipor left immediately, perturbed.

As though in a dream, Gregor dazedly drew on his tunic and went to his post at the gatehouse. Sure enough, Aulus soon appeared from his evening walk in the formal gardens. Gregor drew himself to attention.

"Well, boy," Aulus asked kindly, "has Olipor dealt with you?"

"Yes, sir, he has," Gregor lowered his gaze.

"Your back will keep you awake tonight?"

Gregor hesitated.

"Olipor has whipped you, has he not?" Aulus asked with suspicion.

"Yes, sir, he has!" Worry tensed Gregor's face. Visual proof could be the next request.

"Well?" Aulus pressed him.

"Olipor has whipped me in his own way," Gregor admitted.

"Then he has not whipped you at all." Aulus stated.

"No, sir, he has not."

"You slaves and your confounding ways!"

Gregor met Aulus's eyes with silent appeal.

The corners of Aulus's eyes crinkled. "All right, Gregor, you are pardoned. Olipor too. Return to your watch."

"Yes, sir!" Gregor responded with unrestrained joy. "Thank you, sir!" He saluted smartly and returned to his post, rededicated.

Aulus shook his head and went into the villa.

* * *

The days that followed were brittle with tension. Lucan's past seemed to take a renewed grip on him and to drive him with his old fears and longings. He worried that Olipor must think he insinuated his way into Gaius's position. How can I convince Olipor and Gaius? God knows I don't want to serve the young domine. Aulus tricked me into admitting it too. And then he cornered me into owning up to it that if I do not respond to the young domine, Quintus would have to let me take the consequences of my own folly. He pushed me into admitting that I must make the most of my slavery rather than resist it. The same maddening truisms!

And that new colonate law is a big help too. There go my hopes of pleading the favor of freedom and the cause of free birth. I cannot even leave this land! A damn serf. The domine loves being a serf too, we can tell, by the way he changed almost overnight from cheerful self-confidence to irritable uneasiness. As though he were afraid we were not going to obey him any more. Quintus, aren't you carrying it a bit too far? You too must make the most of your serfdom.

"Hello, slave!" Marcellus greeted Lucan in the stable court. "Where is your fellow slave?"

Lucan started out of his thoughts and answered. "All the slaves are working in the fields, sir. That is where I am going now." Lucan lifted the radish baskets and ties for Marcellus to see.

"Is your fellow slave out there too?"

"Whom do you mean, sir?"

"That newly made slave," Marcellus said casually.

Lucan looked past Marcellus to Marcipor. Marcipor shrugged and shook his head.

"Are you talking about my domine?" Lucan comprehended suddenly.

"Your fellow slave," Marcellus teased. "Surely you know about the new edict?"

"My domine," Lucan insisted.

"Slave to the land. What's the difference?"

"Domine!" Lucan raised clenched fists and eyed Marcellus severely. Too late he saw Marcipor frown a warning, for he already blurted out, "If you insult him I'll . . ."

You will what?" Marcellus took up. "Speak up, slave! Your domine indulges you to speak freely; now speak your mind to your domine's landlord!"

"I'll bash your face in," Lucan returned deliberately with the same threat that Marcellus served him on that day of dubious salvation only months ago.

Marcipor looked shocked.

"Whew!" Marcellus laughed appreciatively. "You're fierce! I didn't think you cared for him. Now you had better mind your manners," he warned crisply, "or I will have to teach you a thing or two. Now where is your domine, Lucan."

Undaunted, Lucan suddenly turned on the formality in his best Greek. "My domine's august landlord will find my domine upstairs in his library, sir. Will my domine's lord allow my domine's worthless slave the honor of escorting him?"

Marcipor grinned broadly from behind his master's back.

"Damn your impudent hide, Lucan," Marcellus retorted in the usual Latin and went into the villa.

I didn't think you cared for him. I didn't think you cared for him. Lucan ran out to the radish field and applied himself diligently, but Marcellus's words burned in his conscience. Dammit, have I been trapped into it again? I didn't think you cared for him.

Absurd idea! Lucan thought. I care for the Roman dog! Is defending him from a needless insult caring for him?

Then his own inner voice picked up the chant. Care for him! You care for him! You do care for him, Lucan.

So maybe I care for him, Lucan reluctantly admitted to himself. He was surprised at his own conclusion. So the impossible is happening. So I am weakening. *I care for him!*

But, his voice broke in with a thought equally preposterous, but *he cared for you first!*

Like something Olipor reads from Scripture, Lucan thought to himself. God loves us first so that we may love one another. God loved the world so much that he gave his only Son, so that no one who believes in him should be lost, but that they should all have eternal life. This is how Supreme Love acts. Does my domine tolerate me on this motive of unearned love rather than on a self-seeking motive? If he does, it is a miracle. If he does, then miracles do happen today. Miracles in human relationship. Man turned into what he is meant to be. Image of God. Does not the Image of God include a capacity to love? Man doesn't give the love he was meant to give. Is this lack of love sin? If man gave love, my family would not have been destroyed. Since this thing has happened—must I—love—the Roman dog? How do you go about loving a domine? I defend him from a needless insult. So 'you care for him'. Maybe I do. Maybe I do.

Meanwhile Marcellus strode boisterously to the stairs and took them two at a time.

"Well there's the slave," he boomed as he walked into Quintus's library.

Quintus looked up startled. "Hello, Marcellus, think I was Lucan?"

"Why are you not working the land, slave?"

Quintus leapt to his feet. "Oh go get kidnapped at the brothel and enslaved for the rest of your days in a bakery!"

Marcellus laughed. "Now Quintus, no offense, no hurt meant. I did not think you would mind so much, you slave-lover!"

"I may be a 'slave-lover' but I am not a slave."

"All right my plebeian friend, easy now," Marcellus soothed.

They clasped each other's arms warmly.

"What do you think of this new edict, Quintus?" Marcellus asked straightforwardly.

"I was going to be a farmer anyway." Quintus said glumly.

"And now that you have to be one? And your children after you?"

"It is a bitter portent. Just think, Marcellus, my family used to own this land! And now I am virtually a slave on it!"

"Especially in the eyes of that Lucan. You are a newly made fellow slave to him," Marcellus fibbed.

"So you think so," Quintus countered, while inside he felt a stab of anger. Will I have to give in to Marcellus's advice and severely show Lucan his place? The next time he steps off the straight line?

CHAPTER IX

I command and you obey!

The field of late cucumbers was ready to be picked over for the August market. The job was to be done on the day preceding market day so that Olipor could travel by night when wagons were permitted on the road. Lucan was paired off with Gaius. The job was a ticklish one. The spiny cucumbers were hard to twist off, and the fleshy vines were easily injured. Lucan soon became flustered. When he took care to hold the prickly vine in one hand and pick with the other Gaius nagged him about being slow.

"See, you do it like this," Gaius said as he dexterously picked with both hands. "Oops, only you don't break a vine. Young cucumbers can't mature on broken plants, you know."

Lucan was in no mood to be instructed on what he already knew. His embarrassment changed to anger as Gaius kept him under close and critical observation. The angrier he got, the clumsier he became.

"You'd better stop," Gaius complained, and went to ask Olipor if he would replace Lucan. Gaius was about a scheme.

Olipor led Gaius back to the cucumber patch, out of earshot of Lucan. "Now you pick some," Olipor said.

Gaius sheepishly began picking under his father's observation. He injured several plants. He couldn't seem to help himself. Sometimes when he just twisted a cucumber slightly, and snapped it off artfully, the vine bent and was bruised. He resorted to the slow method of holding the vine in one hand, picking with the other. He still damaged plants. He stepped on blossoms and immature cucumbers. He finally stood up, flushed.

Olipor laughed. "Want me to scold, now?"

"Well, how do you expect me to pick well, with you breathing down my neck!" Gaius whined.

"You expected it of Lucan," Olipor said quietly. "If you would be a top rate overseer some day you must learn to see both sides before you scold someone. And that takes self-control. Understand?"

"Yes, sir," Gaius answered sullenly. His plan failed, it seemed.

Gaius's plan was actually working very well. Lucan went out during the latter part of the rest hour to start picking alone, before Olipor could assign his work. If Gaius thinks he can have me called off the harvesting, he's mistaken. I'm as good a picker as any of them. And I don't want any critical partner. Lucan made quick work of the first row. When he was half through with the second, Olipor came up.

"Don't you want to work with someone?" Olipor asked.

"No, I'd just as soon work alone." The answer did not reveal the disquietude inside Lucan.

"Well, watch your time, and if it gets near the domine's bath time before you are through, leave the rest for us." Olipor smiled and went to his part of the field.

Oh I'll finish all right! Old fool, Lucan thought after Olipor, don't you see that I have no choice but to work alone? Why don't any of them seek me out? Am I really so set apart? With whom can I be at one?

Doesn't the colonate bother any of them? Undercut their hopes? Anyone with sense can see through their truisms that they answer me with. I wish that there were someone on this earth who could at least look me squarely in the eye and say, Yes, Lucan, I know; I have struggled with it too; it is a real problem. This person would be safe to talk with. This person would love me as I am, the real me, right through my fronts.

They say the Living Christ is like this. Why can't I find him?

Damn! I'm always getting leaf cuts. My hands will never heal at this rate. Dear Apollo, how they burn! And they burn all night. And nobody cares. Nobody gives a damn! I'm only another slave.

I want to be a person!

Why am I so much on edge these days? Because of the domine's touchiness?

Lucan saw Mammercus go out on Niger, ponying Ignis, and he prickled with envy. Soon he saw Gaius drive the oxen in with a cartload of cucumbers. I suppose he's done, Lucan thought. If he comes over here and makes gloating offers to help me finish, I'll tell him where to go. I'm almost done and I intend to show them . . .

Oh for crying out loud, Lucan!

As a deer desires the water brook, so longs my soul after you, O Lord. The psalmist knew how it is. Is his Lord the only one with whom we can be at one?

Suddenly Lucan realized that it was past time to go in. *Crux!* The sun is low. I'll be in real trouble now. As he assembled the baskets of cucumbers he saw out of the corner of his eye that Gaius approached with the team. I suppose he will try to send me in. As though I am not capable of watching my own time! Lucan hurriedly began to load his baskets of cucumbers on his wagon. He spoke bitterly to the footsteps behind him.

"If you think you can bring my baskets in and share credit for my work, you've got a second thought coming!"

"What is the matter with you!"

"Plenty! And you know it! *Ad malem crucem* leave me a . . . !" Lucan turned. It was not Gaius who had answered him. It was the domine! Lucan met his eyes speechlessly.

"That's enough out of you!" Quintus snapped. "Go to my library at once!" he ordered angrily and strode determinedly to his rooms. This is it, he thought. I have to show him his place in no uncertain terms. On his way he passed Gaius and ordered him to get Lucan's wagon.

Gaius pulled up with the team and bore down hard on his subordinate.

"Lucan, how many times have I told you that you must finish your day's work before going in to the domine! You can't expect someone to step in for you like this. Care of your master is not instead of your work out here; it's over and above it!"

"That's not fair," Lucan sputtered.

"I'll dock credit for the whole of any work you leave unfinished," Gaius declared.

"How do you expect me to be two places at once!"

"That's your problem, Lucan."

"Go to Hades, Gaius." Lucan dodged his foreman's hand and hurried in.

Of course this wasn't fair, and Gaius knew it. Gaius knew exactly what he was doing to Lucan.

Lucan went to the slaves' baths to wash himself. He tried to think through his rage to a way out of this predicament but nothing would come. By the time he stood before his master he simmered with resentment at Quintus for appointing him to such a troublesome position in the first place. He faced the master arrogantly, his eyes flashing.

The slave's boldness fired Quintus's irritation. "Lucan, sometimes I think you're not very intelligent or you would learn not to repeat unpleasant mistakes. Now we've been through this time and again about your not coming in to your domine when you should. What is the matter with you!"

"Want the crops to spoil while I scrub your back?" Lucan shot back resentfully.

"When it's time to come in, you come!" Quintus raised his voice.

"To Hades with personal indulgences when work has to be done!"

"I command you and you obey!"

Lucan retorted, *"non vi sed voluntate!"*, turned on his heel and stormed out to prepare his master's bath.

Quintus took his departure to be open defiance. He intercepted the slave with a tackle that sent him sprawling.

Squealing with rage, Lucan attacked.

"I can see why you have been flogged!" Quintus exclaimed, and struck him until he no longer tried to get up but lay sobbing with rage on the floor. Quintus went to his desk but in his agitation could not work. He threw down the scroll and stood over his slave who now lay very still. Unconscious?

"Lucan."

No response.

"Lucan!" Threat sounded in the master's voice.

The slave did not even stir.

"Lucan?" His voice was not kind. "You had better answer me, man!"

Lucan looked his master full in the face and the bitter thoughts rushed out of his contorted mouth. "You dog! You Roman dog! You are as bad as the others and I was just beginning to trust . . ." The impossible concept choked him and he quickly protected his head with his arms and stifled his grief. He wasn't even going to trust that it was beneath the dignity of a Roman to trample one who was prostrated.

The words utterly pierced Quintus. "Get out, Lucan," he commanded hoarsely. "So help me, get out of here! Go and prepare my massage!"

Lucan heard the tremor in his master's voice and obeyed quickly. His master followed shortly and gave himself up into his hands. Even though he had found that he actually enjoyed massaging his master's strong body and took satisfaction in bringing him relaxation and relief from sore muscles, today he hated the imposed closeness.

He scraped his domine in resentful silence. He bore down hard on the strigil.

"Take care!" Quintus warned sharply.

Lucan's scalp tingled and he lightened his touch. Bitter thoughts surged and he bit his tongue. What am I! Dough! To be molded any way you please! I resent it! The dough overflows the pan!

Breaking into his thoughts came the admonition from the Epistles that even he quoted in this household. Now for the first time he really heard the words as though he were beaten into listening. Slaves, obey your human masters sincerely with a proper sense of respect and responsibility, as service rendered to Christ himself. Well, wasn't that what he was doing in the fields? And what about the domine's part? Masters, be as conscientious and responsible toward your servants as you expect them to be toward you, not forgetting that you are responsible yourselves to a Heavenly Master who makes no distinction between master and slave. See how you measure up to this, Domine, you who have just misused . . . Lucan stopped short, for he had attacked his master. He could not justify himself. His hands slowed for he caught himself massaging the domine rather vigorously. True, the domine provoked you into attacking, but you have provoked the domine first, many times, and you know it. Lucan blushed with shame as hot as his previous anger and his hands came to a stop on his master's feet.

"Domine," he pleaded softly and rested his forehead on his master's feet.

Quintus was not ready to relent yet. His tone cut. "Now go serve my supper!"

Lucan bowed. His silence now was of a different sort. He had offered apology, his whole being in the one word laid at his master's feet, and the domine cut him down. Reverting submissively to the Eastern practice, he backed out of his master's presence.

Olipor's sharp eyes immediately detected the marks on Lucan. It was obvious, from Lucan's manner while serving the domine, that these were no accident.

Quintus did not linger at table. Before going upstairs he took his childhood mentor aside into his father's alcove.

"Olipor, you probably noticed my downcast slave. We had a showdown."

"A showdown? He hasn't been serving you very well?"

"No, it's not exactly that, Olipor. You know that he has been working well. It's that he has his own ideas. And they are getting him into trouble."

"I can imagine, Domine." They discussed Lucan's brooding resistance, and Quintus confided his own insecurity after his change in status. He told of the hot words exchanged in the late afternoon and of Lucan's walking out on him in his library.

"I beat him, Olipor."

"Yes?" Olipor sounded non-committal though he was really surprised.

"I'm afraid I struck him quite hard. I was very angry and did not know what I was doing."

"What do you mean by that, Domine?" Olipor was listening for the unspoken words.

"I'm not so sure that it was right to strike him. He's . . . so crestfallen. He wouldn't be, would he, if I had handled him right? He sprang at me. His heart really seemed to be in his attack. Perhaps he was only trying to get out of the door . . . I don't know. Anyway he *wept* when I threw him to the floor. Didn't move when I commanded him. Maybe I'm reading motives into him. I don't know, Olipor. Anyway, I can't imagine myself ever beating anyone! I have believed in the inherent goodness of man!"

Olipor could see that Quintus was genuinely upset at himself.

"Lucan is showing me things about myself that I would have never guessed were there."

Olipor nodded.

"What shall I do next?"

"Domine, to gain confidence you need to be firm yet gentle. It is hard for him to take it from one his own age. You must help him to know his place. Not force him, but help him. Guard him from wrongdoing beforehand and you won't find occasion to punish. When you have to punish, you must make it known to him that you do so and hold high expectations up to him only because you care for him very much!"

Quintus looked down and swallowed. "Send him upstairs when he is through in the kitchen," he said softly.

Alone now, Olipor gave in to thorough alarm. The slave attacked his domine! There could never, under any circumstance, be any excuse for this. Quintus had lost his temper and tackled Lucan, true. But for Lucan to attack back, that was something entirely different. That slave is truly an incorrigible one. Rescued from the streets. And branded for his misdeeds. Olipor knew that Lucan could have killed Aulus that night when Aulus bent over his son's bed. This act had impressed Aulus at the time, and he had assigned Lucan instead of the gentle-bred Gaius to Quintus. Now Olipor felt that he must report to Aulus that he had made a mistake. The sooner Lucan is replaced, the better. No saying what he might do the next time he loses his temper.

Olipor knew that Quintus was becoming attached to Lucan. He could already hear his young domine saying, This is precisely where Lucan needs another chance, Olipor! Perhaps the faith of the young does have something to say to the wisdom of the old. And Quintus would risk his life to prove his faith. Is it hardly worth it? Then Olipor remembered his own record of plots and struggles against Aulus. But not like this! Not like this! Aulus saw him through to loyalty, however, Olipor recalled with gratitude.

Therefore had he, Olipor, any right to recommend anything but mercy toward Lucan? What would tender mercy do to an incorrigible? We shall see. Olipor knew now what he must do. He returned to the kitchen.

"Lucan," he empathized.

"Merely being a slave is torment enough without the added agony of being at odds with the domine," Lucan muttered. Then he blushed for such an admission that he cared was unusual for him. He said no more.

On the way to the stairs to the master's rooms Olipor tried to talk with Lucan. "I know all about what it is like to lose your freedom. And Lucan, being a free man doesn't do away with the problem either. If it's not a domine, it's an employer; if not commands to obey, it's routine drudgery. You need to learn to accept the discipline of everyday life. Really, Lucan, as I have said before, your problem is more basic than slavery; your problem is you. You need never face life's problems alone. There is One who will help you—show you the Way—if you would only let him."

Lucan's reaction was the resentful remark, "You said I wouldn't get beaten here!"

"What do you expect, to get away with murder?" Olipor did not see the alarm come to Lucan's eyes. He saw Lucan to the foot of the stairs but did not wait to see him go up.

Lucan saw that his master was asleep. He wrapped himself in his cloak, crept down the stairway, out through the servant's hall, and bolted to the woods. Except for that galling advice from Olipor, no one seemed to notice his unhappiness and no one followed him up to retrieve him. He threw himself on the ground. No sign of pardon from the domine. Lucan's regrets were now turned to remorse. He had no idea that a broken relationship could matter so much to him. He wanted to return somehow from his desolation and say, "Take me back!"

Doesn't anyone care that I have run away? 'Not by force, but by good will.' Perhaps the domine is letting you free to run off now, Lucan. No—the domine is merely asleep. Go! Far, far away! You are on your own now! You have struck both your masters! They will nail you for it! Acute nostalgia overcame him for the homeland that he knew, for his massacred family who would have cared, forgiven, and loved. Be strong, Lucan, he said to himself. Starve to death—in freedom! he added bitterly.

Lucan bounded up and a low branch bashed him across the face. He slumped to the ground and cried out to the bright presence in the stars before his eyes.

"O God, O God, why do you forsake me?
My enemy stands ever over me,
And lays his hand heavily upon me.
God, come and assert your justice!

With your loving care restore your servant!
Lord God, my heart longs after you.
Where are you? Lord, how long?
I yearn to return to my freedom and my homeland,
And to find you there.
Lord, this is what I am to do:
I am to illuminate the path of men,
So that their feet shall not stumble;
And yet I meet the Tree headlong!
You come in the midst of the people;
They say they have found you here!
And that you chastise through my enemy's hand!
Take these as my family, you say,
And this land my homeland,
And serve my master as I would you.
O God what folly! Do you mock me?
Is it really you speaking thus?
O God I will obey, until I know.
I will not be inert while I seek your Wisdom.
O God help me,
The task is too great for my strength,
Your Wisdom is too awesome for my mind to retain it."

Lucan was answered with deep sleep beyond the stars.

CHAPTER X

Let me serve him

"Lucan, are you awake?" The sun was up, and Olipor cast a shadow over him.

Lucan started in bewilderment. "Am I really out here? Dear God in Heaven, did I really attack him, Olipor, did I attack him? That was a nightmare, please tell me, that was a cursed nightmare!" He rose on his knees in a panic.

"Yes, you do deserve the worst." Olipor regarded him gravely.

"Not by crucifixion!" Lucan cried in horror. "Petros—they didn't beat him half dead first. He took three days to die! They nearly nailed me for driving off the scavengers!"

"There will be no crucifixion," Olipor said firmly.

"*Mio Dio*, you're sending me to the amphitheater!" Lucan bounded up but tripped on his own legs and fell rudely to the ground. He lay there sobbing.

"No heroics, Lucan, nor any quiet hunting accidents."

"Save me, Olipor! Save me! I beg you!"

"Lucan, get a hold of yourself!" Olipor stood over him and waited for him to regain composure.

Lucan finally spoke again, from the ground. "Please don't send me away, Olipor."

"Oh, so now you like this place?"

"Please let me be a farm hand." He got up on his knees.

"Is that all, Lucan?"

"How can I ask for more?" Lucan shrugged hopelessly.

"What would you ask for?"

"To serve him." Lucan dared not look up.

"Eh? What did you say?"

Was the overseer refusing his plea? Lucan reached up to him. "I want to serve him," he declared, then flushed at his admission.

"That, after all, is up to your Domine," Olipor replied firmly.

"He is the best I ever had and now I've ruined it!"

"Has it not occurred to you to ask him to forgive you?"

"Forgive the unpardonable?" Lucan was incredulous.

"That is for him to decide. And you are free to get up on your own two feet and go to him." Olipor remained firm.

"Help me, Olipor, please help me." Beads of sweat ran down Lucan's face.

"My son, I am sorry this had to happen."

"Pater!" Lucan got up on his feet and seized the elder's hands.

"Let's go to work, Lucan. Your domine left early to market this morning. He will be back tonight. You may see him at bath time."

Olipor was for the first time calling him son. The quiet reply nevertheless struck unreasonable terror in Lucan's heart. Fathers sacrificed their sons, didn't they? He worked hard in dreadful anticipation of the master's return, and avoided the villa as much as possible during the day. At the noon hour he asked Olipor if he shouldn't pick the last few hills of cucumbers.

"No, Lucan," Olipor answered kindly, "you have picked more than I intended already. You are a fast picker."

Lucan met his master in the stable court that evening and silently helped him down from the wagon. Quintus handed the team over to Mamercus and without a word led the way to the hot bath. When they were in the water he finally spoke.

"Where were you?" he demanded.

"Up in the woods, sir," Lucan managed to get out.

"Should have known. I'm too upset to deal fairly with you now, Lucan. I'd beat the stuffing out of you."

"Forgive me, sir."

"Forgive you! Didn't you hear me? You don't even know what you are asking me to forgive! Zeus! By the looks of you with your slave's tunic and scars it wouldn't take anyone but two seconds to know that you didn't belong in the streets. You would be apprehended before you knew anyone noticed! Do you know what I am saying?"

Lucan shuddered and nodded.

"I searched to the shadows of Hades and back for you, Lucan. I queried at the rescue mission, at the slave block, the amphitheatre, the iron foundry, the glass works, the bakery and at every damn galley ship in the harbor!"

Lucan was mortified. "Domine, thank you for searching."

Quintus snorted. "What makes you so sure I wouldn't have left you where I found you?"

Lucan blanched. "I'm terribly sorry, sir!"

"You had better be sorry before I'm through with you! This kind of unacceptable behavior you must take on your own responsibility never to repeat again! You can keep yourself out of trouble, Lucan, if you choose."

"Domine . . ." Lucan was reduced to silence and regarded him with awe.

"Let me get the day's grime off and some food into me before I sentence you or I'll be too severe." Quintus led the way to the bench.

Lucan on his knees alongside the bench massaged him carefully, solicitously, giving forth with the best of his skill, seeking out the muscular tightness in his master's neck and shoulders and working it out. Then not stopping short of the sensuous he titillated every inch of his master's body, including the exquisite tug on the joints of the fingers. See what you will deprive yourself of if you do away with me, his hands seemed to plead.

"Thank you, Lucan," Quintus sighed, and made not a move from the bench. Lucan uttered a little cry and pressed his face against his master's shoulder. He must have drifted off also; the crook of his arm had a red impression from his forehead, and his hand was asleep when Quintus arose to be dressed.

However, Lucan did not feel safe, as though the master were waiting for the rooster to relax his head on the chopping block. With downcast eyes he served his master supper, and gave him a little stronger mix of wine than usual.

Quintus watched with amazement that he could have such power over another. He wasn't certain how to handle it, but Lucan must never know.

"Come upstairs when you're through," he ordered, and rose from table.

Olipor intercepted Quintus in the hall and tried to imply that the domine need not be offended by Lucan.

"He was in the woods, sir, collecting his wits. He meant to return last night but apparently was too upset to do so. He feared the death penalty when I found him this morning." Olipor smiled sympathetically. "Poor boy, he is beside himself, sir."

"I should think he would be," Quintus snapped. "Send him upstairs!" Olipor's efforts seemed to have failed.

Letitia was lingering in the peristyle by the stairs when Quintus came by. Their eyes met. She stepped forward wordlessly and searched his face.

"What are you looking so anxious about!" he snapped. "Gods alive! This whole household is acting like doomsday!" He continued upstairs.

She went directly to the servants' hall where all were assembled spontaneously keeping a prayer vigil for Lucan.

Quintus paced his library floor and sorted his thoughts. Crucifixion indeed. Isn't that a bit extreme? Yet he shouldn't have attacked me. But I shouldn't have beaten him. I should have been alert enough to prevent Lucan's getting into trouble in the first place. Now I must uphold my discipline. I must be consistent. Consistent in what? Beating Lucan precisely when the slave was showing, however unpleasantly, a growing responsibility for the farm? Or is a beating the only language he understands? Quintus snatched the chariot whip off the wall and flicked it smartly with his wrist. It snapped loudly and stung him on the ankle. Startled, he put the thing back on the wall. How do I show him that I discipline him only because I care for him very much? How can I make an impression upon him? Give the ragamuffin a good break? Punishment or mercy? "Oh I don't know." Frowning deeply, he sat down and rubbed his smarting ankle.

Lucan chose this moment to enter. He knelt before Quintus as though to help his master change into slippers. He clasped his master's feet.

Quintus chose mercy. "You did not catch cold from your night out in the woods? Ask Letitia to make you some onion soup tonight, if possible."

"Yes, sir," Lucan managed through the lump of terror in his throat. Braced for severity, he was taken completely off guard.

The hoarse voice concerned Quintus. He reached out a hand to feel Lucan's forehead. "Here, let me see." His voice was terribly kind.

The slave lifted his head for examination. His insides froze. Where was the ugly twist? When was the ax going to fall?

Quintus ran his fingers through Lucan's hair at the back of his neck. "Here, you missed one." He pulled off a wood tick, rolled it between his forefinger and thumb, and tossed it in the flame of the oil lamp. Lucan was exonerated. His downcast eyes were brimful.

"My Domine, I have gravely wronged you, and I am utterly miserable. I am not worthy to undo your sandals."

Quintus was momentarily baffled by such dejection. "Nonsense, Lucan! Sometimes we get very angry at each other. I regret that it happened." His voice tightened with anguish. "Does it mean that the world must come to an end? Cannot life continue?"

Lucan looked up in amazement to meet the gaze of his master. "Domine have mercy," he uttered, hardly a whisper. A shudder seized his body. He rested his forehead on his master's feet.

Quintus realized that the slave truly pleaded for his very life! It appalled him to see someone so devastated before him. Now how was he to handle this?

"Serve me, Lucan!" he cried out anxiously.

He who had feared death by crucifixion was speechless. This was the sentence! To live and serve! Quintus touched him on the shoulder and the acquitted one straightened up again.

"With my life, Domine," he pledged, in contrast to his previous response when the fates had held his thread in delicate balance and the Domine had called him to life.

"Tell me, Lucan," Quintus asked solicitously, "that bruise across your face. I didn't do that to you, did I?"

"N-no sir, I-I ran into a t-tree l-last night," Lucan confessed.

Quintus laughed with relief, but Lucan's attempts to laugh came out as sobs. Suddenly they embraced. "It's all right, Lucan, it's all right!"

"Quintus!" Lucan pressed his face into his master's shoulder and clutched him tightly and wept. Quintus held Lucan a moment longer, quite overcome, then released him. And Quintus suddenly became aware of HIM, the Merciful King!

Lucan's bowels melted. He ran out. As he sat in the privy and looked at the cucumber field bright in the moonlight, he comprehended Olipor's words about his picking more cucumbers than intended. In all his determination to show how he could work, he had picked some hills that were to be left for seed.

"Oh Lord," he groaned, "when the Domine finds out about this!" He walked out among the cucumbers to assess his mistake. "Oh my God!" he cried out sharply and sat down, stunned. He had picked the Legerius Early intended for seed.

* * *

Quintus, waiting for Lucan to come up to bed, awoke at every sound of the night. The household rising at cockcrow for the Sunday Eucharist awoke him again and he came down to his father's writing room to get some ink. He heard Dorothea's voice in the alcove.

"We can talk in here, son. My, you are upset!"

Gaius upset? Quintus wondered. He paused inside the writing room door and eavesdropped.

"Meter, it's terrible! I feel utterly, hopelessly trapped!"

Quintus puckered his brow. This was not Gaius's voice at all. It was Lucan's! Quintus sharpened his ears with intense interest. The very boy she would have every right to despise—for had he not taken her son's position?—this very boy she called son.

"What is it, son?" Dorothea was asking.

"The-the c-cucumbers! The s-seed cu-cu-cumbers!"

"We know about them, dear, calm down."

"You do? That I-I p-picked them—the s-seeds—the-the Legerius Early? Oh Meter!" he groaned. "Does he know?"

"He knows, dear."

"I s-set out those seedlings myself, to be sure they'd be done right. The Domine hand bred them."

"And then you contritely picked them for market."

"I did. I was out of my head yesterday."

"So you sat out there last night too upset to come in?"

"Yes Ma'am. I was thinking about yesterday and the day before. And Dammit! The night went by! I never reported back upstairs, and now the Domine is gone from his bed."

"He's probably just gone to the water closet, and assumes you're with us!"

"O Meter, I just can't do anything right. Some repentant delinquent I am! I can't just go up there, see Domine, your delinquent is back, upset because you were absent from your bed!"

"Lucan, please, don't be so hard on yourself. Every person wrongs at sometime or another and gets punished for it. Accept it as part of life; we are not perfect! Your domine cares for you very much."

"Oh but Meter, you don't know the extent of my wrong! And the domine could hardly even like me if he knew. He would have the right to crucify me!"

He really feared a murderer's punishment! Quintus realized, as he listened from the writing room.

Lucan continued. "I would have murdered him if he hadn't stopped striking me when he did, Meter, really I would have! The old fury came back to me and took possession of me! You see, we quarreled. I dared to quarrel! I caught myself and tried to get out the door before I lost control again but he intercepted me. Then I attacked him and he beat me. I just lay there and wept, I was so furious. I didn't trust myself to even move! I have no reason to get so angry in this household. What is happening to me! It is as though I were trapped by the demons of the past. He thought to beat the devil out of me, but instead he beat the Legions into me! I hate him for it! I don't have these shackle scars on my wrists and ankles for nothing!" Lucan stopped and breathed heavily.

"But you don't really hate your domine?" Dorothea asked gently.

"Sometimes I really do!" Lucan challenged with intense uneasiness. He was not sure that she really heard what he was saying.

"Well then, we will begin from there," she said. Dorothea wanted to say, I can't think it of you, Lucan, really, but she caught herself. By refusing to acknowledge and accept what he was intent on saying, she would only drive him deeper into rebellion in attempt to prove that he really meant what he said. She had to accept him as he was, before he could be helped to something better.

Lucan relaxed perceptibly. Dorothea thanked God.

"I really think I do hate him at times, Meter. Except at night . . . when I am doing copywork, or proofreading for him, I am sitting near him then . . . he invites me to talk man to man and . . . and . . ." Lucan faltered.

"Yes, son?" Dorothea prompted.

Quintus in the writing room held his breath.

Lucan thought of saying, I think I know what Olipor means when he quotes the Epistles and the Didache that we must obey our masters as if they represented God. But Lucan was not ready to admit that yet, even to himself.

"Then I am ashamed of my rebellion," he confessed.

"There, there, my child." Dorothea took him in her arms and held him closely. She ran her fingers through his hair.

"But listen, Meter. My domine said that whether or not I get punished is up to me. He wants voluntary obedience from me and I must discipline myself to it. And Olipor said that I can serve Quintus well if I put my heart to it."

"Yes?"

"This is just, Meter, but . . . hopeless. I cannot do it!"

"You cannot expect to do it all by yourself," Dorothea said. "But with Christ, all things are possible."

"All things but me!" Lucan broke in and pulled away from her embrace.

"Including you," Dorothea affirmed. "Christ forgives you as you are and does the impossible with you."

Lucan suddenly stopped fighting. "What do you mean?"

"Christ does not expect you to be perfect all by yourself. He knows you cannot do it alone. He knows you need help and he asks you to do his will only with his help. Christ gives you the power to do God's will."

"Can Christ really help me, Meter? Is he really concerned with me?"

"Why certainly!" Dorothea answered. "Look at Olipor!"

"Olipor?"

"He was freeborn. You didn't know that, did you son. And then the tide changed."

"No I didn't know!" Quintus exclaimed softly from the writing room where he was eavesdropping.

"Oh bitterness of all bitterness!" Lucan exclaimed.

"Until he met the Christ," Dorothea went on. "Then his life was transformed, and bit by bit he learned to obey and love."

"How did that happen?" Lucan asked.

"Ask him, sometime," Dorothea replied. "Come along, it's time for worship. The Domine must know that you are with us. You can watch for him." The two went to the kitchen where the other slaves were assembled.

With a tight throat, Quintus hurried back upstairs. When the tide changed. That must have been when Pater beat the stuffing out of Olipor. Olipor must not know that I found out his secret!

Lucan stood with the other slaves in the kitchen and his thoughts wandered during the worship. So you do know what it is to struggle, Dorothea. You do know! Olipor too! You really have been tried by fire and you have come out victorious! Lucan regarded them with new respect.

Dorothea and the other women, veiled, stood on the opposite side from the men. Behind the table, facing the people, Olipor sat on a stool on one side of Bishop Nicodemus's chair, Gaius on the other. On the dining table before the faithful lay the scrolls of the Living Word.

Olipor read from the twelfth chapter of Paul's letter to the Hebrews. Lucan comprehended vaguely through his own thoughts that Olipor was reading something about running with determination the race with eyes on Jesus the leader. Then Olipor's words caught Lucan's full attention.

> "My son, do not regard lightly the discipline of the Lord,
> nor lose courage when you are punished by him.
> For the Lord disciplines him whom he loves,
> and chastises every son whom he receives."

The words burned in Lucan's breast. Olipor seemed to be reading scripture at him again. Not that Olipor really was choosing the passages for Lucan's benefit; Olipor was in fact reading according to the lectionary. It seemed that the Living Word often spoke directly to Lucan and it astonished him with its truth, and he had to blame somebody for his unwillingness to yield. Little good it does me, he thought, to hear and not have the power to respond.

> "For the moment all discipline seems painful rather than pleasant; later it yields the peaceful fruit of righteousness to those who have been trained by it."

Peaceful fruit! Lucan sank into his thoughts again. Ridiculous! Discipline with a beating only brings turmoil. Whom is he trying to fool!

> "Strive for peace with all men, and for holiness without which no one will see the Lord."

Holiness, Lucan thought. See the Lord. In these people. See the Lord in Gaius. See the Lord in Olipor. See the Lord in Quin—This was too ridiculous for Lucan to consider any further. He came back to attention with a jolt. Olipor had finished reading the first lesson, and Gaius was chanting a psalm while Lucan indulged in his thoughts and counter-thoughts.

> "Be not like a horse or a mule without understanding,
> which must be curbed with bit and bridle . . ."

Why, that's me! Lucan exclaimed to himself and was off into his thoughts again.

"Alleluia," the faithful responded fervently at the end of the psalm, and Olipor read again, the second lesson, from the Revelation of John.

> "'I know your works: you are neither cold nor hot. Would that you were either cold or hot! So, because you are lukewarm, and neither cold nor hot, I will spew you out of my mouth! . . . Those whom I love, I reprove and chasten; so be zealous and repent.'"

So repentance is the door through which God comes, Lucan thought. Repent. For what? For longing for God? Being in despair? Not loving the Roman dog? Lucan thought of the hard knocks that life had dealt him. Could God be working through these? Rather than mere fate? And I have been blind to it?

> "'Behold, I stand at the door and knock; if anyone hears my voice and opens the door, I will come in to him and eat with him, and he with me.'"

Lord, be my guest, Lucan thought wistfully.

Gaius's second psalm reflected the same plea.

> "The Lord hears when I call unto him.
> Be angry, but sin not;
> commune with your own hearts on your beds
> and be silent.
> Offer right sacrifices, and put your trust in the Lord."

The Lord will hear indeed? Lucan, absorbed, sang the Alleluia with the others.

"He disciplines because He loves." Olipor from his seat addressed the group. In his dissertation on the scripture he explained that the Lord works through his people, that the Lord, through Quintus, was disciplining his servants at Good Will. "And we must respond to the Lord by giving our young domine our whole-hearted service. For if we do not respond, if we are neither hot nor cold, but tepid, what can our Lord do but spit us out of his mouth?"

Lucan left off following Olipor there. Because he loves—the young domine beat me because he cared? He became that angry out of concern for me? Lucan was skeptical. He knew well the raging anger of unconcern and hatred. And this beating by Quintus, if this was supposed to be discipline motivated by love, Lucan could never have known it, for the master's furious burst of anger was no different than that motivated by hate. No, Lucan concluded, you don't demonstrate your love for a person by beating him up. There must be another way. If he really loves me, why doesn't he guide me and prevent me from falling into trouble in the first place; rather than punish me when he is at fault for neglecting me.

Perhaps he is trying to guide you, Lucan, and you have refused him, his inner voice said. You have to work through the white heat of your rage and forge a new relationship, well tempered, refined. He cares for you. Lucan wanted to believe it. Lucan needed to believe it. Someone in this world cares for you. Now that someone cares for you, you may come to know that it is because first SOMEONE has cared for us all.

Gaius's voice disrupted Lucan's self-examination. "O catechumens, bow your heads for a blessing." The bishop gave the blessing, and Gaius took up again: "Let the catechumens depart! Let no unbaptized persons remain!"

Lucan and other visitors were dismissed. He went through the door into the hall leading to the peristyle, then he stopped. He could not leave. He pressed himself into the morning shadows, hoping that he would not be noticed. Lord, he prayed, let me stay and find you. Olipor did see him there, and out of pity let him remain.

"Alleluia!" the household shouted, for Bishop Nicodemus had motioned to Olipor who announced the Gospel.

"Alleluia!" for they were about to hear a proclamation from their Great King.

"For God so loved the world that he gave his only Son,
that whoever believes in him should not perish but have eternal

> life. For God sent the Son into the world not to condemn the world, but that the world might be saved through him."

Lucan sank into reflection again, but returned to attention when Gaius read about light; how the light came into the world and every one who does evil will not come to the light for fear of being exposed. He himself is meant to be a light to the feet of man. How is he to do this?

> "But he who does what is true comes to the light, that it may be clearly seen that his deeds have been wrought in God."

"Thanks be to God!" the group cried wholeheartedly.

". . . Yet if I have no love I am but a clashing cymbal . . ." the letter by Paul explained and elaborated on the gospel. Lucan knew that he had been serving well. There was no question about that. But diligent service was not enough. He must give more to his domine; his very heart. How can I? To know is not enough; how can I *do* it?

Bishop Nicodemus delivered his sermon from his chair. He spoke of the power from God to become what we are meant to be. Power and grace. And that power, the Bishop explained, was governed by love of the quality just described. Power to become, and love, these are gifts of God. No man has them except from God.

Lucan felt again, acutely, his sense of unfulfillment. It was as though he were pursued to the edge of a precipice. If I do not commit myself in obedience to God, I will fall into the chasm of final self-condemnation regardless of all my longings. But God can buoy me up like a strong updraft and can lift me to the other side! Lucan was frightened over the leap of faith and trust he knew he must make.

The household of the faithful knelt in prayer. Bishop Nicodemus asked their prayers for the whole church throughout the world, for the Emperor, for peace and security during his rule, for the sick, those afflicted in any way, prisoners, travelers, the unconverted, and for all those who departed this life in the Faith. They prayed silently after each bidding, then the bishop summarized the intercessions in a brief prayer.

Then the bishop said, "The peace of the Lord be always with you."

"And with your spirit!" The faithful rose to their feet.

"Salute one another with a holy kiss," the bishop said. They exchanged the kiss of peace, starting with the bishop who exchanged with Olipor who in turn exchanged with Gaius. Then the congregation exchanged the salutation, the men with the men, the women with the women. Will I be detected and sent away? Lucan wondered. He was detected, but not sent off. Marcipor smiled encouragement.

Gaius removed the scrolls from the table and spread a white linen cloth over it. The people formed a line and each made an offering of a small bun made in the kitchen of Good Will, some wine from their own vintage, and whatever they had of produce and personal allowance. With these small gifts they offered themselves, their lives, to be taken by their Lord, consecrated, and used according to his will. Olipor received the offerings and placed them on the table.

"The Lord be with you," the bishop said.

"And with your spirit," the people responded.

"Lift up your hearts," said the bishop.

"We lift them up to the Lord!" the faithful responded.

"Let us give thanks to the Lord."

"It is right so to do!"

The bishop laid his hands on the offerings of bread and wine and chanted magnificently the prayers of thanksgiving and consecration.

> "We give you thanks, O God, through your beloved servant whom you sent to us in the last days to be a Savior and Redeemer and Messenger of your Will, who is your inseparable Word;
>
> "Through whom you made all things, and in whom you are well pleased;
>
> "You sent him from Heaven into a virgin's womb, and he was conceived within her and was made flesh, and shown to be your Son, born of the Holy Spirit and a virgin;
>
> "Who fulfilling your Will, and acquiring for you a holy people, stretched out his hands when he suffered that he might free from suffering those who had believed in you;
>
> "Who also—when he was of his own free will betrayed to suffering that he might destroy death, break the fetters of the devil, tread hell underfoot, enlighten the righteous, fix the boundary, and manifest his resurrection—
>
> "Taking bread and giving thanks to you, said, 'Take, eat, this is my body, which is broken for you.' After the same manner, he took the cup, saying, 'This is my blood, which is shed for you; as often as you do this, you do it for the recalling of me.'

> "Wherefore, mindful of his death and resurrection, we offer unto you this bread and cup, giving you thanks that you have counted us worthy to stand before you and to minister unto you.
>
> "And we beseech you, that you would send your Holy Spirit upon this oblation of your holy church; that uniting them into one, you may grant to all your holy ones who receive that their faith may be confirmed in truth in the fulfillment of your Holy Spirit.
>
> "That we may laud and glorify you; through your Servant Jesus Christ, through whom be glory and honor to you, Father, Son, and Holy Spirit, in your holy church, both now and for evermore."

The faithful all but shouted their response: "As it was, is and ever shall be, world without end, and for evermore! Amen!"

Lucan, who had followed closely, would have responded too, had he known what to say.

The bishop prayed briefly that the consecrated body and blood be received worthily, and the true benefits thereof be granted.

"Let us attend," Olipor said.

"Holy things to the holy," Bishop Nicodemus said as he lifted up the consecrated bread in invitation to receive.

"One holy Father, one holy Son, one is the Holy Spirit," the people responded.

"The Lord be with you all," said the Bishop.

"And with your spirit," responded the people.

The bishop communicated himself, then Olipor and Gaius, then the others came up for their pieces of bread and sips of wine. Lucan watched intently with wide eyes.

"The Bread of heaven in Christ Jesus," the bishop said as he gave each communicant a fragment of bread.

Each communicant in turn moved over to Olipor holding the chalice and, standing, took three sips:

"In God the Father Almighty," Olipor said as the communicant took the first sip.

"Amen," said the communicant.

"And in the Lord Jesus Christ." Olipor said at the second sip.

"Amen."

"And in the Holy Spirit which is in the Holy Church."

"Amen!"

A joyful spirit is among these people, Lucan observed. They did not come merely to learn something. They didn't come merely for an emotional experience, or to create an atmosphere. This is no mere memorial. What is so compelling about it?

What tortures for the faith do Olipor's scars indicate?

Why had Cara in her youth suffered a state sentence in the Puteoli navel brothel rather than denounce her Lord? And what mercy inspired Postumus to take her to wife and adopt her son Paulo, Postumus who gossips yet tends to be morally rigorous?

How does Sextus the Iberian dare to attend, after being caught in that act of self gratification commonly practiced by slaves during the rest hour, but condemned by the Christian sect?

And why does Marcipor risk his neck to come?

Why, they are *doing something with Someone!* They are eating and drinking with their Living God! The Lord is indeed in our midst! He comes to us, such as we are! Even to me who had murder in my heart! Lucan knelt, overcome with awe. Lord, I believe; help my unbelief! O Lord, I obey; purge away my disobedience!

Olipor then prayed:

> "God Almighty, the Father of the Lord and our Savior Jesus Christ, we give you thanks, because you have imparted to us the reception of your holy Mystery; let it not be for guilt or condemnation, but for the renewal of soul and body and spirit; through your Servant Jesus Christ, through whom be glory and honor to you, Father, Son, and Holy Spirit, in your holy Church, both now and for evermore."

The faithful took up, "As it was, is, and ever shall be, world without end, and for evermore! Amen!"

"The Lord be with you," Bishop Nicodemus said. And when the people responded, he outstretched his hand and blessed them.

"Amen."

"Go in peace," Olipor dismissed them.

Lucan left quickly before anyone should take notice of him again.

"'I wait for the Lord,'" he sang going upstairs to his master, "'my soul waits; in his word is my trust.'" He stood before his master's desk where Quintus in his nightshirt was bent over work. "Would you like me to help you start your day, sir?" he asked brightly.

"Yes, thank you." Quintus tried to hide his surprise. What has happened to this slave! "Then perhaps you could use some rest." Quintus indicated Lucan's bed.

Lucan smiled his thanks, and Quintus smiled back. Before he obeyed his master's merciful command, Lucan made the necessary preparations and carefully, almost tenderly, shaved his master. He gently massaged the care lines on his master's forehead, and ran his fingers soothingly down his temples. Then he bent over and brushed a kiss on his master's forehead. "Peace be with you," he said, and looked deeply into his master's eyes.

Quintus was forgiven. And he knew it.

Then Lucan took off his tunic, and in his loincloth crawled into bed. But he could not sleep. He lay awake, quiet, relaxed, as his mind worked on. He felt that he had been forced to take the leap over the deep, gaping chasm of choice between acknowledgment that God was God, and refusal to admit it. The reluctant Lucan was confronted by God. This was not a matter of belief or unbelief; his Lord was undeniably present. Faith did not mean a leap into the unknown, but rather, commitment of oneself to the unseen divine order, the ultimate Reality, the Lord of All himself, with whom we have personal relationship. Realizing this, Lucan had pledged his obedience. He had leapt. And he had not fallen to destruction! He was borne up! His faith was in his Lord! A warm glow filled his breast. He closed his eyes and basked in that wonderful realization of no longer being a lost sheep. Now he wanted to be able to worship with the flock also. He wanted to receive Christ's Spirit through his Body and Blood, he wanted to receive life renewed and sanctified.

He had leapt. He was borne up!

In gratitude he was to love this Roman here with him, this man who bought him and paid too much for him, so much that he could never repay it! This man gave him love; because he cost so dearly? More than that; Lucan had tested him sorely. The Domine's magnanimity welled from his essential being. That Lucan should be loved by his master, any master, came as a complete surprise. That he was expected to respond with love was, until now, beyond his comprehension. Lucan was almost reluctant to look at the mortal before him, should the transfiguration fade. Yet the Vision was to be lived out with this person in the flesh, in day-to-day living, with this mortal, every inch of whose body he knew intimately in the routine daily care. Yet it wasn't as though he were settling down comfortably with the known. The Domine was growing in stature as he coped with farming, with his staff of slaves, with the agony of the colonate and with life itself. And Lucan as Quintipor was expected to cope with him, faithfully at his side.

About an hour later Quintus left his desk to work outdoors. He looked in Lucan's direction. He walked up to Lucan's couch and bent over it.

"Were you asleep, Lucan?" he asked softly.

"Not yet, sir." Lucan sounded very relaxed.

"Don't get up." Quintus left the room and returned shortly with a goblet of fresh warm milk. He handed Lucan the milk.

Lucan rose on an elbow and took the goblet. "You are very kind, sir," he said warmly.

"And I even know about the Legerius Early seed," Quintus smirked.

Lucan nearly spilled the milk. Then puffs of laughter escaped his nostrils and they had a good chuckle together. Lucan knew he was forgiven. He regarded his master with devotion.

Out in the fields Quintus thought about Lucan. He knew that this was not the first time that he was forgiven by one of his men. This time though he was forgiven by a slave who never before had love in his heart for him. This was more than servile loyalty and obedience. As far as Lucan was concerned, their relationship was really restored. More than restored. Created! To what it had never been before! This slave had swallowed his hurt and bitterness, as though the burden of hurt had been taken away from him, or had been made ineffectual as a warping force in his life. Quintus again felt that old stab of relief and wonder and joy. Lucan had been created! This is the work of more than man alone, the sensitive young Roman felt. As though Lucan had actually met this Christ whom the slaves worshipped. Can I meet this Christ too? Or will I find at last that this God has all the while been seeking me?

Shortly after, Bishop Nicodemus came up again to officiate at St. Lawrence's Anniversary Birthday into Eternity. Lucan heard the early morning knock at the door when he left the vigil to take shaving water up to his master. He opened atrium door and was flustered to see the bishop there.

"The Lord be with you!" Nicodemus greeted Lucan.

"A-and-and with your spirit!" Lucan stammered.

"So you are a believer now?"

"I wish to be accepted as a catechumen, sir. I have been an unbeliever long enough. I think I am ready to commit myself. Also I have studied the Scriptures diligently."

The bishop was delighted. "Lucan, my boy, how did the Lord finally reach you?"

"He made me realize that for the task he has given me I need strength beyond my own."

"The task that he has given you?" Nicodemus queried.

"To love that man, sir," Lucan pointed up to the master's room. "And to serve him as though he were the Lord."

"The Lord be praised!" the bishop said joyfully.

"Who is gracious now and evermore!" Lucan responded.

"You will have long and rigorous training until the Pascha three years ahead. Are you ready to stay with it?"

Lucan did not expect it to be that long. Nevertheless, "I am ready," he affirmed. And for his patron saint he would call upon Lawrence, that 'Roman Stephen' to whose tomb on the Via Tibertina thousands made pilgrimage and kept the vigil last night. Right now at cockcrow those at Rome would be celebrating the Eucharist in which they participate in the saint's death and resurrection. At service Bishop Nicodemus told again the beloved story of true Roman faith crowned as richly with martyr's fame, and prayed that we also, in our suffering may steadfastly hold to the Faith, and, being filled with the Holy Spirit, may learn to love and bless our persecutors.

Lawrence, he explained, was deacon of Pope Sixtus II who was burned alive three days before him, in the Christian year 258, under the emperor Valerian. While the faithful deacon, disguised, followed his Pope to the stake, Sixtus said to him, "Grieve not, my son, in three days you will follow me." The prophecy came about. Three days later the order came to display the church's treasures. Lawrence did not hesitate, but adding guile to victory, hurried to obey. He brought together the poor from far and near, and pointing to this piteous band, claimed these to be the church's treasure. A wondrous sight! As Lawrence claimed the treasureless to be his treasure, his persecutor, cheated, mad with grief, made ready the avenging flames.

"Remember always, my son," Bishop Nicodemus spoke directly to Lucan, "remember that these, the least of our brothers, are God's treasure. You, Lucan, even so you."

And Lucan determined that he would perfect himself unto worthiness of his higher calling.

CHAPTER XI

The Least of my Brothers

Quintus bent over his accounts, trying to close the gone-by summer season's books. He had been insanely busy with the vintage and he had neglected the accounts entirely. Now the fall planting was upon him. Early-ripe cereals had to be sown, also various beans and peas, and fodder. Artichoke plants and vegetable seedlings needed transplanting, and new shrubs and saplings put in place. All this to do before the olive harvest, followed by the January butchering and packing of pork and marketing the storage crops. He had wanted to figure the taxes on the harvests as he went along, not at the last minute, in anticipation of the four-year taxes due at the end of the fiscal year.

No sooner do I increase our profit with improved farming than it gets chewed up with taxes! Quintus groused to himself. How does the Emperor expect us small farmers to meet the increased tax and survive on our land? Thank God Constantine abolished the scourge and the rack! The system will bankrupt us yet! But I'll die trying before I let Marcellus sell out.

He glanced at Lucan, sitting cross-legged, studying Columella on planting instructions. Lucan, why yes! The bet! Obviously won! Marcellus owed him money that could go toward taxes. No, hold on. Marcellus would demand a test, and Quintus did not want to risk traumatizing Lucan just yet. Lucan continued to be visited by his demons at unexpected times. The burning of the brush pile during autumn cleanup sent him screaming to his bed with inconsolable sobbing. No, Quintus concluded, he wasn't going to bring up the bet, and Marcellus certainly was not going to, because he owed. And he probably didn't have it anyway, because of gambling debts.

Lucan, feeling eyes on him, looked up and smiled.

"You know, Lucan, it's a good thing I don't have to pay taxes on your head this time. You are not registered with the decurion yet. As far as he knows, you don't exist. So we will let well enough alone and save us some tax money on you."

"I'm not registered with the tax collector? I am not bound to the land, then?" Lucan's transparent face betrayed a new idea.

Quintus eyed him. "Now just what are you thinking about?"

"Nothing, sir, nothing. Just dreams."

"Planning to run away?" Quintus probed.

"Oh no, sir, I-I it's just too far-fetched to even tell you." Lucan was in fact thinking of asserting his free birth, and of pursuing his scholarly ambitions, his lifelong dream.

"Well, tell me anyway, sometime. I've got some ideas too."

Lucan pretended to be absorbed in the scroll before him.

Quintus returned to his calculations. Months into farming, he was still foxed by the ledger. After some minutes of concentrated work, he fumed. "Plague take it, I can't balance this damn ledger!"

"Please let me help you, sir." Lucan rose to his feet.

"No!" Quintus shouted. He struck the desk with his fist. "I am the master of this estate and no damn slave is going to manage it for me!"

"Then won't you please refresh yourself? The mind flows afresh when the body is stimulated."

"Giving me orders, slave?"

"Only trying to take care of you."

"Like Olipor," Quintus snorted.

"Olipor, sir?"

"Certainly. Want something, offer it to your master as something he wants and he can't refuse. If you're tired of sitting in here, get out! By the Gods, one would think that you slaves imposed your servility upon yourselves! What are you doing standing there! Go outside and do a man's work! I don't have to tell you to breathe! Trench soil, damn you!"

"Thank you, sir."

"Thanking me for sending you out to trench soil, for the gods' sake?"

"For sending me out to do a man's work," Lucan replied with the emphasis on man, and suppressed a smile.

"Well, it would sound ridiculous to order you to do a boy's day's work, now wouldn't it," Quintus glowered at him.

Lucan worked with Old Servius and Sextus at trenching and manuring vegetable beds. Sextus hauled the manure, and Servius and Lucan did the spadework. They each dug two spades' depth and about a foot wide, and put the soil in a basket and Sextus dumped it at the opposite end of the row. Next they worked manure into the soil at the bottom of the trench. Then they dug a spade's depth of soil just behind the open trench, and threw this topsoil into the bottom of the open trench. They took the lower level of soil from the second trench to make the top layer of the first. This they kept on doing until they reached the ends of their rows, and filled the last trench with the soil carried there from the beginning of the row. Then they started on new rows. This trenching aerated the soil better than plowing could do, and provided a deeper bed of usable soil. It also cut down on the weeding, for the surface soil from the last season was buried too deep for any weed seed to grow. But Hercules! It was hard work. Soon Lucan, dripping with sweat, wished he were still sitting cross-legged in the stuffy library studying a scroll for his master. Olipor was at Puteoli marketing fruits and vegetables and eggs, the lucky stiff. Gaius was in the villa—what was Gaius doing there? Soon Lucan saw Gaius approaching rapidly.

"Lucan!" Gaius called. "Lucan!"

Lucan was alerted by Gaius's urgency.

"Your domine wishes you to ride to town in all speed and fetch him two quills and a pack of papyrus sheets."

"My domine?" Lucan doubted.

"Yes, and do hurry!" Gaius said.

"Why so urgent?" Lucan mused.

"I press you," Gaius answered shrewdly, "because the domine is madder than a dog in August. He forgot to ask Olipor to get them. He needs them sooner than expected!"

"Watch your language," Lucan retorted, though he knew very well that Quintus was in a foul mood.

"If you value your hide, hurry, and take the horse."

"What horse?" Lucan asked.

"Ignis, of course, dummy, he's the fastest," Gaius answered without hesitation. "I didn't say gelding."

"What about the money?" Lucan asked tersely.

"Your domine instructs you to get it from Olipor at our booth. You have it straight?" Gaius took the spade from Lucan's hand.

"Yes. And thanks." You messenger from heaven, he thought of Gaius, relieving me of this beastly job. Ride his horse, Lucan thought as he hastily bathed and borrowed a steward's tunic. I wonder? he added as he entered the horse's stall. Oh well, Ignis is faster, he thought as he slipped on the bridle and girthed the saddle. Better not aggravate the master by delaying to check the order. He led the horse out to the mounting post and sprang on his back.

"Come on, boy!" he urged needlessly. With a clatter of hooves on the pavement, Ignis plunged out of the stable court and kicked up his heels with glee. Lucan grinned. This was going to be fun. He waved at the poor fellows stuck with the trenching.

Quintus from his upper room wondered what in Hades Lucan was doing galloping furiously down the driveway on Ignis! He descended to the kitchen to find out. But hearing voices, he stopped in the hall and listened. The kitchen crew were gossiping and jesting as usual, while they made medicinal wines and pickled elecampane. He wondered that they had so much to talk about day in and day out!

"Well here comes Gaius again. What are you up to?" Postumus wanted to know.

"Boy I really played a good one on him," Gaius barely got out between his laughter.

"What are you up to now, you rascal," Letitia scolded.

"I really fixed him. Sent him on an errand in the young domine's name, on the young domine's horse."

"You dare to, even when the domine is in the house?" Letitia gasped.

"No one else is supposed to . . ." Kaeso started to say.

"Ride his horse," Gaius finished. "Exactly. Well, the domine will be angrier than Zeus in a thunderstorm."

"But Gaius," Letitia protested, "he could get flogged!"

"He is a fighter too," Postumus added. "He will probably thoroughly undo himself this time."

"And guess who will serve the young domine then?" Kaeso comprehended.

"Then peace and order will be restored at Good Will," Gaius threw in lightly.

"Gaius, you devil!" Letitia burst out. "The once happy Gaius!"

"As though happy people do not have ambition?" Gaius defended himself against the unexpected perception.

"My God, Gaius, you are going too far!" Letitia was distressed. "You detain him when he takes supper to the domine so the food gets cold, you worked him up to a row with the domine, and . . . Gaius, you're wicked! I don't know that I want to be your wife someday!"

"Sticking up for your brother in Christ, eh?" Gaius retorted.

"He is not my brother! Why, he could be my hus—"

"If you are so concerned about Lucan, why don't you marry him—after I replace him."

"I'm not marrying anyone just now," Letitia declared.

"Lucan won't marry," Postumus tossed in, "and thank God for that. Him doesn't want to beget children into slavery."

"What makes you think so?" Letitia asked.

"I was teasing him the other day about his-ah-good fortune," Postumus said with a wink at Gaius.

"Well, he certainly does not want to serve the young domine," Gaius informed them. "He has told me as much himself. What's wrong with helping him toward his desires?"

"I'm going to tell Olipor on you," Letitia threatened. "Our harmonious household jarred with jealousy!"

"You wouldn't dare tell him," Gaius countered evenly.

"Well, I'm not afraid of Dorothea . . ."

"Want my honest opinion, Gaius?" Postumus asked.

"Yes?"

"Well done, my boy."

"Why Pater!" Letitia exclaimed. "Aren't you with the young domine?"

"Of course I am, but does it mean I always has to agree with that young know-it-all? Him's made a mistake, a bad one, when he elevated that cutthroat off the street to his high position. Sure him will be 'one of us'. Sure him's quiet and obedient. Just you wait until he feels at home here, until he feels familiar enough to show us what he thinks! Give him a couple, three years and see!"

"You've got him wrong, Pater," Letitia said.

"What do you know about him?" Postumus turned upon his daughter.

"Well," Letitia gestured, "he's around the house, serving the domine and all, and I get to talking with him and all . . ."

"And all? What's 'and all'?" Postumus queried sharply.

"Nothing, dear, really," Cara answered for her daughter. "Lucan is teaching her how to read."

"Lucan? Her? Alone?" Postumus sputtered.

"He's sweet on her, if you're asking me," Kaeso informed.

"Well, if he so much as tries to touch you, I'll . . ." Postumus threatened fiercely.

"That's right, Letitia," Gaius chimed in, "we don't want anyone molesting you."

"Don't worry!" She answered in no uncertain terms and flinched at their vehemence. It wasn't Lucan who was trying to feel her up, or who waited in ambush for her and displayed to her when she went to the fruit and vegetable storeroom in the barn. Nor did she dare breathe a word of these disturbances. That was the demeaning part. They would call her a liar. Or deny that she was bothered by these things, because she 'must want it', whatever 'it' was. She didn't like them for making her feel that way. "Lucan is safe," she declared.

"You just remember whose girl you are," Gaius warned.

"A moment ago you were giving me away in marriage to Lucan after you replace him. Not a bad idea! Marriage to him, that is." Letitia turned away from Gaius and pouted at her work.

"Now—!" Gaius began. "I did no such—!"

"You ain't going to do no such thing, either!" Postumus scolded both of them and with that firmly stopped the quarrel.

With that, Quintus turned back to his study. Well! he said to himself indignantly. So Gaius is harassing Lucan. I will have to think this one over! And Letitia. Far cry from the frightened, timid little girl of spring! She's still a young girl in a woman's body. She needs time. I'll grant it to her. All the time she needs, short of rebellion from the men.

Lucan returned in what he considered good time. The afternoon had turned glorious. He enjoyed the outing. He hoped he could persuade his master to take a ride. He went upstairs singing. He buoyantly took the papyrus and quills out of his saddlebag and put them on his master's desk.

Quintus looked up at him. "Well, Lucan!"

"Here you are, Domine," Lucan bubbled, taking his master to be pleased with his promptness. "It's perfect out, how about taking a ride?"

"Well, Lucan," Quintus repeated sternly. "I see how easily you are taken for a ride!"

"Why, Domine!" The squelching pun reduced Lucan's voice to a whisper, and his face blanched. "Domine, you didn't send me?"

"I did not! Why didn't you verify the order?"

"Gaius told me not to take the time."

"Gaius . . ."

"I thought you trusted me, domine, don't you see? Best horse, cash for the asking. An incredible high! I wanted to do my best for you!" His eyes filled with frustration.

"Lucan, go find Gaius and bring him up here," Quintus ordered sharply.

"Oh no, Domine!" Lucan returned with feeling. He blushed because he was crossing his master's will openly.

"Oh no? And why not?" Quintus pressed.

"P-please, sir, it would make things worse." Lucan inadvertently exposed himself.

"Things, Lucan, what things?"

"That . . . that is all, sir. I think that my domine would do well to ignore the joke," Lucan added hastily, and made as to take his post at the door. He did not want to mention the unpleasant to his master.

"No evading me, Lucan, this conversation ends when I say so," Quintus insisted.

Lucan trembled visibly.

"Lucan, come here."

Lucan came beside his master's desk, and Quintus took him firmly by the hands. Their eyes met. "Now what is it."

"Domine, it's just that my domine is taking a long time to see it." Lucan flushed with embarrassment.

"See what?"

"My domine should have spoken to Gaius from the very first. Life would have been a lot easier for all of us." Lucan's voice was low and dejected.

"From the very first, Lucan? What do you mean?" Quintus inquired gently.

"Ignis. Interrupting you at n-night. A-Acribus. Wh-whom I could work with. The-the a-arguments about which t-tool I could use. My q-quota for the day." Lucan wished he hadn't spoken.

"I didn't know anything about it!"

"N-no sir."

"Is that why you started working alone?"

"Yes, sir."

"That's the kind of thing you should have told me at the morning interviews! To help you adjust. You knew that!"

"Y-yes, sir."

"Or were you too busy rebelling?"

Lucan winced. "The interviews made things w-worse. Gaius was j-jealous. I couldn't tell you that!"

"And what else can't you tell me?"

Lucan hesitated. "That Gaius is crushed that I have his p-p-position. You must do something for him, sir, to help him find a new purpose."

Quintus dropped Lucan's hands and stared at him dumbfounded. Many things suddenly made sense.

"I sh-shouldn't have said anything, sir, please forget it." Lucan was stricken.

"You should have! Much sooner!"

"I-I felt it wasn't worth troubling you about."

"That's my decision! I beat you up instead! And you have been living up here all this time and bearing the provocations in silence! I am sorry, Lucan."

It twisted the slave's guts to reduce his master to apologies. "I am sorry too, Domine. I took it all out on you."

Quintus did not reply, nor did he know that what he did at the moment was greater than anything he could say. He put a reassuring hand on the distressed slave's arm.

"Look, Domine," Lucan reached into his saddlebag again and pulled out an abacus. "This is for you. I got it myself. You gave me a silver coin back when—for a haircut."

"The coin that you didn't spend, neither for the haircut nor for the dagger? Is this *bona fide*?" Quintus's eyes twinkled.

"It's honest goods, Domine, from the heart."

Quintus was touched.

Then Lucan asked in a barely audible voice, "Will you have to punish me, sir, for riding out?"

"Yes. Severely." The corner of the master's mouth twitched.

"Then you will have to catch me first."

"What!" Quintus stared at him.

Lucan backed slowly towards the door. When Quintus sprang up, Lucan turned and ran. The chase was on. The household staff in the kitchen gawked with astonishment when they stormed through with yelps of laughter and dashed across the fields.

"Holy Mercury, Lucan!" Quintus gasped when they reached the meadows. Lucan turned and gave him such a look that Quintus thought, this man is running for real!

Quintus brought him down in the woods with a flying tackle, and wrestled him vigorously and pummeled him.

"Domine! Domine! Please! I didn't mean it that way!"

Quintus hesitated a moment and like lightening Lucan seized the advantage and pinned his master down and sat panting astride him and clasped him tightly with his thighs to ride his bucking. He held Quintus's arms to the ground and looked directly into his face.

"Domine, please, it tears my guts to see you this way. I know how much the colonate is eating you!"

"I am in bondage indeed," Quintus surrendered quietly.

"Courage, Domine."

"Really! That's easy to say from your side of things."

"My side of things?"

"Slaves are supposed to be carefree in exchange for their servitude."

"Are they, Domine?"

"Tell me, Lucan, what would you do?"

"Go to the city and earn us some money."

"No, dammit, not what you yourself would do—you know you can't leave this place—what would you do if you were me."

"My surname isn't Oikonomikos for nothing, sir," Lucan persisted.

"With those scars of yours you'd be thrown in the arena so fast!"

Lucan sobered at the reminder. "It does look as though I'd more likely take your place in debtor's jail."

Quintus searched his slave's face. That incredible idea gave him pause. "No one is going to jail, Lucan," he swore vehemently.

"That's the spirit, Domine." Lucan released his master's arms.

"What were you daydreaming about, Lucan? In the city?"

"Scribing, sir. Rare books ferreted out of private libraries to replace those lost in Augustus's scourge and Aurelian's fire. Beautiful books. Scrolls of decorated love poems for men to bestow upon their loved ones. From the Greek. From the Hebrew Song of Songs. Right on up."

"Including Ovid?" Quintus's eyes crinkled mischievously.

Lucan went one further. "Even Dodekatechon of Paramos."

Quintus tittered. "And what about Elephantis!" He tickled Lucan in the ribs.

"Why not!" And they giggled like the two adolescents that they were.

"Tell me, Lucan, where did you get such a notion?"

"My father, sir, and how he faithfully repaired the family scrolls against hope as they fell apart. My father read love poems to my mother while she sewed by lamplight."

"For example?"

> "Such is the passion for love
> That has twisted its way beneath my heartstrings
> And closed deep mist across my eyes
> Stealing the soft heart from inside my body . . ."

"Beautiful!"

"And then—it's from Archilochus, sir."

"And then, Lucan?"

"They made moan together. They thought we were asleep but I lay awake to hear the beautiful words. And—" He wasn't going to tell that he wiggled to their rhythm.

"When they were spent I would sneak under their covers and my sisters after me and they would invite my older brother who thought himself too old for the bunny cuddle."

Quintus stared speechlessly at this incredibly touching vignette but Lucan could not see him for the salty mist in his own eyes.

"Know what I daydream about, Lucan?" Quintus looked up from under his slave. "Making this place into a State Exhibition Farm. People will come from miles around to observe how the soil can be built up with crop rotation and green manuring. This place can be restored to the fertility that our forefathers knew! Campania. Lyrically beautiful Campania. God, how I love this land!"

"Let me help you, sir."

"And let me help you, with books from my clients."

"You are kind, sir."

"Lucan, you are so good to me," Quintus sighed pensively.

"Dear Quintus . . ." Lucan in his emotion let the proper name slip.

They looked into each other's eyes for a moment, then the master reached up and caressed Lucan on the neck where his brand lay. "I would that the hurt go away, Lucan."

Lucan fell on his master's neck and kissed him.

The overflow of mutuality, the pinnacle of shared dreams, the unexpected confessions of tenderness and their bodily closeness overcame them both. Lucan rolled off onto his back and lay panting beside his master. Quintus raised up on an elbow and noticed the pulse in Lucan's neck.

"You too, Lucan?" he murmured.

Lucan nodded and averted his eyes.

And again Quintus felt that stab of wonder and longing.

* * *

Quintus did in due time speak to Gaius about the incident, and the entire matter of his status.

Gaius went directly from his domine's library to his own room. He didn't for the world want to see anybody just then. Olipor would have to be waiting for him there.

"You have been troubled, haven't you, son," Olipor said gently. "Will you tell me about it?"

Gaius reluctantly told his father everything. "It was only a joke, Dad."

"It was really more than just a joke, wasn't it, son?"

"The way it turned out, yes—what do you mean, Dad?"

"Are you jealous of Lucan, perhaps?" Olipor suggested.

"Jealous? He's my friend!" Gaius asserted.

"Except that he has your position and you want it back," Olipor said.

"That's how the domine interpreted it, but really . . ."

"What, son?"

"I guess I haven't behaved very well," Gaius confessed.

"No you haven't, son. You have wronged your domine, Lucan, and our Lord. Remember, our Lord said, 'Whatever you do to the least of my brothers you do to me.' You must learn how to love, Gaius. The Apostle said,

> "Love is patient and kind. Love is not jealous or boastful; it is not arrogant or rude. Love does not insist on its own way; it is not irritable or resentful; it does not rejoice at wrong, but rejoices in the right. Love bears all things, believes all things, hopes all things, endures all things. Love never ends.

Don't waste your energy in envy and self pity, Gaius! You have too big a job to do. You need to pray to do the Lord's will; not seek your own ambitions."

"Dad?" Gaius said contritely.

"Yes?"

"The young master said something like that to me. He sounded so much like our Lord that it seemed as though I were standing before our Lord himself. He said that I can serve him personally and faithfully at any task—that the only way I can fulfill my personal ambitions is to desire the same thing he wants for me."

"Exactly what does the domine want for you?" Olipor's voice was tense.

"To be the next overseer after you, Dad."

"May your obedience be your joy," Olipor replied with relief.

"The young domine," Gaius pouted and let out his true feelings, "the young domine—sometimes he's a little bantam rooster."

"He is your domine nevertheless, Gaius. And he too is under the judgment of God whether he likes it or not."

"Sometimes I think—I think—"

"What, son."

"That God is a big fat rooster!" Gaius blurted out.

"He *is* the Supreme I AM" Olipor laughed.

"I don't always like it. He devours you, like Acribus."

"I don't always like it either, son. Because we each want to be the Big One ourselves. Remember he is our Creator, and we are only his chicks. That is why we must obey him. We can learn to like it, too. Pray for the right mind and heart. Act obedience until you can truly obey. Then your obedience becomes your joy."

"I'd like to believe that, Dad."

"It is a fact, son, and a promise."

"Dad, is the Domine trying to be a Christian?"

"He may be trying to live Christian principles without confessing Jesus Christ as his Lord and Savior.

"Can one do that?"

"Do an impossible task, without Christ's grace and power?"

"I don't think so."

"Now Gaius," Olipor started in again.

"Yes, Dad?"

"You must make peace with Lucan before you can come to the Eucharist."

"Apologize to him? Dad, what can I say to him?"

"He will not make it hard for you. He is having his own troubles trying to obey the young domine."

* * *

Gaius did make up with Lucan before the next Eucharist, though not with words. The loquacious Gaius found himself completely unable to speak. He seized Lucan's arms and pressed them, and Lucan responded immediately.

At worship Lucan stood by the kitchen door so he could slip out should his master need him. He was the one who first saw Quintus approach. Even though it was time then for visitors and catechumens to leave worship, Lucan took him by the arm and drew him over to his side. Olipor was reading the Lord's parable about the Samaritan. Quintus listened with a nervous attentiveness to this and to the Gospel and Epistle passages that Olipor read alternately with the psalms.

Bishop Nicodemus told the faithful to sit down. He talked with them about the great responsibility placed by God upon each person as a member of the Body of Christ to bring God's love to those around him, "Even to the least of your brothers, for our Lord said, 'As you did it to one of the least of these my brethren, you did it to me.'"

The bishop's message kindled Quintus's heart, for had not he and Lucan already done this for each other to some extent? Isn't that why he was so moved by the slave?

"Dear family," the bishop summarized, "'God so loves the world that he gave us his only Son, so that no one who believes in his forgiveness and love should be lost, but should have eternal life.'"

"Amen!" the household shouted, and fell into a deep, vibrant silence. Quintus almost wept. This love was the most wonderful reality that he could experience. God all along had been trying to show him his love, and he had not acknowledged its Source. Through the imperfect actions of his slave men and women, God had been trying to speak to him of his wonderful forgiving love. He was ready now to surrender himself in gratitude to this Kingdom, to God's plan. 'Thy Will be done.'

It was suddenly obvious to him that the real center of everything was not himself, but God. Repentance seemed natural to him, a thorough change of heart and mind from his self-centeredness to the real Lord as his King. His quest was fulfilled, and he found what he was seeking where he least expected to find it—in the midst of his simple, mundane household of slaves.

At the offertory of alms and oblations, Nicodemus whispered to Olipor. "Your young domine is among us!"

"Yes, sir, I know, and Lucan with him."

"Olipor, you have become singularly lax in admitting people to the rites before they can understand," the bishop chided in a firm whisper.

"He understands with his heart if not with his mind, sir," Olipor ventured, who knew from experience the missionary practicability of his disobedience.

"I will give him a blessing if he comes forward," Bishop Nicodemus decided.

"Thank you, sir, thank you very much!" Olipor was moved.

Quintus worried when the faithful moved forward in a line to receive communion. Surely I shall be found out now! But he knew that he could not slip out, either.

"The Bread of Heaven in Christ Jesus," the bishop said.

"In God the Father Almighty," Olipor said, administering the cup for the three sips.

"Amen!" the communicant said.

"And in the Lord Jesus Christ."

"Amen!"

"And in the Holy Spirit which is in the Holy Church."

"Amen!"

Letitia turned to go back to her place. Her gaze met that of her master in the back of the room. Her eyes widened with surprise, then she smiled brightly and looked modestly down.

Old Servius turned next; Servius who the morning before had complained bitterly of a backache, and whom Quintus had excused from work. He saw his young master. Tears started to his eyes, and he raised his hand to bowed head in salute.

Now they will all know, Quintus thought. Quintus looked into each face as the faithful turned to go back to their places.

Sextus the Iberian winked.

Gaius, who because of his recent trouble did not assist this time, smiled and blushed.

His mother Dorothea, the housekeeper, was radiant.

Baltus the plowman grinned through his red whiskers.

Mute Manius, as dark as the volcanic soil he plowed, saluted.

Mamercus the Arab raised a hand softened by lanolin from handling the flocks.

The Gaul Kaeso, rotund because he hadn't quite overcome the unheard novelty of being able to snack freely while cooking in this household, began a smile but compressed his lips to suppress a soft burp.

Next Cara, illiterate and superstitious, who suffered a sentence in a brothel rather than deny her faith, smiled warmly.

Postumus raised his brow and tried not to question the young master's motives.

Their son Alexis the vinedresser nodded superiorly.

Paulo the older, adopted half-brother, assistant vinedresser, quietly met his eyes.

Their youngest, Gregor, whom Quintus had forgiven more than once for sleeping at his night watch, looked up to him with devotion.

One by one Quintus looked upon his household. Only Megas was not there. Marcipor was there. Marcipor pressed Quintus's arm when he passed by to hurry home. They all had something in common as they turned away from the sacrament, and each expressed it in his individual way. Joy. No, you couldn't exactly contain it with the word joy; their worship did not intentionally deliver such an emotional stirring. It would be more realistic to call it confidence, care, Quintus felt. Outgoing concern, if you would. Each of them could have avoided him with that pious and self-contained gesture of downcast eyes. But no. That he was in their presence mattered to them. They each looked him in the eye and greeted him. Quintus felt a surge of tenderness toward his men and women. The Kingdom is indeed in our midst!

Bishop Nicodemus returned the bread plate to the table, then turned to face the faithful. He confronted Quintus with a steady gaze. Quintus instinctively stepped back—right on Lucan's foot. Lucan put his arm around Quintus's waist and steadied his master.

"Draw near, with faith," Bishop Nicodemus invited. Quintus did come forward, bringing Lucan with him. Then he was struck with awe. He did not know what to do. Feeling awkward in the Holy Presence that he sensed, he knelt before his legs should tremble. Lucan knelt beside him. The bishop laid his hands on Quintus's head. "May the Lord bless you and keep you, Quintus; the Lord make his face to shine upon you and be gracious to you; the Lord lift up his countenance upon you and give you peace." Then he laid his hands on Lucan's head and likewise blessed him.

Olipor said to the kneeling young men, "Go in peace, brothers in Christ."

Master and slave rose together, and faced each other. They embraced.

"Peace be with you, brother," Lucan said.

"Peace be with you, brother," Quintus replied.

Quintus turned, met his household with a broad grin, and returned to his place. He had finally done it. The others sang, joyously accepting Quintus's presence as though it were the expected.

Peace. No, that was not entirely what Quintus felt. This faith was no opiate. More like a challenge. A challenge to face the tremendous responsibility ahead. Olipor dismissed the faithful, and as they left for the morning chores, Quintus smiled quietly on them. Then he arranged with the bishop to become a catechumen along with Lucan, his new brother in Christ.

PART II

LORD, I AM NOT WORTHY

Why is my pain unceasing, my wound incurable,
Refusing to be healed?
Will you really be to me like a treacherous brook,
Like waters that are not sure?

Jeremiah 15:18

CHAPTER XII

Paschatide A.D. 324
Keep the possibility open

Gaius had a way of coming in to supper ahead of the others, flopping himself down on the bench at the kitchen table, declaring that he was tired and hungry, and urging the kitchen staff to hurry. Letitia usually went along with his mother's humoring of him until she realized that Gaius was all demands and no give. She could not tolerate that when they were married. She must try now to break his habit. Tonight she would say something to him about it. It would have to be publicly, in the kitchen; she never could get to see him alone. As she was carrying dishes from the cupboard to the table, and her pater was stirring a pot of stew, Gaius breezed in and sat down.

"By Hercules I thought he'd never let us stop digging holes! How many trees does he think we can plant next fall! I wonder how many people will fall in and drown after each rain. Careful, Meter, going out to the throne after dark!"

His comments were met with laughter from the kitchen staff. "Mud bath, that's good for the complexion," Dorothea quipped.

"Letitia, where's the milk? I'm nearly undone with hunger." What he really meant was, get me the milk.

"It's in the pantry, Gaius. I'm very busy right now."

"I can see that," he observed critically. "You're running late in here."

"Well certainly," Dorothea explained to her son, "with all the spring chores."

"Oh my goodness you is here already, Lucan," Cara exclaimed when Lucan walked in. "We certainly is running late. Quick, Letitia, finish setting the table, dear, at least we can look ready. Thank you, Lucan, you're a dear," she complimented him on his habit of helping.

"Yes, move it, Letitia," Gaius ordered from his bench. "And don't forget my cup of milk."

"Just who do you think I am, anyway!" she snapped, "Your slave? If you're so desperate, why don't you help us get ready, like Lucan does."

"Because *Quinti-puer* here is a serf's chattel and I am my own man," Gaius drawled derisively from his bench. He smiled complacently.

"Why Gaius!" Dorothea chided her son.

"Careful about how you refer to the domine," Lucan warned good-naturedly.

"Where is your inseparable, little shadow?" Postumus queried.

"Asleep on the massage bench."

"Good work, little cheesepot!" Kaeso jibbed.

Lucan clenched his jaw and let the comment pass. Contradicting them wouldn't change anything. They would continue to believe whatever they wished.

"How many times have I told you—" Letitia started to his defense.

"Now stop it, all of you!" Dorothea scolded from the pickle jar. Cara shook her head at her daughter and resumed making salad. Lucan looked neither to the left nor to the right but kept his eyes to himself as he prepared his master's place at the table. Postumus turned his back. Granted at least the privacy of turned backs, the fight was on.

"If you're tired of serving me like a slave," Gaius said, "why don't we get married so you can learn to anticipate my needs like a good wife? You're sixteen now, Letitia!"

"The obedient wife. Is that the only way to sanctification?" she pouted.

"You have it," Gaius smirked superiorly.

"Isn't that some kind of idolatry?"

The question stopped Gaius cold.

Lucan turned away to hide a smile. She certainly was a bright pupil and worth all the time studying philosophy, theology and logic together.

"Remember, Letitia, when our young mistress Marcia got married? You couldn't marry me soon enough back then."

"Gaius, I was only twelve!"

"Well, I plan to keep my promises."

Letitia turned away furiously, got more dishes from the cupboard and banged them down on the table so hard that her father yelled at her. When she had spread the dishes, she found words. "Keep your promises, is that all?"

"What more do you want?" Gaius was defensive.

"Some companionship with you. Some giving of yourself."

"Letitia, I'm working on our freedom price. I need my evenings. If you would accept yours first, our children would be freeborn while I were yet a slave, and we wouldn't have to wait so long!"

"Oh, no. It would be the same thing while you worked on yours."

"What's the matter, Letitia, you don't want to be the submissive wife of a slave?" Gaius drawled.

"I don't want to be the submissive anything of anyone!"

"Whew! So high headed!" Gaius feigned awe.

"All the complaining you do about obeying the young master is the same thing, Gaius."

Lucan turned and looked at them in surprise.

"You're even worse about the bellyaching, Lucan!" Letitia snapped.

"Shush, Letitia!" he chortled, embarrassed.

"Can't you concede that I may have similar feelings about obeying a husband as my lord and master?" Letitia addressed them intently. "Isn't that only another kind of slavery?"

"Nope!" Gaius grinned complacently. "It's only natural."

"Ma, am I crazy or something?" Letitia close to tears, appealed to Cara.

"No, dear, you ain't crazy," Cara conceded. "You two has to work it out." She looked at Postumus.

"Read the next part of that epistle, dear," Postumus said, "after where it says wives obey your husbands."

"I have, Pa. And I don't see where I get any such reciprocity from Gaius."

"The what?"

"I've read all of the New Covenant, Pa," she answered thoughtfully. "Know what the Christ says to me? Jesus was the first religious person on God's earth who acknowledged that women are equal to men in the sight of God. He allows me a soul! A precious gift! I owe him! I'll die before I give it up!"

"That's beautiful, Letitia," Cara said, who had herself suffered a term in the brothel rather than renounce her faith.

"And it's gone right to your head," Postumus said.

"Yes, Letitia, what about Paul to the Ephesians, and the Colossians," Gaius challenged.

"That's not Jesus speaking! Christ's message is lost, and women are put right back into traditional servitude," Letitia declared.

"Where do you get that idea!" Gaius scoffed.

"Think about it," Letitia argued. "Christ's truth emerged once again through the Gnostics, then the church Patriarchs buried the message even more deeply. Read for yourself."

"I don't have time for that sort of thing," Gaius answered.

"And what does that have to do with marriage?" Postumus asked.

"It's like this, Pa. If, as scripture says, I must subject myself to a husband in the name of Christ; then in the name of Christ I have to first find out who I am and what I have to give, and who he is to whom I am going to give myself!"

"To me," Gaius said.

"Gaius, you are so assuming and so demanding." Tears ran down her cheeks.

Gaius looked at Lucan and shrugged. Postumus sucked in his lip. The women concentrated on the supper.

Quintus came in and took his place at the head of the table. Lucan brought him a cup of milk immediately with a smile, and a sidelong glance at Letitia. Then Quintus got up and offered help as was his custom when the kitchen was running late. He took a serving dish from Letitia's hands to carry to the table. Their eyes met and he noticed her distress. The rest of the household filed in and sat down. Letitia serving the salads passed close by Gaius and stuck out her tongue at him.

Quintus saw it. "What's with her?" he asked Lucan.

"Lover's quarrel," Lucan replied.

After supper when the men left the kitchen and Dorothea was about the villa lighting lamps, Letitia voiced her thoughts to her mother.

"Be patient, dear," Cara humored her angry daughter. "And when you hears a lot of braying, consider the source!"

"How can I trust myself to a jackass!"

"You knows he ain't perfect but you loves him anyway. Your Pa has been most considerate to me."

"Oh you and Pa," she scoffed, "that's different! You had no choice. Do I have to slavishly take orders and wait and see what happens to me? Can't I take hold of my life and start controlling it?" She planted herself firmly in her mother's path. "Ma?"

"My goodness, you is talking like them patrician women!"

"You know, Ma, Marcia has more rights under Roman civil law than I would have in a Christian marriage! Christianity brings women right back under male authority again."

"My, you has been doing a lot of reading," Cara said. "But Christian marriage is more about love than rights, dear. Scripture say that the man should love the wife as hisself."

"Then woe to the wife whose husband can't love himself," Letitia reflected.

"Does scripture say that too, dear?"

"No, I made it up. But Aristotle says if we don't love ourselves we can't love others. And I wonder how a wife can maintain her integrity as an unequal, even if loved!"

"I don't understand what you says," Cara replied.

Understand. That is the key. Who on this earth can understand? It's no use with Gaius. He has gone to his room, anyway. Doesn't he care that I need him? Lucan. Where is he? She went to the peristyle and sat on a bench on the clipped grass and looked up at the young domine's library door. She longed to see her reading teacher, her mentor. Presently Lucan emerged and came downstairs. She rose and met him in the colonnade.

"I suppose you are on some errand," she said bitterly.

"As a matter of fact, I am. What is it, Letitia?"

"Gaius has shut himself off from me again."

"Letitia, dear, have I taught you how to read for no purpose at all?"

"Certainly, so I could use Apicius's cookbook that you copied for me, you glutton!" She put her fist on his lean stomach. "Really, Lucan, if you cannot expect deep communion with your own spouse in the closest human relationship that God has ordained, where else can your great loneliness be filled? Do you think that God who loves would ordain a union to be made in which love cannot emerge?" She rushed for her room.

He caught up with her in the hallway leading to the kitchen, and grabbed her wrist. "Do you?"

They stood panting, looking at each other.

"Maybe that's what I'm trying to say to Gaius."

"You said some rather heavy things in there," Lucan commented.

"What about your own mother and father, Lucan? Can you remember how it was?"

He drew breath. She was asking him about the golden days, before the unthinkable. Only she could probe into his past without slamming shut the doors of his mind.

"She deferred to my father. It has never crossed my mind that submission to a husband could be demeaning, Letitia."

"How can you say that at the same time you resist your slavery!"

"I'm learning from you," he confessed.

"You are the one who is teaching me how to think things through," she replied softly.

"Say," he caressed her tenderly, "You're some woman!"

"You're the only man here who can see past the boobs and butt."

"Perhaps."

"And what does that do to you, Lucan?" She leaned on his breast and felt his heart pound. "I want to know."

He clasped her in his arms, backed her against the wall, kissed her on the mouth, and rubbed his fully aroused body firmly against her. I want the same thing every other man here wants. I want the very thing that destroyed my mother and sisters."

"Stop, Lucan, you frighten me."

"Sorry," he said. "It scares me too. Listen, dear, it may be that our deepest longings cannot be fulfilled on the human level. Always keep the possibility of communion open between yourself and Gaius." He tried to invade her eyes but could not get past the mist. "Courage, little sister, stay with your convictions." He watched her with desire as she walked down the hall to her room. Unexpectedly a wave of nausea and dizziness overcame him and he leaned against the wall until the demon from the past subsided.

As soon as he completed his errand, Lucan sought the scripture pertaining to the disturbing interlude with Letitia. He picked up Paul's letters to the churches at Corinth and opened the scroll to the first.

> To the unmarried and the widows I say that it is well for them to remain single as I do . . . The unmarried man is anxious about the affairs of the Lord, how to please the Lord; but the married man is anxious about worldly affairs, how to please his wife, and his interests are divided . . . I say this for your own benefit, not to lay any restraint upon you, but to promote good order and to secure your undivided devotion to the Lord.

And I suppose, Lucan thought, in Paul's sense marriage is a distraction also to one who would give wholehearted service to an earthly domine, therefore the practice of keeping personal slaves celibate.

Next to the marriage discussion Lucan came across that other passage which always gave him thought.

> Were you a slave when called? Never mind. But if you can gain your freedom, avail yourself of the opportunity. For he who was called in the Lord as a slave is a freedman of the Lord . . . So, brethren, in whatever state each was called, there let him remain with God.

Never mind! Paul didn't know a thing about slavery, he reflected sourly. But precisely this was the other horn of his dilemma! Stay at Good Will and be fired with passion for a woman he cannot marry. Or, run off to freedom in direct disobedience to the admonishment to remain in fellowship with God in the station in which he was called. Lucan blushed deeply, for Quintus had glanced at him, and was now looking at him intently.

"What is it, man?" Quintus asked. "Why did you excuse yourself from me?"

Sweat stood out on Lucan's forehead and lip and he looked up at his master. He saw that Quintus really wanted to know. He reluctantly showed his domine the words pertaining to that horn of the dilemma about which Quintus already knew, and hoped that Quintus would not guess the other.

'If you were a slave when you were called, never mind . . .'

"There you have it," Quintus nodded masterfully. "Isn't that a fine thing to say to someone stuck in the colonate," he wryly tried to relate to Lucan about his own status. Then his mouth curled into a mischievous smile for he knew what Lucan was really blushing about. Marcellus had told him. Marcellus had come upon Lucan and Letitia in the maze, sitting asleep over their books, her head on his shoulder, his head on her hair. Marcellus had angered Lucan and embarrassed Letitia with some smart comment.

"Do you prefer to be chaste, or chased?" Quintus teased.

Lucan chortled at his master's pun and his perspiration prickled.

"Perhaps you need to read Plutarch's Dialogue on Love to clarify your thinking?" Quintus suggested. It was a cruel dig.

"Domine!" Lucan bound up and glared. He shuddered at the memory of the nightmarish days when he was forced to be a darling. He needed no argument in favor of conjugal love. He remembered the golden days with his parents. He observed the two old couples downstairs.

"I've got some good books under my bed that you may dust, Lucan."

"Domine, will you stop—"

Quintus's eyes crinkled with humor. "Are you giving me orders not to have some fun, slave?"

"Plague take slavery, we're talking—as brothers—baptized in the family of Christ! If you cared, you wouldn't poke fun at my expense!"

Quintus returned a startled look. He had not thought of that before.

"And if you cared at all for Gaius you wouldn't encourage anyone to steal his girl!" Lucan remained adamant. He just made his decision and realized it only after he spoke. He immediately sobered at his confession.

"You love her, Lucan," Quintus said gently.

"My—sister." Lucan now had that innocent look of his.

"You don't have to reveal your private life unless you are willing," Quintus affirmed patiently. Then he probed. "She is not your sister, and you know it! I saw you two down there."

"Now Quintus!" Lucan remained evasive except that his cheeks reddened.

"Come on, Lucan, tell me about it. I would gladly give you permission to marry. Yes, I would like that."

"Marry the forbidden treasure?" Lucan daringly searched his master's face. "Why?"

"Oh, forbidden treasure is it? Where did you get that idea? I would like you to marry. It would help you settle down. You would be much more content, much steadier. You may even find deep satisfaction. Taking a wife would be the most natural thing for a man to do. New love, mutual support and comfort, new responsibilities, new freedom. Someday I . . ."

"Help tie me down more firmly? New freedom?" Lucan protested mildly.

"Ah, there's that side to you also," Quintus picked up swiftly. "Does freedom to you still mean complete release from any connection with Good Will? Does it mean more to you than love? And you would not beget children into slavery? Is that it, Lucan? Really, forbidden treasure?"

Lucan was cornered, and shocked that his domine would use his own confidences upon him.

"I-I don't know my own mind on that," he confessed.

"Lucan," Quintus coaxed, "come here." Quintus moved to his couch and started taking off his sandals. Lucan came to his master, and on his knees, helped him.

"Lucan," Quintus began again, "I would not make you marry if you did not wish to. Rather, I charge you not to marry unless you are willing to see the means of grace in the sacrament of marriage. There are others who long to share God's gifts in your place."

"Including you, Quintus?" Lucan asked intuitively.

"Why not?"

"Why not," Lucan echoed compliantly and proceeded to massage the thong marks out of his master's legs. His mind wrestled with Quintus's desire for Letitia. Somehow he must help his master handle his involuntary celibacy. There was a way. Were they not mutually aroused during the evening massage at the bath? There was that old pledge, and Quintus never made a move to break it, that he would not touch him erotically. Again, while they were catechumens, they had faced together their attraction to each other and had made the mutual decision, because they were Christians, not to indulge in the flesh.

Cheesepot. Round mortar. Kaeso's nicknames for him had a new point to them. Little Shadow. Inseparable. He let them think as they wished. One was always haunted by one's past. Perhaps now he should reconsider the whole matter and help Quintus loosen the warp, in order to save Letitia from him.

Why not? Anointing with oil the well-made body of someone you have come to love is anything but neutral. His skilled hands were more than just massaging, they were lingering, they were loving, and the master knew it. All he had in this world to offer in love was himself, yet that gift was supreme. And if the master desired to take it a step further, one thing remained the same; he was not allowed to refuse. Quintus could reach out to him from the massage bench and draw him close and enter the low road to the heart slowly and gently. It would hurt, it always did, but this master would be careful, and would reach around front to stroke his broad chest and muscle-plated stomach and would titillate his manhood in rhythm to the battering ram until his body was an unbearable explosion of pleasure-pain rending a cry from the heart.

What in heaven's name was he doing thinking like this! To deny his secret ladylove so that he could give undivided devotion to his master was one thing. He could see the beauty in that. To give up his beloved so that his master could have her himself was quite another matter. He could see the everlasting torture in that.

"Lucan, that's enough, thank you."

He was still massaging those thong marks, long gone! He looked up at his master's face.

Quintus reached out and stroked his slave's neck where the brand lay, and his hand trembled. He looked into Lucan's eyes without seeing the hidden anguish for he was preoccupied with thoughts of his own. It seemed that in time his bitter quip about the Colonate came to be not such a bad idea after all, namely that since he was a veritable serf, he was really one of the slaves anyway. He may as well go all the way in associating with them, even unto marriage. He had always held affection for Letitia, but the possibility of marriage had not until now occurred to him. Now this renewed sense of equality with her, negatively through the Colonate, positively through his new faith, augmented his feelings to love. He saw the touching, the intimacy between the married couples downstairs, and he wanted some of that himself.

* * *

"Not as a plaything, Marcellus, but as a wife!" Quintus argued hopelessly with his friend in whom he had confided.

"What! You will take the household—whore—to wife?" Marcellus looked shocked except that his eyes twinkled with devilment.

"She is a virgin of exceeding virtue," Quintus rose to her defense.

"The only virtuous woman is one who knows how to straddle a man," Marcellus declared. "She should be servicing all the single men, and raising the communal brood. I provide at least that for my men, Quintus. They pay me for the privilege, of course. I started talking to you about this three years ago! Let me get her started for you. That's my specialty, you know," he boasted. "Painless. She'll love it."

"No, Marcellus," Quintus said firmly, "you don't understand this household."

"You and your household of ascetics," Marcellus mocked. "You do the strangest things in the name of your religion, against the very grain of human nature. And I suppose," his mockery deepened into derision, "I suppose that you will tell me next that you are still a virgin too."

Quintus was ashamed before the voice of the world to admit that he was.

"Really, now!" Marcellus pounced on his silence. "This will not do—a full grown man like you—what's the matter, Beans, has Lucan corrupted you or something? As a slave she can't refuse, you know. Or are you just a very sad fool? So you've never done it! I'll wager that you have never even so much as—"

"I'll have you know that she has been in bed with me!" Quintus boasted fiercely even though on that occasion he was half dead with chills and fever and Letitia had mercifully, "In the Name of Christ," warmed his body with hers during a severe chill. His very manhood was at stake in Marcellus's terms. Marcellus saw his contradiction before he did and teased him all the more.

"I was sick, Marcellus!" Quintus attempted lamely.

"Holy Venus! To miss such an opportunity!" Marcellus tantalized. He would accept no excuse. "Get her started for the others, Beans, use her for yourself, but marry a wife from good Roman stock to manage your household and bear your progeny."

Quintus would hear none of it.

"You know what one of your heroes says to that?" Marcellus went on, with a mischievous snap in his eye.

"One of my heroes?"

"Our honored Seneca the elder, nonetheless. He says a young man has done no wrong to love a prostitute—a usual thing. Give him time, he will improve and marry a wife. Seneca enjoyed the pleasures permitted to his age and lived according to the rules laid down for young men." Marcellus chuckled. "And you would condemn what our forefathers have always provided for by law? Or is it that you haven't the guts to be a real Roman in your household? Want to bet on it? I'll give you a couple weeks."

"It's precisely because I have guts that I can say to Hades with our forefathers," Quintus said coolly.

"Ah, treason!" Marcellus crowed. Then curiosity got him and he asked, "What do you go by, then?"

"Christ," Quintus admitted.

"And what does your Christ say?" Marcellus grandly offered his friend the privilege of a listening ear.

"He says that we should love our God with all our heart, and all our mind and all our soul, and our neighbor as ourselves. And by his life Christ showed us an example."

"Can't you just see her, in the name of Christ, lovingly administering in her womanly way to the members of the household? Love and self-giving, aren't those supreme Christian virtues?"

"Not that kind of giving, Marcellus. If you love people in Christ you do not use them as though they were objects, tools to your pleasure. You would not use the light ladies, Marcellus."

"But you love Letitia?"

"What are you getting at, Marcellus?"

"Well, you would not be using her."

"Yes I would be. Precisely because I do love her and respect her as a person, I do not want to behave selfishly or irresponsibly towards her. The consummation of love is a sacrament, an outward sign of a permanent union made before witnesses and sealed by God, in which the partners are answerable to God. And Letitia and I have not contracted any such union."

Marcellus became irritated that he could not get through to Quintus, not even on his own grounds. He tried another tact.

"Why don't your forget about love and mystical unions and simply breed your female slave for the sake of her own health. Or have your husbandman take care of it."

"For her health?" Quintus became all ears.

"If you want to be so responsible you have to look after her, before she gets the wandering womb illness."

"The what?"

Marcellus explained. "The uterus moves about inside in its longing to be pregnant. Why, it can shift up against her lungs and give her respiratory problems!"

"Where did you hear that one?"

"It's right there in Galen. Even in Plato. And way back from Hippocrates. Zounds! Don't you have a doctor book? You should know. You're the one who is supposed to be so educated!"

"Hmm." Quintus was embarrassed not to know.

Marcellus pressed his argument. "Even Aristotle said the female state is a deformity, however common. She needs care. You're neglecting her."

"You don't expect me to believe that."

"She really shouldn't have to wait so long after puberty to be pregnant, Beans," Marcellus persisted. "Does she have painful menses?"

"Why yes, I think so."

"See, what did I tell you? As I said, if you haven't taken care of her in a couple weeks, I'll get her."

"Don't be ridiculous, Marcellus!" Quintus dismissed that strange advice. In the animals he butchered, the uterus was firmly attached.

"I'm serious, Beans!" Marcellus waved good-bye and departed.

Quintus wondered why he and Marcellus remained friends, why Marcellus kept coming up here, and why he let him.

Dear Beans, Marcellus was thinking to himself on his way downstairs. This was the true reason he valued his friendship with this plebian farmer, his tenant, that Beans was genuine. And in Beans' household Marcellus was made to feel comfortable, relaxed, at home. The slaves here were informal, vulgarly so, and Marcellus was shocked at first. But among these workers of the soil Marcellus could climb off his high horse altogether and relax, body and soul. He did not have to act the noble knight. He did not have to wonder subconsciously or altogether too painfully, as he did in the company of social equals, whether he measured up to his role, whether he was doing enough, being enough, acting enough. Here at Good Will he could be just, well, you know—just Marcellus! There really was something about Beansie's household. Marcellus had seen the change in Lucan too. That slave had arrived here bitter, tense, defiant, and he has changed. Now his face has taken on a fresh innocent look, which also reveals some sort of inner exuberance. Marcellus himself went home refreshed, in high spirits.

Quintus parted company brooding, depressed. He knew that in a sense Marcellus was right about not marrying Letitia. In this sense he felt obligated to leave slave women to slave men. Yet in another sense he knew that Marcellus was very wrong. In Christ there is no slave or free, and he was a member of the Living Body. Here he could make a clear demonstration. Here also the common faith of the household could be used in his favor. Gaius regarded Letitia as his, and here again, Gaius took too much for granted.

What would his parents say? Quintus knew that of course they would exhort him to choose a spouse from his own social level. But who would marry a veritable serf? Yet he must not steal from his slaves the only woman they had. He could request that Lucan minister to his erotic needs; this was one of the intimate duties expected of a body servant. But because of his new faith he did not exploit that right. Furthermore, he would rather satisfy his drive with the object of his passion. Yet he must not pluck the beloved ewe lamb from the poor man's breast. He continued to walk in daydreams and to dream sensuous dreams at night. He instructed himself in Ovid on the art of love, and in the eroticism of Martial and Catullus, and he looked up that troublesome bit about the wandering womb sickness, until he felt he must see Letitia married to someone else in order to remove the temptation from himself.

Even then temptation would have a way of sneaking in. Roman custom gave him, the master of the Estate and therefore the Best Man, the right to lie with the bride before her bridegroom took her. The custom was helpful to the bride as she wouldn't have occasion to begrudge her husband the pain of her first intercourse.

CHAPTER XIII

Bonded without bondage

"I-I've got something to tell you, Lucan," Letitia said.

"What is it?"

They sat together on a marble bench in the formal garden. Supper was over, and the busy world hushed, shadows had lengthened and evening come. They met briefly before reporting for the night, Letitia to her room and Lucan to his master. Lucan had something to tell her too, a distressing decision, and he did not know how to bring it up. Letitia tremulously presented what was urgent on her mind.

"You know I've said before that I am terribly lonely," she began.

"Yes, I know," he said gently.

"I tried to tell Gaius again. He wouldn't hear me! I have told him many times before, still he doesn't give me enough attention. He becomes impatient as though I have no right to ask it of him. He says I must trust that what he is doing is more important. Imagine! Really, Lucan, it's that he simply can't give himself beyond a certain point. He just keeps on working his head off all day in the fields and bends over his vegetable accounts and planting charts at night, and the only time we get to see each other is at meals when I must help wait on everybody else. You know, Lucan, this won't do. Since he refuses to be companionable, I in my loneliness cannot help noticing other men. If he won't be a companion, perhaps someone else will! He isn't taking care of me; I am lonely to the point of . . . trouble." She looked down.

"So you get the roving eye?" Lucan commented, half amused.

"Of course!" She was startled at the way he put it. They chuckled. He put his arms around her and she leaned against his pounding heart. Being near him made her breasts ache and made her secret place wet and full. Would he do anything to cure it?

"Lucan, make me into a woman?" she pleaded wistfully. "Let's have a child right away so they won't separate us? Please, Lucan?"

"That wouldn't stop anyone from anything," he answered gravely. "We're slaves, Letitia, remember?"

"Why Lucan, Where's your courage?"

"Christ!" He withdrew his arms and held his head, his face screwed up in pain. Then his gaze became far away as the horrors of the past surfaced in his memory, horrors that he had survived solely through gut courage. She tried to comfort him but he turned away to hide the threatening nausea.

"But you do love me?"

"You know it! I love you as my little sister. I'm confused too, Letitia."

"I see." She was taken aback.

"Don't you agree that right now we shouldn't play with fire?"

"Meaning?" She searched his face intently in the fading light.

"I'm afraid the reading lessons must stop," he said regretfully.

"No, Lucan," she pleaded, "I don't agree."

"Must I run away to make us behave?"

"No! No, if the state should get you . . ." her voice wavered.

"What then, Letitia?"

"I need you, Lucan."

Her declaration made him feel very uneasy. "Turn to Gaius again, Letitia. Be more insistent at his door. Be specific about what you want. Call him out of himself."

"Supposing I decide to break my engagement with Gaius?"

"All right! Do it! Then see what you want. But don't turn to me as an out to your problem. That's not loving, Letitia, that's called exploiting. And I don't like being used."

"Is that so!" She rushed into the villa to hide her tears from him. She was trying so hard to avoid being exploited only to find herself accused of exploiting! Of course he was right, but he didn't have to hurt her like that! She was mortified to run directly into Olipor, and when he gently guided her to a quiet part of the house to soothe her troubles, her reserve was gone.

Olipor had been watching Lucan and Letitia meet together, but he hadn't tried to stop them as Postumus had; resistance would make the young people only more determined and secretive. He came to realize that actually Lucan would be the better match for Letitia than Gaius. Even though Olipor had admonished his son repeatedly that in comparison with spiritual riches worldly matters were not worth a Christian's pursuit, Olipor found himself clinging to the selfish and worldly desire to see his household restored. His son as the groom, and the bride, would no doubt receive among other wedding gifts the precious gift of freedom. And Olipor dreamed of grandsons, freeborn, who would restore his real name and line. The house of Ophelus shall rise up again, and diligently manage Good Will, their ancestral home. Yet there was nothing much, really, that Olipor could do to bring this about. His advice to Gaius regarding his son's relationship with Letitia was met with the maddening indifference of youthful rebellion. Gaius wished to work out his own life his own way. As for Lucan, Olipor knew that were he to try, he could not do much about the domine's wishes for his favorite.

Now that Olipor learned from Letitia that Lucan would discontinue seeing her for the sake of Gaius, the old overseer breathed relief. Lucan had better! Olipor thought. Then Olipor perceived the painful discipline that Lucan was imposing upon himself and a profound respect for the youth welled in the old man's heart. Lucan, surprisingly enough, had the right spirit in him. Lucan was giving the household no mere lip service. He would develop into a true servant. In spite of himself Olipor could admit that Lucan had the solid stuff in him that Gaius had not, and could predict that Lucan would surely acquire great responsibility one day.

* * *

Quintus, strolling through the formal garden that same evening, had come upon the two young slaves sitting together on a bench. He hurried on, pretending to be absorbed in the fresh fragrance of the moist chilling night air. Could it be, really? He wondered. Letitia and . . . Lucan? After what he said about stealing Gaius's girl? Clutched by jealousy, Quintus went into the villa. Lucan was nowhere to be seen. Nor was Gaius. He got himself a scroll and settled in his father's office, the alcove of the atrium.

Soon Gaius came into the atrium by the front door, blushed at being caught shortcutting through the family entrance, and turned back to go out and around to the stable court.

"Gaius, where's Lucan?" Quintus asked deliberately.

"I'll find him for you, sir." Gaius went out again and resumed what he was already doing, looking for that renegade who had sneaked off with his girl.

He found Lucan sitting on a garden bench, his face buried in his hands.

"The Domine wants you," Gaius informed him curtly.

"Thanks, Gaius."

"Where's Letitia?" Gaius asked suspiciously.

"She went in," Lucan admitted openly.

"She had better."

"Listen, Gaius, you've got to do something for Letitia."

"Do for her! What do you think I've been doing all these years! I've been preparing for her the greatest gift she could hope to have."

"That gift of yours could come as a wedding gift to both of you," Lucan suggested.

"I'm not counting on that," Gaius had reason to reply.

"She's lonely, Gaius. What she really needs is . . . she needs . . . intimacy . . . with her man."

"And what concern of yours is that?" Gaius's voice tightened.

"It pains me to see you neglect her. I am discontinuing the reading lessons, Gaius, and it may be a good thing for you to take over. Really, friend, if you do not at least take her into your arms, at least tell her you love her, someone else will!"

Lucan dodged the fist intended for his jaw, and went into the villa. He wondered how a son of warmly affectionate parents could have an overdose of constraint in him, whereas he himself who had a background that could really result in withdrawal could accept his own and her human nature. It was as though he were being liberated from the demons by the grace of God.

Lucan sought out his master immediately.

"Why, Domine, you are working down here!"

"And why not?" Quintus snapped. "Can't I do what I please in my own house?"

"Pardon me, sir, I meant that you usually . . ."

"Read upstairs," Quintus finished. "It's as lonely as the shadows of Hades up there with my companion nowhere to be seen."

"I'm sorry I neglected you, sir. It won't happen again." Lucan sadly knew in his heart that he would not be neglecting his domine again for the same reason as tonight. Then he felt resentful. Quintus wanted you at his side always. More accurately, Quintus assumed that you desired nothing else but to be at his side always. He called it companionship. Lucan called it slavery; there was scarcely any room for him to have a life of his own.

Quintus dropped the matter, except that he resolved to speak with Letitia the very next morning about the matter of her marriage. After breakfast he asked her to come upstairs to his library when she was finished washing the dishes.

Letitia irrationally gave Kaeso unprecedented confidence.

"Kaeso, I'm frightened. Please don't tell, but I think the young domine has ideas about me. He has been watching me closely ever since I came of age.

He saw me and my man in the garden last night. He pretended not to see us, but I know he did."

Kaeso's first reaction was, which man? Instead he replied, "Letitia, you know what's in your heart and I know you can take care of yourself. I'll wait for you at the foot of the stairs. Just call if necessary. The Lord be with you." And Kaeso could hardly wait for Postumus to come in from the kitchen garden so he could tell him. While cutting ham and adding it to a pot of bubbling beans, Kaeso stared wistfully at Letitia's well-developed form and nicked his thumb.

With this reassurance from Kaeso, Letitia went up to her young master. When she saw that Quintus was awkward, her fear deepened. "You would see me, Domine?"

"Letitia," he said in attempt to invite confidence, "do not call me Domine. Come . . . come here . . . come sit with me and talk with me, the man behind the title." He guided her over to his couch and they sat down together.

"Remember, Letitia, when we used to be playmates?"

"That was pretend, Quintus."

"And this is for real. I want you to open your heart to me. Would you be married, Letitia? You are sixteen now. We must look after your needs."

Letitia's eyes widened and she chose her words with care.

"Quintus," she addressed him with deliberation, "I would be glad for your permission to marry, only if it is the man of my choice." Her own daring frightened her.

"Would he be . . ." the hesitation made butterflies in her stomach . . . "Gaius?"

"No, Quintus." Letitia intuitively wondered if he were saving himself for the last.

Quintus looked intently into her face. "Is it . . . Lucan?"

"Domine, no other." She watched him closely for his reaction.

"Will Lucan have you?"

Letitia fidgeted with her hands. "I know he would if it were arranged, otherwise he will consider me only his sister and wed nothing but his freedom." Her voice betrayed her frustration.

"And you would marry him on those terms? Marriage is serious, Letitia, it is a sacrament!"

"Quintus, I was about to remind you of that. I won't marry unless both partners are willing."

"And you think Lucan ever will be ready! Letitia, tell me, why do you forgo Gaius? He has been promised to you for years. His love is time tested. Now does Lucan take your fancy because his love is new?"

Letitia answered quickly, defensively. "New? After three years of—" she caught herself. "Lucan is the only man here who . . . " she faltered. "I cannot help but respond to someone who calls me into being."

"Who . . . what?" Quintus was mystified.

She answered slowly, reflectively. "It is as though, while with him, I discover who I am, as though he is inviting me to become what I was meant to be in the fullness of life. And I see not only myself and himself, but also Christ who . . ." she stopped and stared wide eyed at her master, for he was looking at her as though he thought surely she had gone out of her mind.

"And Gaius?" the domine asked softly.

"Gaius does not know that I am human."

"And what must one do to prove that one regards you as . . . human?" Quintus chuckled.

Since he had to ask, he probably would not understand the answer, but Letitia attempted it anyway.

"See my person inside my woman's body, my person whom Christ is calling into being." She was dead serious, though the thoughts had only now come to her mind and lips.

"And that person is different than the submissive Christian wife?"

"Quite, sir."

"Lovely is the Christian wife, like precious oil on the head that runs down onto the beard."

"If you don't have to be a thing, like that precious oil," she muttered sourly, with the emphasis on thing.

He laughed. "Your ideas will get you into trouble, Letitia."

"I know, sir."

"And if you don't win Lucan?"

"Then I won't marry," Letitia experimented with the new idea and trembled in her earnestness.

"Incurably idealistic. We can't let our only young woman go to waste, so to speak. You must understand that you will marry, after all, and whomever I approve," Quintus reminded her firmly of her status. "Every single man here earnestly desires you." His eyes narrowed slightly. "Including myself."

"Oh you beasts! You horny beasts!" Letitia buried her face in her hands.

"Don't you have desire?" he queried sharply.

"Of course. But I don't hide in the cellar steps to steal a kiss and I don't push people into a wall to rub against them, or greet people by groping for their breasts."

"Too bad!" Quintus was amused.

"I would happily be bonded with someone, but not in bondage. Can you understand?"

"Only too well. You feel like a commodity, however precious." Quintus took her hands. "Marcellus thinks we should pass you around for a fee and raise a communal brood. I want to give you a choice."

She shuddered.

"Will you listen to me?" he continued. "You must understand the impact that you have on us men. You must be careful about the choice of him with whom you will share your womanly gift. And Letitia," he added with a touch of awe, "you have the gift of new life in your power!"

"Really, Quintus." She looked at him contentiously.

"After all," his eyes twinkled mischievously, "you are a seedbed of excelling virtue."

"No, I'm Letitia, child of God," she said under her breath.

"And I intend to determine who plants that garden."

"That's up to me, Quintus." She stood up, shocked at her own daring.

"What did you say?" He tried to sound offended but he was actually enjoying her spunk.

"Whatever pleases my Domine," she submitted quickly. Fear prickled the back of her neck.

"No, say it. You haven't finished. Is that what Lucan is teaching you? What to think?"

He is teaching me how to think, to know my mind."

"And I'll instruct you to know your heart," he impulsively changed his approach. He stood and took her hands again. "I saw you two in the garden last night. He had his arms around you. Does he really regard you only as a sister?"

"As some sort of inaccessible goddess!" She was close to tears.

"Then I'll teach you how to become accessible to him!" Quintus offered. "Here. Sit down. Don't be afraid."

She obeyed.

"Now." He took her hands and placed them on his chest. "Caress me. My arms, my neck, my chest. Go inside my tunic. How does it feel?" He had asked Lucan to depilate his armpits for him in anticipation of this encounter. He noticed that Letitia practiced the feminine charm of depilating her arms. Was she depilated down there too?

"By Hercules! You've got muscles!"

"The better to embrace you with, my dear. Now. You must encourage him to caress you like this, Letitia." He reached inside her clothing and gently felt her breasts. "Holy Venus, you have a lovely pair."

"To nurse babies. Do they please you?"

They sat there touching each other, and their breathing quickened and deepened. "Now down here." He guided her hand to the loincloth over his manhood standing like a tree among its protective underbrush. The he put his hand where her holy mountain would be hiding beneath her undergarment.

"Do you understand what is happening?" he asked.

"I understand." She felt the garden gates yielding.

"See how effective that is?" He clutched her to himself and poked his tongue into her ear. A shiver of delight ran through her and she felt desire she never knew existed. She leaned very still against his breast. Quintus could have impaled her right then and there sensing her desire, but it was against his principles to take advantage of her. He nibbled the back of her neck. Then he propositioned her.

"Let me come into your garden, Tish?"

"You honor me, Quintus, but the gate is locked and the key is hidden in my heart." She knew that she had no right to refuse him.

"Good girl, you've learned how to make a gracious and eloquent refusal." Then he added gently, "I can always force the lock."

"No, Quinnie!" Panic seized her. "I mean . . . !"

"Not unless you say so."

"You are most considerate, sir." Why should she refuse? Her body really wanted him, her childhood sweetheart, her strong but gentle master, and wanted him now. Hungry advances from Sextus and promises of painlessness from Marcellus only made her feel degraded. Lucan refused to allow desire in his life because carnal passion had destroyed his family and nearly himself. Gaius seemed not to realize that eros existed. If Quintus would only take her, right now, and get her over with her initiation, then she could offer herself to Lucan without his having to worry about hurting her. Then perhaps she could heal him. But she was afraid to make that little response which would bring her fantasy into reality.

Quintus broke into her fantasy. "Ah, Letitia, how I would like to have you at my side, my wife, my helpmate, my companion, my lover, my cuddly one in the lonely of night. How very much do I want you to surround us with our children. My beloved Lucan, bless him, cannot do all that for me."

"That's exactly what your beloved Lucan can do for me," she replied gently.

"Indeed!"

"I'm sorry, Quintus." She was trembling.

"I appreciate your honesty," Quintus said sadly. "I have already offered him permission to marry. He declined. You'd have to win him over, that is."

"Quinnie, you are such a dear." She brushed a lock of hair back from his eyes, and her hand shook.

"I love you, Tish," his voice wavered with emotion. He touched her lips with quivering fingers and kissed her on the eyelids.

She ran out of his bachelor quarters and left him there, alone, sick with desire, on the couch. Kaeso met her anxiously at the bottom of the stairs.

"He respects me," she beamed.

* * *

During the rest period someone came upstairs to the library, and the footsteps were not Lucan's. Quintus looked up impatiently from his reading. Gaius stood before him. The sensitive slave looked unhappy. When I am most troubled myself, Quintus thought, that is when my slaves will not leave me alone.

"What is it, Gaius," he asked, annoyance in his voice.

At this Gaius knew that things were not going to go well but he could not withdraw. "Domine," he complained, "Lucan has my position. Now you are offering him my woman too? What's to come of me? Domine, is this fair?"

Quintus answered quietly. "Gaius, you take too much for granted. If it is my desire to assign a certain thing to one slave and something else to another, is that any of your business? How can a slave ask what is fair? You must obey me. That goes for all of you!"

Utterly squelched, Gaius turned and left without a word. Of course the domine was right; the domine was the domine. At times like this Gaius could cheerfully hate the domine's guts. Especially for alluding to the Risen Lord's words in his reply. Gaius shuffled dejectedly back to his room.

"Gaius?" Olipor called softly from his door. "A word with you, son."

At times like this Gaius wished that his father would not habitually drag him into his room and offer advice, in the domine's favor, of course. How could the man be so damn devoted! So selfless! He could hate his father for it, except that his father was also understanding and gentle towards imperfection. And his mother, who was in the room, he appreciated for keeping her counsel to herself.

"Little son, what is it?" Olipor asked gently.

"Do I have to yield everything to the domine's wishes? But everything?"

"Obedience is a slave's very nature, my son."

"But when he proceeds to invade my personal affairs isn't there a point where I must plant my feet and stand firm?"

"Gaius, how can you become your domine's utterly dependable steward if you keep seeing to your own interests?"

"Dad, you can't be serious?" Gaius shook his head.

"Nothing but serious, son. Our domine is patient and condescending towards a slave who is not wholeheartedly devoted. Of the slave who gives himself the domine asks even more and expects it. Nothing is enough short of total commitment, and that commitment, by the nature of the task, he tries beyond endurance."

"The tyrant, Dad!" Gaius exclaimed under his breath.

"It seems so, son. However this is not unlike the way God acts; praise be the Lord."

Gaius seized his father's arms. "You're telling me that God is actually placing his finger on me and saying, I will you not to be Quintipor, and not to marry?"

"Sometimes he does that, for example the prophets, his own Son—did you say not to marry?!"

"Can you believe it of me, Dad?" Gaius's grasp tightened with his unwillingness.

"It's possible, nevertheless don't put as much energy toward questioning as toward willing to yield to God's will."

"Oh Dad, this Christianity! This Christian Way!"

"I know, son, I know."

Gaius stumbled over Alexis on his way to the privy, then brooded in his room while Olipor clutched his own breast in prayerful struggle and could not be comforted by his wife.

Alexis got himself up from his rude awakening and went outside to relieve himself. While going by his sister's room he peeked in and noticed that she was not there. He seized upon the opportunity, and looked for her in the formal gardens. She was alone reading, in a niche of the maze where Lucan had transplanted ferns and wildflowers. Lucan was given time off to pursue such projects as this, Alexis grumbled to himself. Silly Greek!

"Letitia!" he spoke abruptly when he reached her.

"What are you doing here, Alexis?"

"Waiting for Lucan? You like him, don't you." Alexis jumped into his subject bluntly.

She studied him briefly. "My brother in Christ," she answered casually. "My tutor."

"Love him? And I don't mean 'in Christ'."

"Whatever gave you that idea?" She didn't think he was on her side.

Alexis would not let her dodge. "If you really love him, you had better leave him alone. You belong to Gaius."

"What do you think I am, a piece of property?"

"I'm warning you, Letitia, if you want Lucan unharmed . . ."

"You're being ridiculous!" she flared.

"I am dictating to your sense of duty," Alexis admonished.

"Duty!"

"You must obey the young domine," Alexis insisted.

"And become his wife!" Letitia retorted.

"His wife!" Alexis was scandalized.

No way could she retract that blunder.

"Well, the same goes for him. We have warned you, Letitia!" Alexis was adamant. "And don't go crying to Ma and Pa either." He left her as abruptly as he came.

Letitia was intimidated. She knew in her mind that her brother was right; she could not let her heart, or her master's heart for that matter, upset the natural order of things in the villa that the top manservant gets the bondswoman. And if she cried on her parents' breasts, her mother would give her a sympathetic ear, but her father, typical man wanting to fix things, would hasten to arrange marriage for her—with Gaius. Yet why should the order of things be right merely because it was customary for the overseer to be married? She was increasingly convinced that an arranged marriage between herself and a man of Gaius's uptight sort would not be right. And must she not work up the self-confidence to say so? Exhortations were quoted to her about how she would be valued inasmuch as she would humble herself, subject herself, obey. What really hurt was the implication that she must deny her emerging self. Doesn't duty at times call upon one to make a stand with the courage of conviction?

Come night, she fretted in bed. Problems, problems. And why should they concentrate at a certain time of the month with her? She had dusted Aristotle on The Generation of Animals thoroughly enough to understand what her menstruation was and why she had to have it, but why did she have to go through this ruthless self-appraisal along with it? That she should produce worthy material upon which some man's moving cause would work? Have I failed? she asked herself. Is there something bad about me that drives them mad? Including Lucan? When I snuggle up against him during the reading lessons and listen to the pounding of his heart, he gets hard in his loincloth and pushes me off. And Quintus . . . he would consume all of me . . . body and soul. Is my own body to be my worst enemy? Then why was I created this way? I'm not sure I want to be a mature woman! She stewed and tossed and turned over her exaggerated problems, and wept over Lucan until nearly morning when she finally slept out of sheer exhaustion.

Her mother, understanding what time of the month was approaching her, would let her sleep. Letitia, for the next five days or so, would not be permitted to prepare food anyway, nor could she walk in the kitchen gardens lest she look at certain vegetables that would surely wither away at her mere glance.

* * *

In the dark of the same night Quintus moaned in his dreams and stirred in his bed. The sound woke up Lucan.

"Are you all right, Domine?" he called solicitously.

"I can't stop thinking of her," Quintus replied. "Oh Venus alive, I wish someone would marry her before I fall on her! When you massage me the way you do, I pretend it's her. Marry her, Lucan, so I don't lose her to them!"

"I can't do that for you, sir!" Lucan was shocked.

"Weren't you thinking of her yourself, there in bed?"

"I won't lie to you, sir."

"Then do it, for the gods' sakes!"

"Own me, share my wife?" His master had absolute right to demand it, but Lucan was incensed that Quintus would even think of using him to gain access to Letitia. It was one thing to be his master's utterly devoted servant, but quite another to be used to exploit another. "No, Domine, *totus tuus* ends there."

"I don't know what I am saying, Lucan. Merciful Venus! Such dreams! The weights on the warp are too damn tight! It hurts! Help me, Lucan, you can help me!"

Indeed Lucan had not escaped being an officer's chamberlain in complete innocence. He knew more than he cared to divulge. Submerging the revulsion of the past with compassion, Lucan got out of his bed, went over to his master and in the name of Christ devoutly ministered unto him with his skilled hands and gave him the gift of peaceful sleep.

CHAPTER XIV

The way of the world

Almost two weeks slipped by in routine hard work. Baltus and Manius hoed the grain fields and weeded the meadows while jackdaws and crows followed behind to gobble up exposed grubs. Gaius, Olipor and Old Servius set out vegetables. Alexis and Paulo pruned and grafted fruit trees and fertilized them with olive oil lees. From his vantage of the sloping orchard Alexis kept a sharp watch on the villa and Letitia's comings and goings, nor did he relax except when Lucan had followed Quintus up in the vineyard to help Sextus and Megas heap soil around the vines.

As soon as he could get his flocks out to graze each morning under the watchful eye of Cerberus the sheep dog, Mamercus worked in the commercial flower beds in the formal garden and was joined by Gregor afternoons. They sowed berries of laurel and myrtle for garlands and set out ivy for wreathes in constant demand at market. Between meal preparations Postumus and Kaeso put the kitchen garden in order, and established new vegetable seed-nurseries according to Gaius's plans. The three women assembled and prepared earthenware jars in which they would soon be packing and pickling fresh sprouts, stalks, and flowers of herbs. Then they began grinding the dry ingredients for making quick digestive syrups to be stored in pots for medicinal purposes.

Gaius continued to flop into bed nights immediately after supper and record keeping while Letitia tried to read of an evening and could not. Lucan was not a little distressed watching this, but he kept firmly to his decision.

On a fine, sparkling morning Mamercus took advantage of the dry air to muck and air out the stalls and sheep pens while the flocks grazed in the meadows and the horses and mules lazed in the stable court. Sextus helped. The sun was burning off the barnyard urine and the pungent aroma wafted up to the upstairs library.

Life was good, and Sextus played his boyish prank again. He let the cocky, aggressive rooster Acribus, devouring, the one that would rush you and claw your face unless you carried a stick, into the pen of hens. Sextus watched with satisfaction as Acribus chased down the already fertile hens and raised general bedlam until he found a hen that would squat obligingly for him. Letitia heard the frantic cackling and leaving her mortar and pestle ran out furiously.

"Get Acribus out of there!" she yelled at Sextus. "The hens won't lay when they're pestered like that."

"Aw, but he looked so frustrated on the wrong side of the fence," he drawled.

Letitia squealed and punched Sextus soundly on the shoulder and charged into the henhouse after the rooster. Sextus followed her, presumably to help. "Got you!" he crowed and pinned her against the wall. He seized her breasts in his hands, smothered her cries with a wide mouthed kiss and rubbed his body against her until he came in his loincloth. She pummeled him with her fists.

"You have to admit that you want it, Letitia. I'm really going to get you one of these days."

"Sextus, get away!"

"What's the matter, Letitia, don't you like being pinned down like a hen?"

"I'm not a hen!"

"Then how about stallion and mare. Meet me in the loft and . . ."

"No, Sextus."

"I won't do anything you won't let me, promise."

"You already have."

"Come with me now, or I'll tell on you in here with me."

"And I'll tell on you and the ewe."

"Holy Priapus, woman!" he ejaculated. "You do that and we'll all tie you to a beam and impale you like only men can and leave you hanging there until you bleed to death."

She knew from her mother's accounts of the state sentence in the brothel that men are quite capable of erotic violence. Her mother had also reassured her that men were capable of great tenderness, that some day she would be giving herself to a young man at Good Will, that both would be instructed beforehand so that the act would be gentle and lovely and would create a bond between them. She refused to be intimidated by Sextus.

"Who would do such a thing," she challenged icily.

"Gaius," he said.

"Gaius! As though he's interested in woman flesh!"

"And there's Lucan," he said.

"Lucan is blocked—up here," she tapped her head. "You didn't know that, did you. Who, Sextus, my brothers? My father? The older men? Megus who lives for his wife's memory? Don't threaten me, you scoundrel!"

"The Domine," he said triumphantly.

"Get out, Sextus."

"Cold woman, I know what will happen to you. One of these days you will be on your bed aching for someone to lie with you, and we will all laugh in your face. Then you'll have to gratify yourself with a dildo like some lonely widow."

She attacked him with her fists. "I said get out!" She chased him out of the henhouse. He caught her hands and stole a kiss and ran laughing to the stable court.

"Get out!" she yelled after him. "Get out!" she yelled at the rooster. "Get out! Get out!"

Through his chortling Sextus managed to tell Mamercus. Only Mamercus did not think it so funny. He immediately left the stable court and went to the chicken yard to help restore order out of chaos. He did not like the idea of Letitia's smooth arms clawed, bleeding. He did not know what had come of himself lately, he who used to laugh at Sextus's pranks. Whereas before, at the Feast of Pales when ewes were bred, and his fruitful flocks were a constant reminder of his own barren longings, he could admit his desires to the Lord and obediently rededicate his celibacy to the Lord's service, he found now that his frustration had the better of him. He yelled savagely at the big rooster.

"So you think you are so smart! You think you are so smart on top of the world like that!"

The fierce voice drew Quintus away from his morning bookkeeping at his desk and he went to the library window and looked down into the poultry yard with an amused chuckle. He saw Acribus beat a fast exit, and Mamercus bow at Letitia's thanks, take and kiss her hand, and walk away with stiff strides.

She lingered at the doorway of the hen house and smoothed her hair. She innocently emanated female sexuality and desire. She was a bright blossom beneath the trees. The spring flowers could be enjoyed by all, but she was to be the *letitia*, the joy, of only one. The current question in everyone's minds was, which one? Quintus found himself rapidly forming his own opinion as to which one. Why not? He nodded in agreement with his own thoughts and went back to his desk.

Lucan, still at his desk, asked to be dismissed, and went downstairs.

Letitia returned to the kitchen where Gaius was now standing at the door.

"I saw the whole thing," he accused.

"Then why didn't you help me!" she snapped back, tears starting to her eyes.

"You can take care of yourself very well," he drawled sardonically.

That hurt. "Gaius, you don't care!" She stepped past him into the kitchen only to bump into Lucan.

"Are you all right?" he gave her one of his searching looks.

"Are you all right?" she flung back at him, and attacked the mortar ferociously with the pestle.

There was that uncomfortable feeling again! That ambiguity as to how she was regarded. It wasn't her imagination, it was true! She knew how she felt! Hurt! Shaken! She didn't like herself when things like this happened to her. She resented the men who imposed such situations upon her. She was uncertain as to whether she were elevated to something special, or thoroughly degraded to an erotic object. Just an object. There was no way to clarify this uneasiness with anyone. They wouldn't understand. You're growing up, the women would say. Bitch the men would call her at worst, or at best, all you need is a good lay. Not even Lucan would understand, for he desired her also in his own painfully guarded way that made her feel guilty for being attractive to him. She must lick her wounds in silence, grim, lonely silence.

An uproar of laughter and jeers broke out in the stable court. Quintus ran down to see. They had thrown Sextus in the horse trough to "cool him down." He was drying himself off by running around in his soaked clothing and embracing everybody.

* * *

During the rest period Quintus stood at his upstairs window. He could hear the hoopoe poo-poo-pooing in the olive grove and the ecstatic skylark over the meadow. He saw Letitia go out the back door, through the kitchen garden to the formal garden. He knew what her errand was, and he prickled with jealousy. He was rebellious at all his noble self-persuasion to be the perfect, unselfish domine, all the while life was passing him by! Marcellus was more than due to return to see if he had taken any action regarding her. He could not dismiss the possibility that the literature was right. He had to put his personal doubts and moral scruples aside and do his duty towards her. More realistically, he had to take the courage of his passions and act accordingly. He was uncertain about how to get her to cooperate.

He went in to the balcony and followed it to the corner bedroom and stood at the window there and watched her disappear into the maze. Well, he concluded, Lucan hasn't come up yet to be dismissed. If I am not around, he will wait until I appear. Quintus quickly slipped downstairs and out the atrium door to the formal garden.

Almost instinctively he found Lucan's fern and flower niche in the maze. He picked a wild clematis blossom and offered it to her.

"Don't get up! Thought I'd find you here. Alone?"

"Yes, sir." She was very alone. Without Lucan. In this secluded place. Panic seized her breast.

"Under-the-bed books?" he guessed. "Don't be embarrassed. Need help?" Laughingly he sat down next to her to help her with her reading. She was cutting her teeth on Greek poetry now. He scanned through the scroll. It was just like Lucan to select the works of Sappho, a poetess, for her.

"Here," he said, "here is a good one for you,

"The Blast of Love:
Like a mountain whirlwind
punishing the oak trees,
love shattered my heart."

Letitia smiled and her eyes moistened.

"And here's one for me,

"Ungiven Love:
I am dry with longing
and I hunger for her."

Letitia drew breath and held it apprehensively.

"And this is a good one for Lucan!

"Shall I?
I do not know what to do:
I say yes—and then no."

"Oh Domine!" Her voice quavered.

"Where is he, anyway?" he asked, knowing very well that Lucan would be waiting in the upstairs library to be dismissed.

"We have stopped . . ."

"The reading lessons?"

"Everything, Domine, everything!" She broke into weeping.

"That must be very painful."

"More than you can realize—" She stopped abruptly, for had she not rejected him, her master?

"You still have me, Tish." Here he was again offering himself, with his ever deepening capacity for tenderness and empathy, forged by his growing relationship with Lucan and tutored in erotic detail from the great love books. His disarming charm and magnanimity struck a response in her.

"Oh Quintus, I would live in your house forever, but how can I be your . . ." Letitia wanted to be more than a concubine but could not bring herself to say it.

"My what, Letitia?" he asked softly, feeling out her expectations.

"Surely you don't intend to marry a mere slave!"

He looked at her silently. Indeed he had no intention of cohabiting with a slave. He would not tell her this. He wanted her to want him for himself, not for her freedom.

"You are right," he answered in a low voice. He saw the hurt come into her eyes. He made as to leave.

"Quintus . . ." she called swiftly and put her hand on his arm. She was suddenly afraid of losing him too.

"Letitia?" He wanted her to admit it.

"You were going to—you said something about a lesson?" She finally got it out tremulously and blushed deeply.

He laughed and put his arms around her.

"Yes. Remember? I am to teach you how to know your heart. May I give you your next lesson, Letitia? I want to search deep in your garden and find that key to your heart."

Not that! Yet now that she had failed with Lucan, how could she refuse her domine? What was Lucan afraid of? What was Gaius avoiding? What was all this violent pressure about from Sextus?

"Answer me, Letitia?"

She had no right to refuse. She wished that her gentle master would just take her instead of pressing her for unwilling consent.

"Tish?"

She wanted a relationship. Not on the condition of freedom in some nebulous future when her purchase price would be saved up, but today, now, so she could live through every day's dailyness. If only she could determine her own life! Not purchased by anyone! And not like this! She felt trapped.

She started to cry softly.

"There, there," he soothed, "it's going to be all right, it will be all right. Lean on me, Tish, just lean on your Quinnie."

He drew her back up closely to his breast and wrapped his arms around her.

"Remember when we were little children and we used to pretend?" he murmured into her ear and she giggled nervously.

"Well, for real there are twelve postures of Venus! Can you imagine? I'll teach them all to you. That will take time. By then we will be bonded, like true husband and wife, and love will be confirmed between us."

When he nibbled her neck and gently fondled her breasts, she felt that tightness in her private place. She could hear his heart race and could feel the firmness in his groin pressing against her buttocks. His breathing came heavier. He was no different than the others.

"We'll work in our separate spheres by day. But at night," he breathed, "oh! At night we'll have private times together, like now. We can read poetry, then put Eros to shame." He slowly undid the knot of her girdle and reached under her dalmatica to fondle her breasts and belly directly. He noticed with amusement that she had not yet depilated herself down there.

"Do you like what I am doing to you, Tish?"

"It disturbs me . . ." She had never let anyone do this before.

"It's a good disturb, isn't it? You can disturb me too, Letitia, I would like that." He placed her hands on the insides of his thighs.

She began to believe him repeating to her how wonderful she was, as the sentiment was becoming reciprocal.

When he loosened her loincloth she permitted it apprehensively. She marveled at how his strong farmer's hands, forceful with pick or shovel, could also be so tender with eros.

"Will you tie your girdle in a double knot for me, Letitia?" Again he was proposing to her.

Her body double-crossed her resistant mind.

He proceeded quietly. "You know how we farmers spade the virgin soil, how we probe lightly to test for resistance, then we set the blade and drive it firmly with the heel."

"Stop! Quintus!" She suddenly wrapped her legs around him to throw him off, but that only allowed him to penetrate completely.

"It hurts!" she gasped, utterly overwhelmed at the splitting pain.

"It isn't supposed to! I followed instructions," Quintus declared, puzzled.

"Says who! What instructions!"

"The expert." He was stricken at having exposed himself.

"Marcellus?!" She suddenly scissored her legs around him and struggled.

"Lie still, Letitia! It can hurt only the first time and you've done exactly as I was going to instruct you."

"I am trying to throw you off, dummy!" she panted. "Please get away from me!"

"Tish, we've already broken ground!"

"I'm going to be sick," she gasped frantically.

"You're going to be just fine." He met her frightened look and keeping her pinned with his body he kissed her gently and made sharp love bites on her neck to distract her and give her time to adjust to his presence.

Is this what her body wanted! All that longing alone at night with aching breasts and moist secret parts—for this! Sextus's threats about their all impaling her and leaving her to bleed flashed into her mind. She recalled her mother's account of being painfully forced when sentenced to the state brothel for being a Christian. And now she was being initiated, not by the Best Man, to prevent her from resenting the Bridegroom the pain of the first union, but by the Bridegroom himself.

"Quinnie," she pleaded.

"I'm making you into a woman, dear," he murmured into her ear.

She clutched at his buttocks to keep him still, but misinterpreting her action for passion he became overcome with excitement and cried out spontaneously with a pleasure that she did not share. She wept softly with bewilderment and deception. He kept her in embrace and caressed her and talked soothingly to her.

"How do you feel?"

"Taken!"

"I'm sorry that I hurt you," he apologized. "I suppose—that's the way it is—and forgive me, I wanted to storm that garden gate myself."

"You stormed it," she sighed.

"You needed it as much as I did," he replied.

"If you say so," she answered in a small voice and felt a twinge of resentment at his male presumption.

They fell asleep in embrace, and when they awoke he began caressing her again. She responded shyly with an exploratory touch. Was he really up to it again?

"Shall we try another posture?" he asked winsomely.

"Not Marcellus again."

"Where else did you expect me to get advice, from your mother?"

"Quintus, don't you dare!"

The absurdity of the situation was too much for them. They broke into giggles, like two naughty children. He pulled her over to straddle himself.

"This is called the Horse of Hector. Pleasure yourself on me, Letitia."

"What do you mean?"

"Hasn't your mother told you anything?"

"I haven't asked," she lamented.

"Well, you had better start asking now. You're a woman, Letitia. You cannot deny it any longer. You should be wanting some of that promised joy." He pulled her down.

It didn't hurt again as he had said it wouldn't, but he had to work at his fulfillment this time.

She tried to think of Lucan, but it was no use. She simply felt forced, like that poor hen, and hated herself for letting herself into this situation.

When he was finished she felt thoroughly rutted.

"How do you like being a woman?" he gloated.

"Is this what the fuss is all about, Quintus?"

"Holy Venus." He sat up. "You have to admit that you liked it!"

"I have to admit that I wouldn't leave my father's house and follow someone to the end of the world for this."

That stung, but he quickly decided not to be offended. "I haven't found you yet. Patience. You'll see. It takes practice."

"Practice?" The idea scandalized her.

"Ah, yes! We've tried only two of the postures of Venus. There are ten more! And you will find joy, I promise!"

"Shh! Someone's coming!" She grabbed up her loincloth and girdle and plunged through the bushes like a scared rabbit.

"Lucan! Lucan!" she called in bewilderment, her insides throbbing.

Quintus watched her quizzically, rearranged his clothes, and picked up the scroll to take back.

Suddenly Lucan appeared through the maze and Quintus met his silent accusation.

"What are you doing here!" Quintus queried sharply.

"Would it be improper for me to ask you the same question?" Lucan returned.

"Most definitely," Quintus retorted.

"I-I couldn't find you. Letitia—didn't she call me?"

"She did. And perhaps now you won't be afraid to take her." Quintus placed the scroll firmly in Lucan's hands and made his way to the villa.

Lucan found Letitia wading into the swollen stream, and snatched her out.

"Can't I even wash without some hot poker out to get me?"

"I told you not to play with fire!"

"So what are you going to do about it, big brother?"

He clutched her to himself and angrily spanked her on the buttocks. She pounded him on his back.

"You're jealous! You give me up to Gaius because you know he is safe. You can't tolerate me with anyone else. Yet you can't take an erotic relationship can you, Lucan Oikonomikos. Have the weights been taken off your warp? So you can't make love to a woman?"

"Letitia, if you don't get into the house fast, I'm going to hit you again, this time with a long, stiff pole, and I won't be gentle."

"You just do that, big brother," she retorted and continued punishing him with her fists.

He forced her roughly to the ground, tore at his loincloth, and slammed himself between her thighs.

"Are you capable only of rape, Lucan?" she gasped, suddenly terrified. "Lucan! Lucan!" she screamed to penetrate that glazed shield over his eyes.

Suddenly he saw not Letitia but his terrified little sister long ago in the clutches of the drunken Roman soldier. Only the soldier was himself! A wave of nausea overcame him.

"*Mio Dio!*" He got up and pulled her to her feet. "Letitia, Letitia, have I abandoned you to this?" He tried to gather her struggling into his arms.

"Yes! You too have betrayed me, Lucan. Everyone! Down to the last man!"

"Did he hurt you?"

"You are hurting me, Lucan."

He released her and saw his white hand-marks on her arms.

"Forgive me!" He stood and watched helplessly as she walked out of his life. Then he returned slowly into the villa by way of the atrium door.

Letitia slipped into the kitchen only to meet the entire household assembled and agitated.

"So you've been out with him," Alexis accused.

"He's had her!" Sextus observed her loincloth in her hand.

"My—laundry." She would have to soak the cloth in her own urine to get out the blood stain. "What! Do you want me to wash my bloody loincloth with yours?"

"You've done with your monthly," Mamercus observed.

"The Domine's had her!" Alexis conjectured.

"What is this! Some kind of trial?" Letitia snapped.

"She screamed for Lucan, I heard her," Kaeso argued, accusing Quintus.

"She screamed at Lucan, I heard her!" Postumus countered, defending Quintus.

"Was it the domine?" Alexis demanded.

"Gaius, take and discipline your bride," Olipor said.

"I make no use of the match with you!" Gaius denounced Letitia.

"Nor I with you!" Letitia retorted.

"Why, children!" Dorothea chided.

"Seriously, now," Mamercus advised Gaius softly, "take the advice of your husbandman. You should mate with her immediately Gaius, then the child will likely be yours."

"The plague take it!" Gaius refused to serve as second cock on the fertile hen.

"What child!" Letitia was shocked.

"This is the fourteenth day in your month, is it not, Letitia?"

"Do you keep a calendar on me too, Mamercus?" she retorted, close to tears.

"Come with me, men! We'll show the young domine what he can and cannot do!" Alexis cried.

"Oh no you don't!" Lucan strode into the kitchen from the atrium.

"This is one battle you won't have to fight for the sun of your life Lucan Oikonomikos," Alexis snarled.

"Lucan Legerius!" Lucan insisted on his allegiance. He seized a cleaver and blocked the doorway. "Not him! Me! It was I!"

They stared at him in disbelief. He sought Letitia's eyes. Without words passing between them, Letitia understood. She was horrified at his self-sacrifice. Her anger at him diffused into anxiety.

"Do you hear," he roared in anguish, "It was I! Letitia! Tell them!"

"What do you want me to do!" she scolded. "You jealous prigs! Lie with each of you, one at a time during rest period?"

She fled to her room, Cara behind her.

"Get him! Cut him! Mamercus, get your scalpel!" Alexis shouted.

"*Ad malem crucem!*" Lucan posed, ready.

Gaius suddenly attacked and disarmed Lucan with a blow on the forearm. Lucan struck him on the neck and sent him sprawling. Dorothea cried out and rushed to her son.

Alexis closed in. Sextus seized Lucan's hands from behind and twisted him, back to his back, and held him spread eagle over his bent shoulders. Paulo quickly grabbed Lucan's legs and knelt and held them taut. Lucan was suspended and quite helpless.

"Mamercus! Get over here with your knife!" Alexis shouted.

"You *carnifex*, you!" Lucan cried in anguish. "Olipor! Help me!"

"Out of the way, old man!" Alexis shoved Olipor aside.

Mamercus closed in. They pounded Lucan murderously with their fists and tore at his loincloth with the knife.

It was more than Sextus could wish on him. He remembered something and interfered before they cut Lucan, pleading Christ for strength, but not before they beat him senseless.

"Wait! He didn't do it!" Sextus rolled Lucan off his back and let him slump to the floor.

"What!" they chorused.

"He can't! Letitia said so!" Sextus affirmed. "He gets sick!"

Alexis shook his fists at the upstairs office. Mamercus and Dorothea carried Lucan to the sickroom.

By this time Quintus reached the kitchen from upstairs where he was aroused from sleep by the commotion. His guilt concerning Letitia released itself in uncalled-for anger.

"Now what is the cause of this beastly disturbance!"

He was met with united angry silence. They could not lawfully tell him that they were rioting about him for that would be direct accusation.

"Will no one be a spokesman?" He looked from face to face. *Mio Dio!* What do they know!

"Olipor?" Quintus challenged.

Olipor avoided his young master's gaze.

"You are the overseer, Olipor, my father's faithful steward."

Olipor faithfully remained silent. He bowed his head.

"Gaius?"

Gaius's eyes narrowed with bitter resentment, and he rubbed his neck. "I am forbidden by law to speak," he answered through his teeth, forbidden as a slave to accuse his master.

"By the Gods!" Quintus exploded, missing their intimations completely. "Are you plotting against me? Someone had better answer, and fast!"

They silently simmered in hot resentment.

Suddenly he had a flash of intuition that he had power over them only because they allowed it, and at this moment they were on the verge of not allowing it. He experienced fear for the first time in his life, real scalp-prickling, gut-freezing fear. If he panicked he could be a dead man.

"I give you permission to speak, Gaius," he insisted firmly.

Dorothea came into the kitchen from the sickroom and addressed Quintus quietly. "Domine, the boys have been fighting. Please, Lucan is asking for you."

"So! You are picking on Lucan again!" Quintus's helplessness before his men made him livid. "Who is domine here anyway," he scolded. "Me? Or you? By Jove you are subtle! Because I am also a serf do you think you can outnumber me? Remember that you are still slaves and I am yet free. Or again do you pull me in as a convert, and in the name of your ever-loving God exert your pressures over me?"

"Yes!" a voice entered from the stable court, "see what love they have for each other and for you their domine!" It was Marcellus. His remark stung like a chariot whip. "I have come to introduce love to Good Will, Quintus."

"You and your love can get back on your horse and go home!" Quintus retorted. "I am introducing discipline!"

"Aha!" Marcellus ejaculated knowingly and turned around at the kitchen door to go.

"And it isn't that either!" Quintus shouted after him, whereupon Marcellus replied "Then forty lashes each!" and chuckling with amusement rode for home.

Quintus returned to his scolding, his eyes blazing with anger. "Now exactly what do you men think you mean by your grumbling about priority and seniority! About certain among you being homebred and Lucan scum off the street! Do you think that you can earn any favor with me? Do you think that you can obligate me with your good service? As though I cannot request you to do more? Fools! The best you can do is live up to your duty, if you can even do that much. For what domine will say to his slave when he comes in from the field, 'Come at once and sit down at table,' instead of saying to him, 'Get my supper ready, and dress yourself and wait on me while I eat and drink, and you can eat and drink afterward'? Is he grateful to the slave for doing what he has been ordered to do? So you also, when you do all you have been ordered to do, must say, 'We are good-for-nothing slaves! We have done only what we ought to have done!' I will have no more talk from you about your reward, what you have done and what you have earned; whatever you shall receive shall be like that which I have given Lucan: pure gift.

"Do you hear? He did not insinuate his way up; I have promoted him to prove my power over him. I chose him. What is that to you? You must obey me. Now get out to work, all of you. I will not sentence you in anger for you would get neither justice nor mercy." Quintus strode resolutely out of sight, then made for the water closet and vomited.

Not a man moved. The domine could not have delivered a more effective rebuke if the problem were merely one of jealousy. But heaped upon their knowledge of his sin, the rebuke based on a parable of the Christ only fanned their fury. They each indulged in self justification until with some pertinence Olipor led them out to work. He set them to hard physical labor and spaced them widely so that they had no choice but to drive their fury into the soil. "Really, my friends," he admonished them, "who among us has not been forgiven a transgression?"

When Quintus entered the sickroom and saw Lucan lying there battered and unconscious, he let out such a cry that Letitia came running from her room. He clutched her in alarm and drew her down beside him on their knees. He leaned across Lucan's breast and moaned and listened for heartbeat.

"Lucan!" he called solicitously. "Lucan! Beloved, don't leave me!"

It is Lucan's father calling to him and pleading from the beam while the soldiers assault his mother and sisters. His brother is run through for resisting. He engages in a terrific battle with the soldiers. One pins him down, but not before the women break away and flee. He blacks out from pain of that elusive source.

"Lucan!"

He regains consciousness at the sound of his name. That soldier is bending over him, with a sister in his grasp. No, it's Quintus. And Letitia? He hadn't rescued the women at all. In fact, another seduction had taken place, however lovingly, and he hadn't been there to prevent it. Then what did he do? The last thing he would believe of himself. Violence. He beat her. Then he lusted after her himself. He was justly punished. He moaned deeply.

"Lucan!" The soldier—no, it's Quintus—called his name again. Lucan was really awake now. He looked at Quintus, bending close to his face.

"The cost of being the Quintipor is high," Quintus mourned. "Preciously high. Lucan . . . are you . . . willing?"

Lucan tried to look at him through puffy eyes. He doesn't know what the fight was really about, Lucan thought. *Mio Dio*, he doesn't know. And I am not going to tell him. The domine's face blurred and slipped in and out of focus. Lucan had a question to answer.

"I am Quintipor," he mouthed through swelling lips. He meant neither commitment nor resignation, but an obedient statement of fact.

It was enough for Quintus. He rested his face on his Quintipor's breast and wept.

The slave, as though willing his semi-conscious body once again to obey, painfully slid his hand across his chest to his master's head resting there and closed his fingers into his master's thick, curly nape, as though clinging to life itself.

It was too much for Letitia. From the many times that she had held Lucan, his head cradled in her breasts, and heard him through his bitterness and anguish, she would not have guessed that there was such a powerfully mutual bond of love between these two. Though she wanted that sort of intimacy for herself, it terrified her that she may come between them. She got up from her knees and departed in awe.

Later Olipor returned from the fields and slipped into the sickroom himself. One thing he wanted greatly to know from Lucan. If the young man were guilty as he intimated, why did he beg Christ for strength during the beating, instead of mercy? He found Lucan in a sweat, his head turning from side to side. Olipor mopped Lucan's brow with cool water until the youth quieted and focused.

"It is finished, my son," Olipor soothed, "you have done well."

Lucan's eyes widened in alarm. "No, no, Olipor, you have it wrong," he murmured.

Olipor ignored the denial and spoke carefully. "This is what the Lord means by taking his cross—the pain of reconciliation—you must bear the consequences of what your domine is." Lucan opened his mouth to protest, and Olipor continued quickly. "Yes, Lucan," he concluded, "blessed are the peacemakers and blessed are those who are persecuted for righteousness' sake, for the Kingdom of Heaven belongs to them!"

"Olipor! Please do not gut me!" Lucan cried out and turned his face away from him.

The overseer seized his arms so that he looked at him again and said fiercely, "I would like to see Quintus take the beating that you got!"

"No, no Olipor!" Lucan groaned and prayed that no one else realize that it was Quintus and not he.

Olipor, convinced that Lucan was innocent, went back to work. Lucan sank under again.

When the world focused again, Lucan was alone. He became only too aware of the impossible task he took upon himself. Lucan . . . are you . . . willing? O God, do you too love me only as I walk the straight line? I am undone for I cannot walk the narrow path. I betray you again and again . . . I am not any good! Oh Lord! Sometimes I wish I never knew what you demand of us! Oh the beast, Lord, the beast that my domine is! And I have to obey him! I have to kneel down and untie his shoes! It is bitter, Lord. I have deeply respected him. I have tried to serve him as I would you, Lord, and he has let me down.

Lucan, are you willing?

Lord, is this really what you want me to do; make peace? O Lord, this is despair to me; this kind of love requires of me a sinlessness that I do not have.

He who unties my shoes shall never be let down.

I would serve you, Lord.

Lucan, are you willing?

Lord, help me. Lucan yielded to the subtle pressures of love and slid into sleep.

CHAPTER XV

A stiff-necked people

Quintus went into a deep depression upstairs. He refused to come down for food and drink that evening and the next day and had the household so worried that Olipor went upstairs to him with a tray of food. Quintus refused to acknowledge him. He even refused to respond to word that Lucan was pleading for his master to come to him.

During the rest period the household consulted among themselves. They were desperate for Quintus to resume command before Marcellus found out and inflicted all hell on them. They tried another approach. They sent Letitia to coax the Domine back downstairs, "whatever it takes."

Letitia went upstairs to her master's room, tapped on the doorjamb with her foot, and entered. She put a fresh tray of food and wine down on his desk and stood at his bedside. He lay on his bed, his back turned. He did not move. She knelt at the bedside and leaned over him.

"Go away," he commanded harshly. I don't want to see any of you. I want Lucan. Only Lucan can come to me. Only Lucan loves me. Only Lucan understands me. All of you tried to kill him. I will have nothing to do with anyone until Lucan is able to come to me himself."

She placed her hands on his shoulders and caressed the back of his head and neck like a mother comforting a child. When he did not respond she felt under his tunic and caressed his chest.

"Will you accept me in his place?" she whispered into his ear and nipped him sharply.

"Tish!" He turned and seized her. "Oh, Tish, you have come to me!" he moaned into her neck and drew her up on the couch. He manipulated her onto her right side and fumbled urgently with her clothing. He was at first shocked, then very pleased to discover that she had depilated herself for him.

Ai! Is this a man's response to everything? She felt a little resistant at first, but she gave in to him. Why not, if it would comfort him? Perhaps she could experience some of that promised joy. Would she get pregnant? The next generation could be born of such compassion. No, Mamercus said something about the fourteenth day. She was past that now. She assumed that like his ewes and sows she would need to be serviced within hours of her readiness to take. She was on her way to her next flow, she knew. She felt the usual heaviness, her neck was unquestionably enlarged, and her breasts were tender. It would be the full treatment, complete with cramps, she could tell. She already had a touch of nausea. Did the ewes experience anything like that? Did they take so long to feel gratification? She would have to ask Marcia some time about this goddess of intercourse and get more information before she married. Meanwhile she would have to bring that tray up tomorrow . . . and the next day . . . and the next . . . She was losing awareness of everything except the two of them. Her toes curled and her head tilted back and she broke out into a sweat and felt a whisper that promised to be a shout. She held him closely when he let out his little cries followed by a sigh of deep satisfaction.

"What posture was that?" she asked dreamily.

"The most restful," he said.

She basked in the warmth and tingling and noted to herself that she hadn't even thought of Lucan.

"You felt that, didn't you? Therefore perhaps you will conceive. I'd like that."

"But we can't even think of such a thing! I'm not supposed to be doing this!" She sat up alarmed.

"Didn't the household send you up here in acquiescence?"

"No! The household sent me up to persuade you to come down and resume command."

"Then why did you offer yourself to me?"

"To get your attention!"

"You have it! And here's my answer to the household!" He pulled her down again.

"Go screw? Is that your answer? Ouch, Quinnie, my breasts!"

"Then stop fighting me! Stop wiggling like a harlot, trying to avert my arrows. If you conceive they can't separate us! I shall give you my quiver full of baby!"

Letitia gasped. She had used the same argument on Lucan. An argument from helplessness. Very well, then, she thought angrily. Exactly what did those men mean using her gender indirectly, instead of appealing directly themselves, to get Quintus's ear? The cowards! Damn them anyway, putting her in a situation like this! And her mother, how could her mother help but know what would happen? Letitia recalled how once Quintus had stood between herself and the rest of a rather exploitative world during a vulnerable time of her life, and she had depended on him to protect her. Only now he was doing no such thing! He was acting frantically from a position of weakness! How dare he use her like that!

"Respond to me, Tish!" he demanded in frenzy. "Answer my call!" He sought her with his hands, his mouth, his whole being, reaching into the depths for her heart.

She responded to him with a vengeance, and when he slacked off, dampened by his self-imposed fasting, she got after him with her hands and teeth so that by the time he emptied his quiver within her she was experiencing some of that promised joy and was quite beyond herself. They sank under embracing, then returned to day, they knew not how much later.

"You felt that too, didn't you?" he whispered complacently in her ear.

"Against my goddam will," she castigated herself.

"Tish!"

She wrest herself free. "Where's your basin and pitcher? I have failed the household."

"No, you have succeeded only too well! With you at my side I know how to answer the household."

"I can't go down there smelling like love." She got up and proceeded with her ablutions.

"Why not? We need more love around here. You're going down with me, the master." He got up and started dressing. "Right now you and I will face them together."

"You want to use me as a shield!" she gasped in shock.

"My shield, my comfort, my strength, my reason to be."

She stared at him dumbfounded.

"Isn't that enough for you?"

"Find it within yourself, Quintus." She shook her head in disbelief and finished dressing.

"You want me to be a rock, a goddam rock!" he fumed.

"You had better be if you're going to stay in command of this place!" She snatched up the used tray and headed for the door.

"The last time someone tried to walk out on me like that I flattened him at the door with a flying tackle," he threatened harshly.

She turned and looked at him full face. "And you've regretted it ever since."

"To Hades with you, Letitia!"

She hurried on her way before he could discern how terrified she was becoming at her own insubordination.

"I have no regrets, woman," he shouted after her. "To the contrary, Lucan and I found out what we meant to each other, and I have the best damn Quintipor that I could hope for."

She faced him again. "Your best damn Quintipor is grieved that you haven't come down to him. He feels that you don't really care for him, that you want him healed only so he can serve you. That's bitter, Quintus."

"Well dammit, doesn't anyone down there allow that I may have feelings too?"

"Am I not someone? I try to attend to your feelings and you knock me up and send me to Hades."

"Now, Letitia!"

She ran out before he could find words. To her consternation her parents were waiting anxiously in the peristyle.

"Well?" Postumus pried and took the tray. "How did it go?"

Tears started to her eyes. "I have failed," she sobbed. "I have failed the household, and I have failed him. Oh Ma, I have made a terrible mistake!"

"There, there, now, dear," Cara took her in her arms. "You did your best." Then Cara looked over her daughter's shoulder and exchanged a knowing look with Postumus.

* * *

Quintus put on his best tunic and dug into his trunk for his toga. He hadn't worn it since the day he was admitted into manhood. He wrestled with the damn thing but could not get it right. He descended to the kitchen and commanded Dorothea to fetch Olipor.

Upstairs again he fumbled through the cabinet, pulled out the codebook and laid the scroll on his desk. He looked through it while he waited for Olipor.

By the books they should all be flogged for quarreling amongst themselves. Marcellus was right. Forty lashes. How was he to do that? Flog Gaius himself, and command Gaius to flog the next, each chastened becoming in turn the chastiser? He smiled at the sting that would deliver.

They should all be nailed up and crucified for gathering against him. And how was he to do that? Hire an executioner? That would be Olipor's problem to carry out the order. Then who would bind Olipor to the beam? "Ha!" he snorted.

And then who would work the farm? Men, God knows whom, that Marcellus would send up? Incorrigibles out of prison? The *desperati* off the ship? One stowaway alone gave him enough trouble!

Olipor would plead for mercy. He knew it. Had he not himself already set the precedent by showing mercy to his own Quintipor? He had no choice. He couldn't dismiss them for disciplinary reasons, boot them off the land. The Colonate bound them to him forever. He was in a bind. He had to remain the master. He must retain control. Justice. Justice? How can one presume to do justice with slaves? That was a contradiction in terms. He threw the code on his desk and slumped on the bed.

"My son." Olipor approached in a conciliatory manner. In days past Quintus would have wept on his beloved pedagogue's shoulder without losing face, talked the matter out thoroughly and gotten on with life. Not this time.

"Dress me," he ordered coldly.

Olipor obeyed, and in gathering up the toga off the desk he swept the codebook to the floor. He picked it up and blanched. Quintus was up to something drastic. Olipor knew what Aulus would do. Aulus would mete out justice to the letter. Was the son, after all, like the father?

"What do you intend to do, sir?" he asked hoarsely.

"Throw the book at them."

"My Lord, have mercy on us!"

"Mercy! Did anyone have mercy on Lucan? I'll give them mercy!" Quintus snatched the code and waved it viciously at Olipor. "I'll give them mercy; not one iota shall I overlook! Now listen to me! I shall have audience with the men. One by one, alone. Send the troublemakers in yourself. You are not to breathe one word of explanation to them, nor they to each other. I shall be in my father's office. Now go."

"At once, my lord." Olipor knew that the life of the household balanced precariously on the reflexive I. He obeyed carefully, thoughtfully, prayerfully. He chose his own son first. Gaius saw him approaching and stood waiting. Olipor clasped his son by the shoulders and penetrated deeply into his eyes. He chose his words carefully.

"The lord of your life summons you to the throne of judgment." Olipor held his gaze until the young man wavered.

Gaius was no fool. He ran in and prostrated himself weeping at his master's feet. Quintus neither spoke nor asked him to speak. Gaius suddenly realized that he himself had nothing on but his loincloth.

"Domine, I have been a blithering idiot. I lie exposed before you, my heart is laid bare. Lord of my life, if you can find it in your heart to forgive, as always my utmost desire is to serve you faithfully."

"Your credibility is on trial, Gaius," the master replied sternly. "Go back to work." Quintus noticed the tremble in the lithe Greek's body as the slave walked out.

Presently Alexis appeared and made for the stairs. His hair was wet from the bath and he wore a clean tunic. Damn, Quintus muttered to himself. Cannot Olipor even now obey instructions?

"Alexis!" he called sharply.

"Domine?" Alexis turned and his eyes widened at the awesome sight of his master wearing the toga and sitting in state.

"What ever are you doing!"

"Olipor sent me," Alexis approached carefully.

"Why?"

"He said that my domine wishes to see me, sir."

"Your domine—wishes—to see you?" Quintus repeated sarcastically.

"That is all, sir. I am here."

"Why did you clean up, then?" Quintus's tone accused him.

"For the kill, sir." Alexis replied simply. He sniffed a little laugh.

"What do you mean by that!"

"A confession, sir. I am the leader of the disturbance. I was not man enough to admit it in there."

Quintus took the confession in brooding silence.

Alexis looked circumspect. Wasn't the domine going to ask him what the riot was about? Wasn't he going to give him an opening? Alexis tried again. "I am most anxious that the wrong man does not get chastised."

"You shall be flogged, Alexis. Report to me tonight."

"My lord is most merciful." Alexis managed a bow and departed in straight-backed irritation.

Paulo was beside himself with trembling. "I was overcome, sir. Believe me, I have learned a lesson."

"Learn your own mind, Paulo. You are not your brother's shadow."

Sextus wet his loincloth in terror. "I won't do it again, sir," he pledged.

"See to it, Sextus. You may go." The youth turned and nearly fled.

Mamercus came in as meekly as the sheep he tended and knelt, head bowed to the floor. "Do with me what you will, my lord. I followed like a dumb sheep. I have no defense."

"Do you expect me to strike down a defenseless sheep? Get out of my sight!"

Kaeso broke into a profuse sweat. "Let me eat the bread of sorrow and drink the water of repentance."

"You do that, Kaeso," Quintus retorted at the miserable, rotund slave. "All of you are to do that!"

Postumus knelt. "Domine, your servant once watched over your boyish steps. Now your manly steps are your servant's command."

"Well said, Postumus."

Megas came in and silently made obeisance in the Slavic manner.

Balthus was serious for once.

"You would see me, sir?" Gregor asked in clueless, wide-eyed admiration and was dismissed immediately.

Manius knelt and saluted, tears streaking his mute countenance. Quintus waved him on before he would try to vocalize in groans and gestures.

Servius bent low, too stiff to kneel without aid. "The Domine's a slave serves the Domine. The Domine's a slave served the Domine's father before a him and his a father before a him."

"Go in peace, Servius."

Olipor appeared before his master once again.

"My lord." He went to his knees.

"Enough, Olipor."

"There is one more, my lord," Olipor spoke dejectedly from the floor.

"Are you accusing the women?" Quintus half whispered.

"No, sir."

"Lucan?" Quintus queried sharply.

"No, my lord."

"Where is he, then?" Quintus demanded.

"It may take him time to reveal himself."

"Just what do you mean!"

Olipor chose words carefully. "He has a long way to come."

"Have you sent for him then?"

"I have imparted to him the message."

"I am waiting," Quintus replied impatiently and Olipor arose and bowed out before he should become further entangled.

Quintus sat there, reviewing, weighing, puzzling. He had noticed who was and was not involved in the kitchen when he interrupted them. Then was it Marcellus, for God's sake? Damn that scoundrel!

Quintus retired upstairs in exasperation, pulled the toga off into a heap on the floor, and threw himself on his bed. He did not come down for supper, and had the household so anxious that they sent another tray up to him. The presence placed the tray on the nightstand and departed. He stole a glance at it. The bread of sorrow. They brought him only bread and water! Damn them! He got up, lit a lamp, sat at his desk and tried to work. Presently another approached.

"Go away"' he commanded harshly. "I don't want to see any of you until that final person reveals himself to me!"

"Domine." It was Alexis. "We have an appointment."

It was almost as though Alexis were summoning his master instead of reporting to him for punishment.

"Are you so anxious to be flogged, Alexis? To set yourself up as an example?"

"I do not deny that I deserve it, sir." Alexis looked him in the eye.

Was there a touch of defiance in his voice? A dare?

"Forty lashes, Alexis," Quintus informed him coldly.

Alexis nodded slightly. The bastard! Is he really going to do it?

"I suggest that you support yourself against the doorjamb."

Alexis returned a look of surprise. Not in the stable court? With witnesses? And an assistant to tie him up? Someone else to mete out the punishment?

When the master picked up a flagellum from the desk, Alexis swallowed. Not a simple whip. He hadn't thought Quintus had it in him. He moved with dignity to the door and placed his hands on the doorjamb. The first blow knocked the breath out of him. Soon he pressed himself as closely as possible to the doorjamb to keep the weighted thongs from wrapping around him. How much longer? Christ! I lost count! How much longer—can I—take it? The bastard!

Will he—never—go down? Quintus panted with effort to maintain the rhythm. God! I'm going to be sick!

Alexis's white knuckled hold loosened and he swayed. The lashes wrapped around his groin. "Mercy!" he cried out and doubled over on the floor.

"As you—had mercy—on Lucan!"

Alexis buried his head in his arms and moaned, and moaned, and moaned.

"Go when you are able." His master's voice cut through his senses. It was finished. "And bring in that final man! Drag him in with wild horses if necessary!"

Alexis got to his feet, bowed with a new respect although his back screamed in protest, and staggered out. He came upon his father in the kitchen.

"What happened to you? Did you fall through a hedge?" Postumus dabbed at the cuts on his son's arms with a dishrag. "Where have you been!"

"My back," Alexis breathed. "My back! What does it look like?"

"*Mio Dio* your tunic is in shreds!"

Only then did Alexis realize that the master mercifully had not requested him to strip. He leaned heavily against his father and broke into trembling. "He can violate my sister but no one can touch his darling. He can go to Hades! He is still hollering for that final man!"

"Enough!" Postumus admonished. "You must turn the other cheek; you must not even think of revenge! If the senior domine finds out, you may be a dead man."

* * *

Quintus continued to sulk upstairs and began to feel trapped in the quagmire of his own behavior. He had made a mistake, a bad mistake, listening to Marcellus and lying with Letitia like that. He made a worse mistake by sulking upstairs. He should have maintained his command immediately after reviewing the men one by one. Maintained! If he hadn't already lost it! He was amazed and not a little taken aback at the depth and magnitude of their anger. A profound resentment undergirded his beloved family in Christ. Beloved? Family in Christ? Perhaps he had been making a one-sided assumption while they still felt very much the slaves, rebellious against their master. He would be the good master, completely unaware of the contradiction of terms, until it all blew up in his face.

He could not bring his slaves to their knees by withdrawing from them, he could see that now. They had minds of their own. He had encouraged them in good faith and now he was taking the consequences. By confining himself to his room he had abdicated his command. Through his depression he tried to formulate his action to get it back.

Why didn't Letitia come back up to get him? When word was sent up to him that she was feeling sickly, he envied her the excuse to be in confinement. Women and their menses!

Plague take it! Even though he was getting a lot of book work done!

Early next morning he heard hoofbeats in the stable court. The final renegade has arrived! He is here! Quintus sat tensely at his desk for an indeterminable long time. What were they doing down there! His head ached. He threw himself despondently on the bed.

Soon he was hearing the rise and fall of singing. Psalms? Is it the Lord's Day again? He longed to be down there with them again.

Presently one of them came upstairs and stood there silently. How dare one of the men come up without permission!

"My son." Bishop Nicodemus finally spoke with deep regret.

Resentment shot through Quintus. Not the Bishop! What does he know? "Please leave me alone."

"Quintus, your household is ready for you to come down to them, so that we may continue."

Quintus sat up with an exasperated grunt. "Are they still trying to pressure me, Nicodemus? Is this fair? Already every one of them could be flogged to ribbons for gathering together as they did against my personal slave."

"Quintus, please."

"Bishop Nicodemus," Quintus entreated, "must I use force? Is there no other way? You know that I use the whip only with deep regret. Is this the price I must pay for trying to be decent? This is the time I wish I never regarded my slaves as any other than so many articulate farm implements! The Way is too involved and painful. I would have at least my personal slave as a friend and see what happens! The others beat him out of jealousy. Can't one rule with love?"

The bishop took a deep breath. This was indeed a delicate situation. He had to proceed carefully. "Quintus, your household is waiting for the last man to appear, don't you see?"

Quintus's intended retort changed into a sharp breath as he suddenly gathered what the bishop meant. They were waiting for him! He himself was the man! He himself plucked the beloved ewe lamb from the poor man's breast! He stared at Bishop Nicodemus through guilty eyes. He almost asked the bishop what the household really knew, but he prudently held his tongue to avoid incriminating himself with a confession. After all, the bishop himself was only a freedman. Nicodemus stood erect and looked through him. Or perhaps it only seemed so to his guilty mind. Your household is waiting for you to come down to them—not that you may forgive them—rather that they may forgive you!

He who had only at this Pascha completed the three-year catechumate and had been initiated into the flock with Lucan his new brother in Christ, had already proven himself most unworthy! This is how I behave within a mere month of dying to sin and rising again to new life! If I had been martyred on Resurrection Day my baptism would have been sealed; now with a whole lifetime ahead, look at me already! Quintus shuddered. 'Purge me with hyssop, and I shall be clean,' he prayed, 'wash me, and I shall be whiter than snow.'

"Bishop Nicodemus, what must I do?" he lamented.

"You are to come down and take your position at the head of your household!"

"I cannot marry the girl now!"

"No, I wouldn't try to do that," the bishop returned thoughtfully. Having been exploited, Letitia may not be able to meet Quintus in a mutual relationship.

"To Lucan!" Quintus added swiftly out of the possibility that the uprising really was out of jealousy toward Lucan and that Nicodemus did not know about his sin. If they didn't know, he did not intend to tell them.

"I wouldn't do that either. What you can do now is to come down to your household." Nicodemus, who had just spent an hour alone with Lucan in the cubicle and almost as long with the others in the kitchen, remained firmly on the sore spot though he was neither going to pressure Quintus unduly to a confession, nor break his own confidence.

"I can't just walk in there and receive communion!"

"I don't think you should either, Quintus," Nicodemus replied gently to his stubborn lamb.

"Excommunicated!" Quintus was shocked.

"You have said it, my son, until you have made peace with God, yourself and your household. You must begin now by getting dressed and coming downstairs with me."

So! Is that what they were doing during all that quietness down there, Quintus said to himself as he grudgingly obeyed. Supposing they really know? Enough Old Roman remained in Quintus to make him highly indignant that the slaves should be concerned with a private affair of his and could be protesting against what the ancients have always held and what his contemporaries still held as a matter of personal rights of the domine. The slaves had no right to interfere with their domine; it was none of their business! Furthermore it was unlawful for them to witness against their domine! And they knew it!

The Christian in him reminded him that it would be their concern, very much so, for his sake as well as Letitia's. He had to go down to them. Well, this was only supposing they knew. As far as he could tell, they did not know. Nor was he going to confess. 'Create in me a clean heart, O God,' he prayed, 'and renew a right spirit within me.' He sighed heavily, sensing his hypocrisy, and reluctantly preceded Bishop Nicodemus to the kitchen.

The slaves all waited there, including Lucan. They had put Lucan in one place of honor next to the young domine's place, and Gaius in the other. See, it was about the jealousy after all, Quintus said to himself when he noticed this.

All eyes went to Quintus as he walked in. The silence was overbearing. Sextus, who had been teasing Letitia about little dishes of oats under her bed, winked. Quintus met Alexis's steady gaze, and the slave raised hand to forehead in a salute. There, see? Postumus smiled hesitantly, and Quintus was even more certain after that. Letitia exchanged only a swift glance with him, such power had he over her that a mere glance brought a shiver to her very innards. Her hand went up to the love bruise on her neck. Lucan searched his master's face and wondered if Quintus knew he had taken the blame for him. Quintus took the long look to be one of encouragement. Good old Quintipor! Quintus nodded to his slave.

Bishop Nicodemus proceeded with the versicles in the Eucharist that look forward to the restoration of God's Kingdom.

"Let Grace come and let this world pass away," he said.

"Hosanna to the God of David!" the others responded.

"If anyone is holy, let him come. If not, let him repent."

"Our Lord, come!" Quintus joined the others boldly.

"Amen!" No sign of repentance yet on his part, the bishop observed.

So they have come around again, out of their jealousy nonsense! Quintus reassured himself. The versicles that Nicodemus meant for him, he took to apply to his slaves. This will end that quibbling for a while. Quintus tried to convince himself that he need not worry about his real guilt.

Lucan was distressed at his domine's confidence. So Quintus thinks that the household does not know about the seduction. Nor can I accuse him by telling him. Am I doing the right thing?

Quintus brought the troublesome matter up that night when Lucan moved back upstairs with him again. Lucan was on his knees before him, undoing his sandals. The slave massaged the thong marks from his calves.

"You have no idea what a relief that is," Quintus sighed. "Welcome back."

"Thank you sir."

"But why did you leave me up here so long? Why didn't you come up to me?"

"Domine, I couldn't walk!"

"Sorry, I didn't think of that. Did they do permanent damage?"

"No, sir."

"Now tell me, Lucan, truly, what was the cause of this disturbance?"

Lucan looked up at him, full in the face. The question was asked in faith. He answered in trust.

"You, sir."

Quintus averted his eyes for a moment. When he looked back he saw that Lucan was still studying his face.

"Will it ever be right again between them and me?"

"It will be, Domine, I am sure, but it may take time."

Quintus clenched and unclenched his jaw several times as emotion swept over him.

"Ah, Lucan, Lucan, why didn't you take command of me and prevent me from this mischief?"

"I take command of you, sir?"

"You're my brother in Christ, aren't you? Aren't you your brother's keeper? Sometimes you have to save me from myself!"

"I saved you from the consequences of yourself." Lucan spoke in a tone that implied, my God, Quintus, can't I do enough for you?

Quintus swallowed. He wanted to lash back at Lucan for holding the painful truth up to him. Suddenly he realized that Lucan was not condemning him. Lucan had given himself up for him! Here it was, the mutuality that he yearned for. They were at one though their unity was born in pain, and Lucan had paid the price. It remained for him, Quintus, to accept the free gift, offered in love. His eyes wavered from his intimate who looked up intently at him. He finally spoke.

"You did that for me, Lucan?"

"Is that not what you desire, for me to love you?" Lucan responded warmly.

Quintus's soul responded, 'more than anything in the world,' and again he was stabbed with wonder and awe. He heard his tongue say something quite different.

"So you couldn't make it with her, eh?"

CHAPTER XVI

House built on a rock

The air was so clear after the storm that Quintus could almost forget. Or so it seemed. While Lucan wrestled with the agony of being a scapegoat, and Letitia secretly dusted book seven of Pliny's Natural History regarding certain symptoms, Quintus plunged himself vigorously into work, his men with him. He had been through the agricultural cycle enough times now to have a firm hold on what had to be done when, and how to fit in extra jobs. His theories on restoring the land were proving to be sound and the fields showed a renewed fertility.

The household conjectured among themselves that the master was trying to bury his conscience in work, and was trying to make them do penance, except that he was uncommonly cheerful about the long summer hours and ordered extra rations all around so that no one would lose weight. Nor could the household get any clue from Lucan, for the Quintipor kept his confidences tightly to himself.

Only the Quintipor knew what was really in the heart and mind of Quintus, what the master felt about his excommunicated status, whether he was using it as a leverage upon the household, or whether he really felt the pain of separation. Quintus accepted more and more the ministries of Lucan's gifted hands that coaxed him into relaxation and enabled him to sleep, or that comforted him out of bad dreams and lulled him back to peace.

In September when Quintus contracted out the bumper grape harvest and wine making, and directed his men to cleaning and repairing the property, inside and out, their conjectures changed to worry. Why, he'll chew up the profits in unnecessary expenditures! Is he out of his mind?

Sensing their uneasiness about him, and to allay their anxieties, Quintus disclosed, a bit premature to certainty, the apparent motive behind his drive.

News had reached them about Constantine's civil victories. The soldier brothers were expected home on leave sometime before the seas closed in November, barring new outbreaks at the front. There would be an extended family reunion "like this place has never seen before. And I don't want any snide remarks from any of you about ruinously farming with a polish."

They laughed at the ancient adage and cooperated willingly at pruning and trimming, raking and composting, scraping and whitewashing, inspecting and repairing. The household didn't want the soldier boys making fun of their little brother trying to farm.

Now the briar hedges bordering the fields couldn't claw a person passing by. Now the steps to the stable court no longer threatened to break one's neck, though the shining waxed floors in the villa did. Removal of cobwebs from stable rafters and corners of rooms made it easier for swallows and bats to catch prey in the out buildings while the indoor spiders had to start patiently from scratch on the slick walls. Lizards in the peristyle had to climb into the potted plants to find sufficient litter, and scorpions were exterminated.

Finally, a messenger arrived at the villa one October morning before daybreak and requested that the young master should be aroused. He delivered a papyrus to Quintus.

"Olipor!" Quintus called excitedly. "Make ready! They are coming! With my parents and sister! Postumus! Prepare an evening dinner—lay on your best! Letitia! Get out the fine family service and set a festive table!

"Gaius! Hurry! Saddle the horses! We must be off!

"Lucan—you stay! You will be serving us at table tonight. Olipor and his family will be having their own reunion."

Lucan, the master's inseparable companion, his brother in Christ, his equal in the sight of God, was suddenly reduced to slave again. Lucan should have known. Of course. This was normal. How else could it be? What hurt the most was Quintus's unawareness, his neglect to acknowledge what was happening. If Quintus had merely said, look Lucan, you and I have to play master and slave for a while, Lucan would have nevertheless hated it, but he would have only too gladly borne it. Quintus was oblivious and Lucan was crushed. His very body reflected it with something he had not been afflicted with nor experienced in nearly three years. A hot twinge of pain visited the pit of his stomach. So he had to be the slave. When the family was around, the master's inseparable was only a slave again. Well, he would do a good job of it for his master. But the betrayal! The wounding! The bleeding pain inside! Again his gift in love, with a price!

So Lucan spent the morning helping the women get out the fine dining appointments and set the dining tables. Then he rehearsed protocol and nervously awaited the return of his master with the rest of the familia. He was not too thrilled at having to be on display at waiting table. He was no good at being on exhibit. He feared that self-consciousness would get the better of him and cause him to make a social blunder.

At sundown the familia arrived and dismounted at the atrium and Olipor's four sons took the mules and four-wheeled *raeda* around to the stable court where the household rushed out jubilantly to greet them. After refreshing themselves in the baths by scraping off the sweat and dust of the journey, the familia assembled on the curved couches around the circular table in the summer dining room. Marius, Aulus and Fulvia's oldest, a kindly and responsible centurion, sat next to his parents. Marcia the only daughter followed him, slender, vivacious, a free thinker. Next to recline came Fulvius their middle child, quiet, given to conformity. Then came Cornelius whom they call the dethroned one when they wish to tease him. Quintus the youngest took his place last.

The first four offspring came to Aulus and Fulvia as rapidly as biologically possible, then the tired womb miscarried between Cornelius and Quintus, and each time the grief stricken mother clung more desperately to Cornelius's babyhood. He was seduced, as it were, to the hugs and kisses that an independent minded little boy repels unless he is either hurt or tired. Then Quintus came along and the worn mother withdrew from the older boy rather abruptly. Cornelius grew up to dislike and distrust women.

Lucan brought in the appetizers of green onions, and pickled anchovies with sliced eggs in piquant sauce. Then he stood at attention a little space off, by the wall. So this is the familia. He listened to the snatches of conversation.

"Did you get enough, Quinnie?" Fulvia the mother asked solicitously, as Quintus was busy being host at table. "Poor dear," she added, "you're not going to have a chance to eat."

When Lucan took out the appetizer platters and brought in the salad, "This will be a real treat to you soldier boys," Fulvia said brightly. "You don't get much else but grain, do you?"

"Actually we do, at the local markets, between combat," Marius got in before Cornelius drowned him out.

"Well hell no!" Cornelius the third son was explaining between mouthfuls, "those bloody—er—excuse me, Mater, Marcia, I seem to forget that you women are at the table. Army talk, you know. A bad habit. Every other word . . ."

Lucan's eyes widened and he stared with fascination. What was it? Here was a family, so closely knit a family that they were unaware of his existence, notwithstanding his being a mere slave. And Quintus? Quintus was being coddled by his parents as the pet baby. And he, the same age? He was torn away and his family destroyed. Ten years ago seemed an eternity, yet recent enough to hurt. In a sense, the hurt deepened as the years went by. He himself needed to be a somebody in the midst of a family. His stare focused on Marcia, initially because he had not seen fashionable beauty before and was intrigued by it. Would Letitia have to help her comb that hairdo? Would the matron jab her in the breast with tweezers if she pulls on a tangle? Then he stared because his mind was really far, far away.

"Well, they didn't have a chance at Chrysopolis!" Cornelius was relating intensely their final battle. "We already beat them at Hadrianopolis in July, you know, and chased them in retreat to Byzantium where we lay siege—do you follow me, Pater?"

Aulus was obviously preoccupied with the salad bowl that Fulvia passed on to him. Surely he wasn't seeing things? Something was really moving between the leaves?

"Eh?" Aulus came to. "Well enough, Corne, go on. My battles were mostly of a different sort," he said, and the soldier brothers knew that he referred to Olipor. Aulus tried to catch Lucan's eye.

Marcia followed her father's signal up to Lucan and found him still staring at her. That's a country slave for you, she thought, so straightforward in their ways. If Rufus were here to see him looking at me like that, fur would fly.

"Will you take this salad?" Aulus meant to the kitchen.

Lucan blinked back the moist film in his eyes and, misunderstanding, proceeded to pass the bowl to Marius, the oldest son.

"Well you know," Cornelius was saying, "the navy already beat the shit out of them—"

"You're slipping again, brother," Marius interrupted mildly.

"Sorry—I mean—we were victorious at the Hellespont. Licinius sneaked across to Chalcedon, and Byzantium opened her gates. After a breather we followed him over and got a cut at him in Chrysopolis. Man, that was another bloody slaughter! We cleaned them up, we really did! We had already killed some thirty-four thousand at Hadrianopolis. Now another thirty thousand of their hundred and thirty thousand killed. Thousands more ran. You should'ave seen—"

"Cornelius, please." His mother quailed at the thought of tens of thousands of husbands and sons slaughtered in a civil war.

"Well, anyway we chased Licinius to Nicomedia where his—wife—negotiated a surrender," Cornelius derided.

"Indeed!" Fulvia came to attention.

"Constantia, the Emperor's half-sister, you know," Marcia filled in, and watched her mother's eyes widen.

"At that, Chalcedon opened her gates to us. Our regiment did itself right proud!" Fulvius said.

"And you do have to give the navy credit!" Marius elaborated. "We were outnumbered, three hundred fifty ships to our two hundred. At first there was a draw—"

"Then there was a mother of a storm," Cornelius took over. "Some five thousand of them drowned."

"Cornelius—" Fulvia appealed.

"Crispus handled our fleet right well. Sailed right on to Byzantium," Fulvius filled in.

"Crispus?" Aulus raised his eyebrows in disbelief. "The Emperor's oldest? That young cockerel an admiral already?"

"Now Pater," Quintus protested, "Crispus is only a year younger than me, and I have been a man for three years!"

Marius looked down at the salad bowl Lucan held before him and laughed too heartily for his little brother's claim alone.

"Well . . ." Aulus didn't really hear. He was trying again to get Lucan's attention. Marius was now passing the bowl along to Marcia.

"No, no Lucan!" Aulus checked the slave sharply. "Out!"

Marcia let out a startled cry and Marius giggled. Then Lucan saw it. Good Lord! Do You have a sense of humor? An adventuresome caterpillar was making its way among the tossed greens. Lucan blushed and retrieved the bowl.

"You rascal!" Aulus muttered.

"Lucan! So this is Lucan," Cornelius commented and scrutinized the slave.

This. Lucan's back stiffened and jerked a little from side to side as he walked out.

"Why," Fulvia beamed, "a mere boy!"

"He would have been made man the same year as I," Quintus said.

Would have been. Lucan was getting his attention indeed, and see what kind!

Out in the kitchen Gaius studied Lucan to determine how well his trick was working. He couldn't really tell.

Now Lucan was jolted back into remembering his instructions. He hesitatingly brought the salad back in, sans caterpillar, and he himself served the bowl to each person. The grain-fed soldiers relished the greens.

But Lucan's confidence was shaken. With solicitous attention he helped his master and the family wash and wipe their fingers between courses. He examined the platter of tunny fish before bringing it on. He brought on the roast lamb, fricasseed chicken and ham with careful manners. He made sure that the beans were done, and that the cabbage sprouts had not been overcooked. The family was seeing him in action for the first time. With the exception, of course, of Aulus. Lucan did not relish being on trial like a specimen. Would they approve of him whom Quintus chose instead of the carefully bred Gaius? Could he make up for the unfortunate incident even though it did bring a laugh? Or would the family take Quintus aside and put him to task on Lucan's behalf? Lucan was anxious that he should not cause his domine distress.

The familia was still talking about the Emperor's conquest of the East. "Tell me, boys," Aulus asked discreetly, "is it true that the army had . . . prayers . . . before battle?"

"We always sacrifice to the standards," Fulvius said.

"I mean prayers to—"

"Didn't you know about that, Pater?" Marius replied. "The Emperor's request. He has been doing that ever since—"

"Oh, just a general non-committal sort of prayer, Pater," Fulvius broke in.

"Ever since when?" Quintus asked Marius.

"Then the Emperor isn't Christian?" Aulus asked openly.

"Well," Marius hesitated.

"What about that bloody—er—what about that Christian chaplain that runs about at his elbow?" Cornelius came out.

"Who?" Quintus asked intently.

"Bishop Hosius of Cordova." Marius searched his youngest brother.

"Take a look at this, Pater." Cornelius drew out an amuletic charm that hung around his neck. "This will answer your question." He slipped the thong over his head and held out the pendant for Lucan to take to Aulus. "A gift from our Captain for valiant service. I'm too damn poor yet to have the crest changed to mine and to buy a gold chain for it. Well don't just stand there gawking, slave, put down that fruit platter and take this here charm to your lord to see."

Lucan took the amulet gingerly. The side up showed a jeweled Chi Rho chrismon where previously there had been a regimental badge. As he carried the charm to Aulus, Lucan turned it over. He nearly dropped it. Yes, he had seen this thing before! Around the neck of his second master! So he's a captain now? Lucan gave the unsettling thing to Aulus and sought refuge behind his master's couch. He searched the three soldiers' faces and scanned his memory. He sensed that their arrival meant the end of his safety.

"See that chrismon?" Cornelius said. "It has power, Pater. It actually saved me from the point of the sword."

"Yes, I know, it was under this sign that Constantine liberated Rome years ago," Aulus was saying. "Surely he hasn't really devoted himself to this god of the rabble?"

"Pater, your prejudices are showing," Marius teased.

"Remember," Fulvius said, "as sole ruler of the empire Constantine is also Pontifex Maximus of the gods, and of the state worship of Augusta. And this rabble is only one-in-ten strong."

"Sure, Pater," Cornelius assured him, "that's all there is to it. No matter what they say." Cornelius took a large bite out of his quince.

"Now I don't know," Marius drawled meekly, "some say that the Emperor achieved through earnest prayer and devotion what you think you achieved by your lucky charm."

"Really now!" Aulus said.

"You might say," Marius proceeded carefully, "that God is working out his purpose through Constantine."

"What god, dear?" Fulvia tried to participate intelligently.

"The One God, Mater, the Lord of Heaven and Earth and all that is therein, who has commanded us to preach and make disciples of all nations in his name." Marius came out with it boldly.

Then he looked down, for his parents were regarding him speechlessly.

"By Hades!" Cornelius muttered, "We would be celebrating the Emperor's triumph throughout the East and South right now if you Christians were obediently preaching baptism instead of preaching scandals."

"What's this?" Aulus exclaimed.

"You know, Pater, Arius and his dispute," Fulvius clarified.

"Are you telling me that squall stopped a jubilee?"

"Squall—Zounds!" Cornelius interjected. "It's a fucking big issue! Beg pardon, Mater. The Emperor fought his way up to top dog only to inherit an empire split by a religious squabble. In a sect he himself liberated from persecution, mind you. That's the damn scandal of it. It is really that damn bad, Pater! Licinius persecuted Christians because they were pro-Constantine. So the Emperor used the persecutions as an excuse to get a cut at Licinius and conquer the East. Then the Emperor sent an order to Alexandria that the ecclesiastical boys straighten around. Didn't work. They sent right back to the Emperor that the whole church had to be consulted on the issue. Imagine a soldier talking back! But these preacher boys get away with it! Constantine has had to call a council. At Nicaea in Bithynia. At least they acknowledge his authority to call them together. The council will take place next summer. In the meantime—well, that's how we got to buy exemptions from duty from the captain and come home."

"So the Christians are good for something," Fulvia beamed on her sons.

"Huh!" Fulvius sniggered, "they're good only for stirring up everybody with their damn controversy. Just walk through the streets and what do you hear! Buy a loaf of bread and ask the price, and they answer, 'The Son is subordinate to the Father.' And those ditties they sing in the shops! Arius put his argument to the tune of tavern dances."

"He did?" Quintus put in with glee.

> "God was not always Father;
> Once he was not Father;
> Afterwards he became Father . . .

You have to really see it to get the total effect," Fulvius elaborated. "Here—Lucan—get Artemas to entertain us. And Felix with the cithara. We want excerpts from the Thalia!"

"No, let's not," Aulus contradicted the order firmly. "We shall have enough of it later. Too much, I'm afraid. For now your old Pater will call for his sandals and retire. You young fellows go ahead and have your wine supper." He escorted his wife and daughter from the table.

"Is Papá angry?" Fulvius looked about uneasily.

"I told you he wouldn't tolerate The Way in one of us," Cornelius shot at Marius.

Marius shrugged off the attack.

The brothers lingered to live together around the table a while longer. Olipor had olives and parched peas and lupines taken in with a fresh supply of wine, sent his sons in to assist, then he bowed out himself to attend Aulus.

The lot fell to Cornelius to dictate the proportion of wine to water. He set it mercilessly high. The slaves mixed the prescribed amounts in the krater and filled the goblets for the first round. Lucan put only a little in his master's cup.

"Say—what's the idea?" Fulvius noticed.

"I do not wish to get raving drunk," Quintus said quietly.

"And why not?" Cornelius snapped. "Slave, fill his cup."

Quintus had to give in, and the soldiers' three slaves winked at Lucan.

"So I hear you are bound to the land by the colonate law, Quin," Fulvius commented. "You should have enlisted promptly on your seventeenth birthday. Now what are you going to do stuck on the land?" He drank deeply.

Quintus hesitated. "It isn't as bad as you may think," he said, wondering why he defended that very thing which galled him.

"Well, I s'pose ya can still enlist," Fulvius suggested, "ya can escape the land that way."

"Don't really want to," Quintus protested.

"Or you can enter the Christian ministry," Cornelius probed. "The Emperor has left you that loophole. Also he has subsidized the church with state funds, so you could be quite comfortable, and he has exempted the clergy from taxes and draft, so you would at least be secure."

"No, I don't have that option," Quintus commented bitterly.

"The draft," Fulvius rejoined, "the draft may get ya yet. So many men from each precinct, ya know."

"The draft is a detestable abomination," Quintus muttered into his goblet. And during the scathing from Cornelius that followed, Quintus spoke to himself. I can see now, he thought, how men bring their own slavery upon themselves. Here I am dying to get the hell out from under the colonate, and see how I deride the source of my liberation!

"Say, why d'you suppose we prepare for war an' fight th' border skirmishes, anyway!" Fulvius added his own rebuke. "To keep from being overrun by da furciferous barbarians, dat's why! To hold on to everything dear dat we have!"

"Sure," Quintus answered. "And see how we got our precious world in the first place. By greedy plunder and murder and injustice toward the less fortunate! Then we sing of our glorious fighting fathers. Of course much good has come of our expansion: a great civilized world under law and order. But where is our justice? Our responsibility? Our engineering is striding beyond our moral ability to use it to our health."

"And ya propose?" Fulvius challenged.

"Restoring the downtrodden—that is the true justice."

"An' how we gonna do this?" Fulvius pressed, "when da captives we spared from da arena and settled on deir home lands are da first ta join da furciferous barbarians dat break o'er da border?"

"I guess it isn't all that simple—I guess I haven't thought it through . . ." Quintus groped, now on the defensive.

"I guess you haven't either," Cornelius jumped at him. "What'd you do about invasions?"

"Fight, of course," Quintus answered quietly. "But . . ."

"But what?" Cornelius mocked.

"I can't help wondering if we are not too afraid to lose dear old tradition when confronted with a greater trust," Quintus rallied. "It may be the lesser evil to be overrun while doing right, than to sell our souls to exploitation!"

"*Ad malem crucem!*" Cornelius ejaculated and drank deeply.

"Come to the front with us and get a soldier's viewpoint of things," Marius suggested mildly.

"I will go when I am called. In the meantime I am not going to run away from the land." Quintus drained his cup. Here he was doing it again. Was he afraid he would be rejected at the draft?

"Hey!" Fulvius jibbed, "who in Hades do ya think ya are with dat holier than thou attitude. You'll stay on the land like you were somebody, nobly stayin' on the land!"

Quintus looked his taunting brother right in the eye.

"I am somebody. You don't have a plant named after you. An award winning plant," he declared superiorly.

"What? A plant?" Fulvius returned.

"The Legerius Early," Quintus announced proudly. "A cucumber."

"A cu-cu-cumber!" Cornelius chortled in a derisive falsetto. "Is it long and stiff?"

They all laughed boisterously and even Lucan had to turn away to hide a smile. He prayed that his master didn't notice or the Quintipor's head would surely roll in their room tonight. Quintus should have known better, he thought.

"Yea, pipinna," Fulvius teased, "an award winning pipinna!"

Quintus hid his head in his arms and his shoulders shook with laughter through tears of exasperation.

"Say, Mari," Cornelius left off Quintus and turned upon his oldest brother with a drunken drawl. "How about 'at? Dose bishops also too afraid to lose good ol' tradition?"

"They are preserving the apostolic faith!" Marius asserted.

"Dat bunch of ragamuffins elected by the rabble? Dey should resort to an oracle or th' emperor himself for a decision, like proper people," Cornelius retorted.

"What could be more democratic than a council to decide the issue?" Marius asked. "Why, it's our beloved democracy resurrected again! Issues probed, both sides heard, free inquiry, research into antiquity, open study of Scripture."

"Aw c'mon, brother," Fulvius conceded, "Dey may assemble like da senators did in the republic, but what will be so democratic 'bout binding deir decision on all Christendom?"

"Those bishops are responsible to their people, you know," Quintus entered in, "and their decision must be true to tradition, and acceptable to the faithful before anyone's bound by it. Furthermore, the Christian Fathers didn't deny the freedom of criticism, Fulvius."

"And wha' d'ya know about dat, brother?" Cornelius drawled.

"I have a household of Christian slaves, you know." Quintus wasn't quite up to admitting that he himself had been a catechumen for three years, and had participated freely in just such discussions. He looked at Marius.

"I see," Marius looked significantly at his youngest brother.

"So!" Cornelius challenged.

"I am not a communicant in the Christian faith," Quintus retorted, high on the defensive

Why, domine! Lucan thought, ashamed to profess your faith? And when his domine's eyes narrowed at him, Lucan understood. Oh—you are trying to avoid the scandalous explanation of your excommunicated status. Very well, we keep the secret.

"Well," Fulvius said, "ya 'aven't seen da kind of men da decision will rest upon, Quin. Ya 'aven't seen dose half-literate bishops of da wilds!"

"The church must 'ave a 'ell of a lot of courage ta trust 'er decisions ta a bunch like dat," Cornelius shook his head. "I can't imagine submittin' myself ta a bunch of . . ."

"Well, I can," Quintus interrupted indignantly.

"'Ows dat?"

"'Cause I've already done it."

"Ya . . . ?"

"To my household. I'm 'one of them'." It was out now, inadvertently.

"Scandalous!" Fulvius hissed.

Marius nodded approval. Quintus drained his cup.

"Ya don' know wha' ya doin', Fidus!" Cornelius pressed Quintus with his boyhood nickname given him for his persistence in following his brothers. "Ya don' know who dese men are! Take dat dere slave of yours. I know now 'ere I've seen dat ragamuffin befo'! At th' Slavic front. Jus' a lad den. A bootiful long-'aired lad. No ugly scars. No brand . . ." Cornelius drank leisurely to heighten the suspense.

"Damn!" Lucan ejaculated under his breath.

"Yeah, an' I notice dat ya keep 'im in short hair too. Is he depilated, brudder? Or does he 'ave bad breath?" Cornelius's eyes narrowed searchingly at his youngest brother.

"What d'ya mean!" Quintus flared.

Lucan dipped some wine as a pretense for bending over his master. "For God's sake drop it!" he whispered into Quintus's ear, but his master elbowed him off. "Dammit, thlave, fill my cup!"

"An' yo' slave looks naive, too," Fulvius said with effort. "You've restored 'im well, Quin, we've to admit dat. 'Cept for those scars, you'd never'd thought Priapus could ever've touched him. He ain't pruned, is he brother?"

"I wouldn't know, I prefer women," Quintus squelched his middle brother.

"Whose services, by da way, we an' our men request," Fulvius persisted.

"Who, my bride?" Quintus asked so innocently that they broke into uproarious laughter. So much for that idea, Quintus thought. Serves her right. He drained his cup again.

"I thay," Cornelius took up, "len' ya boy to me will ya?"

"Len' 'im to ya?" Quintus played naive.

"He hath a weak bowel hathen't he?" Cornelius elaborated.

"How'd I know?"

"All ya 'ave to do ith lithen to 'im fart an ya'll know da anthwer," Cornelius explained and they guffawed.

"Fart for uth, Lucan!" They erupted in laughter again.

"Ya thee, Quinnie, ya thee, dat mean hith arth's ath wide ath da gateth of Good Will, and ya tellin me ya ain't ev'n tempted brudda?" Cornelius examined his brother.

"Dat'th boarding thchool sthuff!" Quintus tried to be indignant.

"Boardin' school! Zounds! We're talking bout da furyfated pedicating army! Da defenderth of dis gloriouth empire!" Fulvius drew himself up momentarily then eased down again with a moan.

"Bring yer bowel and yer bowl over here, Femenella, an' len me have thome of dem parched peath." As the slave bent over to serve him, Cornelius patted him on the cheek with one hand and titillated him in the genitals with the other. "Dese nuth ain't parched."

Lucan backed off stiffly and bent over to fill his master's cup. "Domine, please!" he appealed, but Quintus elbowed him off. Lord have mercy! Lucan appealed frantically. He was no longer safe in this household.

Marius motioned Lucan over. "Listen, Lucan," he suggested mercifully, "you don't have to endure this talk. Why don't you go make us more parched peas and lupines, and take your time. Let Felix bring them in."

"Thank you, sir," Lucan replied gratefully. "Please, sir," Lucan addressed Quintus, "my domine's slave shall wait in the kitchen for his domine's orders."

Quintus responded by raising his goblet for Lucan to fill. Lucan had to stay.

"An no 'holier than thou' from you, Mariuth, you was a'ready wide athed befo' ya was converted!" Fulvius reprimanded.

"Ath wide ath da gateth o' Hades." Cornelius amplified.

"That's enough," Marius protested firmly.

"Whereth your testimonial spirit now, Mariuth?" Fulvius dug.

Cornelius resumed his exposé of Lucan. "Our capt'n's darlin. Fidus, wha' ya doin' wid a runaway darlin'? Ya not goin' ta be seen in da ranks wid uth, wid dis bloody femenella at ya heelth. Tink of ya reputashun!"

"Bloody? Houth that?" Quintus chuckled.

Lucan bent over and poured him wine. "Please do not ask it, Quintus, please forget it."

Quintus returned him a cold look. "Upstairth I may be Quintuth, but down here I am the domine. And don't you forget it."

Lucan's eyes tensed with shock. He looked down, then gave his master a reproachful look and backed off. He was not only unsafe, his master was not going to help him.

Quintus drunkenly pursued the fun at his slave's expense. "So wha' da ya know, Corneliuth?"

Cornelius guffawed. "Da Capt'n—ha ha—he was away couple nights . . . left his darling behind. His lieutenant lusted for da boy . . . 'ere was his chance. Got drunk and snuck in da tent at night. Caught da boy sleepin' or so he thought, chained by da ankles to da couch—da boy alwayth fettered at night, ya see. Den . . . ha ha! Da boy . . . waited for 'im . . . bit his nuts . . . whole damn mouthful damn near off!"

The men roared with laughter. "Lucan!" Quintus shouted, "like da flavor of nuth?"

"Dat soldier drew his dagger ta do a job on da feisty colt. Fainted. When he came to, da darlin' was gone, couch an' all. Dey never could even trace 'im! Gone! Never knew if or how he got rid of da couch!"

"Lucan!" Quintus shouted, "Tell 'ow ya got rid o' da couch!"

Lucan was not there. He was giving forth from both ends in the privy.

"Theriouthly, now," Fulvius backed up his brother, "you ain't gonna break our fraternity . . . with high-falutin' ideas . . . about salvagin' some disreputable critter. We four Legerius brothers are gonna be served by Olipor's four. An' dat means Gaius for you! See, Quin?"

"Now . . ." Quintus began.

"Ya gonna enlist, gonna go to da front with us, ain't ya, Quin?"

"No!"

"Holy Mithras! Is Rome gonna fall because Christ'n men refuse to worship the Roman Eagle? An' because the citizenry ain't gonna give no more undivided devotion to da cult o' da state?" Fulvius glared at his brother.

Quintus replied with great effort at enunciation. "Ith Rome gonna fall becauth of blight an' food shortage from within? The biggest empire ever but threatened with hunger from the inthide. Not enough plowshareth to feed da s-swords! An' wen we can no longer feed da populathe an' it rebelth an' da army ith busy at the borders an' can't keep internal order, what will we do? So ya thee, I have no intention of leaving da land an lettin' dis deth-desperately needed rethource dry up!" He sank down and drained his cup.

"So! 'E's kickin' at th' traces!" Cornelius took over again. "Mariuth! You' our centurion! Give our rookie orderth!"

"Now lithen to me!" Quintus leaped to his feet. "I can't go to da front wid ya! I'm a goddamn therf! An' I can't ethcape into da minithtry; I've fucked that up quite literally. Now will ya thut up? An' lay off o' my thlave. I bought 'im! I kin thow ya hith paperth! I know all about 'im—more 'an he knowth about himthelf. I know hith whole life hithtory thraight from da 'riginal thourthes. He workth well! He'th a fwend! I'll prove 'im! I'll prove 'im to ya!" Now Quintus defended his position not as the master of the villa, but as a little boy trying to justify himself to his older brothers. He reclined again, and held his cup up for refill.

"Paperth?" Fulvius sneered. "What fo'! All he had ta do was tell you who him was and we'd have hith status clarified by next pigeon. Hith master died in combat. Could've saved you a few hundred sesterces!"

Quintus returned a look of sheer frustration. He scarcely dared think of how many thousands of sesterces; they might weasel the price out of him.

"Ha! Ha!" Cornelius jeered. "Ya'd tink dat slave 'ere Lucan Fidelio—Lucan Fidelissimo! An' what he done ta prove 'imself?" Cornelius laughed rudely at his defenseless brother.

"Now, now," Marius deliberated firmly, "It's all right, Quin. It's all right. Let's not get into a red hot family quarrel on our first night home. Felix, go get your cithara! Let's have some songs! Let's have Arius's Thalia!"

"An' dammit, Felikth," Quintus added, "tell that thlathe of mine to quit pampering his weak bowel an' get back in here!"

Finally the wine supper came to an end, and the four Roman brothers called for their sandals and retired upstairs. On the way out Cornelius growled at Lucan, "If ya value ya life you'll come ta my bed tonight."

The personal slaves stayed behind long enough to clear the table; the kitchen and farm slaves had long before gone to bed. Gaius loaded all the stemware on the tray at once. These were not just Puteoli glass, but special Egyptian blown glass, a family treasure, and the slaves had been instructed carefully to carry only two at a time, one in each hand. Gaius knew better, only Gaius was tired. The newly waxed floors became his undoing. He slipped in the kitchen.

"Wouldn't you know!" He stared dumbfounded at his work of destruction. Then his brother Artemas, Cornelius's slave, had an idea.

"Comrades!" Artemas said to the other silent slaves, "Here's our chance to really get rid of Lucan!"

"Make him take the penalty?" Gaius expressed his reluctance.

"Precisely! Lucan!" Artemas strode toward the dining room. "Lucan, come back here!"

Lucan came unsuspectingly to the kitchen. Artemas seized him by the tunic. "You dropped the tray. Understand? You dropped it! You take the penalty!"

A murmur of assent rose among the slave brothers.

"What do you mean by this?" Lucan half asked, half exclaimed.

"You just try to say that someone else did it and you will have all of us to say that you did it," Artemas warned roughly. "Then your penalty will be doubled for lying. Understand? Here! These broken stems have sharp edges, Lucan. Quick and easy way out. Better than a flagellum I dare say."

At this Gaius rushed out, looking for his father.

Lucan glowered. Damn you, he thought, I've come this far; I'm not resorting to suicide.

"Here comes Aulus! Play the man, Lucan!" Leonidas said.

The murmur hushed when the senior domine in his nightshirt entered the kitchen. Lucan stood staring sadly at the broken crystal. Then he squared his shoulders and faced Aulus.

"You! You knave!" Aulus scolded. "Didn't you know that you were to carry those goblets in your hands?"

"No my lord, I didn't know," Lucan lamented. The blame was obviously fixed upon him. "I am to take the blame," he mourned pointedly, and Artemas gestured a threat at him from behind Aulus's back.

"These weren't just Puteoli glass. Do you know that these goblets were worth more than the price of two or three Lucans?"

"I don't doubt it, my lord," Lucan admitted.

"Do you realize that you could be tied down and beaten thoroughly? Or sold at the marketplace tomorrow?"

"Yes, my lord." Lucan's jaw quivered. Indeed from former 'offenses' he knew what could come his way. Many a time he was the scapegoat for the frustrations of his masters.

"I will have the overseer charge the price to your savings," Aulus arbitrated. To take a man's savings was to knock out his very hope of purchasing his freedom, and any slave worth his salt collected toward his freedom price from the start. Only Lucan had no savings. He blushed in shame. He would not admit before this audience that his master didn't make enough to give allowances to his body servant. Nor was he going to remind anyone that because of the colonate law he could not be sold off the farm.

"Well?" Aulus demanded.

"I stand chastised before you, my lord," Lucan murmured and did not look up. Aulus left abruptly and the slave brothers winked at Lucan.

"Go to bed, Lucan, you look as though you need it," Felix feigned sympathy.

"Don't forget," Artemas said, "my master awaits you."

Lucan strode out of the kitchen and bolted upstairs. His master roused when he came into their room.

"Eh Lucan," Quintus drawled, "been waitin' ta ath ya—'ow did ya get rid o' dat bed?"

"What bed!" Lucan answered vehemently. If that information were wrested from him under duress or under torture, a certain blacksmith and some grooms at the front would surely die. He went to answer a rap on the door.

"Who knocks?"

It was Artemas. "My Master says he needs a folding-stool. Come or he'll expose you completely to Aulus," Artemas threatened.

"Tell him to go fold himself!" Lucan hurled back and slammed the door in Artemas's face and bolted it. "*Crux!* The only happy man is a dead man," he ejaculated.

"Eh?" Quintus picked up. "Quoting Oedeputh? Gonna fall for dat gloriouth cwap?"

"Domine, in my worst moments I have wondered if there weren't something to it."

"Thuithide?"

"Got any hemlock?"

"Ya not gonna. Remember what Achilleth thaid to Odytheuth in Hadeth. Bethideth, I forbid it."

"Don't worry," Lucan reassured him firmly.

"Lucan Fidelio. Lucan Fidelithimo." Quintus chuckled affectionately.

Was his master mocking him? Or what outlandish boasts . . .

"Lithen, Lucan, don' let my ruff brotherth get ya down."

"No, sir," Lucan answered ruefully, "with your help, sir."

"They can't fathe me. They wan' me ditch ya an' take Gaiuth ath Quinnipor. But y' know what? I'm not gonna let 'em make me."

"Domine, if you can keep me through tomorrow I'll believe in miracles."

"Len 'em thtorm an' plot! Ya an' I thicking together," Quintus insisted without asking Lucan what he meant.

Lucan knelt down beside the couch. "Please help me, Quintus!"

"My houth ith built onna Rock, Lucan, an' no one ith gonna butht it up." Quintus sank back on the couch.

"This house is already broken by the judgment of that rock."

"Oh, bring your left hand to your aid an' get thome thleep! You've been enuf trouble tonight!"

With that insult Lucan's wretchedness was complete. Lucan Fidelissimo. Lucan disgraced and crushed with need. If only Gaius were the Quintipor! "I am the cause of your troubles, Quintus," he sobbed into the bedcovers.

"Betta believe it, Lucan," Quintus turned his back and succumbed from the effort.

Lucan went dejectedly to his own bed and hid under the covers. He was not safe, not even in his master's room. The brothers could break into the room at will. They must have done it innumerable times as boys when their parents thought them safely tucked in and their attendants snored on their pallets. Slide the bolt from its staple and sneak in together and secretly carry on with boyish rituals amid high pitched giggles. A chill crept up his spine and tingled the back of his head. He lay there listening intensively to the night sounds.

Terrifying nightmares of trying to get rid of that bed awoke him twice, the second time not until he had fumbled part way down the stairs, carrying that bed, lying to the guard about going to sleep by a wounded horse, seeking the blacksmith, only this time in reviewing the harrowing experience a gigantic bloodhound knocked him down and licked his bleeding thigh.

Lucan awoke trembling, clinging onto the railing. No one must find out how he got rid of that bed nor must he leak it out in a nightmare. He made his way back to the room.

Quintus was awake again. "For Chrithake commere, Lucan." He held up his covers. Lucan came over and slid in and pressed himself as closely as he dared to the warm body of the lord of his life, his brother in Christ, his dear friend, all he had, the only one in God's world who was not estranged from him. How he loved him!

"Hold me, Quintus, hold on to me. I don't care what you do to me—please—just hold me tight and don't let them get me!"

"No oneth gonna get ya, Lucan." Quintus was turning his back on reality, at least until morning. He would face sober reality in the morning. With a splitting headache? Despair and desolation diffused through Lucan's body paralyzing him like hemlock.

* * *

Aulus summoned Lucan the next day to his office in the atrium. The usual follow-up on discipline, Lucan knew. He was afraid. When you think you are safe, that is when Aulus strikes.

"Lucan, we both knew that you could not be sold."

"Yes, my lord. I thank you, my lord."

"You also knew that you had no savings."

"Yes, my lord."

"Why didn't you tell me?" The query was sharp.

"In front of them, sir? My domine can't afford—you wouldn't have understood, sir."

"Are you insulting my intelligence?"

"No, my lord."

"Then say at the outset that you were afraid! Don't put a slur on me! Nor on your young Domine."

"Forgive me, my lord. I am very afraid."

"What you accepted last night was no punishment at all."

"Your servant is grateful, my lord," Lucan breathed, fearing that his head was really on the chopping block now.

"Did you think you could get away with it?"

"Please, I thought my lord understood," Lucan pleaded.

"Understood what?"

"That I didn't do it! They are trying to get rid of me! Help me, my lord." Lucan softened his defensiveness with a plea.

"Now why should they want to do that?"

"I was once an officer's boy at the front, my lord," Lucan revealed dejectedly. "They don't want me to go back . . . er . . . with Quintus, that is. If he decides to enlist."

"What! Send Quintus to me at once!"

"P-please, sir . . ."

"Afraid for your skin? Last night was only a foretaste of the treatment guaranteed you back at the front. No way is he taking you there. Now go get him!"

"As my lord wishes." Lucan looked down. So he was relieved of going back to where he was traumatized. That was wise and thoughtful of Aulus. But he was also relieved of the opportunity to run away at the front. He understood exactly what Aulus was doing to him. The ax had fallen.

CHAPTER XVII

Enduring all things

Lucan is having one of his dreams again. His sister cries pitiably and he cannot respond for he too is bound. He struggles out of that horror, then slips into a wilderness setting. A little lost lamb calls for him and he cannot cross the chasm between them. As the lamb's face becomes Quintus's face he awakes out of that dream and dreams that he is getting up to urinate. Finally he did wake up and lay sweating, with his eyes open. He really was hearing the crying. But there was no orphan lamb!

Letitia! Was one of the men molesting her? At the banquet a few nights ago didn't the brothers request her services? And what did Quintus reply? Some remark about his bride. They thought he was joking. Then what did he say? Lucan searched his memory. His master neither consented nor forbade them. Eros be damned! His master had defaulted! Soldiers, he grumbled to himself, returning from combat all horny the way they do, lusting after anything two-legged or more, having ejaculation contests on the exercise field. How could I forget! Lucan castigated himself for being so preoccupied over the request for his own body that he completely forgot about her safety. He started up and made his way downstairs.

The crying came from the direction of the kitchen. It sent chills through his stomach. Only he wasn't hearing it anymore. He shuddered and used the indoor water closet in his urgency. Then he saw lamplight flickering in the kitchen. He went in and was startled at what he saw. Marcia, his master's sister sat at the table. Her lovely bosom was bare and she suckled a baby. He would have withdrawn immediately, but too late. He was caught.

Marcia looked up startled and snapped, "What are you doing here?" She distrusted the motive of her youngest brother's scar-faced slave who had stared at her intently that first night at the family banquet. Her first impression of him had been gentleness, though you can't always tell about these deprived agricultural slaves.

"Where did that come from?" Lucan replied defensively.

"From his mother's tummy, where else?" Marcia retorted without batting an eye.

Lucan had put his foot in his mouth. "I mean—why—it's cute! It's-it's so human!" Marcia's baby was now pulling her hair and laughing into her face.

Marcia felt safe now. She took up conversation. "It? He's my little boy, the little monkey!"

Lucan was really into it now. He looked down. He could not tell whether Marcia was cross, or whether she was teasing. He wished that she would dismiss him.

"Furthermore," Marcia continued, "he is more than just any little boy. He is Flavius. He is your master's nephew! Meet your master's nephew, Lucan!"

"Thank you, madam. I am sorry that I broke in on you. I didn't know that you had a baby with you. I heard him crying."

"Think the crying was some unhappy spirit?"

"Y-yes, madam." Lucan should have stopped there. In his embarrassment he added, "It's so long since I've seen a baby."

"Why Lucan!" Marcia said without thinking, "where have you been all this time!" She took a bite of meat to macerate and transfer to the baby's mouth.

"No place for women and babies at all! When I was taken from home I saw seven years at the battlefront. Then for the past three years I have been right here at Good Will, madam." He just put his other foot in his mouth. He wished that his domine had not let him into the habit of saying uncensored everything that came to mind. And why didn't she dismiss him!

"Why, Lucan Legerius slave of Quintus! Your domine was a baby here! And your domine's brothers! And your domine's sister! And Dorothea's four boys! And three of Cara's four children!" She chewed another bite of meat and gave it to her son. "This place is a home, Lucan, not an island of male agricultural slaves! Your domine himself some day will take a wife, and then there will be more babies here. Then you shall see that this is a place for women and babies!" Upon seeing Lucan's abashed look, she added gently, "And perhaps you yourself. Who knows?"

"Me? A—wife?"

"Lucan, you do know what a woman is for, don't you?" she asked dryly. And determined to expose his real motive for being in the kitchen with her, she added, "Or must I show you?" She chuckled roguishly at the look of alarm on his innocent face.

"Madam, may I please go now?" he asked helplessly.

She became very serious. "I have asked you a question, Lucan."

"Yes, madam, I know what for, I know Letitia. I mean we live together—that is—in the same villa. I mean I've taught her how to read and . . ." The harder he tried to untangle himself the deeper he became embroiled.

"Congratulations!" she was fast.

"I-I mean I am acquainted . . ." He wanted to affirm, that is all! But remembering the confession he had made for his master's sake, he broke off and stared at her speechlessly.

She was giving Flavius the breast again.

"You do know how a baby is fed, don't you?"

"Y-yes, madam," Lucan stammered and shifted his weight. "The joy of motherhood."

"Huh! How would you like to be roused out of a good sleep in the middle of the night!"

"I am quite often, when my domine can't sleep," Lucan answered softly.

"And that's the joy of slavery? Really, I am not supposed to think that way," she added.

"My domine's sister is very beautiful with her baby," he consoled her.

"Down, boy!" she snapped. Then she gave way to laughter. Victory rang in her throat.

Lucan was mortified at her interpretation of his presence. He turned to go without her permission.

"Here, Lucan, hold the baby for me, would you?" She offered her child a sip of diluted wine, then held him out to Lucan.

Lucan sat awkwardly with the baby in his lap while Marcia fastened up her tunica, and rinsed out the cup. Little Flavius pulled the neckline of Lucan's tunic down in attempt to stand. Then the scamp grabbed on to his hair.

"Hey-y!" Lucan laughed. Baby Flavius buzzed into his face and laughed a three-toothed "Heea!" Lucan felt himself warming toward the baby. He breathed in the sweetness of the fine-haired head, and tickled Flavius's nose with his nose and nibbled at the baby-lips to the baby's squealing delight. I want a son of my own, someday, Lucan thought.

Marcia took her baby back, and regarded Lucan with a matronly air. "Back to bed, little boy. A few hours yet before morning."

With an energetic grunt Flavius loaded his swaddling.

"Want me to get you some dry swaddling, Madam?" Lucan asked.

"Thanks, not until morning. His excrement helps make his skin soft and white."

Lucan made a face.

"What's the matter with you?" she challenged.

"How would you like . . ." Lucan began, then remembered his position.

"Oh all right! All right!" Marcia interrupted and turned to hide her amusement. The baby was indeed fussing.

"Here, I'll clean him up for you." Lucan tried to hide a smile.

As she was about to put the slave in his place, a Tawny Owl called tremulously.

"Merciful Picumnus and Pilumnus, what was that!" Marcia cried.

"Only an owl, Madam." Lucan grinned broadly.

"Only an owl, you say! With what witch embodied in it! After my child!" She fussed about evil spirits while Lucan triumphantly cleaned the baby.

"Here," her protector ordered, "finished. Wrap him up, and I'll escort you to your room."

At her door she became confidential. "Lucan, thank you for keeping me company. It gets spooky here during the late hours of the night. I have always been afraid. Please come in with me." With a shiver she reached for his arm.

Lucan swiftly acted the slave again and bowed to leave.

"What's the matter, Lucan, am I suddenly repugnant?"

"Quite the contrary, madam."

"One never knows about you deprived agricultural slaves. Now really, why did you come downstairs? Without your master's permission, I take it?"

"I had to piss. I don't need permission for that."

"Why, Lucan?"

"I thought—someone—needed help."

"Are you accusing my brothers?"

"Not them, madam . . . ah . . . ," Lucan floundered. "A tender lamb."

"Yes, I know, the jealous type. Here you were making eyes at me, but no one can touch Letitia, is that it?"

"Please may I go, madam."

"Get in here before I scream."

He obeyed with a shudder. She put her sleeping baby in the crib and motioned Lucan next to her on her bed.

"Don't you know what is happening to you?" she smiled coyly.

He stared at her helplessly.

"I am accepting your proposition and you dare refuse?"

"Proposition, madam?"

"What's the matter with you, Lucan, have the weights been taken off your warp?"

"Please, madam, I am a man of The Way."

"Oh, so you are one of them! Chaste. Are you also a virgin?" she asked scornfully. "I mean with women, of course."

"I am." He declared it then regretted it immediately; he had just betrayed his cover for Letitia.

"Do you expect me to believe that?" she giggled.

"Whatever it pleases you, madam," he tried to recover.

"It pleases me to initiate you, young man," she informed him smoothly. "Here . . . Zounds! but you are tense. Relax, I am doing you a favor. Yes, you are sensitive! My little brother tells me how you love poetry. Ovid, nonetheless. You copied the *Ars Amatoria* for my brother, I understand. My, how you blush! Come now. You shall be my Ovid and I shall be your beloved Corinna. Come, come," she sang.

Tears of outrage gave way to waves of helplessness. He lay on his back panting, his head thrashing as she aroused him, caressing his chest, his nipples, rubbing his armpits, his groin, his privates, nibbling his earlobes, thrusting a tongue in his ear, and finally lowering herself astride him. He rolled over nauseated. She chastised him on the buttocks, hard, until the fury returned and he pinned her down with his weight and punished her with his thrusts until he climaxed inside her.

She loved it.

Before she allowed him to stagger exhausted upstairs to his master at dawn she showed him everything in the known world between a man and a woman. Conflicting feelings warred in his head and throbbed in his chest as to whether he was now totally degraded, or somehow called into a new being, from a neuter to a sexual being, from a thing to a man, a real man!

* * *

Cara and Dorothea lingered in the kitchen after Olipor had marched the men singing out to work. None of the familia was up yet. Marcia came in soon with little Flavius to feed and nurse him.

"Good morning, dears," Marcia sang. "Another candidate for breakfast!"

"What will you have, dear," Cara asked. "Scrambled eggs? And hotcakes?"

"Um, yes, I am starving! Dorothea, get me some porridge for Flavius, would you? Any men around?"

"No, all gone," Cara answered.

Marcia put Flavius on the floor and unbuttoned the shoulders of her tunica, then scooped the pleading baby up again to nurse.

"Are you going to wean him soon?" Dorothea asked. "Look at his teeth!"

"Juno Lucina! Dorothea, please. I want another child, but not now! Not one a year like Mother."

Dorothea laughed and teased her pagan mistress. "Now Marcia! A dutiful Roman matron must perpetuate the family for the religious well-being of the living and the perpetual memory of the dead."

"Dutiful smutiful—I am a liberated woman," Marcia scoffed.

Dorothea smiled. "Besides, nursing them long doesn't always work, either."

"I found that out," Cara said from the charcoal range.

"When I got pregnant with my seventh, I thought that this would never end!" Dorothea chuckled.

"Seventh?" Marcia asked, surprised.

"I lost three, dear," Dorothea said. "But I got what counts, my four sons."

"Too bad you never bore your freedom son, Cara, just one more to go," Marcia sympathized.

"I never had a chance," Cara replied. "What with the Evil Eye and all the daimones, and whiffs of flowers and extinguished lamps, three sons and a daughter was all I could keep. Then I called it quits!"

Dorothea smiled tolerantly at her superstitious Christian friend. "It was one after another during those childbearing years. It seemed that whoever helped the midwife deliver a baby conceived next. It never failed! All you have to do is just see a midwife, they say."

"Are either of you midwives?" Marcia questioned suspiciously.

"No, no," they laughed.

"Well, Cara delivered my last one," Dorothea said. "Gaius. He came so fast that Cara had him delivered while they were still going after the midwife!"

Letitia came into the kitchen and sang out her greetings.

"Good morning, dear," Marcia greeted her. "We are talking about—you know what."

"Oh," Letitia regarded her with keen personal interest. "How was it?"

"Not bad at all," Marcia said. "I was on the midwife's chair a little less than an hour," she boasted. "Nothing at all to be afraid of. Yes it hurts, but so what?"

"Doesn't hurt more than you are willing to take," Dorothea said quietly. "And each one gets easier."

"I'll go along with that," Cara said.

"I was praying especially for you during your due-month," Dorothea said to Marcia.

"You were praying for me?" Marcia asked astonished. "To your Christ? You mean that he is interested in the affairs of women?"

"He is concerned with everything you are and do, dear," Dorothea answered.

"Did you thank him too?"

"Yes, dear."

"Weren't you afraid?" Letitia asked Marcia uneasily.

"Oh yes, a little," Marcia drawled. "I was mostly afraid during my pregnancy when I thought ahead about the oncoming birth. It seemed so inevitable. So final! No getting out of it. I was afraid my time would be long, like Mother's. Each one of hers took longer than the last. Mother said they had to call Father in before Quintus was born."

"And all the while it was because they failed to remove her eaglestone when her labor began!" Cara broke in. "She was sure the goddess was piqued!"

"Well," Marcia resumed, "I wasn't afraid when the actual time of birth came. I was excited because I would soon have my baby in my arms. Juno Lucina, gracious Goddess, was with me! And my Rufus was a dear. Lookit here!" She held out her hand to Letitia. She wore on her finger a little key shaped into part of a ring. "Rufus gave me this. It was his mother's. It helped unlock and open my womb. And also when my time came he quickened my delivery by untying the girdle of his tunic and putting it around me and taking it off me. 'I have fastened it and I am going to loose it.' Then he kissed me so tenderly before leaving the room.

"Then we laid out our food offering for Juno Lucina and Carmentes Postverta."

"And who?" Letitia broke in, eager for every bit of instruction.

"Carmentes Postverta? She is the goddess of normal quick deliveries with the head first."

"Vaticanus's spirit was with the baby too; you should have heard the child's first cry! Rufus took up the infant with the blanket on the floor and held him in his arms. Then Rufus invoked the friendly spirits, and we kept the candle lit in the room, and put garlands on the door, and oh, everyone was so happy! And I was hungry!"

They laughed, and her account ended with a bright smile.

"Oh yes," Marcia added, "know what I craved? Apples and beets!"

The women laughed again.

"Has Flavius a bright red birthmark?" Cara asked.

"No, thanks to the goddess, though I took the precautions anyway. Whenever I was hungry for an apple or beet and wished I had one, I was careful that I was touching myself nowhere else than on my buttocks, so that if he had a birthmark it would be there instead of where it would show."

"Umhm," Dorothea said. "But I didn't have any particular craving. We could get most anything to eat here on the farm."

"What I desired," Cara said sadly, "was healthy children, then live children! They became jaundiced and died. Then I miscarried time and again."

"Unforgettable sorrow," Dorothea said gently.

Letitia took the baby from her young mistress' arms. "I want babies of my own, some day," she said wistfully.

"Oh?" Marcia took the wish correctly to be an announcement. "And with which young man?" Cara served her the eggs with hotcakes and honey, and mead and fresh pears. Marcia started eating. "You're promised to Gaius, aren't you, Letitia?" she started teasing upon Letitia's awkward silence. "Why don't you tell us these things?"

Letitia looked at Dorothea and then at her mother, and did not answer.

"Or is it Lucan?" Marcia cleverly wrinkled up her nose in mock distaste.

"Lucan is really a good man," Letitia defended him.

"So! And what do you know about that?" Marcia pried for a confession.

"I live with him, you know," Letitia began. "I mean in the same villa," she quickly corrected any misconstruing.

"Oh yes, I know," Marcia said. "Lucan said the same thing. He came through again last night when I was in here with Flavius." She took her baby from Letitia and transferred some chewed scrambled eggs from her mouth to his.

"Lucan?" Cara was shocked.

"Again?" Dorothea questioned the implications.

Letitia stared at Marcia and turned pale.

"Oh yes! Lots of times!" Marcia exaggerated a bit and watched Letitia closely. "The first time he actually came upon me, I was startled, but my youngest brother says he does it quite often lately—gets troubled in his sleep and comes down to walk it off."

"To walk it off?" Cara asked suspiciously of Letitia. "With which leg?"

Letitia was silent and looked neither at her mother nor her mistress.

"He is indeed a good man, Letitia," Marcia giggled complacently. She felt she knew now. It wasn't Gaius after all. And it was much more involved than she had supposed. It couldn't have been Lucan. He was too much of a virgin. It had to be Quintus, the little prick! Little brother has been fooling around. And if Letitia wanted all to believe it was Lucan, well, let it be.

"Dorothea," Marcia hinted for more information, "I am afraid that if you want any grandchildren, you will have to adopt a fifth son!"

"Lucan already is my son," Dorothea affirmed with color rising in her cheeks. She looked at Letitia. Letitia squirmed.

"What do you mean?" Marcia asked.

"My son in Christ," Dorothea explained.

"Oh." Marcia expected more information than this strange religious affirmation. "So this thing happened outside of marriage," she surmised. "Or were you secretly married from the start? No matter, Letitia. I'll be happy to instruct you in all I know."

Letitia returned a grateful glance.

Nobody said anything further, but the older women scrutinized Letitia's figure and then exchanged long looks. Why, she had completely fooled them, skillfully concealing her cessation of the menses by observing her monthly quarantine from the garden, doing her stint in the spinning and weaving room, even doing the expected extra personal laundry! Cara's eyes were widened with fear, fear that the household, or her husband, would disown Letitia. She slipped her arm protectively around Letitia's waist. A woman in trouble needs kindness as never before; not disinheritance. And she shall find kindness from another woman who had been in trouble! She shall find kindness from one who suffered a sentence in the state brothel rather than renounce her faith, from one who was taken in faith to the bosom of a man who knew her past, and who adopted as his own the little boy who came to the villa to live shortly after she was presented to him as wife. She hoped that Postumus would be as generous again, and that Paulo, knowing his own origin, would help temper the heart of his younger half-brother, the zealous Alexis.

Then Cara came out of her thoughts enough to notice that Dorothea's eyes were kind. Dorothea in her goodness shall be kind again, Cara realized. By the merciful grace of God she will be kind. I can count on her. Oh my daughter, my dear daughter, and my poor husband.

"Good morning, dears!" Fulvia the matron strolled into the kitchen.

The slave women rose to their feet.

"Sit down, dearie dears, I should be waiting on you. August thirteenth came and went and I wasn't here to celebrate it with you, so I thought that it would be lovely to do so now." She regarded her Christian slaves with lifted eyebrow. "Or would you remember? Do you Christian slaves celebrate Servius Tullius's day? Do you celebrate pagan holidays?"

"We haven't," Dorothea began, for the Christians had a habit of carefully avoiding pagan holidays so as not to be exposed to idolatry.

Fulvia did not wait for an answer. "How are you, Pet?" She turned to her daughter and kissed her and took the grandson from Marcia's arms. Then she noticed Letitia. "Why, Letitia! What is the matter with you!"

"She's seeing to the next generation, Mother dear," Marcia explained, "and we have been teasing her."

"Shame on you, Marcia," Fulvia said affectionately. "With which young man, Letitia? Your precious Gaius? Or Sextus? Or Lucan? Or whomever? Dear me, do you not know? Never mind, dear, it's not bad." The unspoken justification was, you're only a slave, you behaved as expected.

That hurt. Letitia's color deepened. "It is a secret, Mistress."

"You see, Mother?" Marcia triumphed. "A secret marriage!"

Indeed Letitia's secret was about six months along since the incident with Quintus, a secret that she suspected early on when her neck measurement was slightly enlarged, and that she confirmed with the oat germination test on her urine. And if Marcia mistakenly thinks that there was a secret marriage with Lucan and that she was with child by him, so much the better. It just might be a good thing for the Legerius household if everybody could be convinced in the same direction. She dared not speculate how far Lucan would go along with this.

"Oh," Fulvia said. "And by the way, Cara, a gentle reminder that you are to instruct Quintus in the ways of amour, as you have done so expertly with my older sons."

Letitia took breath, and Marcia winked at her.

Fulvia turned her attention back to her daughter.

"How is your milk holding out, Marcia?" And characteristically not waiting for an answer she queried further, solicitously pressing upon others her unwanted services. "Shall we get you a drink of sow's milk? I never did have to resort even to a sucking-bottle with poor Cara here. Dorothea, see to it, will you?"

"Oh I'm quite all right, Mother dear," Marcia said. "But the rascal is waking me up with his teething. And then he has to eat!"

"Of course he does," Fulvia crooned. "Gamma's little baby boy just gets hungry!" She raised Flavius's amuletic necklace off his chest and put one of the colt's teeth in the baby's hand. Immediately he chewed on the smooth broad surface. "What you need to do is rub his little gums with hare's brains," Fulvia prescribed. "Then the teeth will come through faster."

"Now, Mother," Marcia was getting a little impatient.

"Oh, don't you do that? What's the newest?"

Marcia gave up.

"Alexis can go shoot you a hare," Cara volunteered.

At dinner, Cara asked Alexis to go out and shoot them a hare. Alexis jokingly asked Felix, Olipor's eldest to do it, and in the same spirit of sport Felix requested Lucan, coming back and forth to the dining room, to do it. This led them all to a round of jesting, then they dropped the subject with no one really certain who was to do it, if at all.

In the afternoon Leonidas, Olipor's second son, slave of Fulvius, cornered Lucan alone.

"So you haven't shot that hare yet. Is this what you call obedience?"

"You mean to say Felix was serious?" Lucan was surprised.

"Say, do you know who Felix is?" Leonidas drew himself up. "Slave of the centurion! And know who you are?"

Lucan started to answer, right hand man of the young master of Good Will.

Leonidas checked him, with a snappy "Shut up! You are slave of a mere rookie. Furthermore, you are an incorrigible off the street. You are the sort if given freedom, who cannot ever be a citizen! Why, if you came within one hundred miles of Rome you would be put to death! And you presume to serve the youngest domine abroad as well as at home! You may be the Quintipor, yes, but remember, you are no home born. You are flogged and shackled and branded rubbish salvaged from the gutters where you belong!"

Lucan bristled. "Listen, chum, I don't mind your calling me lower in rank than Felix, for that is the truth. And I may have come to Good Will off the street. But I am no incorrigible! I am not even, in the same sense as you, a slave! I am freeborn! Unjustly taken into slavery! And I can prove it to you if I have to! I may prove it to you yet!"

"Why don't you. Just why don't you. And in the meantime, if you don't go shoot that hare, Felix will bust your ass in four parts!"

"I'll go! I'll go!"

"And when you're done there are some chamber pots to be emptied, and combat boots to be oiled."

Lucan obeyed. He was not adept at bow and arrow, for an incorrigible was not permitted to bear arms, and he did not want to admit it. He shouldered a quiver of arrows and bow in hand set out, without informing his master of his whereabouts, to flush a hare from the hedgerows. By dumb luck he got one, and was treated with special kindness by Fulvia and Marcia, until the women and baby returned to Rome with Aulus. However he bore many other impositions from the soldiers and their men with uncalled-for patience, each as another burden he must endure in the Name of the Lord.

But these things paled in comparison to the events of the last two days the soldiers were on the farm.

CHAPTER XVIII

Having neither to weigh thoughts nor measure words

"Marcellus! What's the news!" Quintus greeted his friend joyfully, glad for diversion from the sweaty task of digging trenches in the vineyard so winter rains can soak deeply. "You remember my brothers, don't you?"

"Certainly! Welcome home! Furlough, is it? I bet it won't last long. The Emperor has had his brother-in-law put to death right where he was in exile at Thessalonica."

"Really?" Marius was unbelieving. "Licinius?"

"They have it noised about that Licinius was involved in a military conspiracy," Marcellus elaborated.

"Such wouldn't be beneath the Thessalonians," Fulvius commented with a pointed look at Lucan. "And Licinius has broken promises before."

"But you know what?" Marcellus said. "According to another account the conspiracy story is a lot of bull. The Emperor did it from outright expediency. Rome is really going to pot when even a Christian Emperor . . ."

"So the Emperor's Christian, is he?" Cornelius was roused to battle.

"Really now, Cornelius," Marcellus soothed, "don't you know I like to tease little Beans, here? Well, out of expediency the Emperor also had Licinius's Caesar put to death. Martinianus, in Cappadocia where he was in exile."

"He did?" Fulvius asked.

"The Caesar was cut down, and the deposed emperor was strang-gled," Marcellus made a playful pass at Quintus's throat.

"A-agh!" Quintus beat his friend off and pretended to die in Marius's arms.

Marius's comment stopped them all for a moment. "I suppose his own son Crispus is next."

"They say that Licinius was allowed to choose what manner of death," Marcellus elaborated.

"Repulsive thought!" Fulvius brooded. "If I were in his boots I wonder what way I . . ."

"Opening the veins is traditional," Cornelius put in.

"I thought falling on your sword," Marcellus said.

"Oh come on," Marius urged. "Let's go swimming before death by hard labor chooses us. Here, I'll show you how to revive Beans."

"No, no!" Quintus came quickly to life before Marius could poke him in the ribs.

"Brr!" Marcellus commented on the swim idea.

"If you think it's too cold, just join us at the front!" Cornelius made a playful pass at him.

"Now don't go stepping on the artichokes!" Quintus warned about the seedlings set out between the vine rows.

"Oh, is that what they are?" Marcellus jibed.

"Quick cash crop, friend."

Up at the pool the young men tossed their clothes in a heap and peered over the drop-off into the clear cold water and jested about who was to take the first plunge. All but Marcipor and Lucan, that is. Marcellus did not let Marcipor swim with him; he did not think it proper. So Marcipor usually sat with the clothes and watched, or stole a dip in the smaller lower pool. Lucan never went in the water. He sat with Marcipor or watched him swim. Lucan did not know how to swim, and he was afraid. Quintus had previously thought Lucan was respecting Marcellus's viewpoint, and let it go at that. Now that the brothers and slaves were back, and they all prepared to swim together with no protest from Marcellus, Quintus put the pressure on Lucan.

"Come on, Lucan," he urged in his slave's ear, "Shadows in Hades! Get in the water and learn how to swim! I want to be proud of you!" But Lucan remained aloof.

As the young men peered over the high bank, the soldier brothers suddenly seized Quintus by the wrists and ankles and with much shouting and laughter swung him back and forth and sent him squealing through the air into the chilly bath. Quintus pulled himself up into a ball and hit the water with a showy, foamy splash. He came to surface with an honest "Br-r-r! What about my Quintipor," he shouted gleefully. "He has to go in too! Come on, Lucan, you're not going to get away from it this time!"

The brothers whooped and seized upon the frantic slave.

Lucan struggled and pleaded. "Please don't! I can't swim! Domine, have mercy! Please stop them!"

The laughing men dragged him, clothed, to the edge. In desperation Lucan grabbed the knotted rope hanging from a tree that the young men used for swinging far over the pool and plummeting into the water. The men let go of Lucan and gave him a push. Lucan swung in a wide circle over the water. He peered down with enormous eyes.

"Let go, Lucan!" Quintus urged.

When Lucan swung back over the bank they gave him another push before he could jump off.

"Dammit, Domine, I'll drown!"

"You just do that," the young men teased and exchanged glances.

"I'll get you when you fall in," Quintus coaxed.

The men pushed him out from the bank again. Then Marcellus gave him only a light push so that he would not swing back far enough to reach the bank. He had to let go and fall into the water now. He hung on until the rope stopped swinging and spun him dangling over the pool. His grip gave out. With a desperate cry he fell into the pool.

He came up coughing, choking, flailing. Quintus laughingly kept his distance. He thought Lucan was shamming.

"Domine, save me!" Lucan gasped.

Cornelius closed in. "Tell about that bed?" he threatened.

Lucan's eyes widened with alarm. "The stream bed?" he feigned innocently and doubled under with cramps.

Cornelius came to the rescue but Lucan's struggling pulled them both under. "Hold still, you jackass, you'll drown us both!" Cornelius's words made Lucan all the more frantic. The others dove in. Cornelius finally had to stun Lucan on the side of the neck to haul him ashore. Cornelius rolled him over and massaged his chest under the wet clothing until he was breathing regularly. Then Cornelius's hands wandered.

"That's some body you have, boy."

"Why didn't you let me drown!"

"That's gratitude for you," Cornelius muttered to the others. "I rescued him and he says why didn't I let him drown!"

"Lucan, apologize to him," Quintus ordered.

Lucan scrambled away quickly.

"Is this how he proves himself?" Cornelius shot at Quintus.

Lucan glared at his master. Quintus was speechless. So I'm not good enough for you anymore, Domine, Lucan thought. He hurried back to the villa, deliberately without asking permission first, to escape the Romans' arguments about him.

"Speaking of proving," Marcellus was saying, "we can prove him when you ride to Rome with your brothers. Our bet, you know."

"Oh that damn bet. As far as I'm concerned I've won that bet years ago." Quintus was disgusted.

"Oh no you haven't, Beans. We must try him, under controlled circumstances," Marcellus challenged.

"Well, damn!" Quintus half conceded.

"What bet?" the brothers demanded. There was no covering it up now. Quintus had to explain.

"And," Marcellus said privately to Gaius on their hike back to the villa, "if you want to do yourself a favor, keep watch on Lucan's moods and tell me how he is doing."

"Yes, sir." Gaius knew in his heart that he must do no such thing.

* * *

"Quintus upbraided Lucan that night as the sulking slave knelt before him to undo his sandals.

"What in Hades is the matter with your head, making a fool of yourself before my brothers like that? I was mortified!"

Lucan looked up into his master's face and his heart palpitated. "Domine, how can you expect your brothers to accept your Quintipor when you yourself don't?"

"Lucan, you have been nothing but trouble since they've come home."

"Domine, what have I done wrong?" Lucan half exclaimed.

"You embarrassed me from the start, at the family banquet, and at the wine supper after."

"Heaven knows what I endured on your account that night, Domine."

"Oh yes, Lucan, you're so faithful."

Lucan was nonplused at the sarcasm.

"And what about the Egyptian glasses, you devious scoundrel, working behind my back to get demoted."

"It didn't happen that way!" Lucan cried out in pain.

"Then why didn't you tell me? You got me into plenty of trouble with my father over that one."

"I tried to tell you, sir, that night."

"Then you wouldn't accompany Marcia into her room one night when she was afraid."

"She wasn't afraid, Domine."

"What do you think you are, God's answer to woman's dream?"

"That's not fair, Quintus."

"And you wouldn't go shoot that hare until Leonidas practically kicked you in the ass."

"I'm sorry, sir, I thought they were joking. I did shoot one, you know."

"And what about all that sneaking out of my room at night after I go to sleep!"

"To protect my loved one, that's why!" Lucan blurted out.

"Lucan you've quite lost your perspective," Quintus chided in cold heat.

"Where's your integrity, Quintus? Must you try to prove something every time the world heckles? Already you damn near destroyed me over my— loved one. Then at the pool . . ."

"They had to throw you in!" Quintus interjected with disgust.

"You didn't bear me up!"

They each knew what the other meant. There had been no mutual trust.

"Are you trying to get rid of me, or something?"

"Enough out of you, slave!" The exposé hurt. For years Quintus had been encouraging his slave to speak his mind, but not like this! This was not the inexpressible comfort of sharing openly, without having to weigh thoughts and measure words. This was not the victory he looked for! Instead they were at each other's throats.

"Once before you chided me for not saving you from yourself," Lucan reminded him in a conciliatory tone.

"I have not parted company with my senses, Lucan." Quintus knew that his own was the greater offense. But the heckling he had taken from his brothers that afternoon drained all the magnanimity out of him. He wanted his slave to apologize, to bow to him, beg forgiveness.

Lucan was prepared to do no such thing. "Quintus, I'm hurting! One more stupidity of yours and I'll . . ."

"You'll obey!" Quintus worried about the test to come.

"No, Quintus, I won't obey. For your own good I'll, I'll . . . refuse!" Lucan got up from the laces.

"Lucan Fidelissimo!" It never occurred to Quintus that his beloved other really would go so far as to cross his will. "After all I've done for you!"

"Done for me!" Lucan ejaculated bitter resentment. "Lifted me up to bolster your vanity! Tried me beyond endurance! That's what you've done!"

"Why you ungrateful son of a bitch!" Quintus advanced angrily on Lucan and struck him across the face. "You are no longer the Quintipor!"

"Damned if I do, damned if I don't. Is that it, Quintus?" Lucan rubbed his cheek.

"You are no longer useful to me, Oikonomikos."

"You're only saying that so you can take Gaius with you," Lucan accused.

Their gazes locked. Beads of sweat started on Lucan's face. Quintus's eyes narrowed.

"Self-control. A slave's first lesson. You . . . you haven't even learned self-control, you incorrigible bastard of a slave wench! You are depraved! I don't want you near me!" He struck him on the other cheek.

Self-control. Quintus could not have chosen more devastating words deliberately. Self-control! These words were the touchstone of the past. The demon called Memory now loomed before Lucan in agonizing clarity. Self-control! The elusive source of excruciating pain burned back from his childhood memory. Self-control! Those words raised the floodgates of terror. Self-control! These were the words *they* said to him! The soldiers buggered him! The tearing pain! They impaled him when they ran his brother through with a sword! The hemorrhaging! They plowed him when they plowed his sisters! The unspeakable cramping! Knocked! The nausea! Silenced! The bleeding front teeth!

Enslaved—worse than death; beaten to silence—a slave's first lesson; Pater tied to a beam—don't weep for me; burned alive—weep for yourself; brother run through by the sword—fathers sacrifice their sons; mouth stoppered—stop your bloody screaming; drawn dagger—Brother, behind you! *His father slits his brother's throat!* Pater, no! Self-control, a slave's first lesson! Pater! No! No!

The voiceless scream reverberated through his heart and soul and shattered his mind. He did not hear his master calling to him. He rushed wildly down the stairs, through the kitchen where Marcia was nursing her baby, out the back door and bolted up to the woods. He stumbled, fell, and crawled frantically, panting, clutching at the clumps of vegetation and fallen branches, the images driving him forward, until he stopped retching at the drop-off above the pool. One more frantic lunge and it would be all over for Lucan. Do it!

"Begone with you in the name of Christ!" Lucan screamed in anguish. The images vanished. He lay there gasping with grief. His hands clawed the ground. Self-control. I did not even as much as whimper until I first came to Good Will! And now that I finally speak . . . Worse than death!

How much must I endure, O Lord! This? Even this? O Christ, what have I done! My discipleship requires a strength that I do not have! You commission us to the impossible task of unconditional love, then magnanimously forgive us when we fail! Oh Lord, how cruel! Is it any wonder that man nails you to a beam?

Beloved, did not I myself cry out in anguish from the beam? "Father, forgive them, for they know not what they do."

Then Lucan cried out in desperation. "Oh Christ, how do you expect me to . . ." And he let the bitter tears come.

CHAPTER XIX

Lord of my life, my heart is crushed to ashes

"Say, where is everybody?" Marcellus asked Gaius, the first person he saw when he strode into the atrium of Good Will the next morning.

"Orders arrived early this morning that the young domine's brothers and my brothers must return to duty. They are getting ready for their journey, sir."

"What did I tell them!" Marcellus said. "Where's Quintus?"

"Upstairs getting ready, sir."

"So he's going?"

"He will try to enlist, sir, in Rome, under his father's address."

"And you, Gaius?"

"Domine said that I should go along, sir. He will take me to the front if he is accepted."

"And Lucan is going along too?" Marcellus was making a plan in his mind.

"I assume so, sir, to bring our horses back from the post, though he doesn't know about it yet. He hasn't been seen since last night."

"Oh no?" Marcellus was most interested in this unusual circumstance.

"They quarreled, sir, you see—"

"Ah!"

Then Gaius realized that he was talking too much. He remembered Marcellus's words in the woods yesterday about doing himself a favor by spying on Lucan's moods. He felt like a traitor. He thought of seeking Lucan out and telling him the whole thing before the Quintipor would finally appear and make his own hasty preparations. But he could not move himself to doing it. After all, there was a bet to be proven, and if Lucan is to prove himself, it must be genuine. Gaius had no right to interfere. So he kept silent, though it did occur to him that such loyalty to the cause may not be honorable at all, but downright treacherous.

When Quintus saw the order, delivered by messenger, that his brothers must report to the regiment at once because of a fresh outbreak on the German front, he was thrown into a predicament. He couldn't bear to be alone again so abruptly in a household broken wide open with hostility. Surely they must all know about that quarrel with Lucan last night. They have known all along what he was now admitting to himself, ah yes, he could see it now. The body of Christ was broken. He was excommunicated. He could never regain their confidences. And he had to live with it; he couldn't pull up his stakes and move on, nor could he sell his household out from under him. They were all bound together to the land. And he had to stay and command them, when in fact he lost his leadership.

Yet he could pull out. He could enlist! If he could get permission to leave the land and enlist, he could leave his troubles far behind. Including Lucan. He could not take Lucan back to his old regiment. He would put Lucan in charge, and give him Letitia in marriage. He would be escaping a situation rather than seeing it through. Not only would he have abdicated, he would also be deserting.

Would I really?

Perhaps not to an outsider, but to the household, obviously so. Especially after that quarrel with Lucan last night, and now Lucan's absence without leave. The greater deed would be to stay through the storm. Our relationships, if they could be restored, would be deeper, stronger, more beautiful because of the abounding grace that would bring about the reconciliation.

Quintus, you're dreaming, he chided himself. Is a reconciliation possible? Or is there a point, we being human, where the accumulative errors of the past cannot be overcome except that the offender leaves?

O Domine God, to whom all hearts are open, all desires known, from whom no secrets are hid—O Domine God! You know how I feel! What am I to do? Live on as though nothing were wrong? Can I trust them with it? Can Lucan and I ever trust each other again? O Domine God!

"I can solve your problem for you," Marcellus took Quintus aside with a grin.

"What problem," Quintus shot back, annoyed. Don't tell me Marcellus knows about it too!

"About leaving Lucan behind. Start out with both slaves then we shall test the bet."

Quintus did not answer. He was not exactly in favor of this. If they would only hurry up and depart now before Lucan reported to him or Marcellus found out he was delinquent, then the problem would solve itself. On the other hand, if they were to test the bet and Lucan were to run away, Quintus would feel more inclined to stay with Good Will, claim Letitia, and attempt a reconciliation with the household. Quintus was impaled with indecision.

As they were all saddling up to leave, Lucan appeared looking like death warmed over and contritely hurried to assist. He led Ignis to his master.

"Don't you know I can't handle that fool horse?" Quintus snapped. "Get me Niger!"

Lucan exchanged horses and helped his domine up. His hand lingered a moment on the domine's foot and he looked up into his master's face.

Quintus was shocked to see the swelling and bruising on Lucan's face. Could that mess possibly be from the blows he dealt him last night? He did not want the others to see, yet he needed to have it out with his recalcitrant slave.

"A miserable job you do of running away!" he chided.

"Domine, please forgive me last night," Lucan apologized obediently.

"Didn't you hear me calling?"

"I don't know what I heard last night, sir. I'm sorry if I seemed—"

"Why didn't you come back upstairs?"

"I couldn't sir."

"What do you mean, you couldn't!"

"Please do not ask, Domine." Lucan rested his forehead on his master's knee.

"Answer me! I have a right to know what's going on in your head!"

"No, Domine, not always." Lucan was not about to disclose what else happened to him last night. "It doesn't matter, sir."

"If that's the way you're going to be then you need not report to me now. You can get lost! Spare us both!"

"Quintus—" Lucan's breath caught in his throat and he appealed with his eyes.

The others, thinking that they had put those bruises on Lucan's face during their mischief with him last night, did not want Quintus to see, and having failed to retain Lucan they were now urging Quintus to come along promptly. He turned Niger away to follow them.

"Quintus," Lucan called softly after him.

Quintus heeled Niger to a trot.

"You can't do this to me!" Lucan ran to saddle Ignis.

The household was gathered at the gatehouse to see them off, all except Letitia, that is. Letitia was confined to her room.

Another difficult menses, Quintus surmised.

Olipor held the entrance gate open. As Quintus went through the gatehouse, Olipor commented.

"I admire your presumption more than I do your judgment."

The remark cut. "When we return you shall admire both!" Quintus retorted and legged Niger on. Now what does Olipor know!

Lucan came clattering after and curbed Ignis at a respectable distance behind his master, with the other slaves. Quintus did not look back.

They were well on their way to the post station where they planned to spend the night, before Marcellus spoke of the bet again.

"Send Lucan home now," he said abruptly to Quintus. "And none of your damn explanations, either!"

"Lucan?"

"Yes, Lucan. That isn't his ghost following you!"

"Oh curses! He knows he can't show his face in Rome!"

"We'll be in the hundred-mile radius tonight. Send him home."

"Marcellus, I can't. It's mid afternoon! He can't possibly get home before dark."

"What's this?" Marius overheard and reined his horse alongside. Quintus told him.

"I see. You may as well get it over with," Marius advised gravely.

"But Marius," Quintus protested, "I can't put him to test now! He's upset about something. It wouldn't be fair."

"All the better proving of him."

"He won't obey. He's been uncommonly insubordinate these days. I don't know what's gotten into him!"

"No, not insubordinate, Quintus. Last night we gave him a taste of what he'd face back at the front. It is only natural that he wouldn't tell you about it. You have completely won over your little brother. He is as solid as a rock," Marius reassured him.

"Because he's a rock I worry about what he may do," Quintus rejoined.

"Do it now," Marcellus insisted. "You must! The post station is another four hours ahead."

"No, Marcellus."

"Forfeit him to me instead?"

"No—wait."

"Can't. I have to turn back myself."

"You're not going back until tomorrow morning, Marcellus," Quintus insisted.

"Very well, I shall return in the morning. Now hurry up!"

Quintus twisted in the saddle and looked at his slave for the first time. The slave's eyes met his and Quintus faltered. Marius had expressed it perfectly. Little Brother. Quintus knew that he loved Lucan more than the slave could love him. The pain of his surrender made his voice sharp.

"Fidelissime, what are you doing here! Stay! Go back!"

Lucan trotted up alongside. "Don't you need me to bring Niger home from the Post, sir?"

Always anticipating, always taking initiative, dammit, when does he stop? Quintus turned in the saddle and answered him full face with an anguished appeal, at once a restoration and an order. He hoped to God that Lucan would get the full meaning of his choice of words.

"Quintipor, go home."

Lucan wheeled Ignis broadside and stared in utter astonishment. Ignis fought, reared and turned around to follow the others. Lucan beat the headstrong horse on the ears with his reins, and dug his heels into the horse's sides. Ignis laid his ears flat back and leaped into a furious gallop homeward.

Stay! Go back! Go home! As though to a dog! As though you were afraid I would not obey! Fidelissime, like a glorified little shadow. Quintipor indeed. I have a proper name, haven't I? He brooded as the horse pounded homeward. 'You can get lost! Spare us both!' My veritable brother! My life! And you don't want me anymore!

Oh Quintus, you patiently woo me into your service, then you press me relentlessly with your demands. Are you never satisfied? How can I reconcile! How can I make peace again, I who have disrupted the natural scheme of things in Good Will! And God, where are you now that I need you the most! Will you too desert me now that the entire household is against me? You have indeed driven me out, by your withdrawal of support! That is it! You have shown me out! Indeed the domine says go home! Indeed I shall! Precisely that! Thessalonica!

Lucan brought Ignis to a walk the last few miles in and arrived at the gatehouse of Good Will by moonlight. Ignis stomped and whinnied and scared Gregor out of his skin.

"Lucan!" Gregor exclaimed. "You are back so soon!"

Lucan retorted bitterly, "The domine sent me back!"

"Why, Lucan? Is something wrong?"

"He doesn't want me any more! He doesn't need me! I am cast off like an old garment!" Lucan galloped down the drive to the stable court. He thoroughly groomed, rubbed down, blanketed, watered and fed the horse, then stumbled upstairs to the domine's rooms. He threw himself down on his bed. No good.

He was up again, pacing. He seized a wax tablet and stylus off his master's desk and expressed his anguish in a single line inscribed deeply in his agitation.

Lord of my life, my heart is crushed to ashes.

He propped the tablet up on the master's desk and turned to go. Changing his mind, he snatched up the tablet and poised the blunt end of the stylus to rub out his line. Changing his mind yet again he closed the tablet with a snap and buried it under the pile of work on the desk. He looked about the moonlit room pensively. Here in this room he had found trust and love. He had learned to respond, to become involved in life again. He had dared to reach out in self-giving and had found the essence of life.

No more.

I am rejected! I am put aside like an old shoe to gather dust and mildew! I have become his everything and now I am his nothing! How can either of us bear to remain in the same household together? It would kill me! My final devotion will be to leave his service!

Letitia. He would ask her to come with him. Is that not what she would want? How he loved her! With Quintus and Gaius gone she was virtually his alone. Instead of lying protectively inside her door, refusing her warm invitation to get up off the hard floor and share her bed, he would give of himself and console her also. Marcia had shown him that he was not a mere boy for the pleasure of men, but a man himself, a man who could give and receive and share with a woman. He would be forever grateful to Marcia. He would finally share his new self with his beloved and with his body seek her forgiveness for the plowing he attempted that fateful afternoon on the stream bank. He would even give her children.

Down in the servants' hall again, he paused at Letitia's doorjamb. All was quiet, though Olipor's curtain was open. He opened her curtain a crack. Moonlight flooded the room from her window. He paused, opened the curtain wider, and stared at her bed. Letitia was not there.

Lucan was devastated. He should have known better. Indeed she must ultimately belong to another, and he must not disrupt the order of things at Good Will. His final service to the household would be to leave them in peace!

Olipor, who slept with his curtain open that night, saw Lucan look into her room, close the curtain, and lean against the doorjamb. He watched Lucan's body become racked with the silent grief of a slave. Lucan had completely lost his composure. Olipor wanted mightily to go to him and comfort him, but dreaded the consequences of invading the ultimate vestige of what the young man owned of himself, his privacy. Olipor did not correct Lucan when the young man slipped out the back door. Yes, let the young upstart slip away. Then Gaius will have Letitia after all. He knew as well as anybody that Quintus and Gaius would be coming back, refused at the recruitment office. Gaius and Letitia would in time come to tolerate each other, perhaps even to love each other. And there would be grandchildren. The House of Ophelus shall rise again.

Yes, when the barbarian hordes swarm over the borders and liberate Rome from the elite and the parasitic functionaries, when the populace in the Eternal City will have to work for their living again, when the barbarians come as God's instrument of judgment, then the house of Ophelus shall rise up again. Not that he really believed he would see this; he only thought this way when he was upset, and consoled himself with apocalyptic thoughts.

CHAPTER XX

The world does not come to an end

Quintus and Gaius returned to Good Will over a week later.

"Good morning, Olipor," Quintus greeted the overseer cheerfully. "Eager to hear your report. Say, where is Lucan? Why doesn't he come in to greet me?"

"Domine," Olipor answered gravely, "Lucan is not at home."

"He isn't!" Quintus exclaimed indignantly. "Didn't he . . ."

"Oh he came back all right. That night you left for Rome, he came directly home. When Gregor asked why he was back he answered, 'The Domine doesn't want me anymore!' Gregor had never seen him more heartbroken."

"I commanded him to go home." Quintus was defensive.

"Then he went up to the woods," Olipor said quietly.

"You don't mean to tell me that he really is gone! Why didn't you go after him!"

"Domine, did you ever see that young man cry? And I don't mean from the nightmares of the past. I wasn't about to add insult to injury." Olipor looked through Quintus.

"Olipor!" Quintus moved threateningly close to his elderly slave. "Why?"

Olipor lost patience. "You would have me go up there and drag him back crushed, on account of an asinine bet designed to substantiate your vanity. As the Lord lives, my young domine, you must not use even a slave in that way. You were not really caring for your man. You abused your slave then expected me to put things right again. I wouldn't add another grievance if you commanded me!"

Quintus furiously slapped Olipor across the face. "You thought . . . you thought him a good riddance! So Gaius could take his place!"

Olipor bowed, deeply humiliated that such thoughts had indeed occurred to him, that now the house of Ophelus could rise up again.

"Put out a search far him," Quintus ordered.

"I already have, sir, including dredging the pool."

"I'm returning to Rome in a few days to receive my orders. I have enlisted. Now I want no more of your disapproval, Olipor. I'm doing what I must do. And—I once warned Lucan that if he ever ran away I would pursue him to hell and back until he was willing to come home!"

"Very well, sir." Olipor hesitated. "Sir . . ."

"What is it?" Quintus snapped.

"The farm report, sir."

"Dammit, Olipor, you are too damned fastidious—at the wrong times! You see, you *are* getting old! Ready for replacement! We will tend to the farm later. Go! I can't stand the sight of you!"

"When Olipor left, Quintus paced and exclaimed, "Damn! Father will have it out with me now!"

In the kitchen, Letitia approached him anxiously. "Domine, where is Lucan? They didn't get him, did they?"

"Who? What are you talking about? I sent him home to you!"

Letitia was not ready to disclose yet the entire traumatic story of Lucan's final night at Good Will, including a threat.

"Quintus what have you done!" she asked in alarm.

"You tell me where he is, Letitia," Quintus returned intensely.

"You tried to get rid of him!" Letitia accused.

"What happened between you two when I sent him back!" he countered.

"Sent him back! You sent him away!"

"Is that what he thinks?" Quintus bore down on her.

"I-I-I don't know . . . I didn't see him return, believe me, Quintus! If he sought me, I wasn't in my room. I was with my parents! If he needed me, I wasn't there! I have failed him!" Her voice quavered.

"You believe me, Letitia, I wouldn't do anything to hurt you, either of you."

"Oh no, not at all," she replied bitterly.

"Letitia, what has gotten into you!"

She came close to tears. "Look at me," she said. "Look at me carefully!"

He noticed for the first time that she girded her dalmatica higher and more bloused than usual.

"Heaven help us! So he has run off and left you . . ." Quintus broke off, knowing his own guilt toward her.

"With child, Domine," she finished timidly, unwilling to press charges against Quintus at a time when it seemed the truth would ruin him, and forbidden as a slave to accuse him, besides.

"Damn!" Quintus ejaculated vehemently.

"Lucan and I . . . oh Quintus you must find him!" she finished with a rush and burst into frightened weeping.

"Tish, he'll be back!" Quintus drew her to himself and comforted her. She clung to him, took in his tender warmth and became all the more upset at her predicament.

Cara, working with Postumus in the storeroom, gestured toward the young couple and commented to her husband, "Them two's so in love and doesn't even know it."

Quintus left Letitia, torn in his soul as to whether or not she were telling the truth. Is she proposing to keep me from providing for my own child? Slave laws be damned! I would never forgive myself. Is she trying to spare me?

Quintus went through the motions of the morning inspection while absorbed in thought. I should have seen the light and married Lucan and Letitia in the early spring when they both seemed ready for it. At the time I thought that Lucan was disinterested, but I guess I just didn't think. How could I have missed it! The reading lessons. The little delays while going out to work. That slave is a man! He must have dodged the truth out of the feeling that marriage was not among the privileges allotted him. That's it. Remember what he said? Marry the forbidden treasure? How could I have overlooked it? But then I was in love with her too.

"Alexis! You will lure the damn birds onto the olives if you don't plow that wheat in as fast as you sow it! Paulo, keep right behind him with the mules!"

Alexis answered with a glance at his master as though to say, well look who's back and whatever has gotten into you!

Quintus trotted out of the olive grove and headed Niger up to the woods. Yes, I loved her too. Dammit, I didn't have the guts to act because I had my own amorous feelings, and besides, it would not have seemed just to the other slaves that anyone else but Gaius should get Letitia. So I left things alone with the hope that the situation would take care of itself. If I had looked upon everyone with real concern I would have seen that the real justice called for marriage between Lucan and Letitia. She was quietly but deeply in love with him. He needed her. Much more than Gaius he needed her, and the comfort and wholeness and stability that comes with married life. Gaius didn't seem to care very much one way or the other. Lucan did care though he wouldn't confess it in words. His actions showed that he cared very much. And I didn't have the guts . . .

Or maybe I'm being unfair to myself. Maybe it wasn't as clear cut as all that back then. Anyway, when I did finally act, see what I did! And Lucan was the one who was to stand by her after that unfortunate incident that I imposed upon her. If I had seen them married at the appropriate time, that unfortunate incident would not have happened. Nor would Lucan have run away. I am the one who would be just. My justice should have considered not a priority ruling, but the needs of the different persons concerned. I mustn't try to treat all my slaves equally with the same rules, but rather according to their individual personalities and needs. But if there were no rules, wouldn't we have utter chaos? Oh shadows of Hades!

That's a good-looking stack of wood Megas has cut. He's a steady worker! Look at Baltus leaning against his ox, and he gets busy at loading the cart now that he sees me coming. Will the farm really deteriorate when I leave for the army? Oh, there's Manius, I couldn't see him behind the stack. No, I won't speak to them after all. I'm in no mood for smart-aleck remarks. Was Alexis really as hostile as he seemed? I hope I am accepted at the recruitment office; I need to get away from this place and think back on it from a distance and figure out where I stand. I suppose Lucan felt the same way; get away from the intensely personal relationship so that he could discover who he is. I'll be coming back to this place; my brothers are soldiers for life. Wonder if Lucan will come back? Will he come begging for help as soon as the law catches up with him? And will I be willing to give it to him?

And what about Letitia? Lucan is gone, and Gaius will be going with me, and Postumus will be asking me what about Letitia and I can't let things ride much longer. I have to satisfy him with some kind of action.

There's the linnet on the hedgerow. Lucan was always looking up from his weeding to listen, and hunting out the nest to show Letitia. Good Lord, could it be that they had already exchanged vows and that I had defiled his wife? He was hurt enough for it that night we quarreled. But no . . . no, can't be . . . she was a virgin. But what did Gaius mean that afternoon he came up to see me? Wish I could remember his exact words. No, it can't be—yet the way Letitia would have me think now—Quintus, you are trying to excuse yourself, and you know it. If only I had had the guts to act against the corporate opinion of the slaves!

Now Lucan gone! Quintus felt anxiety and yet he was surprised by a sense of relief. Lucan really gone! And his departure was on his own conscience! Perhaps this was a blessing in disguise! If he were rejected at the draft he could settle down at Good Will his way, only without the help and support of his Quintipor. With Lucan gone, who would defend him now?

At the end of the inspection tour, Quintus was thoroughly upset. Nor was this the end of the problems that streamed to him from his disrupted household. If people would only leave me alone, Quintus thought. O God! If I could only be left alone a while. He needed solitude to collect himself and evaluate his situation. He could hardly wait to start back to Rome where he hoped to spend some time alone between his military appointment and the actual marching date. He had to get out of Good Will!

By afternoon his tension mounted unbearably. He had given the slaves their instructions personally. He was writing out some last-minute instructions when he heard footsteps ascend the stairs. Deliberate footsteps, weighed with a problem. He experienced a moment of panic then disappointment that it could be Lucan. He trembled at the sound. His eyes shot frantically around the room impulsively looking for a place to hide. The footsteps were at the door. He was trapped. He quickly resumed writing. He did not look up until he punctuated the last sentence with an emphatic period. It was Marcellus.

"So you have to take on the neighboring swamp lands and cultivate them," Marcellus stated bluntly. "What do you propose to do about that?"

"What?" Quintus drawled, absolutely finished.

"See for yourself, friend. Twenty-five additional *iugera*." Marcellus tossed Quintus the edict.

"Twenty-five!" Quintus studied the parchment and stroked his chin thoughtfully. "Well, this could be worse, Marcellus. In fact, it could help me out of a predicament."

"Out of a predicament?" Marcellus was puzzled.

"You see, I can easily establish a family on the additional land. And I propose that Postumus should move his family over. Then Letitia cannot refuse to take a husband with her. They will need another young man. That should take care of her. In fact I shall send Sextus up. He and Alexis have become quite inseparable. In close proximity Sextus and Letitia ought to come to—"

"What are you getting at?" Marcellus interrupted impatiently.

"You didn't see her on your way in? Haven't you noticed?"

"Noticed what?"

"Dammit, Marcellus, she's pregnant, and the one to whom she implies she is secretly married has inconveniently run off."

"Lucan has run off?"

"Yes, Marcellus."

"Well damn his hide! What did I tell you, Beans?" Marcellus rubbed it in just a little. "I shall go after him."

"No, no, Marcellus, hands off! He came home first. And get this straight, Letitia isn't pregnant by him, but by me. I am quite sure. She was a virgin. And she didn't even have to assume the lioness posture to conceive!" Quintus's voice betrayed a hint of a boast.

"Well, congratulations! Did she like it?"

"I hurt her at first."

"What did you do that for, Beans! Now she'll be man-shy."

"Well, hardly, but it was a mistake."

"Why, man? You have made a conquest!" Marcellus conceded.

"No, I have exploited her."

"How's that?"

"There is no double standard for a follower of Christ," Quintus insisted.

"How inconceivable!" Marcellus tormented. And when Quintus only snorted impatiently at his pun, Marcellus became irritated. "Why do you have to think of everything in terms of Christ!"

"Because Christ should be the center of my life," Quintus answered quietly.

"Ah, Beans, you are incorrigible."

Quintus lost patience. "You try to be good by yourself. Just try it! Then perhaps you will be able to hear what the Christian message is!"

"Perhaps you are coming to understand it better yourself," Marcellus cooed. "I didn't mean that impossible morality, Beans, I meant your stubborn concern for your slaves. Your love will kill you yet."

"I am worried about the child, Marcellus," Quintus confided.

"There are many ways to handle that, right now or later," Marcellus said. "Sometimes seedbeds get weeded, you know."

"The abominable practices of the world won't do. Am I to follow the first sin with a worse one?"

"Well, just raise the child at home as others do," Marcellus suggested. "You'll have a darling little pet."

"The child may be held up as a constant reproach."

"Can't your Christian household take life naturally as it comes?" Marcellus asked impatiently.

"This sort of thing is not natural to a Christian household," Quintus suggested quietly. "We were behaving like children of darkness, not children of light."

Marcellus shrugged. "Your problem, friend. I have spoken. But it sounds as though you Christians are about to commit the real sin. By Jove you don't have to make such an issue of it! Go ahead and take her to wife! Enjoy her! Raise a large brood!

"Do you suppose I could?"

"I give you my permission, dummy," Marcellus replied facetiously, "and I will teach you how to make love. I will school you beyond the Western tradition of seeking your own pleasure to the Eastern tradition of pleasuring the woman, so that you will become quite irresistible to her.

"Would you, Marcellus?"

"You are going to pursue her, then?"

"That's a secret I'm keeping from myself."

"Oh, dear Venus."

"I've enlisted, you know," Quintus reminded him.

"You know they won't accept you. They need farm boys on the farm."

Marcellus was half irritated, half amused when he departed. These Christians get on your nerves sometimes.

"Taken to horseback riding, Letitia?" he quipped at her in the kitchen and laughed crassly at her puzzled look.

On his way out to the stable court he came upon Gaius and did not restrain what came to mind. "Happy now, Quintipor?" he asked sarcastically.

Gaius went to his room and pulled the curtain. He had betrayed Lucan. If he had truly loved, or even if he had acted responsibly, he would have warned Lucan. Now—Lucan gone—Letitia estranged. Gaius upbraided himself while Marcellus rode out of the stable court and sang a bawdy song from the wineshops.

* * *

The remainder of the week was absolute hell on wheels for Quintus. He worked himself to exhaustion each day only to find himself wide awake with arguments racing through his mind as soon as his head touched the pillow at night.

Lucan has caused him so much grief; should he simply let the fugitive slip through his fingers and to Hades with his safety?

Should he go all out to get the slave back for Letitia with the expectation of escaping the land himself by enlisting?

Perhaps the Recruitment Office will take him but will not permit him to bring Gaius along. Then it would be better if Lucan were not home.

Or should he tell the Recruitment Board to go to Hades, stay on the farm, plow his life back to shape on the land and perhaps plow her too?

Supposing he were found out giving his father's address in Rome as his own, instead of his Puteoli address? Would he be penalized for falsification?

Quintus reported back to Rome and passed the time away for another week touring his school-day haunts before he was finally summoned to receive his orders. He was to stay on the land. The gamble failed. He was fined moderately for falsifying his address, scolded for being overzealous to defend his country and ordered home with a stern lecture on the importance of farming the land. The authorities in Puteoli would be watching him carefully now.

Quintus slumped on a chair in his parents' apartment and tried to tell his mother something that Olipor would have understood, but which he felt that he could not disclose to his Christian overseer.

"No Mater, it's not being rejected at the draft board that's getting me down. I knew when I applied that farmers are desperately needed. It's only that I have to go back to Good Will and there I feel . . . well . . . unclean".

"Yes, dear, it's dirty work. It's a pity that my youngest son, the only scholar among you, must soil his hands so—permanently!"

"I don't mean it that way, Mater."

"You have been bathing regularly, dear?" Fulvia made certain.

"Yes, Mater dear. It isn't anything external, Mater."

"Oh? Then it's in your head? Then you must need a physic, dear; sometimes the need for that makes you sluggish in the head," Fulvia prescribed brightly.

"No, Mater, not that either. I've been having a little trouble—it seems that our young—" Quintus gave up. He saw that he was not getting across at all. His mother was hearing only what she wanted to hear; she was not really listening.

"I'll really have to go back there and take a firm hold of the situation," he concluded.

"Yes," Fulvia said confidentially, "that's what you will have to do."

"The situation being," Quintus tried once again, "that Letitia's pregnant, Mater."

"Is that what's bothering you?" Fulvia opened her hands and dropped them on her lap in relief.

"Yes." Quintus looked down.

"That's nothing to concern yourself with. These things are natural. Of course she is a little frightened. Marcia and I have instructed her on pregnancy and the impending birth."

"Will you instruct me too?"

"Cara should be doing that. It's a pity that I live too far away to see to the finishing of your adult education. I have ordered Cara to instruct you in the ways of amour. Has she not done so?"

"No, Mater," he laughed and spread his hands in chagrin. Ask Cara how to make love to her daughter? "Don't you think I am capable of—"

"Not making an ignorant blunder? No!" she interrupted with feeling. "Animal instinct is not enough. The very dogs have that. Now what's the matter? Being Christian, does Cara have religious scruples?"

"I don't know. I'll ask her." Quintus's cheeks reddened. "And I did mean instruction on childbirth, not on amour."

"What for?" Fulvia gave him her full attention now.

"It's my child," Quintus confessed.

"She says it's by Lucan!"

"No."

"She was afraid to admit it, then. No matter. You are both young and not to be blamed. And freemen aren't allowed to acknowledge or adopt their slave progeny even after freeing them, you know.

"Where does that come from, Mater?" He watched her curiously.

"Marcia," she sighed. "The slave laws. There are certain little pets in that household. We're not supposed to know."

"I couldn't live with that at Good Will. I'm going to do something about it, right away, you'll see."

"That isn't necessary. You'll get over her."

"Supposing I want to marry Letitia?" Quintus experimented.

"Your father is looking for a bride for you, Quintus."

"I am a serf, Mater. Pater won't be able to find anyone."

"Yes, that is indeed a big problem," Fulvia sighed.

"She is literate, and intelligent, and industrious. The makings of a good matron, don't you think?"

"Well, I suppose so," Fulvia conceded. She herself was of low birth.

"Furthermore, I love her."

"This is more complicated than I realized."

"Tell Pater to look for a slave woman for Gaius, instead."

"Why, that's a good idea," Fulvia brightened. "If your pater should find a woman of good breeding in the saepta near the forum he would only be outbid anyway."

"There now, you've got the point. Will you please talk to Pater for me?"

"Of course. And ask Letitia to instruct you. It will bring you two closer," Fulvia advised warmly.

"Mater, you're such a dear. If I could be so blessed with one like you." They rose and embraced. "Good Will shall come alive with families once again."

"How exciting!"

* * *

Back at Good Will, during the afternoon rest, Quintus requested to see Letitia in her own room. He followed her in, motioned her to sit down, and sat facing her on the bed. She fidgeted with her fingernails and waited for him to speak. He plunged right into the subject.

"The child is really mine?"

She hesitated. "Supposing it were? Isn't that what you wanted?"

"To tell you the truth, I . . ." he flushed deeply and took her hands tightly in his.

"You only wanted to lay me, Quintus? Is that it? Your privilege; you're the master."

"It was for your own good. If I didn't, Marcellus was going to, and there would have been nothing I could do to stop him."

"What are you saying!"

"Calm down, Letitia. We wanted it for your health. It's right there in the doctor book."

"The doctor book! Why don't you ask us women what's good for us. What does Galen know about women!"

"See for yourself."

"Then why didn't you have Mamercus do it! He's in charge of the breeding program!" she lipped bitterly.

"Yes, there were others only too happy to oblige. But I couldn't have tolerated that."

"Then why did you have to degrade me so!"

"Degrade you? I didn't degrade you! I was doing it for us."

"For us?" She cried out in exasperation. "Exactly what do you want of me!"

"To bear me children and raise them strong and true."

"Is that all?"

"Of course I hope for more. Much more."

She snorted.

"Letitia." He groped for words. "Letitia . . . this is most awkward . . . are you . . . married? I mean . . . to him? In your own way?"

"Quintus, if you were anyone else I'd swear at you."

"You're unclaimed, then." Relief sounded in his voice.

"Deserted is a better word."

"No, not deserted. You have me. And our child. I was trying to reach you, Letitia, if by no other way, then through our child." His eyes twinkled. "And according to instructions I intend to see that you keep this pregnancy." He stroked the inside of her thigh.

"So shall I spread my legs for you now?"

"Stop it, Letitia. I'm not propositioning you, I'm proposing to you. For the third time. I want to give you the honor of being my wife. I need someone who is strong, intelligent, willing to learn, and hard working. Someone who loves this farm as much as I do. And that sounds like you, Letitia."

"I don't even own myself and you expect me to rule a household?"

"Listen, Tish, right now my father is looking for a bride for me, even a bride with chalk on her feet."

"From the marketplace!" she exclaimed in disbelief.

"Do you think a self-respecting freewoman would marry me and become a serf?" It was an untactful choice of words.

"So you would take for your bride some self-despising slut?" she retorted.

He nearly struck her.

"Don't you lift your hand at me, Quintus Legerius!" She trembled at her own insubordination.

"Dammit, Letitia, use your head! Do you want some self-despising slut from the market to rule the household with me?" He was nearly shouting.

"Of course not!" She raised her voice.

"Well, then?"

"Do you think I will be self-respecting? You own me, Quintus!" She was nearly shouting. "The men in this household think that they own me! I am not entitled to my own life! My own body! Do you think that I could refuse you?"

"Don't give me any of that servile horseshit!" he retorted. "This is Good Will. When have I ever lorded it over you? When have any of you had other than kindness and consideration and even love? By the Gods you slaves do bring your own servile attitudes upon yourselves!"

She stood, white with anger. "How can you be so naive! I can't stand you when you act this way, Quintus. Get off your high horse and be a human being! Open your eyes and see!"

"Tish, help me!" he cried, taken aback.

"Help you!" she shot back. "I am the one who needs help! I'm the one who's stuck with this innocent parasite who's taken me over to be born into a life it won't want! I'm appalled at myself! And you . . . you!"

"What about me, Letitia," he demanded evenly.

"Do you really want me to tell you a thing or two, Quintus Legerius?" She began pacing to maintain courage. Her stomach was in knots, and her fetus fluttered.

"Yes." He stood at attention. "Tell me."

"This is Good Will," she lowered her voice. "That proud moment when you were admitted into manhood, was the first mortal wound to your childhood companions, who were not admitted into adulthood with you. Then you were made master over us, with life and death power over us. That's when we suddenly had to rethink who we were. We started despising ourselves for continuing to love you.

"Then you raised Lucan up over us to prove your power over him. That was playing God, Quintus. Bad! Nor did you stop there. You pressed for the last bit that he owned of himself, his mind and will. And when he didn't willingly give them to you he had to beg your pardon. *Mio Dio*, Quintus!

"Then there's Gaius. Think what you have done to the once happy Gaius! Don't you see, our so-called self-imposed servile attitudes are our only remaining defense. If we don't show a mind and a will, then you cannot take them from us! And it's sick to love you so completely; that means hating ourselves!"

Quintus remained standing and looked down at the floor.

Letitia experienced a moment of fear, then she became angry at herself that she feared him. She turned on him before he could speak.

"So what do you have to say for yourself now, boy?"

"You're beautiful when you're angry, Tish."

"What!" she cried in complete frustration, "here I am cutting you down and you tell me that I'm beautiful!"

"You fascinate me."

"Like another empirical study on 'slaves are people.'"

"You're letting me see the real you. And I like what I see."

"I'm wasting my breath. Out!" She gestured toward the door.

"I hear you, Letitia, and you have cut me to the quick."

"No deeper than you have cut me, Quintus."

"Forgive me, Letitia."

"You don't even know what you are asking! Get out of my life."

"Tish, no!"

"Now," she emphasized with her whole being.

"Hear me out, Letitia. I've learned so much from Lucan. About myself. About the human condition."

"At what price, *Mio Dio*, at what price! Now get out!"

"I cannot bear it!" he cried. "Letitia think of the price yourself, and do not disown me!"

"What am I going to do with you!"

"To begin with, please let's sit together."

She was silent for an agonizingly long time, then she sat and patted the bed next to her.

He sat down, but did not look at her. This was a critical moment. He must not do anything that would take away her vestige of self respect.

"Well, Quintus?"

"Tell me about our child," he asked cautiously. "When did you know?"

"From the start. My neck enlarged. Then my breasts were tender. Remember? Upstairs? And when I missed my menses I did the oat germination test with my urine. They germinated. Fast. Later I had Mamercus examine me internally as he does his ewes."

"He knows!"

"I swore him to secrecy."

"In exchange for which . . . ?" he queried suspiciously.

She avoided his scrutiny.

"And who else has . . . examined . . . you?"

"You really don't want to know."

"Really! Tell me, Letitia," he demanded.

"Get off that damn high horse or get out."

"Zeus!" He got up and turned his back. "Please come clean with me," he requested firmly.

"No incriminations?"

"Lucan, I suppose," he growled.

"Lucan?" She hadn't intended to mention him.

"He came down to your room nights and . . ."

"To guard me! On a pallet inside the door!" She was defensive now.

"Do you expect me to believe that?"

"He's blocked!" She gestured vehemently at her head though Quintus's back was turned. "Up here! He gets nauseated! A demon from the past! Didn't you know that?"

"Come, come, Letitia."

"He was the only one who listened to me that the soldiers and their men were after me!" Her voice was raised.

"What!" Quintus turned on her.

"No incriminations, Domine," she got up quickly and bowed her head. Slaves were forbidden to accuse their masters.

"To Hades with this Domine stuff. What about my brothers and their men?" His voice was raised.

"Don't look at me that way."

"I am giving you permission to tell me, Letitia. I demand an answer." He turned his back again. "Speak!"

"They-they each th-thought L-Lucan was one of them . . . in my room. Then they found out—abducted us together—took us to the corner guest room . . . and . . . and . . ."

"Say it!"

"Quintus, you know what an orgy is. They made love chains with Lucan. They made me play Messelina."

He spun on her and glared, his eyes wide with disbelief and anger. She matched his gaze. Then his eyes narrowed, and he spoke, his voice dangerously soft.

"Well, you must have enjoyed it, you daughter of a whore."

She struck him full face and viper quick he caught her wrist. They stared, panting, he in pain, she in terror.

"Christ alive, woman, am I no better than they in your sight?"

Her lower lip quivered.

"I'm sorry," he whispered. "*Mio Dio*, Letitia, didn't you tell them?"

"Tell them what, Quintus, that they mustn't molest me . . . because I was pregnant . . . with my master's child? They'd call me a liar. That was how Manius l-lost his tongue, wasn't it? Accused of lying?"

"Did they hurt you?"

"I started to hemorrhage! I nearly lost the baby! Everyone thought I was confined with my menses when you all rode out for Rome. I was trying to keep the pregnancy."

"You wanted to save our child?"

"And they really did try to drown Lucan."

"Curses!"

"And now I am quite undone," she sentenced herself hoarsely.

"No, you're not! I want you, Tish, and I want our little child."

"Do you expect me to believe that?"

"Tish!" Her words pierced him.

"It's Lucan that has comforted me through troubled times."

"Letitia . . ." Quintus was mortified at his neglect of her.

"And now you have all betrayed me, down to the last man! Even Lucan is gone! He won't be coming back!"

"I don't blame him!"

"Please remember that you said that, Quintus Lottius Legerius."

"You remember, Letitia, that as his master I am entirely in the right." He spoke firmly, then he relented. "*Mio Dio*, Letitia, *Mio Dio*, what am I doing! I have hurt you so much!"

Such an admission from the lord of her life overwhelmed her. "I have let myself in for it and look what I caused! Can anyone ever forgive me? Oh Quinnie, I am so scared!" The tears came.

He sat her down on the bed again and sat next to her and comforted her.

"I'm scared too, Letitia, that is why I have been avoiding you."

"You coward!" she cried. "And you want me to entrust myself to you!"

"Want me to lie to you?" he pleaded. "Or when I dare to climb off my high horse for you, will you let me be a human being?"

"I'll try," she sobbed.

They wept together, clinging to each other. She was shocked to see how vulnerable he was, with needs, not always in control of his world. The master! Of their lives! This was the intimate burden that Lucan bore. Now the master was asking her to share that burden as his wife, to nurture him and submit to him in a rather one-way street. The thought of committing herself completely to another vulnerable human being shook her to her very core. What could he give her in return besides the pain and heartbreak that drove Lucan away?

"You have told the others?" he asked.

"That the child is Lucan's."

"Why!"

"That was a terrible beating he took for you."

"The Gods! I'll handle it, Letitia. I'll handle it."

"You do that," she cried.

"Help me with the accounts tonight?" he asked. "In the kitchen?"

"You're the master of this estate and you don't want any damn slave to manage it for you," she sniffled. Can he only make demands?

She had him startled for just a moment, then he recovered and smiled. "What else has Lucan confided to you! I'll see you later, Tish. You don't need to get up now. I mean, would you like to rest?"

"Yes I would," she replied softly. "You're learning, Quinnie, you do learn."

"I love you, Tish."

He smiled and strode out buoyantly and she followed him with her eyes. "Damn," she uttered under her breath. "Is this the only way you know how to relate to me, Quintus, to make demands upon me like a child to his mother? Or a master to his slave? And am I going to give in to you?"

After supper Quintus helped Letitia clean up the kitchen. Then they worked on the accounts until bedtime when gradually the entire household retired. Going groggy and yawning, Quintus put his arms around Letitia's shoulders and rested his head. He dozed off. She sat there nearly a quarter hour with his head heavy on her ample breasts. It became obvious that this was no catnap. He was under for the night. She sighed, drew the lamp closer, and blew it out. She put her arm firmly around his waist and guided him stumbling and grunting upstairs to his bed.

Seeing Lucan's cot over there in the corner, in the dimness of the night-light, she wandered over and snuggled down closely to the Lucan-smell deep in the bedding. She was surprised by tears and gave in to grief, quietly, copiously.

Quintus awakened at the sound of the jagged breathing. Was Lucan having one of his nightmares? Then he remembered. He raised up on an elbow.

"Tish?"

She sat up, immediately in control again.

He held out his arms to her. "Come to me?"

She walked up just out of reach. "I'm trying, Quintus," she cried and ran downstairs to her room.

Quintus sighed and lay there immersed in loneliness. Then he fantasized that he ran after her to her room, that he said he would help her forget Lucan, that he made love with her with careful attention to her pleasure as the Easterners do, that she responded ardently, and that it was better than in the erotic literature. She praised him after, saying that he gave her what she needed.

In lonely reality he realized that she was deeply in love with Lucan. But tell the young woman that she was not so much seduced by her master as surrendered to him in obedience by her beloved and you'd have seething rebellion on your hands. He must wait for her to accept him out of her own free will. Yet the longer she put him off, the harder it may be for her. He wished that he could be more resolute. Isn't she terribly lonely herself right now, no doubt crying in her pillow? Couldn't she use some creature comfort?

He did it. Quintus got out of bed and quietly went down to her room and gave her such creature comfort that she forgot about Lucan, lost herself in himself, indeed lost awareness of everything but the extraordinary sensations in her body, and finally lost consciousness itself to a deep fulfilled sleep.

The next morning when Quintus emerged from her room, barefoot and in his nightshirt, everybody was already assembled in the kitchen for breakfast. All eyes were on him. Letitia gave him a nervous smile.

"Good morning, sir," Postumus greeted him, not too stiffly. The others followed his lead.

"Good morning!" Quintus yawned and stretched, and a burp escaped his lips. He went over and enfolded Letitia in his arms and kissed her lingeringly on the mouth.

And the world did not come to an end.

PART III

BUT THANKS BE TO GOD!

Therefore thus says the LORD:
"If you turn, I will restore you,
And you shall stand in my presence; . . .
And I will make you toward this people
A fortified wall of bronze; . . .
For I am with you to help you,
And to deliver you,
is the oracle of the LORD."

Jeremiah 15:19,20

CHAPTER XXI

Lent, A.D. 325
Light of my life, shine on me again

March saw the beginning of a new fiscal year, and this was tax year again. Quintus found himself up against one of a series of civil and military administrative innovations by the sole Emperor of the Roman world. Constantine was founding a new capital in the East, Constantinople, by renaming Byzantium and rebuilding the New Rome to the glory and perpetuation of his august name. It was a massive undertaking at the site of his most glorious conquest. The incomparable Byzantium was strategically guarded from attack by mountains on one side and sea on the other two sides while at the same time admirably seated at the heart of commerce. Constantinople would be the mistress of the East as Rome was the mistress of the West. Divide to control, seemed to be the Emperor's new policy. This would mean double the required civil and military servants paid out of the imperial treasury which would be replenished from you know where.

Quintus was already having a hard enough time meeting his four-year taxes without having to meet the new land taxes levied across the entire Empire. Assessments were drawn up at the provincial level, on cities within the province and upon individuals within each community.

The foreboding of doom crept through Quintus's bowels like a slow cancer when the surveying team arrived to assess Good Will. Livestock and slaves were counted. The lands were measured, including the additional twenty-five *iugera* tended by Postumus's family. Fields were classified in detail as being cultivated or fallow, pasture, orchard, vineyard, or woods. Quintus explained to the officials that certain fields would ordinarily be fallow except that he was experimenting with them. The officials nonetheless classified them as cultivated. Quintus was trapped by his own innovations. He was betrayed by success, the bitch!

The next step was a careful examination of his farm records. Marcellus as the landowner had to swear an oath on penalty of treason and sacrilege that these records were true and not falsified in any way. The tax in kind, deliverable at harvest, from each of the categories of farm products would be calculated on the basis of the average of the past five years.

The final blow was this actual assessment. This was Quintus's reward for restoring his ancestral land to fertility; not a state prize that he dreamed of, or the recognition as an exhibition farm, but an exemplary tax levy. Indeed he was held up to the rest of the farm community as an example. If Good Will could produce this well, then why couldn't the rest of the farm community? His friends at the marketplace resented him as the real cause of the elevated assessment of their farms. Marcellus was too upset to even say I told you so, you shouldn't have farmed in such high style.

This was to be a perpetual tax now, the next assessment coming before the previous round could be completed. There was no regard for good and bad harvests. Quintus was already headed for trouble on the charge of delinquent taxes. Furthermore, word had reached Titus the Magistrate that Quintus had a missing serf.

Marcellus galloped up to his tenant's farm to offer his friend consultation and help.

"I feel like running off to the army and throwing myself out in the front line of the next border skirmish. At least I may go down with honor. I certainly cannot do as much here," Quintus muttered.

"Oh come on, Quintus, it can't be that bad. Here, let me see. Beautiful bookkeeping; that certainly isn't the problem."

"Letitia's hand. She keeps the books now. I wish the balance were as beautiful."

"What's this big outlay for repairs, Quintus?"

"Wheels for the first wagon, shafts for the second. Plain worn out."

"And here?"

"Tiles for a leak in the roof. You don't want the building to deteriorate, now, do you?"

"We may have to, in the long run. And this?"

"Replace ruptured pipes to the baths. That was a mess!"

"I remember that. That's almost a luxury item."

"You can't be serious, Marcellus!"

"And why this lot of amphorae?"

"Bumper crop. I contracted it out, remember? I needed to maximize the harvest. Why not save steps by selling it right off the vines? The next crop may be an off year and I was counting on this crop to make up the deficit. But the new taxes don't take into account bumper crops and off years! Ceres and Bacchus just don't work in averages!"

"If only you hadn't done such a blessed good job of it! By your own success you've raised your own levy." There, Marcellus said it.

"It's a five year average, Marcellus. Remember, I started out rather miserably."

"Not as miserably as your impudent household would lead you to think. I was personally surprised."

"Listen, Marcellus, speaking of impudent slaves, whenever you need to discipline a slave, don't flog him. Send him up here for a few days' hard labor. We can use the help."

Marcellus guffawed at the idea of his self-important chamberlain up here, stripped to the waist, his fishy white belly exposed to the sun, trenching soil. The idea tickled him tremendously.

"Women too, Marcellus."

"They shall see a new discipline that they never dreamed possible. I'll send help every week. Now what's this fine?"

"I was hoping you wouldn't notice that. It's for Lucan. Even if he should return and I am spared this perpetual fine—not a chance! Damn him! Oh damn him!"

"Think he will come back?" Marcellus asked, with twinges of conscience.

"I don't know," Quintus sighed, thoroughly discouraged.

"I suppose you think that he couldn't live with himself until he repaired his wrong toward you." Marcellus was sarcastic.

"Oh sure!" Quintus burst out bitterly. This was the fleeting hope that he struggled to keep.

Sarcasm and Quintus do not go together, Marcellus was thinking. "Don't you believe in the inherent goodness of man, Beans?"

"Hell no!" Quintus retorted. "Man is inherently selfish!"

"Now Beans!" Marcellus was alarmed. Quintus was the only person he knew who retained a charitable outlook toward mankind. If Quintus fell into the brine of cynicism, then what hope remained?

When Quintus perceived that Marcellus was not teasing, he admitted, "Dammit, Marcellus, I love Lucan anyway. After all, he is still a child of God. And God also loves his unthankful and bad children. He suffers for them."

"So you are not going to torture Lucan to desperate incoherence when you get your hands on him again?"

"Well, hardly, Marcellus."

Marcellus, moved by Quintus's forgiving attitude, confessed that the testing of the bet was weighted; he had a spy report to him when Lucan was in a dark mood. And he insisted at that time that the bet be tested for he could be certain that Lucan would not come back. "Really I-I . . ." Marcellus fumbled.

"Lord God!" Quintus cried out in high agitation. "You have betrayed the Lord Christ again!"

"No, not that, Beans! The state never got hold of him! He took a merchant ship to Alexandria! Last November!"

"Alexandria! Why of course! I'll write Leander."

"I have already circulated notices."

"Marcellus, do you have to meddle?"

"I was only trying to recover lost property," Marcellus answered defensively. "You realize he is my property now."

"Property!" Quintus was shocked. "He came home! He's mine!"

"He ran away," Marcellus insisted. "He's mine!"

"But he did come home! That's all the bet said!"

"Prove it!"

"Here! By his own hand!" Quintus opened a wax tablet and showed it to Marcellus. Inscribed deeply, with the date of that traumatic night was a mere sentence. 'Lord of my life, my heart is crushed to ashes.'

"He could have written that before we all departed! He joined us at the last moment, you know."

"Look at the date. The next morning."

"So he postdated it."

"Marcellus, he returned the horse!"

"Any horse will come home without his rider."

"He took care of the animal himself!"

"Nonsense. One of the slaves did."

"It was Lucan. Gregor spoke with him."

"They're lying, then."

"My slaves don't lie."

"All slaves lie, by definition."

"They're Christian!"

"Interrogate them properly with torture and you'll see."

"If you insist, then you pay the penalty for his absence," Quintus retorted.

"Oh, no, Beans, that part is on you!"

"You disgust me!"

"I can't stomach you either!"

"Marcellus, you are not my friend any more! Get on your horse and go home!" Quintus leapt up and showed Marcellus the door.

Marcellus rushed angrily out, furiously stung that Quintus who could extend his charity to an incorrigible slave would not have forgiveness for his aristocratic friend and landlord.

"Go to prison!" he muttered on the way home. "Suffer torture on the *equuleus* for your ungrateful reprobate! Ride that horse for your delinquent taxes, you who refused my recommendations on marketing because they would be 'unfair'!"

Lord God! Quintus moaned when he was alone again. Why did this all have to happen? Best friend at sword's point. Lucan refusing to come home. The whole household is convinced that I sent him away. Why did I have to find out the truth about myself? All my talk about being kind, and just, and merciful. Why did I have to get angry at Marcellus? Why could I not show my friend the forgiveness that I was more than ready to give a wretched slave! It is myself that I despise. Why did I ever let Marcellus challenge the bet! Lord, I have betrayed you again!

Quintus picked up Lucan's wax tablet, opened it and regarded the anguished inscription: 'Lord of my life, my heart is crushed to ashes.' Quintus inscribed his own anguish on the opposite side. 'Light of my life, shine on me again!'

He closed the tablet and put it under Lucan's pillow. Then he went out to the fields and buried himself in work.

* * *

After supper that evening Quintus could neither work nor sleep. He was too upset to face another tense and nightmarish night. If Lucan were here, he would give him sleep. He stood gazing out his window at the spot of light that came from Postumus's cottage up the hill. Must the domine's lot be such a lonely one? Will this estrangement never end? If I called for Letitia would she come to me? Will she ever love me? With whom can I be at one? I've got the burden of their entire world on my shoulders. Don't they even care? Letitia, Letitia, bright light on the hill, come to me! I'll send for her!

Letitia did not comply. She was preoccupied with her infant who was going through one of those unexplainable fussy spells. When Gregor made the next round of night inspection of the premises Quintus intercepted him and sent him up the hill to get her.

"Tell your big sister that if she knows what is good for her she will get herself down here. Now."

"You had better go, Letitia," Gregor urged. "He's fit to be tied."

"That's precisely why I don't want to go. You can tell him that if he wants me to visit him he needs to make his invitation a lot more attractive."

"Is crying need ever attractive? Come on, Letitia, I need to get to work."

"Then go!"

Gregor sought out his mother and appealed to her to reason with his sister. Cara went to her daughter's room. "Ain't you going down to your man when he needs you?"

"What do you mean, 'my man'? Did he give me my freedom or did he only want his son to be freeborn?"

"How are we to survive if the young domine gives up?"

"Do you want me to sacrifice myself again for the household?"

"Goodness, you is so sensitive!"

"Ma, I've had my fill of men. Is that so hard to understand?"

"No, only you is so young to be feeling like that."

"I've been taken for granted by the first, deserted by the second, burned by the third and exploited by the rest. Can you blame me?" Then she added by last minute inspiration, "Perhaps Sappho knew something we don't."

Cara was silent for a moment, then answered patiently, "Child, I was burned by some three-thousand, but when they brings me up here and led me to Postumus and placed my hand in his and his eyes were kind and his bearing gentle . . ." Then impatience sounded in her voice. "Is you going to pass by maybe the best thing that happened to you?"

"What?"

"Your Pa thinks so too. I don't know if you is supposed to know this but him asked your Pa permission to marry you."

"He did? When!"

"Well, some time ago, before the child was born, before him came up to lie with you during the rest periods."

"Don't I have a say in that?"

"You've been having your say all along. All resistance."

"Now Ma!"

"What ever is it that you wants, child!"

"To be cherished, not used."

"Then would you please stop fighting him?"

"Whatever changed Pa's mind?"

"Quintus. Him listens to you. Him cares. Him cares more than the others ever could. The daily visits, the water buckets, the woodpile, your brothers ain't doing them things for you. And when you went into labor, and tied your girdle, finally in two knots, for him to undo, how happy him was! And when you was giving birth him was pacing outside like a dispossessed midwife. And when you cried out for the Lord Jesus Christ and Alexis went galloping off to fetch the Deacon to hear your confessions, him nearly broke the door, him was so anxious to get to you. Lucan's child indeed. And how tenderly him held you on the midwife's chair. And when he took up his son from the floor and held him in his arms . . ."

"Yes, Ma, I was there. Supposing it was a daughter?"

"Now, Letitia! Him is simply precious waiting for you so ardently. You is serviceable again, ain't you? Here you is in the full bloom of womanhood, and doesn't you desire him, just a little bit?"

"And get myself on the midwife's chair again before the year is out?"

"Is that what's bothering you?"

"A lot of things are bothering me."

"Listen, dear, you're nursing. And there's the citrus juice, and the sponge. Go love your fool bottom off! Now what else is bothering you?"

"Is that what Pa wants for me?"

"Try, Letitia, him wants you to try."

"I should let myself in for a new form of servitude? Wasn't slavery enough? Haven't I been exploited enough? Am I to compromise myself again this time in marriage?"

"Think of Quintus. Give yourself a chance to love him. Make his concerns your concerns, and you won't feel that way."

"That's exactly what I'm talking about. All my life I've made his concerns my concerns, and it has been called slavery. Am I to become his slave again in the name of love?"

"Slave? Why no, Letitia, Matron of the villa!"

"I don't want to be put in that lonely spot."

"No lonelier than you is willing to let it be."

"Ma, I saw Quinnie grow up and the wall close around him. The household wouldn't let him remain one of them. Not even when he became Christian. Lucan was the only one who came close and now Lucan is gone."

"All the more reason he needs you at his side, dear. You can speak to his soul. Who else can a man trust his real feelings to except the woman he loves?"

"Really, Ma. Does Pa?"

Cara rolled her eyes heavenward.

"Furthermore, his real feelings are crying needs! He's so vulnerable! The Lord of our lives! He isn't in control at all! And I am to entrust myself to him?"

"So what's new, dear?"

Letitia stared at her mother in shock. "Ma, what am I going to do?"

"At least think about your security."

"What security! As soon as his family returns for a visit . . ." she made a chopping motion with her hand. "If he wants to dump me and marry someone else, all he has to do is bribe the magistrate, or get some poison or bring false charges."

"Pay no mind to that court gossip!"

"It's true! And you saw how in this house they already tried to get rid of Lucan."

"Do you still believe that?"

"Besides, if I marry, I lose my right to my children."

"Letitia!"

"Roman Law, Ma. I've been doing some reading. So don't belabor me about marrying for security."

"My goodness, child." Cara took her daughter in her arms.

"And if I go down there with the baby fussing like this . . ." Tears of frustration stung her eyes.

"There, there, my dear," Cara soothed. "Go on down to him. Help him to understand what it means to love you as hisself. Him owes that to you."

"I'll be hard on him, Ma. I won't let him put anything over on me."

"So be it. But remember two things, my dear. First, never cross him in public. If he hasn't your absolute loyalty, how can he rule the household? Second, be good to him in bed. Remember my instructions."

"Oh Ma," Letitia scoffed affectionately. "I'll go." She gathered up her infant.

"Now wait a minute. Where's your nice dalmatica? And let's comb your hair up. Have you been using your depilatory?

"My dropax?"

"Whichever. And where's your lavender? His lovely gift to you. Ah, Letitia, him's such a good man."

"Thank you for listening, Ma."

Gregor escorted Letitia down the hill to the villa.

"Thanks, Gregor, I guess." Now in the villa her resolve waned and her fear of Quintus's power over her prevailed again. She went to her old room in the servant's quarters. She couldn't seem to help herself when the old slave mentality overcame her again. At times like this she could only think of the many times she had broken the rules of subservience, and was certain that something dreadful would happen to her. He must be seething with anger. Maybe he was going to punish her this time. But what would he do? There were no devastating words he could use on her comparable to those that he used to undo Lucan. He would have to get physically violent. Then what could she do? He was so much stronger! Would he hurt the baby? Yes! That's how he would get at her! Really, what could she do? Here he was now!

Quintus from his upstairs room saw the progression of the lantern down the hillside. When the time had passed that she should have arrived at his room, he went downstairs to find her. He closed the curtain behind him with a smart snap. Their infant threw open his arms in a startle reflex and started crying.

"Careful, Quintus, you're startling Lucian."

He was staring in astonishment at her unexpected beauty, the upswept hair giving her stocky peasant figure an air of elegance and the delicate tendrils at her temples and down the back of her neck giving her the appearance of fragile vulnerability. Her hostility took him by such surprise that he flung it right back at her.

"Why didn't you come down to me when I first sent for you?"

"Couldn't. The baby."

"Can't you just leave that thing when your man needs you?"

"No," she said firmly. "That thing needs to suckle for an hour every two and a half hours, day and night, cracked nipples and all."

Quintus shook his head and heaved a sigh.

"The baby needs one end of me and you want the other. What am I supposed to do; choose between you?"

"Come upstairs, woman, and I'll show you what you are supposed to do."

Letitia did not move. Look at this man, she thought. He gave me my freedom. He asks for my hand in marriage, but he is commanding me as though I were still his slave. She glared at him.

He strode for the door, then turned on his heel to see if she were coming. In one reflexive action she snatched up the infant, clutched it to her breast, and backed up a step. She was still terrified of him when he was angry. He came back to her and reached for the child.

There was coaxing in his voice now as he spoke her name. They both knew the power of his touch. It would send shivers through her body and she would melt to his will, in sweet surrender it would seem to him. Don't they say all a woman needs is a good lay? The surrender would seem like a little death to her, a little more of her dying each time she was not met on the level and taken seriously.

"Don't do this to me, Quintus," she warned sharply.

"You're belligerent tonight."

"Because you're on your high horse again."

"You put me there by your servile attitude."

"I did no such . . . !" The insight blindsided her.

"Afraid of divine retribution or something?" he quipped sarcastically.

"Maybe that's the way it is!" She was defensive.

"Oh women are such sweet hell." It was his turn to be perplexed.

She offered a truce. "What's the first line of that poem? 'Offered a sexless heaven, I'd say no thank you'?"

"So you've been dusting Ovid's love books under my bed?"

"You told me to didn't you?" She giggled and he caught her around the waist.

"You're lovely," he whispered and nibbled her on the neck. That made goose bumps rise on her thighs. She leaned briefly against him and came along willingly. Upstairs in his rooms he threw himself on the bed and she settled next to him.

"Letitia, I am crushed with problems. I need release. Help me, Letitia, please help me with your womanly charms. I need to lose myself in your embrace. Totally. To oblivion."

"What is the matter?" She caressed his temple.

"The taxes. And that damn slave has done me in again."

"Lucan? How!" The mention of his name unsettled her.

"How can that slave run off like that, after all I've done for him? But I don't want to go into it further, Letitia. I want to get some sleep."

"Oh, I should just swallow your bitterness whole and sympathize with you?"

"Don't fight me, Tish," he requested wearily. "I don't want to talk about it any more."

Ordinarily she would just let him close the topic, and resent him that he upset her. No, no, she would console her self, that's little. I won't bother him with it. He's upset. But tonight the hurt in her could not let it pass. The hurt in her welled up in reply. That's right, let him get away with it. Teach him that even in an intimate relationship he doesn't have to bother with your feelings. You want to be cherished in a two-way thoroughfare and you are letting him insist on being nurtured in a one-way alley. Letitia, that will consume you slowly and you know it will destroy you! She spoke, her throat dry with fear.

"Look, Quintus, do you realize what you have just now done to me? You have just now immersed me in a kettle of boiling oil, and you're walking away and leaving me there. That's cruel, Quintus."

"Gods alive, woman!"

"How many times have you done that to Lucan?"

"Crux!" Quintus's outburst startled the infant into crying. Quintus paced the room.

"Actually you drove him away, Quintus."

"Do you think I don't know that?" He was nearly shouting.

"Now let me finish!" she persisted. "Even when he begged you for help you devastated him."

"Is that so," he returned coldly. "And what else has he told you?"

"Everything, Quintus, everything! Oh how I have wept with him and agonized with him and ushered him through the dark valleys of the past and the present!"

Quintus was stung with jealousy. He did tell all, and he told it to her! She was his confidante, not him, his brother in Christ. She was his love. She loved him!

"Are you going to drive me away when I need you?" Quintus asked angrily.

"I hope not, Quinnie," she softened. "But you are going to drive me away if you continue to rail against Lucan."

First Lucan, now the infant commanded her intimacy. He could hardly bear it. "Doesn't that thing ever stop crying?"

"He's upset . . . because we are. You will have to tolerate a lot of crying if you want me down here with you. And I can't suckle the baby under stress. The milk won't let down! I need freedom from care to raise our child." She put the infant to breast to quiet him.

Quintus knelt before her and buried his face in her lap. He sighed deeply.

"I hear you, Tish. Forgive me! Forgive me about Lucan! He was the only person in this big world who would be close with me. Dear God, I miss him! I need someone close so that I can bear to be human."

"Quintus please . . ." Such a confession was completely unexpected, completely unprecedented. She felt very uncomfortable with it.

"Sometimes, Letitia, when I'm birthing this farm, the labor seems quite hopeless and like you women I cry out in pain and desperation. Is that so bad? I have to persevere, the way you women do. I supported you on the midwife's chair so that you could be delivered of a difficult birth. I need someone to support me on the midwife's chair and to coach me soothingly. Is that so hard to understand? Is that too much to ask?"

"No, Quintus." She stroked his head and neck with her free hand. The idea that he needed her and that she had power over him overwhelmed her. Underneath all that authority and command was another human being asking to be recognized.

"I'm here, Quintus," she said shakily.

He snuggled his face more deeply in her groin, then looked up at her again.

"The responsibility on my head—for all of you—it scares me, Letitia. It really scares me. Can you understand?"

"I understand," Letitia whispered and kissed their infant on the fontanel. She also understood that she must always be prepared to take care of herself and her child independently, and that thought was terrifying.

"You really love our little child, don't you," he commented with wonder.

"Something fierce," she murmured.

"I hope you can say that of me, someday."

"Oh Quintus!" With a surge of compassion she put the infant down and drew Quintus up and seated him beside her. Then she maneuvered to straddle him and impale herself on him simultaneously while she picked up and suckled the infant. He lowered his head and tasted the sweetness of her free nipple and looked up at her with awe.

"What's the name of this posture, Quinnie," she giggled.

"Feed our baby," he replied, and tenderly stroked the pulse on her neck.

The stimulation of feeling his fullness inside her and the pulling on her breasts released among other things a generous flow of milk and the infant finally suckled itself into oblivion. Then she gave herself completely to Quintus.

Quintus slept. And when Letitia settled down in bed every few hours after nursing the infant, he reached for her, seeking reassurance, always giving pleasure. Sometimes he didn't even wait for her to finish, but spooned up tightly behind her as she nursed and reached around in front to pleasure her with his hands. She responded generously and experienced overflowing chalices of that promised joy.

CHAPTER XXII

The penalty has already been paid

The pascha found Quintus in prison enduring quiet agony straddled on the narrow pole of the *equuleus*, a torture trestle. He felt his patience slowly give way. The windlass was not yet turned enough to dislocate his hips, not yet, though he was not spared considerable torture. Damn fool nonsense, he thought bitterly. When I get my hands on Lucan again, when I get him again! He bore his affliction in outraged silence. Constantine had passed an edict that floggings and the trestle should be dispensed with in dealing with the delinquent taxpayers. And the news of that decree had reached Puteoli. But little good the law did him now as he sat sweating and racked on the trestle.

There was no use either, in appealing to Titus the Magistrate who jailed him. For it seemed that Quintus, at his booth in the marketplace, had displayed the unfortunate impropriety of jesting with his fellows about Titus, and of coming up with a Quintilian slur on Titus's ostentatious parades to the baths complete with fanfare, the latest style of the perfumed dandy's clothing, and the placement of flowers in the folds of his toga.

It seemed that indeed this had something to do with the jailer's failure to observe Constantine's ban on torture.

Furthermore, Quintus was accused of aiding the escape of a serf. If true, that would be a serious offense. But nonsense! Damn fool nonsense! Worthless nonsense! And where is Marcellus? Why doesn't he come to me!

A breeze accompanying an April shower found its way in through the narrow prison window. It brought relief, but only for a moment. The moving air soon chilled his sweat-drenched body to the bone. Quintus's muscles began cramping.

Lord in heaven, Quintus despaired, his patience spent, is this what obedience even to death means? No greater love has a man than that he gives his life for a friend?

For a friend? Lucan a friend?

"Christe!" he cried out in anguish. "Let me faint! *Christe! Christe!*" There was no escape from this.

A guard unlocked the door and a figure entered the cell and removed his rain-drenched cloak. "Peace be with you!"

"And with your spirit!" Quintus gasped in relief. It was Bishop Nicodemus.

"I brought you the sacrament." The bishop fumbled with the windlass, found it unlocked, and released the ratchet to ease some of the tension. Then he pulled out a water flask from under his cloak and gave Quintus a drink. Finally he released the ratchet again, by increments, until Quintus was relieved entirely of the crippling weights. Then the bishop lowered the young Roman to the floor, and fell to massaging his cramped muscles.

"I cannot get you out of here just yet," Nicodemus said, "but at least I got you off this thing. I bribed the jailer. It is our hope to have you out on probation soon. You must hold on."

"No . . . Lucan?" Quintus asked without hope.

"Yes!"

"You found him!" Quintus's face lit.

"At Alexandria! Secretary at the Basilica. Deacon Leander took down the Man Wanted posters."

"With Leander! I thought of that."

"Deacon Leander wrote you as soon as the seas opened. Olipor got the letter at the docks today."

"Only a letter? No Lucan?" Quintus groaned in exasperation.

"Here, listen." Bishop Nicodemus read Deacon Leander's letter. "Your little brother in Christ has indeed come into my custody. You have restored him to a fine young man. I was thanking God that you finally cleared him of former obligations and saw it in your heart to lend him to me at such a critically important time for the church. It was with a heavy heart that I read and took down the Man Wanted posting in the marketplace. Lucan does not know of this notice. He had simply told me that he was free to come to my aid. I thought it best not to proceed with any drastic action until hearing from you. Furthermore I would like to wait until he is willing to return heart and soul before I send him on the long journey home. As Paul wrote to Philemon, 'Perhaps this is why he was parted from you for a while, that you might have him back forever, no longer as a slave but more than a slave, as a beloved brother, dear especially to me, but how much more to you, both in the flesh and in the Lord.'"

"I could have had the scoundrel home by now! On this same ship!" Quintus burst out bitterly. "If only Leander had sent the man instead of a letter! A fine position I'm in now to go after him and drag him home! But when I get out of here, I'll . . ."

"Quintus! Please!"

"See what my 'brother' brings upon me!" Quintus stormed. "I still have to come up with the fines on him! Bishop Nicodemus, is there no end to what I must endure in the Name of Christ? Even this, Bishop? Isn't this rather beyond the call?"

"Quintus, are you tempted to deny Christ when He suffered to the death for you, for your brother's sin?" Nicodemus put it to him gently.

"Sorely tempted!" Quintus's face screwed up stubbornly.

"Would you have had the Christ put a limit to his obedience?"

"It is my salvation that he didn't," Quintus sobered.

"Quintus, pray for trust in God your Father. Your suffering shall not be in vain! Not that you are accomplishing anything by it, but he is. Offer your pain to him that he may use it for his creative purposes!"

"That is easy to say from your view of the trestle," Quintus grimaced.

"That's better now," Nicodemus approved. "Now look at this. See, Quintus, see what your family in Christ at Good Will has done for you!" The bishop pulled a bank receipt out of his purse and held it up for Quintus to read. It was a payment toward the taxes and the fine for the missing serf. "Their life savings, Quintus, all they had. Two of them even offered to sell themselves, and we had to remind them that they couldn't be sold off the land."

Quintus nearly wept. His slaves! His dear family in Christ! He was reconciled to them at last.

"They pray for you too, Quintus, constantly. Every minute one of them is keeping watch for you. Including Marcipor. And here." The bishop showed him another receipt. "From your business associates on the Via Serapide, and their slaves. They got to wondering why you yourself no longer came down to market. Then when Letitia and baby came down and appealed to them . . ."

"Letitia!" Quintus whispered.

"Letitia has moved down to the villa, to your rooms. She says that she can manage the bookkeeping easier from there. There is more. You won't be angry? She started a new consulting service, door to door to the resort villas, helping the matrons plan their banquets according to the produce in season at Good Will. They are charmed by her. She goes out as your wife—matron's hairdo, borrowed clothes from Marcia's room, a locket from Dorothea. Olipor helped her with letters of introduction. Mamercus cleaned up Marcia's two-wheeler and hitches the bay mule. Gregor accompanies her. She hopes to have you out of here shortly, at which time, she says, you may deal with her as you see fit."

"Tell that remarkable woman that I'll deal with her with due respect. Warn her that I shall claim my bride!"

"Now that's my man," the bishop smiled. "Listen. She is arranging to visit you in prison and tend to your needs, food, massage, love."

Quintus smiled. "She must get Megas to escort her past the guard."

When Quintus recovered from his emotions, he dictated a reply to Deacon Leander regarding Lucan. "I am deeply concerned about my brother in Christ, Lucan Oikonomikos. I want to reassure him to feel free to come home; the penalty for his absence has already been paid. Lucan, I entreat you to return to me. Signed, Quintus Legerius of Good Will, Puteoli. There. That's done. How long will this letter take to get to Alexandria?"

"About four weeks by the next merchant ship."

"Four weeks . . . let's see . . . will it be at the end of May?"

"Yes."

"Oh damn!" Quintus suddenly had a hunch.

"What is it?"

"The Council, Bishop Nicodemus, it would be just like Lucan to have run off with Leander to the Council. Have the letter forwarded if necessary."

"The Ecumenical Council," the bishop breathed as he wrote, "Emperor's Palace, Nicaea of Bithynia."

"Now how long would that take?" Quintus was impatient.

"The letter would arrive at Nicaea late June."

"And then another two months or more for Lucan to journey home. Not until September. And to think that he could have been home already!" Quintus gave in to pure frustration.

As Quintus waited out the slow hours of pain on the cold prison floor, the bishop's words repeated in his mind. Trust in God that your suffering shall not be in vain! Offer your pain to him that he may use it for his creative purposes!

Then he remembered some double-edged words of Olipor concerning Lucan that had impressed him even when they were first spoken. Now these words shook his soul. Domine, sometimes a worthwhile conquest comes only at the price of much pain. And Jesus Christ conquered at the price of nothing less than pain unto—death!

"So be it, Lord," Quintus prayed. "So be it." Then Quintus resigned himself to his Lord without reserve. "Take me, O God. My pain is all that I have to offer you now. Lord, I had no idea when I followed you that my discipleship would mean even this! I had no idea the extreme to which my obedience would have to go! If I could have known beforehand I would not have been willing. If I had known that The Way was to be the most difficult and consequential challenge in my life I would have quailed before I even thought of acknowledging my sonship. Father! Father! Great is your wisdom that you let us see only as much as we have the strength and faith to endure! Father, I know not what is yet ahead of me! My trust is in you! Here I am. Forgive me. O merciful God, I have been acting toward you as my runaway slave has toward me. And yet you forgive. You forgive me my trespasses. And I forgive Lucan. Take me as I am and use me as you will, where you will, when you will, with whom you will!"

Lord of my life, my heart is crushed to ashes.

For the first time Quintus began to intercede for Lucan.

Light of my life, shine on me again.

* * *

"Merciful Apollo!" Marcellus retreated from the atrium where he had just received Bishop Nicodemus, and threw himself down on his bedroom couch. Marcipor sought out his master.

"Does my domine wish the presence of his slave again?"

Marcellus answered the query gloomily. "Bring me some strong wine, Marcipor, I wish to be put out."

"My domine is not well?"

"Oh I'm well all right, it's just Bishop Nicodemus, of all people!"

"Does my master care to say what about?" Marcellus dared to press his master in an unservile manner.

Marcellus became evasive. "Tell me, Marcipor, what do you do when you have wronged your friend?" Marcellus never, no never, asks a mere slave for advice.

Marcipor took it without surprise. "Ask his pardon, sir. How is Quintus, sir?" he asked apprehensively.

"What do you know about him when we haven't been up there for a dog's age?"

"My domine's slave has been up there every week praying with them and for him!" It was out now.

Marcellus's eyes narrowed. "Unfaithful slave! Your beloved Quintus is in prison, riding the *equuleus*! So what are you going to do now; leave me and run to him?"

"God have mercy on you, you are crucifying the Christ again!" Marcipor cried out in horror.

"This has nothing to do with The Way!" Marcellus protested.

"Everything, Domine, everything to do with it!" Marcipor dropped all formality. His time had come. He spoke the hard words quietly, in love. "Marcellus, this is appalling. Quintus in prison! Chained to cold stone! Roaches! Rats! Fleas! Disease! First a deliberate demoralization of his slave. Then a whispered implication to an authority that he assisted the fugitive. Quintus in agony on the trestle! Legs could be wrenched out of their sockets by the weights, muscles torn from the bones by cramping!"

"They're not doing that to him!" Marcellus was defensive.

"How can you say that! 'Pressure him', that's what those words mean. He is indeed on the trestle. Half starved. He could die of pneumonia! And you, engaging in your pleasant distractions, forget what you have abandoned him to while your stooges carry out the order."

"Pleasant distractions?!"

"I know about you, pressing Quintus for the last penny he owes you so you could order a purple cloak and silvered armor for the equestrian reviews."

"Not just any review, Marcipor, The Great Equestrian Review at the Emperor's upcoming Vicennalia! It's my chance to be noticed! Perhaps get a commission! Redeem my family name."

"Marcellus, at what cost!"

"You dog!" Marcellus bared his dagger and advanced on his accuser. No slave of his had ever dared to speak to him like this.

"You didn't know how much evil you could initiate, did you!" the slave maintained his rebuke fearlessly. "You refused to help Quintus with the taxes, too. And if Quintus should inform his father, the old man would commit suicide and his wife with him, rather than resort to the only way left." Then Marcipor caught himself. "Pardon me, sir, I quite lost myself . . . I lost my family . . . I lost my . . . please forgive me".

"Are you telling me that not even the overseer has sent for the senior domine?" Marcellus lowered his hand.

"Olipor is under strict orders not to, and he has his own reasons for obeying."

"What reasons?" Marcellus snapped.

"Think he would willingly be the messenger of doom?" Marcipor evaded the real reason.

"Damn you slaves! Don't you know you aren't supposed to have reasons?" Marcellus muttered at the insight.

Marcipor smiled at his master. He really loved this blindly arrogant Roman.

"Well I'm in no position to go to him," Marcellus sputtered helplessly. "Go on, Marcipor, you were going to suggest?" Marcellus had never before condescended to a slave.

"I was going to say, sir, that you yet have time to stop this one before it is too late."

"What do you mean, Marcipor?" Marcellus opened himself up with effort.

Marcipor returned to the usual formality to ease his master through the difficulty. "Is my domine deciding to rescue his friend?"

Marcellus took the opportunity to save face. "I have already decided." After a moment of thought he added, "And what else do you suppose I have decided?"

"To forgive. And my domine decided to confess his wrong".

"What!"

"My domine decided that he has to acknowledge his wrong if his friend's pardon is to be real." Marcipor was firm.

Marcellus had his doubts. "And what do you suppose your domine intends to do if his friend refuses pardon?"

"My domine will patiently wait until my domine's friend is willing," Marcipor answered.

"What if Quintus disowns me again?" Marcellus came out with it directly.

"Domine, you must take the risk," Marcipor pleaded.

This advice came hard to Marcellus. He would rather open his veins than lose face before his friends and his plebian tenant. His eyes narrowed to slits and he mouthed slowly to his slave, "Marcipor, you can go to the dogs."

Marcipor was not surprised. "If you allow me, sir, you need me here," he bowed. "If your slave must go, first may he remind his domine that the domine knows what he must do?" Marcipor stayed courageously at his position.

Marcellus leapt at him in amazement. "Now listen, Marcipor," he charged, "it isn't fair, you, a slave, pressuring me like this. Will you hold your tongue about this conversation?"

"What conversation?" Marcipor assured him.

Marcellus thrust his dagger at his slave's face. "At the pain of losing your tongue, and consequently your life, will you pledge silence?"

"My domine's slave doesn't know anything about this."

"Your domine's slave is prudent." Marcellus sheathed the blade and regarded him with profound respect.

* * *

Marcellus stormed into the prison and found Quintus chained to the wall to 'wring from him the truth concerning the whereabouts of his runaway serf, and to wrench out of him the delinquent taxes.'

"Of all the damn fool things!" Marcellus raged at the jailer. "I'm reporting you to the magistrate! Cut this man loose! He tells the truth! He is innocent! He did not help his runaway serf escape! As for the tax money—it shall be paid to the magistrate in full! See, look at the promissory. And here is the promissory for the fine."

Though it was the magistrate who ordered the trestle and the chains, the jailer released Quintus, in fear of Marcellus's influence.

Marcellus carried his emaciated friend out and laid him in his carriage. "You are going home to your family, Beans," he said tersely.

When Quintus finally found words, on the way home, he murmured, "Why, Marcellus, why?"

"Letitia is pregnant," Marcellus answered deviously.

"Pregnant! What kind of joke is this, Marcellus?"

"You with your debts and runaway slave could have hung there and rotted, for all I cared!" Marcellus retorted. "I have been angry with you, Beans. Very angry."

"You are not angry with me any more, Marcellus?" Quintus asked weakly.

"Quintus, can you forgive me?" Marcellus unexpectedly pleaded without telling what it was that Quintus had to forgive.

"Oh, so I'm Quintus now?" He mustered a smile.

"Dear old Beans!" Marcellus had never before been on the receiving end like this, and scarcely the giving end. "I bet you," he said with a grin, "I bet you that I can recover Lucan before you do."

Quintus smiled weakly. "Hands off, Marcellus, I beg you!"

"I've posted notices for him, you know."

"And I've ordered a search." Quintus wasn't about to tell that he knew where Lucan was. "I'll get him back when the right time comes. We must be patient. I know of myself that I am incapable of persuading one who may be unwilling. And I'm not about to drag him back in chains."

"You incapable, Quintus?"

"I would only lose my temper again and do something unfortunate." He rose on his elbow.

"Lose your temper? Again? Beans, you have much patience."

"No . . . no . . . during the times that Lucan needed my patience the most, I beat him and undercut him instead." Quintus slumped back on the carriage floor and started coughing.

"You beat him? Your brothers and men roughed him up a bit that night, but you?"

"I had at him first. That's how he came to run outdoors and fall into the hands of my brothers on the way in."

Marcellus was unexpectedly disappointed. "You tried my way, then! But you are a Christian!"

"My dear friend," Quintus attempted between coughs, "Christian, and good, are not synonymous."

"What is a Christian, then?"

"One who knows that though he is not good, he is loved by Christ."

"So?" Marcellus shrugged.

"So one tries to respond to that love, knowing that without Christ's help . . . he . . . cannot . . . even . . . do . . . that," Quintus managed between coughing before he gave in to exhaustion.

Marcellus shrugged. One thing I do know, he thought to himself later on his way home, is that though your life is not perfect, Beans, there's something about you . . .

That night he tried his new thoughts in words.

"You know, Marcipor, strange thing about Quintus. It is as though—well—he has rescued me, and not I him."

"Rescued you, sir?"

"From meaninglessness," Marcellus experimented. "You saw the love and joy when I returned him to his household. Such love could bring meaning to my life."

"Then thank God," Marcipor said quietly.

"What has God to do with it?" Marcellus asked on the defensive.

"He has been able to work through his servant," Marcipor explained.

"Isn't that rather far fetched?" Marcellus parried the idea.

"Indeed you have come far, sir," Marcipor dared.

"Meaning what?" the mystified Marcellus demanded.

"Whatever it pleases my lord." Marcipor became quite the slave again.

* * *

Quintus was bedded down in the sickroom, in the bosom of his household, where they could keep an eye on him, help him to the privy, the table, offer some companionship, and bid him 'Good Health Quintus' whenever he sneezed. Letitia and their infant stayed in her former cubicle next to him. Marcellus sent up a masseuse to relieve the pulled muscles and tendons of Quintus's hips. He prescribed hot and cold packs and demonstrated how they were to massage out the cramping.

In due time Letitia gave Quintus a thorough accounting of her catering efforts, and took full responsibility for the borrowed clothing. They went over the farm accounts together. The bookkeeping was impeccable.

"Now Letitia," he confronted her, "there is something else that you need to tell me."

"There is?"

"Marcellus said that you were pregnant."

Letitia giggled. "Wherever did he get that idea!" Then seeing his worried look, she added quickly, "I stayed out of his reach. I sent the Bishop."

"You sent the Bishop!"

"Only look at our staff and you will see how many times we have helped the rescue mission at Puteoli. Don't you agree that it was most natural to suggest that it was our turn for help?"

"I am indeed a charity case!"

"On Marcellus, among others!"

"Clever woman!" They laughed and kissed. "When I'm better", he threatened with his smiling voice, "when I'm better, look out; I'm going to claim my self-proclaimed bride, and redeem that lie."

"Redeem me, my lord," she whispered.

* * *

Quintus was beside himself with anticipation when the next round trip of ships arrived from Alexandria. Lucan could be on one of those ships! Reason against hope, he told the household nothing. The runaway could be at his feet in a matter of hours now. He rehearsed to himself privately how he would receive him, what he would say. He debated whether or not to take the fresh berries, greens and honey to market himself that morning and meet Lucan on the docks or to stay at home in case Lucan would miss him in the crowd. Home won. He could not concentrate at the books so he went out to work in the fields where his men were earthing up the soil around the fruit trees to protect the roots from the oncoming fierce summer sun.

He was summoned by shrill screams from Ignis the stallion, wild barking from Cerberus, and a commotion in the stable court as though the whole place were being kicked down. He ran over to find Ignis dancing, tail up like a plume, powerful neck arched, around an exquisite Arabian filly with a bright chestnut coat, mane and tail that reflected light like a rainbow. The filly was delivered to Good Will complete with an Arabian groom off a ship from Alexandria. Her name, Rainbow in Hebrew, and Quintus's name and address in Latin were tooled into her fine leather halter. The young groom spoke no Latin nor Greek and could explain no more to Mamercus in Arabic than that he was only making a delivery, and would the domine permit him to stay with his beloved charge?

Quintus surmised the source and accepted the astonishing gift as though he expected it and let the household believe that he was fulfilling an old promise to Mamercus. Tears streaked down Mamercus's face when he received the filly. The young groom responded with obeisant gratitude to the word that since he was included in the purchase price of the filly, he would be allowed to stay. Letitia, holding firmly to what she believed, kept silent.

Quintus understood. First it was a fugitive in place of a filly, now it was a filly in exchange for the fugitive. He pondered her Hebrew name. Of course! The message behind the name was God's promise to Noah of no more destruction of the known world, the rainbow being the sign. Lucan was promising that he would no longer visit upon Good Will the disruption of his presence. Presumptuous slave! It would be harder to get him back than Quintus anticipated. He would give Rainbow to Titus the Magistrate if necessary to demonstrate that he didn't aid Lucan's escape and wasn't accepting bribes. Titus wouldn't make the connection between the filly and the fugitive, though. And a body was filling the open spot on the roster. That ought to satisfy him.

Lucan, I entreat you to return to me! Rainbow was Lucan's answer. Lucan, you cannot bargain with me, Quintus grumbled to himself.

CHAPTER XXIII

If your brother has something against you

Lawrence, an under-secretary to Bishop Alexander, joined the congregation at the large old gymnasium in Nicaea of the East. He was late. He found standing room in the back, next to a column.

Anyway I finished transcribing the final draft of the creed, he thought to himself. The Nicene Creed! And the mound of outgoing mail is off with the morning post. The gym is packed! Some of the parish must have come also to celebrate the settlement of the controversy. Never dreamed this Arian heresy could involve so many. Who's celebrating? Can't even see into the apse, it's so packed. Sounds like Theognis, Bishop of Nicaea. Oh look, you can spot that sunny-haired Goth anywhere! And there's the Metropolitan of India. I'd like a closer look at him. The prayer of consecration already; I really am late!

Now that the controversy is settled, it seems to have happened quickly. July already! Lord, I have been working hard. Debates and Canons to capture in writing, and to transcribe. And the letters! You'd never have guessed there were that many churches.

His attention came around when the assembly spoke as one mighty voice what would be known as the Nicene Creed:

> "We believe in one God the Father Almighty, maker of things both visible and invisible. And in one Lord Jesus Christ the Son of God, begotten from the Father as only begotten God from God, that is from the very substance of the Father, Light from Light, Very God from Very God, begotten, not made, being of one substance with the Father, by whom all things were made, both things in heaven and things on earth: who for us men and for our salvation came down and was

> incarnate, became man, suffered, rose again on the third day, went up into heaven, and is coming to judge the living and the dead. And in the Holy Spirit."

He knew it by heart now after all those sessions.

Then a priest intoned:

> "And those that say there was once when he was not, and before he was begotten he was not, and that he came into being out of nothing, or assert that the Son of God is of a different essence or being, or created, or capable of change or alteration, the Catholic church anathematizes."

"Amen!" roared the assembly.

The Arians can't get around this repudiation!

Three-hundred and eighteen bishops according to Eusebius of Nicomedia, two-hundred seventy according to Eustathius of Antioch. Add their secretaries, and clergy, and laymen like me trained in dialectic, all crammed into this city! Over two thousand! We are making history! The first Council of the entire world-wide church. Granted, only seven came from the West and all the rest from the East. And only one-sixth of the total body of bishops are here. I can't believe it how these men of God go in to the auditorium in the palace and out to the streets fearlessly, unescorted, while the palace guards must protect the Emperor's comings and goings with drawn swords.

So James "The Moses" of Nisibis wears his wild beast outfit even at the Eucharist! And didn't that old shepherd, Spyridion of Cypress, have a time with mule thieves, his own colleagues!

"Taking bread and giving thanks to God said, 'Take, eat, this is my body which is broken for you . . .'" The celebrant's words drifted in and out of Lawrence's consciousness as he indulged in observation.

Oh there's that old hamstrung Paphnutius, Bishop of Thebaid. A wonderful defense he made for the marriage of clergy. And he a hermit! He also is one of those who lost an eye during the persecutions. There's old ascetic Potammon whose right eye was dug out for the cause of Christ, while they say Eusebius of Caesarea escaped by sacrificing to an idol! Some lost their right arms. Most everyone here is mutilated in some way for Christ's sake! And there's an example of Licinius's cruelty. Paul of Neo-Caesarea lost the use of both hands. They say his nerves were contracted and destroyed by a red-hot iron. Horrible.

We believe in one Lord Jesus Christ, of one substance with God . . . These men are living their lives as witnesses. They are at one with the host of Christian martyrs who went before, many of whom owned not even themselves and had no power of their own except the power of their death.

The Emperor. He is magnificent. And when he was about to enter the Council for the first time—the absolute silence in the council hall; all that debating could actually stop! The intense expectation. First the three officers of the court entered one by one. No spears, no shields. Heathen guards didn't enter, only the Christian courtiers attempted the hall consecrated by the presence of the holy occupants. Finally the torch, the craning of necks, then he came—the spontaneous rise to the feet—the unanimous "Ahhhhhh!" as the magnificent one entered.

Constantine. The Conqueror. The August. The Great. Then that towering, broad-shouldered Deliverer, Angel from Heaven, blushed! Wonder if certain comments about him can be true? He betrayed his own excitement, his footsteps faltered, he hesitated with downcast eyes until the bishops motioned him to sit! The Emperor! Lord of the civilized world!

His opening address, like an affectionate son addressing his fathers, exhorting us to unanimity and concord, won most the Council to sound doctrine. I liked his speech—interpreter did a good job translating to Greek—not the same warm manner, though.

Constantine evidently became bitterly disappointed at the noisy process with which we arrived at our unanimity. True, we were quarreling over matters properly determined by study of Scripture and guidance of the Holy Spirit. But where's his church history? What does one expect of a Council? How else did Paul settle with Barnabas, and Peter with Paul? And the Synod at Arles with the Donatists?

"Let us attend," the assistant invited the worshippers, and Lawrence snapped to attention. Sounds like that Abrahamic Hosius of Cordova, the Latin church's chief counselor to the Emperor.

"Holy things to the holy," Bishop Theognis lifted up the host in invitation for all to receive communion.

There goes Presbyter Victor from Rome. What's he doing squeezing in before the dignitaries? Vincentius isn't with him. Where is Vincentius? Oh well, he'll never recognize me, not with this beard. Of course not, Lawrence, you're not that important.

Now there's Bishop Eustathius of Antioch. He lauded the Emperor for his diligent attention to the management of church affairs. No small task Constantine had, either. He united the empire with the sword only to find it divided by doctrine.

What a Council! Ex-presbyter Arius's insistence on the inferiority of the Son to the Father. Some song he sang, disproving the Divinity of Christ, set to the tunes of bawdy dances. Arius himself breaking into dance! Hands raised in horror! Ears stopped with fingers! Eyes screwed shut! Bishop Nicolas of Myra so angry he punched Arius in the jaw! Oblivious of the Emperor's presence! Quintus, you would have laughed . . .

"Quintus," he whispered. When Lawrence realized what he caught himself thinking, a wave of homesickness came upon him for his former inseparable. I am fulfilled here, Quintus. Once I thought that I'd never find myself realizing my life ambition, fulfilling my life work. Now I've been too occupied doing the work of my heart to think of you. I haven't been much of a beloved brother in Christ, Quintus.

You should have seen Deacon Athanasius blast Arius with arguments that held up the eternity and divinity of the Son. He didn't trust Marcellus of Ancyra very much to spell him off, either. And how they tore up that creed presented by the Arians for endorsement! The Emperor tried his best. He set another meeting date and dismissed us all, then tried conferences and gifts in the meantime to reconcile the parties.

Only it didn't work. The Arians assembled for deliberation and worked out how they could get around any scriptural phrases proposed. They could put their own interpretation on them! So when the Council reassembled and Bishop Eusebius of Caesarea proposed his baptismal creed, the Arians found that they could accept it! How they nodded and winked and whispered! They must have had a jolly time over it in the baths and wine shops after hours!

Eusebius of Caesarea was really taken down a few pegs when the orthodox exposed one of his letters on the floor. Wretched theology. To defend himself he turned against his Arian friends and declared them all excommunicate. He proposes to write the Emperor's biography. Is he honest enough a scholar? Oh Lawrence, quit being an intellectual snob. Professional jealousy getting hold of you already. After all, he's the most educated man here.

But the majority . . . really . . . not everyone was an expert at technical questions such as those dealt with in this controversy. You have to admit it. Take those uneducated bishops from the wilds. In fact, most present did not know how to formulate and express an opposition argument against the Arians—wonder if that's why they were invited? Instead, they could only hold to what has been handed down, word for word, no questions asked. Let's not be too exacting with the Arians, is their line; the Arians are sound at heart. They don't seem to realize how Arianism diverges from traditional teaching.

There you go again, Lawrence, looking down your nose. Well hell, it's true. The orthodox leaders were really put to it to uphold the true divinity, and the true manhood of Jesus Christ the Son.

That word which the Emperor insisted upon really pinned the Arians down. Consubstantial—of one substance—with the Father. Not a biblical word, but precise. That's what we need. Precision. But not many are happy over using a non-biblical word. The Arians, all but two gave in rather than be excommunicated. They can still get around even this modern Greek word *homoousios*, 'of one substance'; it is too much like the word *homoiousios*, 'of like substance'. Merely the difference of an iota in the spelling. They could always say that they took the Council to mean the latter. We shall see.

Imagine! A vast Empire cemented together again, not by swords, but by dropping a single iota.

Pay attention now, and go on up. Your turn. Don't hold back the others.

"The bread of heaven in Christ Jesus." Lawrence, among the last, moved with downcast eyes from Bishop Theognis to one of the assistants administering the chalice. The chalicist did not offer the cup closely enough. Lawrence reached out with his hands to bring the cup closer. The bearer drew the chalice up to himself. Lawrence looked up inquiringly and met the eyes of Presbyter Vincentius, one of the two proxies from Rome! The very man he had been carefully avoiding!

"Do not drink to your damnation," Presbyter Vincentius whispered. "Meet with me after the service, at the main doors."

So this is it, Lawrence thought gloomily as he returned to the back of the church. I ought to run off right now and become an anchorite in the desert. Or join Pachomius and his monastic colony in Upper Egypt. Or how about that robber band at Cilicia? Or something wild like that, but safe. You've had it coming, Lawrence. Quintus! Beloved brother in Christ! Lord of my life! My heart is crushed to ashes.

"You and I have an appointment, Lawrence," the Presbyter said when Lawrence greeted him last of all at the door. "With Papa Alexander. At his office."

"About . . . ?"

"You shall see." They walked briskly, talking about the Council, and Lawrence's work. When they were in the prelate's office, and had exchanged formalities, and were seated with the door closed, they quietly came down to matters.

"I have a message for your secretary, my lord," Vincentius said, "that concerns you also. It seems that Lawrence must go home rather soon."

Lawrence blanched. He rose to his feet in the presence of his superiors, and darkness rang through him. Terrified of an exposé, reluctant to be a cause of trouble to his beloved prelate, he stared at their faces.

"I am sorry to hear that," Bishop Alexander sympathized, "what is the matter?"

"We embarked at Puteoli, Lawrence, in March, on our way over here. Presbyter Victor and I spent the night at Good Will. Quintus Legerius was our host. I was his guest a few years ago, you will remember. He spoke of you, Lucan. He needs you." The priest leaned forward on his stool and studied the young man's reaction to his real name. Lawrence maintained a steady gaze so Vincentius continued. "I am sorry I had to refuse you the cup this morning, Lucan. But how can you come to the Lord's table when your brother in Christ has a grievance against you, and you are not reconciled to him?"

"Sir, I am keeping peace with my brother precisely by staying away. I am doing what I see is my duty. I cannot go back on my convictions. I cannot go back there and displace Gaius again. Furthermore, Quintus requested me to leave him!"

"Your domine did not seem to think so. Here, he asked me to give this to you." Vincentius drew out of his tunic a little scrap of Egyptian papyrus.

Lucan unrolled it and a shock jolted through him as he read his master's hand.

'Light of my life, shine on me again!' Lucan closed his eyes and breathed a deep sigh.

"Your domine?" Papa Alexander asked gently. "Not your patron?"

Lawrence hesitated, then looked the prelate full in the face. "Yes, my lord," he admitted quietly, "I am in reality his slave."

"And you are really a fugitive?" Alexander asked.

"You may call it that, sir," Lawrence confessed, still looking at him.

"Why, Lawrence?"

"My domine and I have crossed each other, sir."

"And you won't return and confess your guilt, and plead for pardon?" Alexander remained gentle.

"He is guilty too!" Lawrence insisted.

Vincentius answered him. "You are to understand, Lucan, that we are not here to judge who carries the most blame between you and your domine. You must realize that you have committed capital crimes by running away and by posing as a freedman and a citizen. We are trying to help you."

"Lawrence," Papa Alexander resumed, "under my employment you have shown yourself to be a mature and responsible young man. Yet you are being dishonest, using the church as a refuge from reality. We are here to defend the Biblical faith, and you are here using the faith to live a lie, to perjure yourself. We cannot let you do that. Can you understand our position?"

Lawrence nodded. "Yes, my lord, I can understand."

"Can you prepare yourself to obey, then? To return? With repentance and forgiveness?" Alexander entreated earnestly.

The fugitive looked down and did not answer. He was thinking that men use the faith to control their subordinates.

"It's not as though I were sending you home to be torn to pieces by some ravening wolf, Lucan!" Vincentius urged.

Light of my life, shine on me again!

"I-I don't intend to bargain for my safety," Lawrence coolly assured Vincentius. Meeting Alexander's eyes again, he pleaded. "It's that I . . . must I go now? There is so much to be done here! I would regret burdening you with unfinished work. I would regret most leaving you at all."

Alexander smiled. "I regret having to give up one of my best lay secretaries. Yet Vincentius is right, you should return in all speed. You had better start climbing those steeps while you still can. You see, later you may find yourself so accustomed to your rebellion that you are no longer able to change. That is the real urgency."

Lawrence surrendered. "Then I have no further arguments; I will go."

"You persist in good judgment, my son," Alexander said. "You may clear your desk today and make the necessary preparations to leave. You are to ride tomorrow morning with the prelates taking the decrees of the Council to Rome. I will give you a scroll to deliver in person to Bishop Sylvester at Rome's Lateran Cathedral. And another for your domine, recommending you highly to him. God speed you."

"You are most gracious, my lord," Lawrence knelt and kissed his prelate's ring.

"Very well, Lucan," Presbyter Vincentius warmed in parting. "And take heart; your domine referred to you as brother, and Olipor called you his son."

"A young woman there," Lawrence asked cautiously, "Letitia. Is she married?"

"Why yes! And they have a son."

Ah, Gaius, I am recalled, to disturb the peace again. "Is she happy?" his voice deepened with anguish.

"She is."

"*Ai!* Then thank God!"

Vincentius noticed the blush, and the young fugitive's brimming eyes.

CHAPTER XXIV

Of one substance, to be obeyed

More restless than sleepy on the eve of his departure, Lawrence joined his roommate, Deacon Leander, and the others in the hotel common room and talked over wine.

"How are you, man?" Leander greeted him quietly.

Lawrence sniffed. "Maybe when I get out of this damn humidity my sinuses will clear up." He ordered some wine.

"Oh? So you're leaving us?" Leander asked, wondering what sort of private business Presbyter Vincentius of Rome had with him in the prelate's office this morning.

"Yes, tomorrow. Errand-boy to Rome," Lawrence casually announced.

"And The Marketplace, Capua, Puteoli, and all points south?" Leander probed with Vincentius's touristy reference to the outposts of Rome, and the others laughed.

"To The Marketplace, Capua, and only the next point south," Lawrence answered poignantly and looked tensely at Leander who returned the scrutiny. Each wondered what the other knew.

"What impressed me most was at the beginning when the Emperor burned those written accusations." Paulinus was saying.

"What papers?" Lawrence joined in for diversion.

"Those accusations the bishops wrote against each other and sent to the Emperor."

"Oh yes!"

"And to think that he didn't even read them before burning them, but sealed them up together in a packet, and swore an oath that he did not read them."

"Wasn't that magnanimous of him," Lawrence commented.

"Huh!" Skeptikos retorted. "Plain politics. To avoid a messy smear. Remember, the Emperor said that the crimes of priests ought not to be made known to the public, for fear that they should become an occasion of offense or of sin."

"I can very well see his point," Lawrence said.

"Well, I question it!" Skeptikos countered. "The Emperor went on to say that if he detected a bishop in the very act of gross licentiousness he would have thrown his imperial robe over the unlawful deed rather than have anyone injured by witnessing the deed."

"All right, all right, we were all there," Marcus drawled. "Pretty shocking, wasn't it? How many cover-ups do you suppose . . ." he added and they all talked at once.

"No, not a bad idea, really," Lawrence mused. For had he not attempted to do this very thing for Quintus and Letitia? He tried to cover up the domine's sin so that the other slaves would not be offended by it. And it seemed to have worked. According to Vincentius it was working out for Letitia very well. She is married. Letitia! Letitia! Have I not been punished enough? I am healed, Letitia, and I long for you! My forbidden treasure, how much I desire you!

"Why not such a bad idea, Lawrence?" Marcus drew him out.

"Wouldn't it be more in accordance with God's love," Lawrence reflected out loud, "if such an offender were forgiven by his people and reconciled to them, rather than banished from them? Would this not be a true demonstration of God's mercy if a shepherd could be pardoned by his own flock?"

"Stupid old sheep can't pardon," Skeptikos chewed the analogy.

"It would be effective," Leander spoke through the laughter, "providing the offender submitted to the appropriate discipline." He had been trying to lead Lawrence to such an insight.

"Like the proposal by Eusebius of Caesarea to restore Arius to the communion and to his parish," Paulinus said. "And I'd be in favor of that."

"Eh?" Marcus said, "We should pardon Arius rather than excommunicate him?"

"What do you mean, man, we have excommunicated Arius to preserve the faith!" Skeptikos protested.

Yes, Lawrence thought, in the same sense that I exiled myself from Good Will to restore order. What kind of peace is that? "You can't flatly assume that excommunication is the best way," he said.

"What do you mean, Lawrence?" Leander took him on.

"That love requires too many 'ands' and 'ifs' and 'buts' and 'howevers' to be confined to a set of principles."

"Yes, love does require ends and butts," Marcus punned crassly, mimicking Lawrence's seriousness, and the would-be gem of a sermonette was lost in hilarity.

"Damn earthy Roman, you," Lawrence returned, and laughed at his own gravity.

"And I suppose you are satisfied that the Emperor has thrown his cloak, so to speak, over Eusebius of Nicomedia?" Skeptikos resumed arguing. "Eusebius of Nicomedia appears to favor Papa Alexander and Deacon Athanasius, but he and Arius are personal friends, you know. Came from the same Alma Mater, Lucian's School of Theology in Antioch. I'll bet Eusebius signed because the Arians are outnumbered and he doesn't want to lose his see; not because his heart is with the creed.

"Eusebius gets what Eusebius wants; he has it made with the Emperor, you know. Constantine wanted only to get a majority vote and settle the controversy. He didn't care which way. You could tell that he couldn't follow all of the theology. Now you would let Eusebius get away with it, according to your line of thought, Lawrence?"

Lawrence busied himself with his wine, then answered slowly, "I would not so much presume to pass judgment on my superior as I would presume personally to obey the demand of the Council's decision."

"The demand?" they asked.

"*Seeing that the Lord Jesus Christ is of one substance with God the Father, therefore we are to obey him! Totally! Without reservation!*" He took quick refuge in his cup. He himself had already passed judgment on his superior; he had run away instead of staying to forgive and reconcile. 'Be obedient, rendering service with good will as to the Lord . . .' I am to obey the Lord! Totally! Without reservation!

The voices argued on. "Yes, the Son is True God from True God. The same substance. Inseparable. 'I and the Father are one', and, 'He who has seen me has seen the Father.' In John. Athanasius knows what he is talking about and he won his point straight from scripture. We weren't bullied into it by tradition or episcopal authority."

"As Paul puts it in Colossians, 'He is the image of the invisible God.' Like in a mirror."

"Arius knows what he is talking about too," Paulinus countered. "How can a Son possibly exist in the beginning with his Father? God made him for us and the Son is a god in that he is divine, but he is not the Father."

"Naw, that's idolatry," Skeptikos countered. "We don't worship one who is less than God."

"Uh huh! It's in John. Thomas said, 'My Lord and my God!'"

"Then Jesus said, 'I am ascending to my Father and your Father, my God and your God.' He was sent by the Father as a sacrifice for our sins."

"So," Lawrence became agitated, "so according to Arius, the Divine Father sacrificed his Son, one of his creatures, and what's to stop him from sacrificing his adopted sons?"

"Calm down, Lawrence," Leander responded, "the Son is a manifestation of the Father. God Incarnate. Quite a different matter than delegating a subordinate son to die."

"Aw, you can't push a mystery too far," Skeptikos answered him. "Jesus tried to relieve our minds of the mystery when he said, 'No man knows the Father, but the Son, and no man knows who the Son is, but the Father.'"

"I go by John," Marcus asserted, "'In the beginning was the Word, and the Word was with God, and the Word was God.' We don't worship one who is less than God. We worship one who is fully God."

"Of course! That was never the question in the West. The question was, how could he be fully God, and fully man? God didn't merely send a representative or messenger; but 'Christ Jesus . . . though he was in the form of God . . . emptied himself, taking the form of a servant, being born in the likeness of men. He humbled himself and became obedient unto death, even death on a cross.' How else are we saved?" Leander gestured eloquently.

"Oh you westerners mustn't be so fundamentalistic with your *homoousios*," Paulinus commented, "you must interpret the faith you know, apropos with the times."

"You easterners need to wean yourselves from your Neo-Platonic *homoiousios* and steep yourselves in biblical thought," Marcus retorted. "Otherwise the faith is lost in interpretation."

"Well," Skeptikos gibed, "the easterners can always say that the secretaries accidentally dropped the *i* from that word while inscribing the proceedings or while dictating to the copyists. What do you say, Lawrence?" he winked conspiratorially.

Lawrence leapt up defensively. "I did no such thing! I do not drop letters! Not one iota!" He struck the table with his fist. "Not one iota have I omitted!"

The entire common room was hushed and they all stared at him.

"Calm down, calm down!" Marcus admonished him.

"Sit, Lawrence!" Leander pulled him down gently by the sleeve.

"I'm sorry. It's that this controversy is so close to me."

"Christ! One would think it was life and death!" Skeptikos chided.

"It is! If Christ is truly God, then he is to be obeyed! Down to the letter!"

"Then obey him!" Skeptikos heckled.

"I intend to!" Lawrence declared bitterly.

"By Hades!" someone at the next table commented, "though the Council has come to a settlement, the Arian controversy has only really begun."

Round and round it goes, Lawrence thought to himself. Over and over again. Same old obscuring truths in semantics, and, when they get to arguing for the sheer pleasure of argument, thoroughly laughable. For how can man presume to understand the mysteries of God? Our call is rather to responsive obedience to the great commandment of love. Serve him, and you will get to know him. Serve your domine as you would your Domine. You have run away from your domine, Lawrence. Are you trying to avoid your Lord also?

The arguments revealed the perennial uneasiness of his conscience. If we are to truly love each other, we have to grapple with our differences as well. Quintus had said that. And indeed the Council was a battlefield for hostilities, prejudices, issues. Disappointingly so. Shamefully so when the pagans pointed fingers and said, "Look at them; where is their love now?" And then the Pagan theater produced satire on the heated discussions and violent public demonstrations.

But what did you expect, Lawrence? Super-human harmony? You came with ulterior motives, and do you think that the others didn't have their motives too? Their private concerns to settle? Their private interests to promote? And don't forget that for the most part we have drawn closer together in harmony. How thrilling to see a world-wide body gathered together! And how strengthening! And you, Lawrence, have made some lifetime friends.

Friends? He challenged himself ironically. We'll see how many friends I have when they all find out about me. I am a vessel of the church. Have no illusions about it. Vessel. People here great and small greet me and befriend me only inasmuch as they can benefit from my connection with Papa Alexander. Without that function I may as not exist. That's why I have sought ways to make myself increasingly indispensable. I have a calling to develop. And now . . . and now . . . what good are my friends to me? Bicker, bicker, bicker, like a bunch of schoolboys! This is how the great decisions of Christendom are made! This is how human lives are shaped and broken, including my own.

"Listen," he re-entered the conversation peevishly, "perhaps as Lucian and his school think, everything can be solved logically. Perhaps it really can't. Perhaps we really are talking about a mystery. And by calling it a mystery we honestly are not trying to dodge using our heads. Anyway, all this theologizing becomes itself an idol if we suppose we are serving our Lord well by our intellectual understanding of things, and all the while we are neglecting his real command to us that we love one another."

"Say, man, how do you think you could even hear the Gospel today if it weren't carefully preserved and defined so it doesn't get lost in the reinterpretations of each age?" Skeptikos retorted.

"How can we do our duty of love if we don't discover what it is?" Marcus wanted to ask.

"Hey!" Paulinus put in. "Are you trying to make like that old Shepherd of Cypress, stopping our philosophical speculations with earnest simplicity?"

Deacon Leander's word to Lawrence was, "Excellent, dear brother, excellent! You are like a surgeon's knife, and we love you for it."

"Now can't we talk about something else?" Lawrence was thoroughly wrung out.

"Aw, go jump in the Lake!" Skeptikos gestured toward the Ascanian Lake that filled nearly the entire valley.

"Or go get lost in the woods!" Marcus indicated the dense Bithynian steeps.

"No-no, pardon me. It's only I'm tired. I'm going to bed. Big day tomorrow. Back to Rome with the envoy. You fellows keep it up." Lawrence drained his goblet and stood up to go.

"Sure, we'll keep it up," Skeptikos replied, and his eyes snapped. With his fine tenor voice he pitched a tune and launched into a mock panegyric.

> "Old King Coel is a merry old soul,
> And a merry old soul is he.
> He called for his pipe, he called for his bowl,
> He called for his pipers three."

"Twee tweedle dee, tweedle dee went the treble pipe," Paulinus sang in falsetto.

"Tweedle-diddle-dee went the alto," deliberated Skeptikos in tenor.

"Did-dle did-dle dee went the big—bass—pipe!" Marcus drawled in his deep bass voice.

"Tweedle did-dle did-dle did-dle did-dle dee!" the whole room took-up.

"Tweedle dee!"

"Diddle dee!"

"Did-dle dee dee!"

"That's disrespectful of the Emperor's grandfather, you know," Lawrence put in a last word with a smile.

"Oh tweedle dee dee!" Skeptikos tossed back. "Stay awhile and join us! We've made up a new version. When the Emperor's father sends the Emperor's mother back to Coel in obedience to a political marriage, the pipers turn sour.

Then we've included the Emperor at the Council. And we've added a good one about Arius and his feminine celibates too. Even predicted Arius's death . . . you know . . . how he throbs and trembles as though ready to erupt! Coel's bowl and Arius's bowel. The whole history after the style of Colchester. But it won't take all night!"

Lawrence made a wry face at the poor pun. "Oh you and your paraphrases! Lay off of Arius, won't you?" he said with no little irritation. "I think the Emperor is right about cloaking deeds." The gossip about Arius, Lawrence thought as he shuffled away, hells bells, just because a priest is an ascetic must we become extra gossipy? It's a good thing they passed that canon prohibiting the cohabitation of clergy and the women's religious order. It's as bad as being a slave. You are immediately accused of mischief merely because you are a slave. Can't a fellow even talk with—it's a good thing I left Good Will. God knows what they are accusing me of because I befriended a lonely girl there. I cloaked a deed.

* * *

Back in his room, Lawrence dropped down on his bunk. He buried his face in his hands. O God, he moaned, am I truly as far away from you as I am from my domine, and as unreconciled? He sighed in anguish.

Presently Deacon Leander, his roommate, came in.

"What's with you, Lawrence?" he said. "I can tell that your position on the controversy is real with you."

"It's real," Lawrence said.

"You are a true Israelite."

"How is that?"

"Like Jacob, you wrestle with God. And, as with Nathaniel, the Christ shall be the ladder by which you ascend and meet God face to face. I want to be with you when that happens. Care to share your struggle with me?"

Lawrence paced the room, picked up his stylus and tablet, and threw them down again. 'Light of my life, shine on me again.'

"Leander, am I to throw myself away?"

"Throw yourself away? Certainly not! What do you mean?"

"You know what I mean, the teaching on the new life. Denying yourself and taking up your cross and following Christ."

"I think I know what Christ means by it," Leander reflected, "but I'm not so sure that I know what you mean."

"I mean, shall I hide my light under a basket? If I do not use my talent, but bury it for the sake of denying myself, God may well say to me, 'You wicked and slothful servant, you ought to have invested the talent I have given you.' This has given me no little thought, Leander. On the other hand I fear that yielding to his will means losing my identity and frankly I am terrified of ceasing to be me, of emptying myself of my personhood so that I will become something someone else wants me to be in the name of Christ." Lawrence flinched. "I fear being annihilated as a person. I resist it! I fight it! I want to live!"

"Of course you do!" Leander could not suppress the upward twitching at the corners of his mouth.

"Leander, you're laughing at me!"

"No, Lawrence, I'm not. It's that you are being that surgeons knife again and it's refreshing. By self-denial Christ does not mean to become a doormat, or a mere cipher. He means devoting all you are to the glory of God, rather than to selfish pursuits."

"Yet see what the Church is asking me to do!" Lawrence nearly shouted in his agitation. "Slavery has already robbed me of myself, and the Church tells me that even in the name of Christ I cannot be myself. Not me, but Christ in me! Those are words of death to a slave who has already been deprived of himself! Those are words of a living suicide! I'll tell you what those words mean to me and to other slaves, two-thirds of the Roman Empire! A new slavery above the earthly slavery! Not the freedom in Christ to become what I was created to be, but a mandate, in the Name of Christ, to keep us subordinates in our place, in my case a farm slave!"

"'Slave', Lawrence?"

"Mio Dio!" Lawrence cried and knelt before Leander. "Now you know," he surrendered, and sweat oozed from his face.

"Lucan, you have been recalled?" Leander himself had taken down the advertisement in the marketplace of Alexandria for this runaway serf kneeling before him, posing as a freedman and a secretary. He had been waiting for the right time for Lucan to face up. Now was the time.

"Leander, I am not on loan. I am really a runaway slave. Forgive me, I have deceived you!"

"Don't kneel to me, Lucan," Leander cried, "you have become like a brother! That's better! Now listen. Your domine and I did not want you to be dragged back by the hands of a reward-hungry public who would not care about your welfare. We preferred waiting for the time when you would go back willingly yourself."

"My . . . domine?" Lawrence was astonished.

"He has known from the start that you are in my custody," Leander said gently.

"Your . . . custody?" Lawrence's eyes widened and he blanched.

Leander nodded gravely. "I have not betrayed you, Lucan, I have assured your safety."

"Jesus Christ, Leander!" Lawrence rose swiftly to his feet. "Safety? To return to slavery? I'm going to vomit!"

He fell face down on his cot and dry heaves of abject grief racked his whole being. Slavery! They violated me! Buggered! Impaled! Plowed! Knocked in the mouth! Stuffed with phallus! Everywhere! At the Crossroads! At the Front! At Good Will! Now the church is about to give me the shaft! Slavery—worse than death! Dear Lord, my heart is crushed to ashes.

Leander knelt at the side of the cot and soothed the anguished one across the shoulders.

"Remember, Lucan, you are going to an underground rescue mission."

"Good Will at Puteoli, where freedom is procured for everyone but the members of its own household. Isn't that ironic, Leander? Furthermore, I have been demoted there. You will send me back to be, as Varro puts it, 'an articulate farm implement'!" Lawrence threw out the words bitterly. "Not a person with God-given talents to invest and a creativity to let shine. Merely a serf who is to find life by throwing away individuality and sinking into mere function. Since state and church both say that I cannot be, I may as well commit suicide! I die anyway! The penalty for running away is death. The penalty for claiming citizenship is death. The penalty for claiming my own body is death. The penalty for claiming my own soul is spiritual death."

"Your domine will not destroy you. He entreats you to return!" Leander pleaded.

Lawrence's being rebelled. They tried to kill me there! With great effort at self control he said, "You see, Leander, there is more to it than my offending my domine by running away. He has also offended me."

"Of course," Leander sympathized. "Otherwise you would not have had reason to run away."

Leander's understanding released Lawrence. "I tried to tell Vincentius this, but he wouldn't listen! He didn't even hear me. Isn't my side of the story worth consideration too? Just because I am a slave are my personal feelings naught? Must I always be giving in, Leander?"

"It is true that as a slave your personal feelings are worth nothing. As a Christian your personal feelings are irrelevant to the task of reconciliation given to you. Lucan! Light! Let your light shine in reconciliation!"

"Can I not serve Christ best in my present capacity? Am I really dodging him by serving in the Church?"

"Yes. You may not continue living a lie with us. Return to live, placing Christ in the center of your life, not yourself," Leander persisted. "Satan, that fallen Angel of Light, would have you think that you are furthering the Kingdom by doing good works in the church while dodging your real responsibility. Think about it, Lucan, which kind of light will you be to light the feet of men?"

"So I must deny myself, and take up my cross, and follow him, whatever that means." Lawrence shook his head and moaned from the depths.

"You will find the true meaning to those words, and the true freedom, in your act of obedience to God's task of reconciliation."

What do you think I am! Feebleminded? Is forgiveness any answer? It enables you to live with the past, but does it necessarily change the future?"

"Ask Christ, Lucan, for he is an expert at that."

"Then I suppose I'll have to try forgiveness to get the answer."

Leander clutched him to his breast. "Dear Lucan, whatever you do, I shall always be available to you. You know where to find me."

Lawrence wept in gratitude.

"Grant me one more kindness, Leander?"

"What is it, brother?"

"On our return trip I so hoped that I could ask to make a divergence to Thessalonica, to my childhood countryside, go to the Crossroads, inquire at the local Inn about the burned down farmstead and the family that once lived there. Try to find my sisters."

"You couldn't do that anyway. It would be too dangerous."

"What do you mean?"

"Only two years ago they were looking for you there."

Lawrence paled. "Who?"

"Your former master. The soldiers. When Constantine ordered his experienced troops to assemble at Thessalonica, in preparation for renewed war with Licinius, and the second siege of Byzantium. While waiting there they inquired of you at your old farm, and at various taverns. Your captain—he was promoted after that siege—subsequently lost his life during the pursuit of Licinius at Chalcedon. And your description and your family name is fresh on the minds of your reward-hungry countrymen."

"How did you find out?" Lawrence nearly whispered.

"I had already put out a tracer on your family."

"Leander! Bless you, brother, bless you! Lysistra would be a woman of eighteen now, and little Lucia . . . little Lucia! Why, she's sixteen! I've been searching for girls too young! All that wasted inquiry!" He choked with grief at the futility of it all.

"Easy now, Lawrence."

"They would look a lot like me, Leander. Meter always said so."

"A feminine version, I hope," Leander jested. "So you're not a pedophile after all."

"A what?"

"One of your disgruntled brethren, out of jealousy of the favors shown you, tried to bring charges upon you for your unseemly interest in young girls. I put a stop to that. Fast."

"Leander!" Lawrence felt as though he had been deflected from the claws of destruction, but only to be sent unerringly to the jaws of death.

Light of my life, shine on me again.

Lord of my life, my heart is crushed to ashes.

* * *

In Rome, Lawrence delivered the scrolls in his charge. He forwarded the Puteoli scrolls to Bishop Nicodemus with a personal note and an anonymous bank draft for use at Good Will, via the envoy to Capua, Puteoli, and all points south. Then he gave in to exhaustion. He cared not that he was finally in the Eternal City that he had so longed to see. To his tired eyes it was only another big over-crowded noisy city even if it did gleam in sparkling September sunshine. He sought out the first mission flophouse he could find in the Suburan Quarter and collapsed, caring not if he were robbed or murdered.

The next he knew he was awakened by a solicitous youth.

"What's the matter?"

"You owe another day's fee."

Lawrence groaned.

"Are you all right?"

"Only tired." Lawrence raised up on an elbow.

"You sure?" The youth regarded him with curiosity.

"Well, if you'd been pounding your guts out on post horses for the past six weeks, and when the state's done with you your reward will be . . ." he drew his finger across his throat.

"Where are you from?"

"Nicaea. The Council of Churches. Broke the time record."

The youth whistled. "Which side?"

"One substance. *Homoousian*"

"Are those scars for the faith?" he asked in awe. "What are you?"

"A Secretary. Scrivener. One of the best."

"And you're out of work?"

"Well . . ." At this, Hell caught up with him again. "Well, yes." Lord of my life, my heart is crushed to ashes.

"I know where they've been advertising for help," the youth volunteered enthusiastically. "The Chi-Rho Bookshop, at the Argiletum. Christian proprietor. Stephanos. And it would be damn good for a change to have someone with an understanding of the Christian works. Stephanos wants to build up his inventory of literature of The Way in preparation for our Defender's great Vicennalia Celebration here in Rome next year. Come with me, I'll take you to him."

"What's your name?"

"Cleophas."

"Bless you, Cleophas. I'm Lawrence. Give me time to get cleaned up and I'll be right with you."

CHAPTER XXV

Vicennalia, A.D. 326
Fathers sacrifice their sons

The anticipated Vincennalia of the Emperor Constantine's rule was the dominant talk of Rome for the entire new year. Preparations were vast with parades to plan, spectacles to arrange and provisions to make for the predicted influx of guests and visitors. The staff at the Chi-Rho Bookshop at the Argiletum worked overtime for months preparing huge selections of souvenir books for sale. They expected to make an unprecedented profit on the occasion. Enough to expand on! Stephanos the owner speculated gleefully with Lawrence his junior partner about another shop in Constantinople.

Lawrence's fine scholarship and artistry in copying books led him to many contacts and commissions. The rapidly expanding churches wanted Holy Writ, and wealthy patrons wanted his finely decorated classical literature and copies of rare old books.

Otherwise, to Lawrence Rome was onerous. Extremes of wealth and poverty, beauty and decay, weighed heavily on his consciousness. He was sobered by the great old buildings, reminders of the Republic that was shattered by conquerors who were then commemorated by triumphal arches. Why conquerors? The tyrants? Certainly Roman law, civilization and engineering were spread over the known world by conquest, but who needed them by the sword? Was it so impossible to spread desirable benefits by peaceful means? Constantine was already The Great in the same sense that Alexander was The Great, for uniting the known world under the sword. Ambition and power become adulated if you become top dog. Noble conquerors are a contradiction of terms, Lawrence contemplated sourly. Fools that men are! Will we never learn? Does the end justify the means? Does the *Pax Romana* justify the sword? State and tribal squabbles were put down by a super tyranny. Who needs that kind of peace? He would rather see a triumphal arch to a statesman like Cicero.

Lawrence realized that he thought like a subordinate. It would never occur to the citizen, the average customer of the Chi-Rho Bookshop, what it was like to be conquered, to be subject to another's will, to be defined by another, to have to study another and defer to another, weighing words and timing responses, to be totally aware of the other and totally subject to the other. That would require a tremendous awakening, a great sensitivity, a consciousness that the average citizen never even considers worth his bother. It would take a Jesus Christ. Few citizens in Lawrence's life could understand this. For one, there was Quintus Legerius who had enlightened moments yet who was very much the master. There was Deacon Leander, empathetic but holding to the patriarchal position. Then there was his senior partner Stephanos who believed that Jesus Christ was man's only legitimate master.

Lawrence, himself a freedman in Christ, was living dangerously in outright disobedience to what law and custom ordained for him. The Flavian Amphitheatre was a stark reminder of what happens to those who disobey the *Lex Romana*. He would be in there himself facing justice during the Games before fifty-thousand spectators, if he were found out to be the runaway slave that he was, and not a freedman, if he were found out to be the shackle-scarred incorrigible that he really was, and not a scarred hero of The Way that he seemed. If people thought him a citizen, so much the better, so much more easily he could mingle among them professionally, but so much more awful the consequences.

That looming Amphitheatre near his workplace in the Argiletum was a daily incentive to pursue his talents, and to involve himself with life and service and love of the little local flock at the house church in Stephanos's apartment block in the Suburan Quarter. He was their Deacon, and therefore the keeper of the sacred literature. He could forget entirely that he was an impostor, so well received was he in the mission and in intellectual circles, until a rude reminder would hit him now and then. Such a rude reminder occurred during the Emperor's jubilant entry into Rome on the fifteenth of July.

Lawrence found that he was no exception to the epidemic of excitement. Against his better judgment he joined the crowds on the Sacred Way and pushed forward to the best vantage point for a good view. The splendid trumpets pierced their way to his primordial responses and the drumbeats were his very heartbeat. On parade mornings he also gave the slaves a holiday. Slaves? Yes, slaves. He shook his head at himself. He and his senior partner actually owned slaves, though these men were already part of the business when he came along from Nicaea with a bank draft tucked in his tunic and bought into the business. He preferred to forget that they were slaves, no different than himself really, and he treated them like men and expected them to respond like men. They would have freedom by the kindness of himself and his partner after seven years' service, according to the Biblical tradition. Today they had the entire day off. He would return to the shop and open for business when people poured into the marketplace after the parade.

Again the Emperor was absolutely beyond words! Magnificent! Any wonder that the crowds of pagans would deify him! They worshipped him! The cheers lifted one off the face of the earth! Lawrence, however, saw through the Emperor's showmanship. He wondered if some of the blossoms and garlands strewn before the Imperial Chariot could have been shipped up from Good Will.

The cavalry were formidable in their lamellar armor corselets, triple layered *pteruges*, domed helmets with cheek, nose and nape guards, flowing cloaks, full length trousers and solid leather boots, broadswords at side and great round shields in arm. They rode securely in their four-pommeled saddles draped with fringed cloth. They were splendid specimens of manhood, the fittest of mankind destined to be murderers in the name of greatness. Nonetheless Lawrence couldn't help but look for the standards of his own Legion. Listen to me, he thought to himself, my old Legion, even though soldiers did destroy his family back then. He felt a creeping uneasiness that they might find him and clap him in irons again.

He kept a wary lookout for the Legerius brothers, and was careful that he blended in with the crowd when the legionaries in their light armor passed by smartly.

When more cavalry passed he thought momentarily of a certain bright chestnut filly with highlights like a rainbow and speculated that, covered by the fiery stud she was paired with, her offspring would rival any of these. If a particular troop of horse were to pass by, he would slip through the crowd to the stables at Mars Field and throw himself into the arms of a certain groom who long ago had cut him free from an army cot with hoof nippers and had unshackled him with cold-chisel and mallet. Only that particular unit of horse was not in evidence yet. Or was it? What was that he heard?

"Lucan!"

Yes, he heard it again! He turned, trying not to appear responsive, and looked directly up into the visored face of Marcellus.

"Get the hell home, slave!"

Lawrence melted into the crowd. Since Marcellus was riding, Marcipor must be about, and Lawrence daringly sought him in the stables at Mars Field.

He sought the standard of the Metropolitan Noble Order of Knights and patrolled, asking for Marcipor by his real name, Andrew. He found him. Marcipor did not recognize this Lawrence at first, but when convinced it was his lost brother in Christ from Good Will, he was overjoyed. When Lawrence learned that his brother in Christ Quintus of Good Will was in prison for the second time for lack of payment of taxes and debts he responded unhesitatingly.

"I must go to him at once."

"No! It's too dangerous!"

"Then please tell him that the light shall shine on him again."

"Neither that! Everyone knows that means you."

"Andrew, I have put you in jeopardy, then?"

"It wouldn't occur to Marcellus, should he find out that I saw someone called Lawrence, that it was you."

"I want to send Quintus some money."

"Only anonymously."

"Yes, of course, by a bank draft to the church at Puteoli. I shall return, when the Equestrian Order is scheduled to march again. Do not fail me, Andrew, please."

"I shall be here."

"How is Letitia?"

"Happy with two children."

"It worked out, after all, for her and Gaius."

"For her and Quintus."

"Quintus!?" Lawrence's face became wet with emotion. He held Andrew intently in his gaze. "Please tell her, Andrew. Please tell her that she need only call and I shall come running."

Marcellus rode again in the war games with the haughty young nobles of Rome. He hoped to earn merits toward some sort of commission to give his life purpose. He earned demerits instead for foul play. Then he had to flee for his life in the street riots that followed the Emperor's cutting remark against the phony Equestrian Order. The mishap gave Lawrence the opportunity to get an anonymous bank draft into the hands of Andrew to be delivered to the church at Puteoli and deposited toward Quintus's tax account.

Then the shocking news reached Rome that Constantine had murdered his son. Lawrence was nearly prostrate with anxiety. Fathers kill their sons! Will the Divine Father kill his adopted sons? The old, dimly perceived demon of the past coursed again in his mind, and ravaged his bowels.

The gossip was that the amiable Crispus, firstborn and heir of Constantine and a great favorite of the military and the people, had been arrested and spirited away unnoticed during the celebrations. No one knew exactly the charges, but there were rumors of secret conspiracy, accusations by his stepmother Fausta of sexual indiscretion, of invitations and rewards to informers who supported the jealousy of the Emperor towards his rising son. The magnificent Emperor revealed clay feet, bloody clay feet. Crispus, it turned out, was taken far away to Pola, tried there, and put to death.

Fathers sacrifice their sons! Not only did the Holy One sacrifice his Son, but the Magnificent One sacrificed his beloved Crispus, and Lawrence's own Pater slit his first son's throat according to certain nightmares.

Oh Heavenly Father, who spared not your own Son, will you send me, your adopted son, to my death if I return to Good Will in obedience? The shock and revulsion was enough to drive Lawrence back from any drifting toward the Arian shores of *homoiousios* regarding Christ as a subordinate creature of God sacrificed by God, directly to the more demanding shores of *homoousious*, of obedience to God Incarnate who came to us himself in love and reconciled humankind to himself even at the cost of self sacrifice. The Arian controversy was by no means over. It warred. It spread by subterfuge and treachery throughout the empire, even during the very Vincennalia celebrations, and it especially warred deeply in Lawrence's breast.

* * *

Letitia went to the Magistrate's villa to have audience with him and ask permission to visit Quintus in prison. She took heart and aimed for what she really wanted, nothing short of his release. Her turn came after Titus went through the morning ritual of receiving clients in order of rank. She had enough opportunity to observe him hearing out supplicants to see that he was reasonable and humorous, though ostentatious, and that the admirers loved it, and the nervous clients were quick to laugh with him. However when her turn came, he became the terror that he was reputed to be.

"Your name?"

"Letitia Legerius, my lord."

"Address?"

"Good Will, my lord."

"Ah, yes. Tenant farm near the intersection with the Via Solfatara. So you are the young female slave there. Yes, yes, I heard that you were some dish. Not the greatest to look at, but well spiced. Look at your hair done up in the latest style. Daughter of a prostitute, eh?" The audience buzzed.

"I am a freedwoman, my lord. Wife of Quintus Lottius Legerius."

"Now! Tell me just how that is possible when I, the magistrate, have signed no such writ for you? Nor a marriage license?"

The audience became deathly silent.

"The church married us, my lord. The papers are in the strong box." Letitia did not waver. "I have come to appeal for my husband."

"Want something from me, throw your woman at me," Titus brooded sourly. His wife had pulled that one on him only last night. "Don't you realize that you have just incriminated yourself? On two accounts. First, posing as a freedwoman, severely punishable. Second, by the new decree of the Emperor Constantine against rape and seduction."

"It was by mutual consent, my lord!"

"Ah! You implicate him! You were indeed seduced to leave the bosom of your parents. Freedom was your bait."

"Not at all, my lord. He loves me. He needs me."

"You are well under the age of twenty-five," Titus observed harshly. "And you claim that your lord and master, with life and death power over you—needs—you?"

"Isn't that part of the mystery between men and women?" At once she realized the blunder of trying to reason with him. The audience muttered ominously.

Titus became furious. "Presumptuous woman! You are already condemned by your own mouth. As a freedwoman you share the penalty of seduction! Simple death is inadequate punishment for such sin. By imperial decree the guilty are burned alive or torn in pieces by wild beasts in the arena."

Letitia recalled Lucan doomed before Aulus because of the stolen dagger so zealously applied, yet keeping his presence and courage. "Our Emperor must have been deeply hurt to devise such a horrible penalty against human nature."

"He had his own son put to death!"

Letitia bowed her head. She could not know that the real purpose of that law was to get rid of rivalry in high places.

"Hear me, woman! If parents shirk their duty of prosecution, if they cover the deed by having the couple married, they are subject to exile and confiscation. Slaves, male or female, who are accessory to the seduction are either burned alive or put to death by melted lead poured down their throats."

Letitia's mind reeled. Did he really know all this about Quintus and herself and the household? Did Marcellus tell? Why? How could anyone benefit from their destruction? She held firm.

"Please, my lord, I did not think I was on trial. I came myself to appeal to you for my husbandman's release. He cannot raise crops in prison, sir."

"Pure mettle! Hear the final clause of this decree, woman. There is no time limit to the penalty. The offspring of such an irregular union are subject also to the punishment. Now what say you?"

"Please, my lord, Quintus and I have an infant at home who awaits her next feeding." She indicated the wet milk stains appearing through her clothing.

"Women," he snorted derisively, "always exuding, if not words, then blood or milk." He wondered that she was not at his feet. Did not she believe him? Didn't she realize she was only a slave?

Letitia was cornered. She knew that if she withdrew her declaration about her status and pleaded that slaves aren't liable under this law, she and Quintus would be safe, but their children would be slaves. If she upheld her freedom then they were all doomed.

"Please, my lord, may I see Quintus," she requested.

"Then your master does not even know that you are here!?"

Letitia did not answer. The trap was closed.

"By Juno, you and your Quintus shall be an example to all of Puteoli!" He wrote on a papyrus and handed it to a messenger. The audience murmured tensely. He gestured her aside and called up and interviewed more clients and kept glancing expectantly at the atrium door.

Letitia waited in misery and swayed on her feet as sickness passed over her.

Then the guards brought up a lame prisoner in farmer's clothes. Letitia was at his side at once. She slipped her hand into his.

"Tish! My Tish!" Quintus clasped her to himself and kissed her desperately.

"Attention!" Titus barked. "Your release is at stake and you let this delinquent piece of property distract you?"

"My wife, sir," Quintus corrected him with dignity.

"Why is there no marriage license, then?" Titus demanded.

"My wife did not wish to sign just yet and I have respected her feelings."

"You see? Livy is right!" Titus raged. "Give loose rein to women's uncontrollable nature and you cannot expect that they themselves will set bounds to their license. Quintus, I have brought you before me to retrieve this runaway slave and to teach her how to behave! Appearing at my court like this! Think of her bad example! Presuming to leave the premises without your permission. That is one hundred lashes! You must punish her so that she will remember her bounds!"

"You are right, sir," Quintus boldly agreed with his adversary. "I agree with Livy." He took Letitia by the hands and looking deeply into her eyes he resumed the saying in Livy. "Give women complete liberty, and the moment they begin to be your equals, they will be your superiors." He regarded Letitia with outright admiration.

Letitia returned a startled look.

"How will you punish her?" Titus demanded.

Quintus pressed her hands against his breast where she could feel his pounding heart. His eyes did not waver from hers. "I will punish her soundly, sir, with my beater stick until she is swollen beyond recognition." He watched the corners of her eyes crinkle as she comprehended, and he clutched her to himself. The audience roared with cheers and applause.

She spoke into his ear. "Quintus, I appealed for your release and have undone you instead!"

"No! You have done me proud! See! I am here!"

"There is this horrible new law!"

"I know."

She clasped him in terror, and he explained quickly, "There is no writ either. That law cannot touch us."

"Then our little ones are but slaves! Quintus, I cannot bear it!"

"Trust me!" To hide the betrayal and horror on her face he tilted her head and kissed her passionately, like a bridegroom. Faint from shock, she clung and leaned against him as though in a romantic swoon.

The audience burst into a new round of applause and held their thumbs up. Titus was seemingly outwitted, though not really. Since Quintus had once delivered a sting on his masculinity in public, he would make Quintus demonstrate his virility publicly on his own woman. What could be truer poetic revenge? With great dignity he ordered his clerk to write two parchments while the onlookers strained to catch his words. He handed the documents to Quintus one at a time.

"Here, her freedom tax is paid. And here. Consider the marriage license fee covered. You both need to sign. But first things first." He motioned Letitia to kneel for manumission by the rod, and indicated to Quintus that he should strike her three times on the shoulder. Then Quintus knelt beside her so that he could write comfortably, signed the writ, handed her the quill, and she signed. Her hand shook. She was a freedwoman, antedating the conception of their first child, so that taking their mother's status, both were freeborn. The second document, the marriage license, was antedated so that their son was a legitimate heir. Quintus signed the marriage license and handed the quill to Letitia. She hesitated, returned his intent look, and paled. Freedwoman, citizen, she would subject herself as wife.

"I love you," Quintus mouthed.

She signed, and blackness rang in her ears.

He caught her in his arms.

Titus checked the documents, and marked them with his signet, while the clerk recorded them, and handed them back to Quintus with a smirk. He had called their bluff. Now was the time for his final stroke.

"Consummate the marriage," he ordered, and suppressed a smile. It wasn't for nothing that he had Quintus straddle the trestle. If not dislocate hips when the weights were applied, the trestle would at least emasculate its victim as he rode precariously on that slender rod bruising his groin. And if the victim were fool enough to change to the other side for relief, well, then the complete job was self-imposed, so to speak. Titus would have his revenge after all, both in public and in private.

"Here, on the couch," he said to the astonished couple standing silently before him. "Or must the Best Man take the Bride first?" He stepped toward Letitia.

Quintus resolutely picked up his bride and somehow managed to limp to the couch. What followed was not the mortification that Titus expected, but sheer poetry. Titus had not anticipated the solicitous communication between a couple finely tuned to each other. Nor did he know anything of Bishop Nicodemus's bribe. The object lesson was reversed, touching the heart of every awed male in the room. The couple stood before him again.

"Take good care of each other," Titus admonished. "Quintus, you shall be the envy of every man in town. Letitia, we need your husbandman's produce and taxes."

Letitia and Quintus bowed and departed promptly, Quintus leaning on her arm for support.

"You were lucky," one of the guards said.

The other queried Gregor in unabashed admiration as he stepped up anxiously to meet them.

"Are you from Good Will?"

* * *

Quintus and Letitia lay together reading in bed upstairs. Their two children were tucked in for the night in their little beds in the adjoining room. Quintus was restless. There was something he had to tell her.

Letitia sensed his uneasiness. "Quintus, dear heart, something is troubling you, I can tell."

"My legs hurt."

"Here, want to chew on some willow bark? It's fresh."

"No, it's not that, really. Letitia, joy of my life, I am only too aware of how I burden you with care."

"Quintus, we're in this together, remember?" She gently caressed his temple.

He caught her hand and kissed her finger-tips. "I really need to relieve my mind of something. I've done a lot of thinking while in prison."

"Lord of my life, whatever is it!"

It startled him that she used Lucan's phrase. Yet it wasn't entirely Lucan's phrase. After all, she was formerly his slave. "Letitia, it's Lucan." He noticed her worried look. "He's only three days' journey away. In Rome."

"You found him!" She searched his eyes.

It irritated him how her face glowed. "Dear wife, if something should happen to me again—I may not survive another incarceration—you must send for that . . . light of your life . . . at once." He tested her with his own words from that tablet.

"And become the wife of a slave? Don't you know private law?"

"Is that all I'm good for? Your freedom?" he retorted.

"God!" She forced herself to meet his eyes. Does he know who the anonymous donor is? Will he have Lucan's life when he finds out? "Exactly what is the matter, Quintus?" she demanded.

"You have never said that you loved me."

She sighed in relief. "I was given to you as a peace offering by the household, and you expect . . ."

"I am well aware of that, Letitia," he answered defensively.

"Quintus, you are such a sweet dreamer." She caressed him tenderly. Her eyes snapped with mischief the way they did when he asked the obvious. "I have sacrificed myself for the household. It is a blessing in disguise, and yet you ask me, do I love you? Twice you were taken from my bosom and twice I have restored you to my bosom. And you ask if I love you?" Gentle reproach was in her voice.

"Nonetheless I would like to hear you say it. It would be like precious oil that runs down to the beard." He sighed. "I realize that those are fighting words to you, Letitia."

She regarded him empathetically. Here is your basic Quintus, she thought. He wants all of you, body, mind, heart, and soul. Is that why men insist that we wives love and obey our husbands as our Lord? Are men indeed afraid for themselves if we women put our Lord first? We cannot serve two masters? And a husband should come first in our lives though that condemns us to idolatry? And to cover up, men would deny that women are equal in the sight of God? She knew regardless of her rebellion that she did love Quintus. Perhaps it was sinful to love him as much as she did. If only Quintus could see! She had only to bring herself to confess her love, yet she was afraid to commit herself to those simple, earth-shaking words. It would feel like compromising herself, selling out. She wrapped her arms around his neck and murmured in his ear. "Dear Quintus, you have been such a good husband and lover. Truly I could not ask for better."

He kissed her hair. He should have accepted her appraisal graciously and let well enough alone; instead he was prompted to blurt out his thoughts. "I accuse myself, Letitia, hear me out! I need to unburden. I took you from him."

"He rejected me himself!" she returned swiftly.

"Wrong! He gave you up in deference to me. It's true! Can you live with that? Do you expect me to?"

"No ! Yes! Oh Quintus, Quintus!" she protested into his breast.

"You don't hate me for it, Letitia?" He stroked her hair.

"Sometimes I do. Help me!"

He upturned her face in his hands and looked deeply into her eyes. "I will not condemn either of you for anything that may pass between you," he pledged magnanimously.

She stared at him in disbelief. He was not jesting. Though they had just escaped that morality law with their lives, he was truly offering her license. Shock and anger steamed up to the surface. She managed to answer, her barely audible voice gaining strength as the anger presided. "What do you think I am, Quintus, a whore? Do you think that I take my bond to you so lightly that I can simply—let—something happen? Do you think I have no feeling for you? No integrity in myself? Quintus, you do me an injustice!"

"I'd kill him if he tried anything! That however does not take away my guilt. Dear Letitia, my guilt!"

"Your guilt can go to the crows! You should understand that I shall always love Lucan, yet not as you think! He speaks to my very soul! In many ways I am yet a slave, like him. He dares to express our condition in words. His words are my words, his agonies my agonies, until we are all freeborn and equals in the eyes of men. How long will that be, Quintus? Oh Lord how long?" She flung herself over to her side of the bed and wept silently into her pillow.

"Damn woman harping on slavery again," Quintus lashed at her in anger. "Isn't it enough that I regard them as equals? 'Free them all!'" He gestured in exaggerated mimicry of her appeals. "You know that I cannot give them manumission. I cannot give them wages. You keep the books. You know that it would ruin us, send me back to prison. Is that what you want? Is that my purpose in this household, to rot for you in prison?" Quintus turned his back on her in disgust.

She turned and reached toward him. "Forgive me, Quintus. Do not say such things. Your household loves you."

"Their freedom on my deathbed is not soon enough for them," he sputtered, "so that they must plot my early demise."

"Why Quintus! You don't trust them!"

"Human nature."

"You haven't really forgiven them that uprising, have you, Quintus."

"Have you? Except for that, you could have been married to Lucan! Forbidden treasure, he called you."

"Quintus, you need not castigate yourself over that."

He turned and met her gaze and the lovelight in her eyes shone through the agony on her face.

"Quintus, dear Quintus, I . . ." Again she tried to say it, commit herself in words of love to the lord of her life in an admission that would be a self condemnation to pain, tantamount to a sentence to be exploited and betrayed. She and Quintus were childhood sweethearts. As a young girl she had given her heart to Gaius, as a young woman to Lucan. Now she was about to hand Quintus voluntarily this power to hurt her again. Again the contradiction silenced her.

"I know, Letitia. Dear Letitia." He met her embrace at the center of the bed. "I am your slave. I am your slave of love."

"Not slave! You do not know what you are saying! I free you, dear heart. Only the free can love," she insisted.

"I act freely. I give myself to you, Letitia."

"I give myself to you, Quintus."

"We shall both work through our marriage to a new covenant, better than a paper bondage."

She wept in his arms. "Let Lucan stay in Rome. Unless he wants to come home."

"We can't have our anniversary orgy in the maze if Lucan comes back," he teased.

"Why not?" she lipped. "You can sneak out of your library again while he is waiting to be dismissed."

Quintus guffawed. The tension was broken and they giggled together. They began to fondle each other slowly. She pleasured him with her hands and mouth, knowing every inch of his body and how he would react, the muscled breast heaving over the raw-boned ribs, the platelets over his stomach quivering to the touch, the ticklish depilated armpits evoking giggles, the bite on the sensitive back of the neck provoking goosebumps on the thighs, the dimples appearing at her stroke above the hard buttocks, his manhood springing from the forested groin.

He knew well how to orchestrate her body, caressing her neck, snuffing in her ear, taking a mouthful of breast, nibbling the nipples, then tonguing her with circular strokes. He played her with firm caresses down the spine, tried her with light fingers above the knee, unbearably ticklish at first. The wonder of bodies and the delicious sensations amazed them anew. They played with each other until they could not withstand the undertow of passion any longer, whereupon he plunged to the depths and wave after wave of pleasure undulated through them until a big breaker crested and smashed over them both and swept them swiftly in sparkling, snapping spume to the shores of oblivion. Those of the downstairs people who were awake could hear the moans of passion trickling down in the soft night air and they also partook of the ecstasy.

Quintus awoke in the dark of the early hours and shifted position to relieve the dull pain in his hips. He thought of the crock of willow strips but was too sleepy to reach for it. His mind drifted back to the earlier years when he first started managing the farm alone and would wake up anxious and lonely in the small of the night. With whom can I be at one? He smiled, reached for Letitia's warm body, and cuddled up. Dear Lucan, he thought to himself, dear old Lucan who had schooled him in intimacy and whose disappearance made this wonderfulness with Letitia possible, dear old Lucan would not be recalled to interfere with such bliss. Not for a while, anyway. Quintus drifted back to sleep.

CHAPTER XXVI

Lent, AD 329
Acting on one's convictions

Scarcely two and a half years and two love children later, Quintus found himself journeying to Rome overtly to visit his parents and sell some fine country goods, covertly to find Lucan and to recall him. Quintus was beside himself. It was bad enough to confront a man with slavery and to demand obligations to the master. Furthermore he had to accomplish this task without alarming his parents about the underlying reason, his ever-threatening economic disaster. Worst of all were the intolerable prospects of bringing Lucan the mentor, the soul mate, the burning flame, back into contact with Letitia, the forbidden treasure. How could he endure Lucan in the house? Could Letitia withstand the flame? Would his beloved helpmate, a source of great strength and encouragement to him, a tenacious partner through thick and thin, be able to keep her heart in the marriage? Of course he hadn't told Letitia about this third worry at all, and how it had motivated his resistance to recalling Lucan, and he could see that she floundered helplessly before the closed door of communication.

He took Gaius along on the three-night journey with the mules and a wagon load of Letitia's quality homespun and Gregor's artful baskets. Gaius would be hawking these at a bazaar for a fine price while he went about his own unpleasant business. He also offered among his friends to do errands and bring back for them on his return trip a wagon load of big-city purchases. Bishop Nicodemus asked him the favor of an errand at the Chi-Rho Bookshop at the Argiletum. Now that he was going there Quintus sneaked one of Letitia's favorite scrolls into his pack. He would have a present made for her in the same format.

Gaius's natural reserve, though at his side on the wagon bench, and the soft darkness of night travel gave Quintus time and virtual solitude, to think, to fortify himself, to dare face up to the pressures of the past six months, an eternity of hell, that forced him to take this action. The Magistrate had commanded him to apprehend the runaway himself and thereby avoid dire consequences. Quintus no more trusted Titus now than he had six months ago when he had responded in person to the initial summons from the Magistrate.

Every painful step of the way to that late September hearing had reminded Quintus of the hip-wrenching torture on the trestle, then the more recent bone-chilling cold prison wall. The interview was about the delinquent taxes in produce and his concrete plans for meeting his obligations. Though he had approached this meeting with well-justified apprehension, he was completely unprepared for the interrogation that followed.

The Magistrate had leaned forward confidentially in his chair. "Quintus", he spoke kindly, "you have been dealt with unjustly in the past. That is regrettable. You will never again be imprisoned unjustly. I will make every effort, I will bend over backwards to keep you out of there, I assure you."

The reassuring words effectively evoked the desired fear and dread. "What is it that you want of me, sir?"

"Your taxes."

"How can I pay what I don't myself have?"

"Listen. I shall be liberal with you and allow you to substitute gold for produce."

"Gold! How in heaven's name!" Quintus chortled incredulously.

"Lucan!" Titus declared.

"Lucan?" Quintus groped in astonishment.

"All you have to do is find him and let me talk with him," Titus proposed. "No harm shall come to him. You can even send him back."

"You chose to disregard the law before," Quintus spat out suspiciously. "How do I know that you won't choose to do so again?"

"Don't you accept my apologies, Quintus? Now then, we understand that Lucan is well-to-do. We need his help, that's all."

"He is rich?"

"Didn't you know?"

"No, sir, I honestly didn't."

"Hadn't you better find out about him? And recall him before we have to? We need to sequester his income. However if you decide not to, no harm shall come to you personally. We need you on the farm."

"I don't know a thing about Lucan," Quintus declared.

"Oh you will, soon enough," Titus assured him. "This is not a bribe; it is a clever, sensible idea that would help us all, don't you agree?"

"I can't do that to him; drag him down to the farm."

"To Good Will? That bright island of refuge in a turbulent sea of corruption and exploitation?"

"The sea wall is crumbling," Quintus sputtered.

"Exactly. That is why you are here. We don't want you to go under. You can keep the tide back a little longer. Tell you what. I'll give you a few weeks to find Lucan. But you won't mention it to anyone, will you. We don't want anyone to panic him into bolting."

Quintus had plenty to think about during the peak grape harvest and wine pressing. Yet he had done exactly nothing. What he did not know could not be wrung from him.

At the next several meetings in October the Magistrate's tone had turned threatening. "It would be a shame, wouldn't it, for us to have to go after him and arrest everyone who is aiding and abetting him?"

"How can you go after him when you don't know where he is?" Quintus had a moment of anxiety that they were trying to wring from him something they already knew.

"You refuse to turn Lucan in?"

"I don't know where he is."

"If we have to find him ourselves the penalty will be maximum," Titus warned.

"It's a big world, he could be anywhere," Quintus shrugged stubbornly.

"Protect him! Get to him first!"

Soon the threats had become more personal. "Someone will have to go to debtor's prison if those taxes aren't met, and it won't be Marcellus or me. Nor can it be someone who isn't in residence now, can it. You know, then, who it must be, Quintus."

"You promised that no harm would come to me," Quintus had reminded the Magistrate coldly.

"I don't write the edicts." The Magistrate shrugged and spread his hands, typically using more tact than honesty.

"I have no information to give." Nonetheless Quintus had to answer something, make some sort of statement to get the Magistrate off his back and to put an end to this prolonged disruption of his workdays. He had to do something soon to keep out of jail. But what?

"How can you not find out?" the Magistrate scolded. "Use him! Save your neck!"

"I cannot do that to him, sir!"

"To your slave? Your piece of property?"

"My brother in Christ."

"Ah! I should have known! Pardon me! Tell me about this! We have always envied you, Quintus, for the devotion of your slaves. How do you do it? What great thing is it that we can learn from you?"

Quintus earnestly had sought to work around Titus by evangelizing him. He was released several intense hours later, with the request that he should return on the next day to continue, and the next day, and the next, until the entire week was taken up, while Olipor contracted the olive pickers and the women cooked to feed the harvesters. Quintus talked with relief to be doing something that satisfied the Magistrate. He flowed. He went into intimate detail about his history with Lucan. Titus invited him to sit at table with him as a peer. The Magistrate appeared intensely involved. Not until some time later would Quintus realize that he was trying to use the faith to save himself while Titus was using the faith to break him. The self revelation was to nearly destroy him.

"What a true shepherd you are of your little flock at Good Will," the Magistrate had acknowledged. "How they love and admire you! They depend on you to look after their safety. Perhaps you need to enfold Lucan with your love and safety also. All you need to do is to agree to seek out and bring Lucan to us so that we don't have to apprehend and interrogate certain members of your household, your house church and your father's household in Rome. What a tremendous responsibility you bear toward them! Keep them safe! Save your father unnecessary grief!"

Quintus had to agree with Titus on the responsibility he bore. Still he remained firmly silent on anything about Lucan's whereabouts. The personal cost of his resistance was considerable. After the November olive harvest and oil pressing he had nightmares reliving the seasonal burning of the oil-soaked straw. Sometimes he helplessly watched Good Will go up in the leaping flames. Sometimes, as in that first November long ago, he watched Lucan become rigid with terror before the bonfire, then flee shrieking into the servants' hall. He had dashed after him and wrestled the frantic slave on his pallet until he had the flailing boy restrained in his arms, enveloped in safety and outgoing concern. "Lucan, I must bring you home," he mumbled in his sleep at the pillow that he clutched to himself. "You are afraid and I must enfold you in safety."

Then Titus had sympathized with Quintus's agony. "You may feel terrible about recalling Lucan but you have to rise above that and do the courageous act of a true leader: recall one to save all. Otherwise Good Will would have to be put up for sale, and who knows what would happen to all of you then?

And what could you do about it from prison? Prison, Quintus. Do you want to rot in prison? Brought upon your own self by your misguided refusal to cooperate? What is your household thinking about this? What are they dreading behind your back?"

"You requested me not to inform my household."

The Magistrate erupted. "How can you be so stupid! Do you indeed think that your secrecy has been that effective? Do you think that in all these months of meeting with me that they have suspected nothing? Think you that they are not overburdened with anxiety, afraid to approach you, afraid that you will sink the entire ship for one person overboard? Do you think for a moment that a responsible sea captain would jeopardize the entire ship for one of the crew? You had better believe that he will sacrifice the one to save all!"

"However a good shepherd will leave the flock unattended and exposed to go find the lost lamb," Quintus rose to the bait.

"Well, you do that." The Magistrate had him. "If you bring Lucan back, then you would all be safe from disaster. Otherwise the police will have to uncover him. His associates will get arrested and interrogated in the process. And you know how slaves get interrogated. Spare the fine family he must be with. Spare the slaves agony. Spare his patron harassment and embarrassment and spare yourself the patron's wrath. All you have to do is to go to him and command him to return and be counted. All he needs to do is to make an appearance. I will then speak with him and make the necessary arrangements with him. That is all."

"I will do what I can."

"Without delay, Quintus."

Marcellus, who had offered sympathy and council, also pressured Quintus under the guise of concerned advice regarding Titus's threats.

"You've got to get him back before Titus goes after him with an army. Remember our bet, Quintus. He did run away, you know. If you can't handle him I will. At least get the Magistrate off your neck. I don't want trouble at Good Will, giving the state an excuse to confiscate it. You don't want to be a serf of the state, do you?"

In the recurring nightmares that followed, Quintus became the worshipped Roman Eagle dislodged from the standard and he soared over the fields looking for food. Only he no longer saw a lovely, fertile Campania from his vantage point in the sky, but a vast desert stretching from the Tiber to the Silarus, between the sea and the Apennine. Yet he knew that this must be his Campania, for he recognized the dry, rocky promontory that once was the drop-off ledge to the swimming hole. He wanted to alight but the trees were gone, the mighty oaks and chestnuts, elms, beech, ilex and poplars. He tried to alight on the roof of the ruins of the library but the tile and stone crumbled at his touch and he fell with the debris and woke up screaming.

During the December butchering Quintus dreamed that he himself was strung up like a stuck pig. He gained a new understanding of Lucan's former nightmares.

Letitia was so concerned about him and the unspeakable torments beleaguering him that she urged him to ask Lucan home to relieve his mind and restore his peace of soul. Quintus became furious.

"You and your tirades against keeping the household in slavery, the sinful exploitation of other human beings, using them, not loving them; and now you want me to drag the only liberated man back down to the mire! Letitia, how can you!"

"I worry about you, Quintus. He can help. He once told me that if I needed him all I had to do was call, and he would come running."

"Sacrifice Lucan for me; that is really something coming from you, Letitia." Quintus's sarcastic retort couched not a little jealousy and anxiety. Surely Lucan would return to steal Letitia away from him. Furthermore this was no trivial matter, to call a man back to slavery. Quintus was not about to play with this young man's life as he had done once before when he had made that damned bet about him. Except that now he had to save Lucan from certain disaster, and somehow perhaps they all would be saved in the doing.

The final impetus had come from his trust in The Way. Bishop Nicodemus of Puteoli, on his Lenten visit to the house church, preached on the disturbing issue of how you cannot make an offering to God when you and your brother were estranged. Here was the ultimate moral reason for finding Lucan again, but with an ugly twist. Not only was he estranged from Lucan, but also he must find him in order to use him again. At the next interview with Titus he had confessed willingness to comply.

"You're too late," Titus had declared at the outset.

"What do you mean?" Quintus tensed.

"Didn't you know when he left Rome?" Titus queried sharply.

"He didn't!" Quintus rejoined, then became sullen. He had just been tricked into revealing knowledge of Lucan's whereabouts.

"Get him," Titus had commanded in no uncertain terms. "Now."

Quintus obeyed, with the spine-tingling sense of relief that he was acting not a moment too soon.

From the wagon bench as they made their final night's journey into Rome, Quintus thought of Lucan. How did Lucan live with this directive of our

Lord to leave the gift at the altar and seek reconciliation with the estranged brother? Amazing, isn't it, how a person guards a cherished purpose in the recesses of the mind until that purpose can be brought forward to fulfillment. Does Lucan to this day truly think that he is freeborn? Should I have told him the truth when he first came to me? He wasn't ready for it then. Will he be ready for it now, before it is too late? If I really loved the slave, Quintus thought, I would not have let him wear deeper and deeper into the groove of rebellion. Instead I would have taken immediate personal action to bring him back. Surely he is afraid to come home.

So close to the eye that I cannot see him, like the brow, is that how he's been hiding? In Rome Quintus immediately sought out Presbyter Vincentius who informed him that Lucan was following Bishop Sylvester in his Lenten rounds of the churches in the Eternal City and that he also assumed the name of his patron saint, Lawrence.

"I doubt that you can inspire him to come home," Vincentius warned. "You have to demand obedience. For what use is inspiration in getting one through life? It quickly fades away and leaves one as indifferent as before. Inspiration has no muscle. Now take obedience. Obedience is strong muscle. Obedience has back bone. Obedience calls for guts."

What Vincentius did not add, and what Quintus knew, was that the Holy Spirit in his mysterious ways can take hold of a person's inspiration, however insipid, and work wonders with it. With this trust Quintus therefore decided to continue with his gentler approach. Not by force, but by good will. He followed the round of the Lenten devotions himself, with the expectation of encountering the lost sheep. He uncovered exactly nothing but an overwhelming sense of the size and power of the Body of Christ.

* * *

On the morning of his return journey Quintus limped from his parents' apartment near the docks to the bustling Argiletum. Ah! Here it is, the Chi-Rho Bookshop where that renown researcher and copyist is supposed to be. He turned in. At the same time a youth breezed in.

"Lawrence back there?" the youth asked the shopkeeper.

Quintus's heart quickened. Now it couldn't be the same Lawrence?

"Yes, he's dictating to the copyists, Cleophas."

The youth's face fell. "Oh—I only wanted some advice. Tell him I'll see him at dinner."

"Very well, I'll tell him," the shopkeeper replied good-naturedly. He turned to Quintus with a grin and shrug. "Lawrence lives up to his name all right, but not entirely how you'd think."

"His name? Oikonomikos?" When the shopkeeper nodded, Quintus couldn't believe his luck. "Useful, eh?"

"People come for his advice, and then they buy books. He is a good listener, keeps his confidences, and remembers names. That's his real talent, not only books, as he thinks, but people. He's the junior partner here, and he earned it. Why, he can dictate four books at a time without dropping a line! And he is uncanny at digging up old manuscripts and rare books. The head librarian at the Trajan Baths has sent him to Alexandria numerous times on research projects. And, who knows? He may be a state librarian himself some day," the shopkeeper predicted with pride and anticipation of the reflected glory on the Chi-Rho Bookshop. "What I mean about his real talent is that he really cares about his customers and they know it, and such customers keep coming back. And that part is good for business."

"No doubt." Quintus wondered whether to play the detective or to come right out with his claims. "How long have you been blessed with this Lawrence?"

"Well, let's see. Autumn before the Emperor's Vincennalia Celebrations here. Almost four years."

"The same year as the Council, then?" Quintus became more specific.

"Council? Oh yes. You're up on the Council?" the shopkeeper warmed to him. "We sold a lot of Bibles on account of that song and dance. Yes, that was the autumn Lawrence came. September, in fact."

The date figured. "He came from the east, then?" Quintus asked with friendly interest.

"Egypt. Had some sort of high-power secretarial job there until the 'Ariomaniacs' got too frantic. You can see the shackle scars on him. You know how quarrelsome they are down there."

"So he's Christian," Quintus smiled.

"Oh yes. He's a Deacon in a house-church in the Suburan Quarter. Now sir, what can I do for you?"

"As a matter of fact," Quintus grinned, "I want to see Lawrence myself. Does he not take private commissions?"

"Lawrence Oikonomikos? Yes indeed. He does outstanding private commissions. Beautiful ornamentation, you know. Expensive, though."

"Will he have mercy on a provincial Bishop? I am doing this errand for Nicodemus of Puteoli. And lookit here. I myself have an original Lucan." Quintus pulled a scroll out of his tunic and handed it to the shopkeeper.

"An original Lucan?"

"That's what he called himself back then."

The shopkeeper examined the scroll and regarded Quintus with curiosity. The contents were not religious. Since he owned such a thing, however currently censored, the rustic must be safe.

"Yes, this is Lawrence's hand. You should see how his calligraphy has improved! He also specializes in other classics that the church has suppressed." The shopkeeper's eyes twinkled now. "Lawrence travels widely for his clients, to copy rare manuscripts." He watched the rustic for another undercover sign for censored material, but there was none.

"So in addition to scribing he pursues scholarly research," Quintus commented.

"Yes, he's doing a fine piece of detective work in Alexandria on a suspected forgery, a possible insertion in St. Ignatius's letters making it appear that there was authority from the primitive martyr for a diluted form of Arianism. Do you follow me, sir? An exposure of this forgery would knock out the supposed precedence by an early church father. Now our Lawrence here has tracked down a possible original letter. It would never have surfaced if Lawrence hadn't asked the privilege of going through the private collections in the homes of old families as partial payment of their commissions for just such material as you have in your hand. Clever, wouldn't you say?"

"He manages to have his way," Quintus commented with admiration. "Could I myself presume to command the favors of this personage in such high demand?"

"So you also have some private business for my partner, eh? May I write up your orders?"

"Ask him if, for old times' sake, he would consider a temporary commission from Quintus Legerius of Good Will, Puteoli."

The quiet request, spoken almost apologetically, shattered the shopkeeper like a battering ram. He strove for composure.

"Certainly, sir. I'll ask him, sir. In the meantime here is an example of his present work."

Holy Mary and all the Saints help us! Quintus Legerius! How did I not know! The shopkeeper hurried to the copy rooms where Lawrence and the copyists were still at work. He would enlighten Lawrence slowly, obliquely.

"Lawrence, men, excuse the interruption. Dinner time, anyway. Aren't you on your way out to dinner with Cleophas? There's a . . . rustic . . . out front from Good Will who wants to see you also. Shall I ask him to come back after dinner? Or go back to Puteoli? Or go to Hades?"

"No, I'll see him." Lawrence's eyes widened.

"Lawrence, what about the St. Ignatius scrolls? Your forgery case? Did you remember to arrange for the next ship to Alexandria? Shouldn't you be going down to the docks?"

"Yes, perhaps I should," Lawrence replied, fully comprehending. Before his partner could protest, he strode determinedly to the display room of the shop.

Quintus was surprised that Lucan had not disguised his name more. He examined the scroll that the shopkeeper handed him. It was an exquisitely ornamented rendition of the Nicene Creed. He opened the scroll that Lucan had made at Good Will, and compared the script. It was the same hand, though Lucan's artistry had indeed improved through the years. Quintus went through the motions of examining the creed. His mind worked hard. The shopkeeper seemed to have no notion of Lucan's status. At least he didn't seem to be hiding Lucan from the public. Or perhaps he is warning Lucan right now. Should I claim Lucan and take him home with me? I don't want to make a scene. I don't have Lucan's papers with me, dammit. What am I going to say to him? Lucan come home, just like that? Quintus heard footsteps. With butterflies in his stomach, he looked up. The young man that approached him was bearded, tan, muscular from regular workouts at the gymnasium, handsome, in the prime of life. He wore a fine white tunic bordered with the Greek key design and girdled with soft fine leather. Quintus was awed. Here he himself was, a broken down tiller of the soil, in a plain brown patched tunic, in a shop where he in all appearances did not belong, about to order this successful professional man back to slavery. He could not do it. No, he simply could not do it. Flustered, he groped for words.

"Good day, sir, may I help you?" The familiar voice was masterly, not servile.

"Well Lawrence," Quintus managed. "I should have known that we would meet again in a place like this."

"Sir?" Lawrence saw before him not the exuberant, idealistic youth that he once knew, but a care-worn man, old before his time. He scarcely knew him.

"Wasn't that an impressive celebration yesterday?" Quintus covered awkwardly.

Lawrence laughed, embarrassed. "You must have mistaken me for another, sir. I am the junior partner here."

"No I haven't mistaken you, Lucan, not at all." Quintus spoke as though he had last seen his slave only yesterday.

"Well, no matter," Lawrence chortled. The young man did not yield any sign of recognition, except that his cheeks reddened.

Doesn't he know me? Could I be mistaken? Quintus wondered an awful moment. He swiftly tried to save face. "And Lazarus came out—risen to new life in Christ! Weren't you at St. Peter's yesterday? Wasn't it wonderful?"

"Yes it was," Lawrence took up, glad for something to talk about. It gave him a chance to recover. "Think of it, sir, next week the Christians at Jerusalem reenact for the first time the Messiah's triumphal entry into the city."

"So I hear!" Quintus responded. "The world shall see more of us Christians now that the church has peace."

"What peace," Lawrence muttered.

"How's that?"

"You know that the Arians have been recalled from exile, don't you sir?" Lawrence asked. "And that the Arians took the See of Antioch practically by storm? Clergy aren't supposed to move to another charge, you know."

"Yes I do know. A certain Leander and others sought refuge at Good Will when things got too hot in Alexandria."

Lawrence's stomach seized. He expanded on the news as he stalled for a way out. "Eusebius of Nicomedia finds a formidable opponent in Athanasius of Alexandria, if you ask me. Athanasius is unyielding, and ready to make any sacrifice for the cause—"

Quintus could have jumped at that perfect opening, of making a sacrifice for a cause, but he passed it by. "Do you know Bishop Athanasius in person?"

"I met him at the Council when he was a deacon, secretary to Bishop Alexander, God rest his soul."

"Ah!" Quintus interjected. Lawrence had inadvertently revealed some of his past.

Lawrence continued quickly to cover his blunder. "Know what he has done now? When Constantine demanded the rehabilitation of Arius, Athanasius refused—and had his way!"

Another good opening for Quintus. Again he passed it by, not ready to bring this magnificent person down. Besides, Lawrence was going on, digging himself deeper into a hole.

"So now I hear Athanasius's opponents are working up some absurd political slanders against him."

"Why political?" Quintus led him on.

"Because Constantine doesn't give a damn about the religious issue. He's too busy building his new city. If I may say so, sir, Constantine was mistaken in recalling the Arians and trying to reestablish them. Once I wasn't in favor of excommunication, but now I've changed my mind. Why, they may gain power and refute the whole work of the Council! You can't force an overall rehabilitation on them. Men's hearts have to be changed first, don't you think so, sir? Otherwise offer them a new relationship and see how they refuse . . ." Lawrence ground to a stop, appalled at what he had just said. 'Deeply concerned for you . . . feel free to come home . . . already paid the penalty for your runaway . . . Light of my life, shine on me again'. Leander had told him what was in that letter from the domine, from this man before him who cared enough about him to come in person, or was desperate enough, he couldn't be certain which.

Quintus took this opening. He regarded his slave with all seriousness.

"Then you are not a *homoiousian* but a *homoousian*?"

"Most decidedly, sir. Not one iota missing in that word."

"If you are so positive, Lucan, about the heresy and the truth, why don't you act upon your convictions? Or are you too busy building your new livelihood? Clinging to the extra iota after all, in the reflexive, capital form?"

"I?" Lawrence returned a startled look. "My convictions?"

"That the Christ is truly God, to be obeyed." Quintus put Lawrence's own words to him, as relayed by Leander.

Lawrence broke into a cold sweat. He spoke slowly.

"Supposing that I have been acting on my convictions by staying away, even at personal risk?" He revealed himself plainly, inadvertently.

Quintus was mortified at the slave's intuition. "Then you are indeed my Lucan Fidelissimo," he chortled.

"Quintus!" Lawrence felt a surge of the old camaraderie.

Quintus responded generously, "Good Will is nonetheless your home, and the family there your family."

"Thank you, sir, you are most gracious." Lawrence felt that he had just been given permission to live.

Again Quintus hesitated, unable to lay the mandate upon him. He groped in his mind for a kind way to do it.

Lucan noticed and courage leapt to his throat. He became personal.

"How is it with you, sir? And with Good Will?"

"I cannot keep up with my taxes." Quintus's lamenting tone surprised them both. "And it appears that I still have a missing serf. How can I get away with scratching him off my roster when both my landlord and my magistrate know that he flourishes in Rome? I need him home for the census. We need to work something out with the Magistrate. Otherwise we are in unspeakable trouble." Quintus's voice pleaded and he lowered his gaze. It was pathetic.

"How much time do we have, sir?" Lawrence asked with great apprehension.

"A week at the most."

Their gazes locked. Beads of anxious sweat stood on the faces of both master and slave. Quintus lifted his hand, tremulously reached up and touched the brand mark on his Quintipor's neck. Still locked in his gaze, Lawrence reached up and gently took his master's burning hand off his neck and clasped it in both of his.

Then Quintus spoke quickly in a raised voice for he saw that the senior partner was emerging from the back room.

"Consider doing your work at my villa; you'd enjoy the country. Now—to be sure you have your order straight—I want this set of scrolls made for Bishop Nicodemus of Puteoli like this, see, the Early Church Fathers." Quintus opened the scroll and watched Lucan receive a jolt. It was not the Early Church Fathers at all, but Sappho's lyrical poetry that Lucan had copied as a present to Letitia. It was her favorite.

"Permit me to double check, sir. Where shall I start?" Lawrence recovered. A twinkle came to his eyes for the Early Church Fathers would fill cabinets.

Quintus floundered and lowered his voice. "Dammit, Lucan, don't do this to me!" Out loud he said, with deliberate double entendre, "Start with the Nicene Fathers and work back. Nicodemus is eager to have our own Shepherd of Hermes who's strong on a second chance. Then Polycarp, also gentle toward the erring, but tough against heresy. I want the Gospel of Thomas myself, and the Gospel of Mary. Actually you should do the Gospel of Mary first, decorated. Like this. I'll leave this with you." He handed over Lucan's earlier work. "Deliver the scrolls as soon as possible. For now I need a copy of your usual work order, and I need a strong letter of recommendation from your senior partner describing why you are worthy of this commission."

Lawrence picked up his old work, copied and decorated himself during his happiest time at Good Will, and inadvertently raised it to his lips. "How is she, sir?" he whispered.

"Well and eager to see you." Quintus watched closely for a reaction to the bait.

Lawrence raised his voice. "I am grateful for your generous offer, sir. I shall consider it with great care. If I cannot accept your hospitality to do my work there—I know that your mansion has many rooms and that a place would be prepared for me—should circumstances not allow my acceptance, I shall see that your scrolls are delivered promptly. Without fail." Lawrence bowed and retreated quickly with his partner.

So that is Lucan's answer, Quintus thought to himself, that ambiguity which he means me to interpret both commercially and personally. Did I get through to him?

In their office the senior partner confronted Lawrence.

"What's that homespun fellow from out in the sticks trying to do? Fill his cabinet with a set of matching scrolls to impress somebody? Or enhance his decor?"

"No, it's *bona fide*. For the Bishop of Puteoli," Lawrence chuckled humorlessly. "That man is the Domine of Good Will, the market farm and house-church near Puteoli."

"I know who he is. I took down the Man Wanted ads, remember?" The shopkeeper watched Lawrence's face closely.

"Stephanos," Lawrence shrugged and spread his hands, "I would enjoy a quiet breather out in the country."

The shopkeeper's words tumbled in panic. "What about the St. Ignatius papers? Let the Arians get away with it? And what about our subsidiary in the new Rome? I'm counting on you, Lawrence! You wanted to be there next May eleventh when Constantine dedicates his new city!"

"Stephanos, calm yourself! I shall be there! That's not until next year! Right now I need to go to Good Will for a visit, that's all."

"After four years of evading him?"

"He came to me. He needs me. He saved my life. I owe him."

"He *owns* you, Lawrence, and he wants to use you again!"

"It's more like give and take, and it's my turn to give."

"What makes you think it won't be forever?"

"I shall make it profitable to him to let me return!"

"You shouldn't have to do that! One should have no master at all except Christ. Where is your fortitude?"

"In Christ I am a freedman. Therein is my faith and my strength. I am going back to my brother in Christ."

"Goddamn, Lawrence, we've gone through all this effort to keep you free, and now you really are going to walk through that gate? Submerge yourself in agriculture? Forever? If you survive, that is?"

"Stephanos, where is your faith? Try to understand what The Way demands of me. Pray for me. If I'm prosecuted, you don't know my real identity. Is that understood, Stephanos? Protect yourself!"

"Not pull my right hand from the fire?"

"Promise me!"

"I need you, Lawrence!"

They embraced, then resumed their routines in the pain of anxiety.

When Quintus started to limp out, work order and recommendation from the senior partner in hand, Lawrence checked him quietly. "Quintus?"

The lame farmer turned.

"Would you like—can you use—a post horse, sir?"

"Save it for yourself, thank you. I have the wagon and team."

The master truly expected the light to shine on him again. Lucan watched after him speechlessly, his heart crushed to ashes.

Quintus journeyed home with a tremendous sense of relief. He had fulfilled his mission, he had survived the encounter. And was not Lucan receptive to him, taking his hand like that? He fully expected to have his Quintipor back home in a week's time. He could almost regard Lucan as some sort of savior. Lucan was indeed well-to-do! Through him, though he wouldn't press the point, Quintus owned the junior partnership in an evidently lucrative business. Quintus congratulated himself that he had patience with Lucan over the past several years, that he had given Lucan time to grow and flower. He greeted everyone at Good Will euphorismatically and declared that the best results of his business trip were yet to come.

Then came the remorse, while he was trenching soil, brutal work, slave labor. My God, what have I done! Recalled Lucan only to betray him to the Magistrate? Will the Magistrate torture him? Shall I slip him a knife first? But Titus needs Lucan alive! Can Titus be trusted?

In his anxiety Quintus came to realize under what circumstances Olipor—Ophelus—must have been relieved of Good Will and made a slave on his own ancestral property. To this day Olipor was not telling his bitter story, but the evidence was undeniably there. The old family lares that Letitia rescued from the waterlogged trunks when the atrium store room flooded, looked a lot like Olipor. The old overseer had them repacked in a hurry before anyone should ask too many questions.

Conceivably Lucan could come back with the deed to Good Will in his hand. The gathered household waiting anxiously in the atrium to greet their new landlord would reel in shock at his presumption. They murmur among themselves whether to salute their savior or bow to their new master. Not waiting for an answer, Alexis and Gaius plant a knife between Lucan's ribs whereupon the dying Fidelissimo cries out that Good Will goes down with him. Come, come now Quintus, such thoughts!

As you have done to the least of my brothers, so you have done to me, the Celestial Judge declared to him in his sleep. I didn't betray him! I saved him from arrest! He cried out in the dark and Letitia soothed him. He did not share his burden with her but contained the agony in his breast.

Letitia in her concern for Quintus began to long for Lucan, her big brother, her mentor, her champion, her . . . she wouldn't admit it to herself. She felt a shiver in her abdomen at the thought of him, or was it only that her infant was pulling at her breast? How can she love two men at the same time? One was real, here, however distraught, the other was in absentia, a glowing memory, anticipated like a savior. Her closeness with Quintus now rivaled anything that she had ever known with Lucan and in some way surpassed it. What was the real Lucan like now? Could he disturb their conjugal unity? She worried that Quintus would be very sensitive about that and she feared for Lucan's safety. She was careful that Lucan would be returning to his master, not rushing to her side.

Furthermore she explicitly refrained from asking for his manumission. She sensed that such a favor would be cloaked with danger. If she insisted on his freedom, or if he appealed and gained freedom, he could only leave Good Will a dead man. She was torn between wanting Lucan home for Quintus's sake yet not wanting him to walk into a nest of hot wasps. She sent him no signal except to will him home in her mind.

* * *

In the privacy of his lodging Lawrence fought desperately with necessity, that relentless adversary which dashes personal hopes and aspirations when confronted with the demands and needs of corporeal and corporate life. Go to him, Lawrence, he needs you; he needs to use me. He rescued you; he enslaved me. He called you to life; he raised me up to use me for his own vanity. He gave you courage to be; he claims my very being. He has paid the price of your absence; until he can recover it from me. He has offered you clemency; until he gets his hands on me again. He elevated you to a peer; as long as I don't cross his will. He came to you man to man; I subordinated myself with my first gift. He has called you to a supreme act of love; he has saddled me with guilt. You are free of slavishness; in his hands again I will be subject to whatever personal violation anyone cares to inflict on me. You must deny yourself, Lawrence, and return to your domine; I must assert myself and invest my talent here at the Chi-Rho Bookshop.

Why cannot talent be a true calling? Why should personal rights conflict with personal responsibility? Duty without authority is nothing less than slavery! A slave's hard work is rewarded only with more hard work! Why should there be any question at all? O Domine Christ, who fasted in the wilderness for forty days, and was tempted by the devil concerning the use of your talents, help me!

How many times he had been raked with this torment! First of all he was sent home from the Nicene Council. No one followed up his failure to return all the way home. He was guided instead into an excellent calling. Marcellus had run across him on the Ides of Quintillis during the Vicennalia year. Again the world did not come to an end. Two years ago he had come across Presbyter Vincentius while following the joyous procession that escorted the relic of Christ's true cross from the docks of Rome to St. Peter's. The cross had been unearthed and sent across the sea by the Emperor's mother Helena.

"What are you doing here?" Vincentius had asked. "You belong at Puteoli."

"For the occasion, sir."

"Festival or no, you are an incorrigible, and forbidden to enter a hundred-mile radius of the city. Go home before you are apprehended, slave!"

Lawrence had almost returned on that occasion for, confronted with the relic, the Reality struck him between the eyes. On a huge rough crossbar, perhaps this very one, the Son of God had actually stretched his strong arms in redeeming love for the world.

Does God sacrifice his adopted sons also? The bitter struggle with this question surfaced again until Lawrence reminded himself that he was thinking as a *homoiousian,* thinking in terms of God the Father sacrificing his Son. Shining through the dark clouds came the *Homoousia,* One Substance Incarnate, to dwell among us and give himself for us. Quite a different matter. Not one iota missing in the Divine Word. Yet Jesus did not speak of himself in these words. Though he acknowledged that he was the Son of God, he referred to himself as the Son of Man, the Christ, the Anointed One. He spoke of God as the Father. How could he do otherwise, seeing how he was truly man? In and out of the shadows turned the mystery of the religion about Jesus, and the religion of Jesus, like two vines intertwining, supporting each other, growing toward the light. The agonizing mandate was to respond in obedience to such Divine Love.

Again nothing happened, after all that. The nightmares came and went of his father chained to the burning beam after he killed his son, and of Petros lingering for three days on a cross, the carrion crows attacking his eyes before he was really dead. Then Lawrence had become detached from the true cross, no longer struck by it as at first. He certainly had no advantage over Christians who have no access to the relic. Perhaps he had considerably less advantage and considerably more guilt since his detachment was toward the real thing, placing him in grave danger of apostasy. Yet he had felt unready and could only trust in the Lord's understanding, and then his master's.

Now perhaps he could get by once more. Why not? If the domine were going to do anything he would have already. See? The staff were acting quite the same towards him. Of course the copyists knew nothing, and Stephanos was on his side.

Lawrence continued his work into the week, copying and dictating as he wrote the words of Athanasius upholding the true divinity of Christ. *Homoousia.* Therefore we are to obey him. Totally! Without reservation! Lawrence himself had insisted upon this at the Council of Nicaea.

Perhaps, then, he could go to Good Will for only a visit and make it profitable to continue at the bookshop. He would see Letitia. Letitia! Of course! Why didn't he realize it sooner! She sent the old scroll! She called! And he had promised that he would come running. He renewed the pressure on his copywork staff. During the long mid-day breaks and evenings he cloistered himself in his apartment above the shop and worked on the Gospel of Mary.

At night in his room thoughts of Letitia stole softly into his mind as the purple and gold shadows stole upon the apartment walls and roof, and the daytime noise of humanity was replaced by the nighttime noise of delivery vehicles. He recalled other evenings, hushed, in a lovely garden where purple shadows fell, the brook gurgled, and the marble bench felt cool.

She belonged to Quintus now.

For a while she was his, a stolen heart on stolen time together in his fern and wildflower niche hidden deeply in the maze, a secret refuge away from daily life without actually being away without leave. What a bright pupil she was, learning to read, opening her mind to worlds beyond the villa walls, questioning him intently with her soft brown eyes, or furrowing her lovely brow thoughtfully at something controversial, or pressing against his breast with delighted laughter when she grasped a passage, her closeness filling his nostrils with woman scent. How it would excite him! What a traumatic trap the niche became for her! He was cast out of her life. How he buried his exile in work!

He yearned that it could have been different. Think of what could have been! In their own little cubicle at night instead of working at his books to the point of exhaustion he would read beautiful phrases out loud to her while she stitched little baby things, and love would steal into the soft parts of his heart. Then he would clasp her to himself. God! How he would cling to her and peg her to himself with his manhood!

Suddenly the dream was severed apart by the Master's sword. Her mouth was wide open in horror as it was that final night at Good Will when they were apprehended together by the brothers. Letitia! Letitia! How I wanted to take you away from that place! Why weren't you in your room? Why didn't you meet me? He awakened, clutching his pillow to himself and buried his face in his bedding with grief.

How can I go back and be consumed with passion for a woman I cannot have? Letitia, you must protect me from myself! You belong to the master.

Slavery! I am going back to be a slave! Your slave! Not allowed to acknowledge my feelings!

* * *

Lawrence was among the faithful who followed Bishop Sylvester to his station at the Lateran Cathedral on Palm Sunday. He brought his anguish with him. 'Everyone should remain in the state in which he was called,' the Apostle Paul had written. 'If you were a slave when called, never mind. But if you can gain your freedom, avail yourself of the opportunity, as no one should be a slave of man. If you cannot, never mind. Serve your master as you would your Lord.'

Lord, is your apostle truly speaking your Will?

The old hymn of praise floated across his troubled mind.

> "Let Christ Himself be your example,
> having emptied himself,
> taking the form of a servant
> he became man and humbled himself
> by living a life of utter obedience,
> even to the extent of dying . . .
> that is why God has now lifted him so high . . .
> so that at the Name of Jesus every knee shall bow . . ."

There it was, precisely. Let Christ be your example. In grappling with it, Lawrence scarcely heard the worship that followed.

He was well aware that his disobedience in not returning to Good Will four years ago, a mental unreadiness, had jelled through time into a deliberate decision. He had a prior task to accomplish before he could return. He would then be utterly at the mercy of his domine that his goal, once accomplished, would be acceptable. That was his gamble, and he was willing to play his life on it. The odds were that he would become so set in his disobedience that he would be unable to change. The tension in the situation was to keep an openness to the right time to act. The agony was that actions often had to be made out of the sequence in which one was prepared to take them.

Oh Christ, my freedom!

'He who was called in the Lord as a slave is a freedman of the Lord.'

Obeying the authorities placed over me!

'He who was free when called is a slave of Christ . . . there is no partiality with him.'

Will God sacrifice his adopted son?

Beloved, I am one with the Father.

Lord I am not worthy. Help my doubts! I am afraid.

Go, beloved servant, and be faithful; I shall fit you for the task to which I have commissioned you.

You have spoken, Lord. Praise be to God!

Thus Lawrence watched and prayed with Christ through the bitter struggle between self-will and selfless-will, until, with an agonized sigh, he approached the unqualified 'Not as I will, but as you Will.' He left the basilica on trembling legs. He had entered, Lawrence Oikonomikos, slave of success. He was going out, by the grace of God, Lucan Legerius s. Quintus, brother in Christ, freedman in Christ. Lucan, 'light'. 'You shall be a light to the feet of men . . .' His particular light was not only scholarship as his father had aspired for him, but the ministry of reconciliation, as the Light of the World had been trying to show him.

Light of my life, shine on me again.

CHAPTER XXVII

Passion Week, A.D. 329

A living sacrifice, giving thanks

Lucan loaded his saddlebags on a post horse, mounted and started directly home from worship that Palm Sunday morning. He arrived at the last bend in the road at sundown, Tuesday. Only a short distance now lay between him and uncertainty at Good Will.

Lord, I am not worthy . . . Lucan was sorely tempted again to shirk responsibility and to use human imperfection as an alibi.

Lucan, do you refuse to accept in yourself what God has already forgiven in you? Words of Paul came to him again.

> Having this mercy of God, therefore,
> offer your body in a living sacrifice
> that will be holy and acceptable to God;
> that is your spiritual worship.

Lucan, do not evade life because you will find it imperfect; go, be reconciled with Quintus.

Lord, you have spoken. He was going to do it. The first step of a journey is the most difficult—the old Roman proverb was very true. He had taken that first step and the momentum would help carry him through his hesitation. A prayer of the Apostle came to his lips.

> "Grant that I may be strengthened with all power
> according to your most glorious might,
> for all endurance, and patience with joy,

giving thanks to the Father who has qualified me
to share in the inheritance of the saints in light."

Nonetheless Lucan was unnerved that Gregor had not begun his watch at the gatehouse. The watchman could not help by escorting him in. Everyone would be at supper now. Lucan led the horse around the buildings, and felt ready to run at the slightest provocation. He entered the stable court. Cerberus barked. Ignis poked his head over his stall door and neighed. Lucan shoved the post horse in a stall, grabbed his gear, fled to the kitchen garden and climbed through a window into the slaves' bathrooms. He debated whether or not to take time to clean up. His urgency pressed him, yet out of respect for his master he wished to wash himself and trim his beard, and put on fresh clothes. As he cleaned himself, he listened to the voices in the kitchen. I can't just walk in there as though I belong! God help me! Why doesn't someone find me here and take me in?

When he was barely done, he heard footsteps enter the hot bath. Losing his head, he sneaked out of the cold bath to the stairs and bounded upstairs like a scared rabbit to the safety of his master's room.

* * *

Immediately upon hearing Cerberus bark, Olipor went out to the stable court. The sheepdog woofed at the strange horse and looked at Olipor intently. Lucan must be about. Surely it is Lucan, and he is afraid to come in. This is what the domine meant that the main results of his business trip to Rome were yet to come. Olipor inspected the row of stalls, the pens, and called insistently in the barn. He attended to the horse. Then he returned to the kitchen with a strong hunch to go look in the slaves' bathrooms. At first he put off the hunch as being ridiculous, but in the middle of a conversation he shrugged and gave in. He found wet foot prints on the pavement, a towel and dirty linen clothes on top of a travel pack and a shaving knife left by the mirror, as though hurriedly. Olipor checked the master baths and the office in the atrium, then started up the stairs.

* * *

Letitia reclined bare bosomed on the big bed in the upstairs bedroom, nursed a newborn and read a scroll. She tried to read, that is. Quintus was late in returning from his summons before the Magistrate and she was worried sick about him. Lucan had not shown up yet and Titus was threatening jail.

Quintus had told her that yes, he had found Lucan, at the Chi-Rho Bookshop no less! that they had a good, quiet talk, and that he expected Lucan home, but that she must tell no one. Now that his anticipated return was to be a reality, another aspect of the intimate triangle loomed as a threat. Supposing that Quintus became so close with Lucan that he no longer needed her for advice and companionship? Would she indeed be relegated to second place? Would Quintus, out of jealousy, prohibit her to resume her former closeness with Lucan? Why, she could be left completely out in the cold!

Lucan! Lucan! How I want you! How I fear your return! So vividly did she visualize him that she let out a little cry of surprise when he suddenly materialized, then became flustered and tried to back out quickly as though he had not been noticed.

"Oh Lucan! Come in! Thank God you're here!"

"Letitia! So the reading lessons have served you well!" He approached and knelt beside the bed and kissed her on both cheeks. Then he buzzed the infant, and leaned his cheek against her bare breast and looked up at her. "Oh Letitia, to see you face to face again! I am quite overcome." He lifted his head and sought her lips. He didn't care if he seemed too forward.

"I see that you are indeed healed," she whispered when he released her. He flushed with pleasure. They gazed at each other deeply, mentor and pupil, soul mates, former confidantes, fellow conspirators.

"Mama? Comes the Daddy home?" A small boy came in from the adjoining room.

"No, Lucian, not Daddy. This is Uncle Lucan. Come greet Uncle Lucan, Lucian."

Lucian. Named after him! A moment of anxiety gripped him. His child? How could it be? Then he looked into the likes of Quintus's eyes. Truly Quintus's son. Lucan held out his arms.

The child's face lit. "Uncle Lucan! Uncle Lucan!" he cried shrilly. "We love you, Uncle Lucan!" He climbed onto Lucan's thigh. "Tell me a thory, Uncle Lucan! When you and Daddy were boys. Tell me about when you fell into the thwimming pool!"

"Mama?"

"Come here, Libra."

"I want to hug Uncle Lucan too!" A little girl came over and sleepily settled on Lucan's other thigh. "Tell me a story? How the cork go boing on your head!"

"Later, children, later," Letitia replied gently. "Where is Dulce? Show Uncle Lucan how you can go back to bed before little Jocelyn wakes up and comes in here too."

Lucan hugged and kissed them. Then the children took hands and quietly returned to the adjoining room.

"Letitia, you amaze me. You have yet another in the nursery?"

"My goal is a fourth son, Lucan, my freedom child."

"You can't mean it! Didn't Quintus give . . ."

"Yes, of course. He freed me before our first was born. Yet I cannot feel free as long as the others in this place are in bondage. You know what I mean, Lucan."

"Bless you, Letitia." He leaned forward and kissed her between the eyes.

"I have argued with him unremittingly about freeing the household. I have threatened, stormed, and even withheld myself."

"And?" An edge of expectancy sounded in Lucan's voice.

"He was furious, of course. He quoted Corinthians at me about spouses giving each other their due. He threatened to take one of the slave women. I said that if he did, the consequences would make Medea look pale. He said he could do whatever he wanted in his own household. I said so could I. He tried to stare me down; I wouldn't yield. He said, 'So you care that much!' I called him a blind fool. 'Blind!' he exclaimed. 'Don't the blind see by feel? And don't I feel my woman right here next to me?' He tried to possess me whereupon I shoved him away. Lucan, you would have been proud of me! He went out to work in a huff, but by nightfall he apologized, and so did I. He begged me not to—desert him—again; it left him too desolate. I'm telling you this Lucan so you'll know what you are coming back to." She blinked back the tears.

"Then we discussed the household and farm situation and reached a working compromise. He claims that we are economically locked in to slavery. I can see that, though I refuse to accept it. The women have an out; we have our freedom child. The men, poor dears, get their freedom only on their deathbeds. Not that they can leave us." She watched Lucan closely, anxious that he didn't harbor any false hopes.

"I can understand that," Lucan mused, thinking of how his own slaves, when given their freedom, were bound by law to stay with their trade, and most stayed with the bookshop.

"Olipor says it's best that way seeing how we are bound to the land by the Colonate Law. They're guaranteed a living and we can't afford wages. Furthermore, he says, we have our faith. I challenge the faith, Lucan. It shouldn't have to be that way. I don't see why we can't challenge scripture that exhorts slaves to accept slavery if they can't earn their freedom; why we can't challenge scripture on submission of women, or on obedience to corrupt civil authorities! Certainly those set in authority over us are subject to the same Lord, but we are his hand and his mouthpiece! Olipor says, where would it end if we start challenging?"

"You have changed," he observed quietly.

"So have you, Lucan," she sighed in relief. "Now how did we get onto that? Yes, the children. Understand that Quintus and I are close in more ways than one. When we wrestle with life together our souls touch, and our bodies become as one, and these little ones spring forth."

Lucan nodded. It was as it should be. But these beautiful children could have been mine, he reflected remorsefully.

A neophyte woman with heart shaped face and large eyes peered around the doorjamb.

"Come in, Dulce."

"Don't get up, Lucan, please," Letitia checked him, and motioned Dulce to come closer. "Dulce, meet Lucan, the Quintipor. He won't hurt you. Lucan, Dulce is my nursemaid."

"Are you my big brother?" Dulce stared transfixed at Lucan who looked mystified.

"She asks everyone that," Letitia explained, "seeking her lost brother. The Rescue Mission sent her here from a brothel. Hysterical. Hopefully a man with understanding will step into her life. Perhaps . . . perhaps?"

Lucan regarded her with sympathy. "Peace, Dulce." He offered his hand to her but she quickly backed up. "You have had a fright, I can see. I am sorry. My sisters," he added on impulse, "both of my sisters—and I was forced to watch—" His eyes filled.

"Oh!"

"Would you like me to be your brother, Dulce? I would like that."

She moved toward him, watching him intently, and shyly reached toward his extended hand. They touched ever so briefly. She reached out and traced the scar on his face with her fingers, through the eyebrow and down his cheek to his beard. Then she laid her hand on his forearm and he gently clasped her arm.

Letitia looked on with amazement; Dulce just doesn't let anyone touch her.

Then Dulce turned toward her. "Will you be sleeping in the nursery tonight, Mistress?"

"No . . . Quintus will be back." Letitia handed over her sleeping infant to Dulce, and pulled up the top of her garment from the waist. The young woman hummed a little nursery riddle that Lucan recognized from his childhood, and retreated to the children's room.

"Now, about Quintus and you and me," Letitia courageously led him to face their situation together. "You did warn me that you would run away to make me behave," she reminded him firmly, but her eyes twinkled.

He took her hand in his and touched his forehead to it. "I have agonized about that decision."

"You thought of me? Your little sister?"

"My forbidden treasure." He had to confess it, to be at peace with himself.

"Why, Lucan!" She cried out breathlessly.

"He wanted you for himself, Letitia. And I couldn't claim his child. Please understand! Please believe me! Beloved, it would not have been fair to you."

"You dear, compliant, self-effacing . . ." she groped for a word. "Slave!" she spat out bitterly with her whole being.

"Forgive me, Letitia!"

"Dear Lucan, you are trembling so!"

Suddenly they embraced. A sob escaped his throat and her eyes flooded.

"Forgive me, Lucan! I did what was necessary!"

"Letitia, you are not to blame."

"You don't feel that I had abandoned you? I couldn't give birth without him! I couldn't deny him his child and wait for you! I-I . . ." She started to tremble in his arms. "I knew you weren't coming back."

"Letitia, I must confess that I did come back for you."

"You came back for me? When! What do you mean?" Her eyes widened and she felt a moment of panic. She knew the Lucan of her fantasies but here in her arms was the real Lucan with power over her and she feared any disruptive claims that he may make on her.

"That night, I came back for you. Didn't you know that I returned? I came down to your room. To ask you . . . to run away with me."

"Lucan, oh Lucan," she gasped.

"You weren't there . . ."

"I was crying my heart out on my mother's breast."

"I was crying my heart out at your empty room. Then I came to my senses again. I must not disrupt the order of things at Good Will. I . . . abandoned . . . you."

"You gave up your happiness for me," she breathed.

"And found it in myself," he affirmed, "who I am inside my skin, not defined by anybody else. And you, Letitia? How is it with you really?"

"You did right by me, dear, you really did. God! It was hard at first! It is still hard! When there is contention between Quintus and me I become mute, and it takes a day or so for my heart to touch my mind and to know what to say to him. I'm a slave, Lucan, I'm still a damn slave! Then he lifts me out of the quagmire of slave mentality and gives me the courage to be. I love him, Lucan, I love him something fierce!"

"I prayed it would be so. And I wouldn't for anything interfere," he pledged as he clung to her.

"Is that why you stayed away?"

"Yes. Just look at me, Letitia, how do you think I could have endured it?" He pulled away from their embrace.

Indeed she was impassioned by his high level of arousal. "Dear big brother, I used to wonder about you, how you agonized over everything you did whereas I seemed to be able to . . . ," she drew a long tremulous breath, "just act."

"And now?" he asked gently.

"I agonize. You see, Lucan, I was very reluctant to marry."

"You were?"

"And become a piece of property again? You know the age-old agony: to be loved without exploitation; to be pair bonded without bondage."

"Is it that bad, Letitia?"

"I don't see you submitting to any kind of bondage, Lucan."

"I'm here, am I not?" he answered in anguish.

"Oh Lucan, your return is an act of love and I have not so much as told him that I love him."

"Letitia, how could you withhold such a confession from him!"

"I have been so upset over you. Then it became a battle of wits. Now it's a matter of principle. I can't compromise myself to confess it."

"How does he take it? Your reluctance?"

"Personally. He blames it on my love for you. But he is very empathetic. He also attributes that to you."

"He does?"

"He has said that during those years with you he gained insight into . . . our . . . viewpoint. He learned how to be more completely human."

"That is mutual," Lucan reflected. "Letitia, how does he take my unwillingness to be in bondage?"

"He understands."

"But he must be after my blood!"

"Not if he wants to live with me," she pledged. "Oh Lucan," she burst out, "he's been unbearable! Couldn't you see how downcast he was when he came to you at the bookshop?"

"I saw him through guilty eyes. He was formidable. Looking back, you're right, he was meek. He did not make a scene. There was some hesitation, as though he didn't really recognize me at first." Lucan chuckled. "I didn't help him, either, Letitia. He has every right to be furious. He intimated that he needed me home. Not asked. Not ordered. He gave me your signal."

"My signal?" Letitia queried swiftly.

"Didn't you send for me? The Sappho scroll? You didn't?"

"I did not! That underhanded rascal! Keep me out of this, Lucan. Don't play with his heart! That's dangerous! He ordered you to come back for himself! Didn't he? Lucan?"

"He suggested that I was needed home to prevent some disaster. I gave him an ambiguous answer. He accepted it."

"He is a broken man, Lucan. It took him great courage to come to you."

"Courage?" Lucan's brow puckered. "To come to me?" Wonder sounded in his voice.

"Please, dear brother, you are not supposed to know that."

"I had a premonition of what you are saying. When he turned and limped away he seemed so . . . so . . . crestfallen. I-I . . ." Lucan's voice tightened with compassion. "I would have come anyway. For him. For you. I . . . you . . . both of you . . . you have shown me the way. You two have given me the courage and the will to live and love again. You have given me a family again, a place to belong, forever. You have given me a glimpse of the eternal Gift."

His testimonial struck disquietude in her. "Lucan, please," she protested, "you do not know why you are here." She was anxious to prepare him without startling him.

"Why? Letitia, you must tell me what is happening!"

"Hard times, Lucan. We can't seem to balance our books, and it isn't his bad math, either. You see, the Emperor is grinding workers of the land into the ground for taxes to build his New Rome, and we can't produce enough to meet our quota. My catering business collapsed; people aren't throwing big parties anymore. I've tried to supplement with homespun goods. We've economized here to bare bones. We've even opened the villa to city guests who want a country hideaway. They don't always pay. I've never seen Quintus so depressed. I'm at wits' end and there is simply no one that I can talk to!" Her eyes filled.

"Dear little sister!" He enfolded her in his arms again. "It will all work out!"

"No! We're drowning, Lucan! We're all drowning here at Good Will. Excessive taxes, the Colonate, debt to Marcellus; Quintus is not taking his bondage very well. We have to face the fact that our bright little island of Good Will is going to be overwhelmed by a floodtide of economic disaster. Good Will may go up for sale, and all of us with it!"

"For sale! Nonsense! You must tell me where Quintus is!"

"He is pleading with the Magistrate!" Her voice trembled.

"Come with me, please. I will show you to your domine."

"Olipor! How long have you been standing there?" Letitia demanded uneasily.

"Long enough," came the even reply.

"Thank God, he is back." Letitia closed her eyes and drew a deep breath.

Olipor did not contradict her.

"Here, dear sister, please give this to Quintus. He requested it." Lucan drew a package out of his tunic containing his old scroll and the present for her copied and decorated in his own gifted hand, a book long suppressed by the Church, the Gospel of Mary. He nearly pulled out another parchment for Quintus, but preferred to present it in person. "I'll talk with you again, later, little sister."

"Later, big brother."

Olipor escorted Lucan downstairs to the family baths off the peristyle. He was ominously aloof. "The domine is away and his delinquent slave is discovered in his bedroom with his wife. Very good, Lucan," he chided.

"It's not that, Olipor."

Lucan entered the baths with trepidation. He could not be positive of his standing with the domine. He was evidently some sort of hero in absentia, to be sure. He had already been forgiven generously before he even repented. There was that letter which the domine wrote to Leander at Nicaea, and that scrap of paper delivered to him at Nicaea: 'Light of my life, shine on me again.' Yet Quintus let him be at the Chi-Rho Bookshop until he came in person and asked him to come back. For the census, he said. But now that Lucan was actually through the gate surely there would be some sort of reckoning. His stomach knotted. The Roman scraping himself with the strigil wasn't Quintus at all, but Marcellus!

"Well I'll be damned!" Marcellus exclaimed. "So fate brings you here!"

"Not fate, sir, but an act of God. Where is Quintus?"

"An act of God, poppycock! How desperate did you have to get before you would resort to Quintus?" Marcellus tore at him with disbelief.

"Marcellus, I left an excellent position on my own free will to come home. Please, is Quintus in here?"

Marcellus blocked his passage. "Come home, you say! Quintus? What is Quintus to you, presumptuous one, first-naming us!"

Lucan lowered his voice. "Even when one has wronged, one does not cease to be a member of the family."

"Now you imply that you are his brother or something! Zeus! If you are what you claim to be, then how could you have done what you did to Quintus, you bastard castaway of a slave wench!"

"I know I deserve rebuke, sir."

"Listen, slave, rebuke? I'm merely stating a fact! Do you hear? Facts!" Marcellus proceeded to aim a barrage of outrageous statements at Lucan, moving on to the next claim before Lucan could respond to the previous, each question jabbing persistently at his vulnerability with studied accuracy. The effect was like that of the dreaded battering ram on a city wall.

Lucan stood on a crumbling rampart. "Marcellus, pardon me. Where is Quintus?"

Marcellus pressed relentlessly. "You admit it, then, slaveborn?" Arms across chest, he now waited for an answer.

"Admit what?" Lucan tumbled.

"Those crossroads!" Marcellus shot at him.

"Rocky and Broad Street?" By association Lucan came out with the highways from which his family farm had gotten its name The Crossroads. It was a wrong move.

"So you confess knowledge of that too, you foundling slaveborn exposed to die."

"I-I d-didn't say . . . !" Lucan floundered.

"No, you didn't say Oikonomikos was your father because you knew all the time that he picked you up, and your mother threw herself at his feet and he bought the desperate slave wench from the landlord."

Is it possible? Meter's bastard son? Exposed in desperation at the crossroads? Adopted by Pa? Not freeborn at all? Raised out of love? "Oh Pa!"

"Yes, your old master, that landlord is your pa. And his name?" Marcellus barked.

No, it can't be, Lucan shook his head.

"Telling me you don't know!" Marcellus thrust his face close to the slave's. "Lucan is the name. Where else did you get your name except after your procreator?"

"From Oikonomikos, after his aspirations for me!"

"No! From your old master the landlord who begot you and had you educated. Know what happens to slaves who lie?"

"My father educated me."

"Old Lucan was illiterate, you liar!"

"Oikonomikos . . . educated me . . ."

"How could a filthy agricultural pig have educated you?"

"A freeman! Himself educated!" Lucan rose to his father's defense.

"Oh so?"

"Noble!" Lucan dared.

"Prove it!" Marcellus challenged.

"In the register!"

"What register?" Marcellus asked triumphantly.

"Thessalonica!"

"You haven't seen that register, have you, Lucan," Marcellus taunted. "It lists him as a slave of old Lucan on The Crossroads farm. It lists your name as—Spurious!" Marcellus circled Lucan for emphasis. "Spurious s. Lucan!"

Lucan's eyes narrowed. "You prove it, Marcellus."

"What! Accusing me of lying now?" Marcellus unfolded his arms with a vicious flathand to Lucan's face. "Ask to see your papers, sometime, in the household strongbox, slave. By the Gods if you knew what was written about Oikonomikos you wouldn't claim to be his son. You yourself admit he was a noble. He was really a ruined decurion from Southern Italy, hiding as a slave in Thessalonica. There's another register that you haven't seen, Lucan. Right under your nose. In our neighboring province of Lucania. It lists Oikonomikos and his son but it doesn't list you."

Lucan swallowed bile. Marcellus continued to batter him with words.

"You think that your family was destroyed by wanton lust, for resisting uninvited dinner guests who got out of hand. You prig! You obviously don't know what happens to the family of a deserting decurion! Why do you suppose your so-called father put his own son to death before your eyes, then torched the house, himself with it? Not a word from you now! Listen!"

Lucan listened in dazed silence.

"You think the soldiers killed them, don't you. Well, there's a lot that a ten-year-old child doesn't want to see. Think about it. Do you think that the soldiers representing the world's most just government would wantonly kill? Don't you think that a doomed man would want an easier way out than a public trial and spectacle of himself and his son in the arena? He slits his son's throat and torches the hut. But the soldiers get to the rest of you before he does, whereupon the crazed man chains himself to the door. As for your sisters you should know Roman Law well enough to realize that they don't execute virgins without first violating them."

"They didn't execute them!" Lucan declared.

"Oh so you admit that!" Marcellus closed in on Lucan. "And why do you suppose you were spared, you fool, bastard slaveborn of old Lucan's slave wench! And why do you suppose that you and the women were sold, dummy, why else but that old Lucan wanted to recover something for damages. Coming home on free will, indeed!"

Lucan breathed deeply to force back the nausea. Pater wept for me from the burning beam. 'Do not weep for me but for yourself. Slavery—worse than death!' Father sacrifices son, but the slave is spared! The demon of the past stood starkly before him. The source of his hidden anguish was finally revealed! His mind rebelled. What was the truth?

"Where is . . . my . . . domine?"

"Ah, so it's not Quintus anymore; now you are calling for your domine? Slave, I am your domine."

Lucan's vision darkened. "You are lying, Marcellus."

"So you still think I'm lying!" Marcellus struck him down. "Kneel before your lord! There was a bet, you know. You didn't think of that, did you, when you came back on your own . . . free will. You belong to me, slave. Before I turn you over to the Magistrate for trial I will examine you with a flogging to get the truth. When the state is finished with you I will compost you."

"Marcellus, please do not destroy yourself!" Lucan bent forward clutching at his vitals. He wished to High Heaven he had given Letitia the scroll that was soaking up the sweat of his breast.

Marcellus regarded him in amazement. "Zeus almighty! How desperate can you get under the pretext of compassion! You should have thought of compassion before Quintus was hauled off to prison. Prison!" Marcellus emphasized over his shoulder and made a dash for the chilly pool.

"Prison?" Lucan repeated incredulously and followed on his knees to the edge of the pool. "Prison? Quintus? Now?"

"You ass, Lucan. What else? Taxes. A runaway serf. Trouble with the Magistrate. A fine. Prison sentence until every penny is paid. Torture on the trestle. And you think he can still forgive?"

"He didn't tell me! My savings—I could have—Marcellus, you must tell me where he is!"

"What about your savings?"

Lucan made a lost gesture. "How can a runaway claim anything?"

"I see you admit that too, you incorrigible one! Freeborn son of a decurion, indeed! Some economic asset you are, Lucan Oikonomikos! All those fines, let alone the outrageous price Quintus paid the slaver for you in the first place, and then that ransom Quintus had to pay old Lucan in Thessalonica for a legal ownership because the soldiers defaulted on your purchase price. And finally he lost all investment in you when you ran away. And now that I have recovered you, you are telling me that you forfeited your savings? That was my money!

You are a pain in the ass in more ways than one! As though Quintus would forgive if he could!" Marcellus dove under.

"If he could." Lucan, on his knees, leaned over the pool. "Is he . . . is he . . . ? Marcellus? Marcellus! Doesn't Letitia know? Am I too late?"

"Why do you ask! Have you come to take his place in prison? Like a self-sacrificing Christian?"

"Mio Dio!" Cold sweat oozed from Lucan's face. "He wants me to take his place in prison?" The household would frantically expend themselves to get their Domine out of prison, to save their own skins. But to get another slave out? One who was not necessarily loved by the household? They would let him rot!

"Why do you suppose he asked you to bring home all that copywork!"

Lucan rose to his feet and staggered for balance in the blackness that overcame him. Pain stabbed him in the stomach. "No . . . no . . . you're mistaken!"

"You had better go back out through that door while you still can. I shall not pursue you until morning. Now get out!"

"Marcipor in there?" A voice called from the hot bath. "Send him in when you're done, will you, I want a massage."

"Get out while you can, slave," Marcellus warned.

"Right away!" Lucan answered loudly and strode at once not to the exit, but to the door to the hot bath while Marcellus gaped in astonishment.

Quintus's back was turned when Lucan entered. In the actual presence of his master, Lucan's relief turned to guilt.

"At your service, sir," he murmured.

"It's about time!" Quintus chided. Then he turned, for that was a long-absent voice. "Fidelissime!" he uttered. That was all. Nor was there reproach in his tone.

Quintus emerged out of the hot bath and limped to the bench for his massage. "Fidelissime," he repeated in a quavery voice and hid his teary face in his arms.

Lucan blushed at this salutation from one who had been his closest friend, one with life and death power over him, one whom he had wronged grievously but who had forgiven him before he even repented. He took in the domine's care marked face, the broken health, and disfigured hip that therapy could not cure. Self-will murders the Christ, Lucan could see it now. Why hadn't he swallowed his hurt and obediently returned at the outset? His domine would have been spared this body-breaking torture. This reflection of himself on his master was appalling. On his knees he started the massage and he could feel

Quintus stiffen under his cold hands. He rested his quivering hands on his master's feet.

"Quintus . . ." he pleaded, "Quintus . . . I should have ridden that *equuleus,* not you."

"I would have found your horseback ride none too easy," Quintus replied. "Now thank God both rides are over."

"Amen." Lucan could only proceed with the massage. He felt that old pleasure of living warmth under his gifted hands, and as of old his master moaned with pleasure. When he finished he cushioned his head against his master's shoulder as he had done many times before, and they both drifted off to sleep.

"Ah, Lucan! We were both tired," Quintus mumbled when he roused himself. "Refresh yourself, eat; Olipor and Marcipor will attend Marcellus and me. You and I can talk after. But do not visit the household just yet. Take the west bedroom upstairs. I'll send for you."

"You are most kind, sir."

At supper with Marcellus, Quintus, with a hint of complacency in his smile, requested Olipor that he should summon Lucan to his office when they were through eating.

"Well, how do you like your slave presuming upon your mercy?" Marcellus asked.

"What do you mean?" Quintus queried.

"Why," Marcellus spluttered, "he carried on with me as though he thought he were—pardon the insult—your brother or something! I had a talk with him, you see."

"So you laid it on him heavy, eh?" Quintus looked worried.

"Thought you would be too easy on him so I . . . well . . . I told him a thing or two. I didn't want him to think he was doing you some great favor."

"You got through to him," Quintus said. "I was going to tell him too. Gently, Marcellus, gently! Or as a last resort, if he didn't come home on his own."

"Home," Marcellus repeated. Even you say that. And now that he has?"

"I'll send him back to the bookshop to make us some money!"

"To Rome? Quintus, there's the Colonate."

"I suppose you're right."

"And he's incorrigible!"

"Oh. I forgot."

"Forgot! What do you mean, forgot?" Marcellus demanded. "How can you be so . . ."

"He has returned to me, Marcellus, as, well, more than a slave. Can't you understand?"

"Zounds! How can anyone understand a lunatic?" Marcellus retorted.

"Don't try," Quintus replied.

"He's mine, you know."

"That's debatable," Quintus asserted. "He came back."

"The state will get him anyhow. Neither of us can claim him."

"That remains to be seen."

"I must interrogate him with you."

"No, Marcellus." Quintus was adamant. "This is private."

"Quintus, you're impossible!"

"Stay out of sight, if you must. Absolutely no interference."

"Unless he pulls a fast one on you."

"He won't," Quintus asserted.

CHAPTER XXVIII

To stand before you as a man

Lucan attempted his master's presence again, in the office off the atrium. Even though he would have to make an accounting and perhaps stand judgment, Lucan approached with a light step and warm heart. It was a reunion after some four years apart. He felt a growing mutual return to the old rapport. He was impatient to help the household, but of course he had to hear his master out and wait for the appropriate time to present his offering.

Quintus was the more anxious. Here they were bound together by imperial decree to the Colonate, and Lucan had run away at risk of his life. They were brothers in Christ by sponsoring each other in baptism, and he had virtually driven his brother away to a death sentence. They were both deeply in love with the same woman, and only one could have her. These hard realities had to be faced together and resolved.

"Come in, Lucan. At ease! Relax! I'm not out for blood. Please sit down."

"Letitia told me that I'd find you here," Lucan replied warmly.

"I thought I told you not to visit the household!"

"That was before I found you, sir," Lucan soothed.

"Lucan, do you realize what you just said? How it sounds? You sought her out first?"

"I sought you, sir. Before anyone knew I was here, I went to your upstairs study. I was rather surprised," Lucan chuckled with a humor that Quintus did not share. "Please forgive me the blunder. She is beautiful, Quintus. Your family is beautiful."

It was almost as though Lucan smiled a benediction on his master and Quintus felt somewhat relieved of his guilt concerning her.

"Has Letitia told you how we came together?"

"Not yet, sir."

Quintus was eager to explain himself. "She went up to live at her Pater's cottage on the new acreage. She wanted everyone to believe that she was pregnant by you. She had a long labor. We were worried for her safety. She kept crying for you, Lucan, to unlock her womb. Then she cried for the domine. They thought she meant Domine Jesus and they sent for the Deacon who immediately let me, the domine, into the room. Well, Lucan, she confessed, and I confessed and we were absolved. Then she was able to deliver, and I held her while she was on the midwife's chair. A miraculous experience! I attended all her deliveries. Old custom, you know. She protests, but I got her that way, so why shouldn't I support her on the midwife's chair? She delivers more easily then. She is my dear little rebel. She has worked hard to overcome the slave mentality. You can understand what I mean, Lucan."

Lucan smiled empathetically.

"I haven't always helped her," Quintus added. "It was convenient to have a servant wife. But more than interesting to have an equal. She keeps me honest! She gives me the courage to be. I'll do anything for her. You have mentored her well, Lucan."

"Thank you, sir. I am happy it has worked out for you."

"Is that why you ran away, Lucan, so that . . . things . . . would . . . work out?" Quintus probed gently.

"Something like that, sir." Lucan broke out into an anxious sweat. How deeply will the master dig?

"Did you know about the bet?"

"The bet? No, sir."

"Then why, Lucan, do you remember?"

Lucan began to tremble. He could not speak of the dagger that his master had driven into his heart. "I saw myself as the cause of the disturbance of peace at Good Will. I honestly thought I was doing you a final service by leaving your service."

Quintus rose to his feet. "You had no right to make that decision!" He tried to sound stern, but his own guilt made it agonized.

"I confess my presumption. I prayed that it was the right thing to do."

At the least sign of submission on Lucan's part Quintus would have saddled him with his own guilt. "I was counting on you to manage the farm if I were drafted," he confessed.

"A scapegoat manage the farm?" Lucan replied incredulously.

"Precisely. And go under with it." Quintus sat down. "That's where I was, back then. Ready to sacrifice you. Your departure jolted me out of my apathy. I really can't blame you for going. But why didn't you come back when I sent for you at Nicaea?"

"I-I couldn't come back empty handed, sir."

"You had no reason not to. Now Lucan, really, why?"

"I had just found myself, sir, my life work. I wasn't willing to give it up. I could not return until I was certain within myself why. And how I felt about you, sir. About myself. About . . . slavery . . ." Lucan stopped suddenly.

"Yes, you do have that streak of independence in you, don't you?"

Lucan spoke boldly. "You had to know where I was in Rome, sir. I told you in my letter."

"Your . . . letter?"

They stared at each other and slowly realized together what must have happened to that accompanying letter with a copy, in Lucan's own hand, of the new Nicene Creed. Neither wanted to admit it. Lucan continued quickly.

"Both Vincentius and Marcellus knew I was in the city. When you needed me, I trusted that you would recall me. Right or wrong, I put my life on your understanding."

"You trusted me so much that you postponed your obedience and pursued your trade as long as possible," Quintus interpreted.

"Yes, sir," Lucan admitted dejectedly. "I didn't know about the trestle, sir."

"I stupidly made fun of the magistrate. Wouldn't have made any difference if you were here or there. I'll admit, Lucan, that I could have easily found you and sent for you. The truth is that I was not prepared to handle your return. You see, it could have been . . . very difficult . . . for Letitia. I-I . . . we . . . she had a hard time, Lucan, transferring her devotion from you to me. I'm not certain that she wouldn't yet be powerfully attracted to you."

"She tells me that she is close to you, Quintus, in more ways than one," Lucan reassured him.

"How I lean on her! How she bears me up! Even if we lose the villa, I have it all in her! It would devastate me to lose her, Lucan, do you understand what I am saying?" Quintus rubbed his forehead.

"I understand, sir." There was a slight tremor in Lucan's voice.

"Twice back then I tried to give her to you, and twice you refused."

"And both times I declined on my own free will, sir."

"I did not deserve your deference, Lucan."

"That was for me to decide, Domine."

"Supposing I had run off to the front?"

"I made certain that you were back, sir, before I left Puteoli."

"Damn! You can be so annoyingly . . . thorough!"

A flicker of a smile came to Lucan's mouth.

"You love her, Lucan," Quintus challenged suddenly.

"M-my s-sister!" Lucan protested. He was trembling visibly now.

"Lucan, you dodged me with that once before! Lucan?"

An intense sensation of danger shivered down Lucan's spine. "How can I put your mind at ease? Shall I leave immediately after the census?"

"Yes do! No, don't go! Stay awhile," Quintus acquiesced. "We both love you. Letitia and I have to work things out. You can help."

"I will need to see her alone, Quintus, can you tolerate that?"

"It will drive me insane, but I trust you will maintain your impeccable virtue."

"She loves you, Quintus, how did she put it? She says she loves you something fierce."

"Really?" Quintus's face shone. "She said that to you? I want to believe that!" Those words were like sunshine after a thunderstorm, like puddles of shouting frogs in the spring! If only he could hear those words from her lips!

"Don't let self-doubt get between you two," Lucan warned.

"Self-doubt?" Quintus's old problem.

"Perhaps I've spoken too freely."

"No, not at all, Lucan. You really should have come back sooner," he added appreciatively.

"I really intended to come home, sir. But not empty handed. I owe you so much."

"Home, you say, even though I ordered you back?"

"It would have been terribly hard to go through that gate without an immediate incentive."

"And now that you have?"

"I trust you, Quintus."

Quintus took a long breath and regarded him a moment. "Will you continue to trust me, through some difficult things that I have to tell you?"

"Yes, sir."

"About your status."

Lucan rose spontaneously to his feet and blanched.

"You are safe with me," Quintus tried to reassure him, "but you may want to sit down."

"I am ready, sir." Lucan remained on his feet.

Quintus was relieved that Lucan did not debase himself before him.

"First of all, Marcellus. The things that Marcellus hurled at you are true. About your background. Your illegitimate birth. If you were indeed freeborn and named after your origin rather than after your progenitor or your step-father's aspirations for you, then to this day, as a hereditary decurion of Lucania you would be liable to be hauled back in chains, bled for everything you've got, and put to death for deserting. Your adoptive father was a runaway decurion from Lucania. He really was old Lucan's slave; he had exchanged his freedom for your mother's so that he and his son could hide more effectively and so that their children would be freeborn. I knew that before I asked you to be my Quintipor! I did not think that you were ready to handle it, then."

Lucan's vision blackened. He bent and clasped wildly for the chair. When the ringing passed, he stood erect again. "I couldn't have been ready, sir," he admitted, and covered his face in grief. Pa! Oh Pater! Father sacrificed son—as an act of love! But the slave was spared. Lucan braced for the thunder in his head and the nauseous rebellion in his gut. Nothing happened. The demon of the past no longer had power over him! Conquered by a revelation of love!

"I also put out a search for your mother and sisters back then," Quintus continued gently. "Nothing. I am sorry."

"How can I thank you, sir!" Lucan spoke through the pain. Quintus waited silently for Lucan to recover himself.

"Now, Lucan, the bet." Quintus's uneasiness made Lucan shiver with apprehension. "That night when I sent you home to Good Will, Marcellus and I were testing a long standing bet. You went home. Then you ran away. Marcellus thinks he has claim over you. I think not."

"I pray to God . . ." Lucan began to tremble again.

"Having run off like that, are you aware of the civil charges on your head?"

"Yes, sir."

"Be advised that you have the right to a mediator. Shall we get one for you? What are your wishes?"

"To be alone with you, sir." What Lucan intended to do required privacy. As he stood before his master to face his charges, his ears rang with dread of the unavoidable accounting that would follow. He could not have anticipated that he was going to be so mortified before another human being. He knew that he could be a dead man on three counts. Quintus began to enumerate them before him. It was excruciating. Soon he had a white-knuckled hold on the chair back and molten lead swirled in his stomach.

"You are a runaway serf. Penalty, to be dragged back in chains and put to death. You posed as a citizen. Penalty by civil law, to be beheaded. You are branded as incorrigible, not allowed within a one-hundred mile radius of Rome. Penalty by civil law, death."

Safe in his master's pardon Lucan dared to confess with downcast eyes. "I am guilty as charged." He looked up in supplication to speak further. He had nothing more to lose and everything to gain.

"Yes?" Quintus prompted.

"If you do not press charges, sir, then who would prosecute me?" Lucan was outrageously presumptuous.

Quintus was overwhelmed. "What do you think I am," he cried out, "Christ or something? Do you think that I can influence the world? Do you think that I can bend the imperial law? Influence the Magistrate?"

"The consequences of my choices are entirely on my head," Lucan rescinded.

"The hell they are! Lucan, Lucan, I can hardly keep up with your . . . your . . . I can't find the right word! And the others! Have you thought about the others?"

"I have thought only of my family in Christ, sir."

"Your senior partner, Lucan. The families in the house church! They are all aiding and sheltering a fugitive, incorrigible, posing as a citizen. How can you possibly think that you alone will bear the consequences of your actions?"

"The shopkeeper will testify that he knows nothing of these. And the families are completely innocent."

"Silence, you fool! What I don't know can't be wrung from me!" Quintus cried in anguish.

Lucan was suddenly horrified at himself and his presumption. He sank low on his knees and quaked.

"I rest defenseless before you," he admitted dejectedly.

"You had better believe it!" Quintus emphasized.

"I am utterly and completely at your mercy," Lucan unconditionally surrendered.

"Absolutely. And at the Magistrate's mercy! You . . . must . . . understand!"

Lucan gasped.

"At least I didn't have to drag you home in chains."

Lucan drew breath slowly. This was no gentlemen's agreement, no brotherly reunion. Abject fear prickled the back of his neck. By some grandiose imagining he had returned to Good Will as God's commissioned emissary. In reality the master had lured him back to spare him chains and certain death. The commissioned one was but a blind worm under his master's heel. He was literally floored. He could not even move, paralyzed by the truth, the awful self-revelation.

"Lord of my life, my heart is crushed to ashes." He did not realize that he uttered it out loud.

The barely audible answer came swiftly. "Light of my life, shine on me again."

Did he really hear it, or was this more grandiose imagining? He could hardly get his next utterance out.

"Will I stand trial, sir?"

"Over my dead body!"

"Save me, Domine!" The plea escaped Lucan's lips even upon faith that he was safe.

"Save *me*, slave!" came the pained rejoinder.

Only their augmented breathing broke the silence.

"Domine, I am unworthy," Lucan finally acknowledged, still bowed.

"That is for me to decide, little brother," Quintus replied with compassion.

Little brother. There it was, that affirmation upon which Lucan staked his life. He slowly straightened on his knees and lifted his face and regarded his master in gratitude.

"Brother," he murmured, and their eyes met.

"Sit, Lucan, and listen to me. The Magistrate shall be here in a day or two to question you. You must take care that he has no cause to interrogate you in the manner customary for slaves. You wouldn't survive. He will ask you for your defense. You have not one pebble of civil ground for defense. But don't stand silent before him or you may be a dead man yet. You have matters of the heart for defense, Lucan! Tell him how it was with you! Tell him why you ran away! Tell him about your family in Christ! Tell him why you came back! If he does not press charges, then as you say, there will be no one to prosecute you. I have interceded with him at length. I have told him our story in detail. I have pleaded for your life and you shall plead for mine!"

Lucan was on his feet again.

"Brother, we must trust whatever Titus has in mind for you," Quintus cried in agitation. "Your voluntary return has already saved me from the jaws of the jailer."

Lucan searched his master's face and paled. Take his place in prison? "What does Titus have in mind, sir?" His voice was heavy with dread.

"Lucan, I have become quite adverse to being incarcerated in debtor's prison."

"Christ! I have grown quite unaccustomed to being a slave! Confine me and I can no longer contribute to your household. Release me, and I shall be as a jewel on your crown."

"Forgive me, Lucan! I cannot release you!"

They regarded each other in anguish. Lucan shuffled to catch his balance. Has the master truly betrayed him?

Quintus buried his face in his hands and leaned heavily on his desk. "I am condemned to use you, Lucan, don't you see? As I have asked you before: Lucan, are you willing?"

As soon as he said it, Quintus realized that it was wrong. Who do I think I am, anyway! God? Look at the shock on his face. Gods alive! If any man or god made such a requirement of me, I'd either tell him where to go, or kill myself. Self-giving is one thing, demand of human sacrifice another. How barbaric of me! What a presumptuous, bumbling fool I am! It's too late now. I've already said it. Look at the determination set in his face. He is not going to acquiesce this time. He's too strong. Look at him standing there in judgment of me. My God, he's dangerous!

"Lucan . . ." Quintus's face contorted in agony. Lucan, his creation! Lucan balanced on sword's edge between life and death! How he loved him! One misinterpreted word, one move, one jot or tittle or iota threatened catastrophe. He must not lose him!

Lucan knew that his time had come to act. He walked over to his master's chair, knelt beside him, put his arm around Quintus's shoulders, and clasped him tightly.

"Here, Quintus," he said softly, "here is my answer to you. Nobody is going to prison." He reached into his tunic.

"Oh Christ my family!" Quintus emitted a voiceless scream of terror and tensed for a dagger.

Marcellus eaves-dropping in the shadows of the colonnade drew his sword. Olipor and Marcipor monitoring him from behind restrained him silently.

"Quintus!" Lucan cried in horror. "Do you have no more faith in me than that?" He pulled a scroll out from his tunic. Its wrapping was soaked in his own sweat. He laid it on his master's desk. It was his savings and investment gains, in a bank draft made out to Quintus, for a large sum of money, more than enough to cover delinquent and current taxes and fees, and to buy his freedom many times over, and to free Quintus from being in debt to Marcellus. Quintus wept in relief and gasped behind his hands.

Marcellus let loose an expletive in the shadows and sheathed his sword.

"Domine?" Lucan called softly. "Domine? Quintus! Quintus, this is yours. Please accept it. Dear Brother, please, you have forgiven much. Please do not be so hard on yourself." Lucan released his master from his hold and started to leave.

Quintus opened the scroll, swallowed, and stared at it.

"It was you!" he uttered in sudden comprehension. "That anonymous donor when I was in prison! Damn you, slave, are you trying to buy me?" His voice rang out after Lucan so that the entire household must have heard.

Lucan faced his master again. "Quintus, I owe you so much."

"Lucan, I *own* you!"

"I realize that, sir."

"Then that is why you sent money?"

"Because of your need, sir."

"Did you think that you could save me?"

"Did you not more than once save me?"

"To repay me then, is this why you came home so willingly? To put me in your debt, perhaps? To relieve me of Good Will? And go down with it?"

Lucan turned his heel on his master's raving.

"Lucan if you walk out on me you're not coming back alive!"

The master's intensity spun him in his tracks. He scrutinized Quintus's face, his every pore alert.

"What else do you expect?" Quintus lashed at him.

Lucan hesitated and studied his master's face before he answered.

"To stand before you as a man."

"Very well, man, you shall!" Quintus bounded to his feet and his hip rebelled so that he had to grasp the desk for balance. He grabbed a key, fumbled with the lock of the strong box, snatched out a parchment, unrolled it and turned it toward Lucan. "Here! Sign!"

Lucan was stunned. It was his writ! That was not what he meant! He didn't even know that such a thing existed. But here it was, dated on the day Quintus rode to Rome with his brothers and tested the bet. It was signed, waiting only to be countersigned. Here before him was his heart's desire. But the writ of manumission, because of broken laws, bore the sting of death. With his demise all of Good Will would fall. His beloved family in Christ would sink to the depths. He met Quintus's eyes.

Quintus's look was excruciatingly anxious. Lucan's was profoundly sad.

"Forgive me, Lucan, that I did not give this to you before we were trapped by the Colonate law."

"Put that thing back," Lucan whispered hoarsely. Manumission or bondage would not change one iota of what he intended to do for this household and for this man before him who had saved his life and given him a family.

"Actually Titus promised me your life if I never give you your freedom," Quintus replied with immense relief. "Should circumstances change, you need only countersign before witnesses."

Quintus put the writ back. When he turned toward the desk again, Lucan couldn't be certain what happened. Did Quintus falter? They were in each other's arms in tight embrace, weeping openly, Quintus in sheer joy and gratitude that he and his household were saved, Lucan crucified by the truth that had he signed himself away to detachment from this household, as of old he would have been forced to watch helplessly while his beloved family went down to certain destruction before his very eyes, while the state buggered him and stoppered his mouth to silence.

Quintus began to comprehend the totality of Lucan's sacrifice. He sank slowly to his chair. Lucan sank with him to his knees and pressed his face into his master's breast and trembled, trembled.

"We shall each stand before the other as man to man, I promise you," Quintus affirmed, and stroked Lucan's neck where the branded cross lay.

"In the name of Christ," Lucan cried. They clasped each other again in complete mutuality, in resurrection of their love.

"Oh for Christ sake!" Marcellus jeered under his breath and retired with Marcipor to his guest room.

Olipor slipped away to his room before he should be found out.

CHAPTER XXIX

Restored and commissioned

Quintus dragged himself upstairs to his bedroom. He was dismayed to find their infant and Dulce on his bed with Letitia. Without a word Dulce took up the infant and vanished.

He stood there looking like doomsday gazing down at Letitia so that she called out his name in alarm.

"Quintus?"

"I don't know whether to embrace you or thrash you!"

"Quintus, what is it!"

"You knew," he accused her, "you knew all the time!"

"Knew . . . what?"

"The anonymous donor. Who he was. Where he was hiding."

"I honor confidences," she stated simply.

Quintus cussed.

"You didn't tell me about your interrogations, Quintus, the anguish that Titus put you through. I could have sent for Lucan."

"You didn't need that worry," Quintus retorted.

"We're in this together," she reminded him.

"You should talk! What did you do with that letter?" he demanded.

"What letter?" she blanched.

"What letter," he mocked. "Rather, which letter! Which of how many?"

She evaded his glare.

He seized her by the shoulders and forced her to face him. He hurt. She had done wrong and she knew it. She knew it at the time, that it was a rebellious act of protectiveness. Suddenly she was that little slave girl again, in the clutches of the big bullies who held her by the wrists and stripped her of her clothing. Then her savior had galloped up on a pony and had charged into them with a pony whip. The 'punty whip' still hung on the wall. Only now the savior was threatening her with male brutality and with his male betrayal was shattering their mutual trust so carefully nurtured over the years.

Crushed to the core, she reverted to abject female submission.

"What letter, Quinnie," she managed.

"That he sent with the copy of the Nicene Creed written in his own hand."

"I was afraid of what you would do," she confessed.

"You could have ruined us by holding back like that! By God you still love him!" His accusing look bore into her.

Terror seized her throat. She got up on her knees and took his hands and pressed her face into them.

"I did it for us, for you and me," she wailed, and the tears overflowed. "Because I love you, Quintus!"

"What!?" he whispered, the anger inside him abruptly becoming a hushed silence straining to hear any intonation of the long desired words. He sank down to the bed and drew her close to his breast. "Repeat what you just said?" he whispered tremulously in her ear.

She answered, afraid of her own voice. "Gentle, compassionate Quintus, my patron, my husband, I love you. I love you something fierce!"

How long he waited for those words! She was finally, actually confessing! Like gentle rain hissing into the parched soil! Like every alfalfa seed in the hayfield leaping to life! She truly meant it! Good Will could sink but he would survive on that firm foundation!

"It's all right, Tish, it's all right! We're saved! Do you hear? Marcellus will not have to sell out from under us! I no longer have to be indebted! You'll see!"

"The anonymous donor?" Her tone was suddenly anxious.

"I didn't have to take it from him, Letitia. Our salvation was by his own initiative! It was volunteered! Freely given! Unconditional! God! It's humiliating!"

"And you? He . . . ?" Her voice refused to ask it.

"I have no choice but to accept what is already mine! And I finally understand what must have happened between Aulus and Ophelus—Olipor. I'm quite certain I finally uncovered Pater's secret! And I have one better over him!" He laughed through tears and they wept for joy in each other's embrace.

"Yes, you're entirely right, they did a switch about."

"How did you know, Letitia?"

"Every room of the villa is open and functional under my supervision, as you know. Those old family furnishings I restored, the old trunks I rescued when the atrium flooded, they all tell a story, Quintus. And a certain person, delighted to see old treasures, talked."

"What a devoted little honeybee you are!" he complimented her most highly.

* * *

Meanwhile Lucan went to the sickroom and rummaged in the cupboard for a tonic to relieve his raging stomach. Then he retired upstairs, buried his face in the pillow, wept in sheer catharsis, and grieved the slave's fate of being forever exploited. "Slavery!" he uttered, visualizing his father shouting from the burning beam. "Worse than death! Weep not for me, but for yourself."

A barely audible sound like a stifled gasp came from the darkness.

What was that! Had someone set him up? Was not Marcellus still in the house? Is this why Quintus did not want the household to know of his return?

"Who's there?" he demanded. "Answer me!" He bounded onto the floor on the other side of the bed from the presence, every nerve taut for defense. He scanned the darkness for any sign of movement. Suddenly he was back at the frontier fending off the enemy who would steal into a soldiers' tent at night and slit the throat of only one infantryman among the eight. Damn that he hadn't gotten out his dagger! Terror prickled the back of his neck.

Only the enemy started to hum softly that haunting nursery tune.

"What are the words to that?" he breathed with relief.

"Say hen hen without the rooster?" she sang lightly.

"Hen hen," he heard himself sing back and they fell across the bed, reaching for each other, weeping and laughing in each other's arms.

"Lucia! Lucia!"

"Shh! It took you long enough to recognize me!"

"Doesn't anyone know?"

"No one! I'm just another underground refugee to the House Church at Puteoli. Off the ship from Alexandria. Running from the Ariomaniacs. It was enough for me to walk the same paths, and breathe the same air, and use the cookbook in your hand. Then they said that you were located in Rome, and that you would be coming back!"

"Were you really a prostitute?"

"I cooked for them. My hysteria about . . . other services . . . is only half real but it spared me."

"How did you ever?"

"That Man Wanted poster all over the Alexandria marketplace! I took a poster to my room! It had to be you. Who else had a Latin and Greek name like that?"

"That was four years ago!"

"Are you telling me?"

"How on earth?"

"I'm an Oikonomikos, you know, resourceful. Actually Deacon Leander who brings the sacrament to our house recognized the poster. Then things happened fast."

"Leander," Lucan whispered. "Bless you, brother!"

They talked quietly for what seemed hours. The late, waning moon illuminated the room. Then there was a tap on the door.

"Dulce? Are you in there, Dulce?" Letitia stepped into the room.

Dulce got up and embraced her. "Mistress! Oh dear Mistress! Thank you so much! My brother was dead and now he is brought to life again! Restored to me again!"

"Brother?" Letitia gave Lucan an annoyed look. "Very well, Dulce. Listen, the children are awake and whimpering for you. Please, before they awaken Quintus."

"Right away, Mistress." Dulce dashed down the moonlit hall.

Letitia put her hands on her hips. "Lucan, I don't think I know you anymore," she chided.

"My sister!" He started to explain, then changed his mind.

"Where have I heard that before? Go back to bed, Lucan," she ordered and went back herself.

He must have slept, for he was next conscious of daylight and whispering and giggling at the side of his bed. He turned toward the children.

Lucian stood up. "Daddy said you can come riding with us!" he declared. "I get to ride with Olipor."

"Daddy says you can take me!" Libra piped up. "And Daddy can take Jocelyn."

Lucan regarded them through half-slits. "Wake me up," he smiled. With whoops of delight the children were on the bed. They threw aside the covers and tickled him until he was on the floor in self-defense.

"Enough! Enough! I'm awake!" he laughed, and hugged them both and sent them off with pats on their behinds. "I'll meet you at the horses."

Because Wednesday was a station day in commemoration of the Lord's betrayal, Lucan did not eat or drink anything but toured the farm directly with Quintus and Olipor on horseback, each holding a child in front of him in the saddle. He rode none other than Rainbow.

"Well, here's the reckless rider," Mamercus greeted him back at the stable.

Lucan lost face at the reminder. "I didn't ruin Ignis, Mamercus?"

"Not ruined," Mamercus replied. "Sired some outstanding foals. How did you like our darling little brood mare?"

"Where is the little Arab groom that came with her?"

"It was you who sent the filly!" Mamercus realized. "The boy died! Got sick on the spring fava beans!"

At noon Lucan went to the kitchen and visited the household there. Dorothea, lovely with expressive wrinkles and a halo of snowy hair, met him at the kitchen door and embraced him.

"Look!" she cried out. "Our little son is back!"

"Why, here's the little filly!" Sextus exclaimed.

"There's the little cheesepot!" Kaiso slapped Lucan on the back.

His greeting forced a chuckle of surprise from Lucan.

"Kaiso!" he took up. "Are you head cook now?" He regarded Kaiso's obese figure. "The position has done you well! Who helps you?"

"There are new women in the villa to help," Dorothea laughed.

"Here! I'll show you!" Sextus declared. "Cloemene!" he shouted into the servants' hall. She appeared, exquisite, obviously pregnant. "A gift from Marcellus, his flute girl. On the condition that I keep her perpetually in the condition she came in . . ." Sextus gestured generously with his arms.

"Well, you're the one who can do it!" Lucan quipped, and they laughed. The embarrassed woman hid in her husband's arms and he kissed her hair.

"Ask Marcellus to find you one," Sextus said.

Lucan shook his head.

"Anyone special in Rome?" Dorothea lifted her brow in interest.

Lucan's lips curled in a melancholy smile. With the weight on his head, he could never marry.

"Come on in, dear, and meet Lucan," Dorothea moved toward the door to the hall and brought in a sophisticated young woman whom Aulus had snatched from the dealer before anyone touched her. "Lucan, meet Demetria."

Lucan stared, astounded. "Sis? Lysistra?"

"Bug off," Gaius growled. "My wife."

"Pardon me! Hello Gaius."

"Alexis has a wife also," Dorothea continued, "a refugee through the church underground rescue."

Lucan glanced around to see if Alexis's wife were there, and noticed the diminutive boy sitting in the corner, clasping his arms around his knees and rocking on his buttocks.

"And you are . . . ?" Lucan asked.

"My fourth son," Cara beamed, "my freedom child, aren't you, Bobo," she crooned at the boy who smiled back and rocked even faster, controlling his head movements with effort. Cara's fourth son, born out of change-of-life passion, was a spastic.

"Peace, Bobo!" Lucan greeted him. He embraced Cara.

"Bobo queried with a touch of disdain in his voice, "Are you the runaway slave?"

"Yes, only a runaway slave," Lucan replied.

"Ha, ha! You gonna get flogged!"

"Bobo, that's not polite!" Cara chided. "Him is the first among us!"

"Pray for me, Bobo," Lucan said.

"We already does. We will!" Cara responded. "Come, come, Bobo, we goes back up the hill now."

Lucan continued greeting others as they came in. "Well, old plowman," he took Baltus's hand. "Do you plow the new fields or do we have to . . . trench soil?"

"Trench soil, you bum," Baltus grinned and black Manius his mute assistant leered.

"I will, when I need a rest from my copywork."

"Copywork?" Gaius repeated. That explained the tunic.

"It does sound strange, doesn't it, that the runaway comes home with a commission?"

"Home," Sextus echoed.

"Really presumptuous," Gaius said.

"You'd be interested, Gaius. St. Ignatius's letter, the forged insertion laying a precedence for Arianism, and the long recension in the Ante-Nicene Fathers."

Gaius returned a blank look.

"Postumus has some young men to help trench soil," Baltus filled in the awkwardness, "rescued, you know."

"And Megas? Does he still supply you with wood?" Lucan asked Dorothea.

Dorothea glanced away and replied quietly, "Megas has run away. On the last anniversary of his capture."

"The domine and his brothers located his family," Olipor explained. "Megas was sent on trust to escort them down here. They made a break for it instead. You can guess the rest."

"The state, Olipor? The state hunted them down before Domine could bring them back . . . and . . . and . . . ?"

"The soldiers. He resisted. We lost Marius. Megas and his entire bloodline went down."

Olipor evaded Lucan's eyes and Lucan shuddered with horror.

"He wasn't as . . . fortunate . . . as you," Gaius stood off and commented.

Lucan acknowledged the rebuke. He now understood Quintus's own reaction of terror the previous night. "And old Servius?" he inquired, looking past Gaius into the servants' hall, "where's old Servius?"

"Yes, he's sleeping," Olipor said.

"We buried him three winters ago," Dorothea explained. He died quietly. The young domine nursed him himself in his last illness."

"That sounds like Quintus," Lucan said appreciatively.

"You were afraid to face him?" Sextus asked.

"If you want the honest truth, yes."

"Come on," Sextus urged, "we want to hear your story, man!"

"Some other time, when we have a long evening."

"Are you going to be staying with us?" Kaeso asked.

"For a while . . . I . . . depends on . . ."

"Depends on how long he can keep the peace." Gaius's sarcasm bit.

"That's about right, Gaius," Lucan laughed nervously.

"Gaius! What is the matter with you!" Olipor openly chided his brooding son.

So unusual was a public rebuke from his father that Gaius's scalp tingled. "I've been displaced, that's what!"

"And what have you done to . . ." Olipor began, somewhat shocked.

"Done! What have I done!" Gaius answered his father with a burst of temper. "First of all, I didn't desert the farm, and what about that lousy dealing with Letitia! Getting her pregnant so she'd marry him!"

"Gaius, please!" Demetria took him by the arm and tried to escort him out. The house of Ophelus had some fine material upon which to rise, but Demetria was childless.

"Leave me be!" He shook her off and turned angrily on Olipor. "And then my savings. I've spent nearly all my years working day and night toward the freedom price and . . . well . . . in the last generation when desperate domine sold himself out of life imprisonment for his steward's savings, there was a switch about in status."

"Gaius." Olipor checked him sharply.

"You can't tell me you're not disappointed, Dad. Look at me . . . little I've gained for my faithful service. Instead he!" Gaius pointed at Lucan. "He runs away, comes back with his freedom price, and is treated like a savior or something. What kind of justice is that!"

Olipor answered his son with cool heat. "In the first place, Gaius, we . . . you . . . were as much saving your own skin as the domine's and you know it.

Secondly, you have Lucan completely wrong. He comes back not for his own gain but as a savior of us all, and your domine's most beloved brother."

Gaius stormed out of the kitchen. Demetria apologized and followed. The others gaped. Lucan, deeply embarrassed, turned to go.

"A word with you first, son," Olipor regained himself and led the way to his room.

"Olipor, you still call me son."

"If I didn't know the truth about the cussedness of human nature, I'd disown you!"

"Pater!" Lucan seized Olipor's arms. The old man was on his side.

"You have taken upon yourself the wisdom that was beaten into me."

"Olipor . . ."

"It hurts. I know it hurts. Lucan, I salute you."

"Please . . ."

"What Gaius says is true, about the switch about in status, when the rescued master sent the steward back into the city to insure a steady income. Your domine is brooding upstairs. You can expect him to until he accepts the fullness of what you have done," Olipor meditated.

Lucan released himself. "Olipor, I am only doing my duty as his slave."

"That is not how he is taking it, Lucan."

"I owe him! I am not trying to buy him! Is Quintus still worried about that?"

"He is raking himself over for accepting your sacrifice so readily."

"Mio Dio."

"He was as completely unprepared for your gift as you were for his. You have done a good thing, Lucan. And I think that you will be relieved to know that Marcellus has forfeited his claim on you."

"Olipor! You nearly had us all done for, when you ushered me into the hands of Marcellus!"

"I was sick with worry when I realized it. He thought that you used your savings to extricate yourself from your senior partner. He is astonished that you have ransomed your domine without changing places with him. I pointed out that your position with your domine had already changed; it was transformed. And do you know what he said? 'By the gods you'd think this nonsense was God's Truth!'" Olipor clapped Lucan on the shoulder affectionately. "I will arrange with the bishop to have you restored to the flock at worship tomorrow morning, in anticipation of the Resurrection Day!"

The penitent bowed his head in gratitude. He saw clearly now that he was a new man. Fifteen years ago, his secure world had been destroyed. Eight years ago he had stormed these gates broken, and God had made him whole. Now he entered again, sent, to be broken and forgiven and healed many times over, certainly, but commissioned. Go, beloved, and I will fit you for the task to which I have commissioned you.

I obey, Lord. Lord, help me!

CHAPTER XXX

To wash one another's feet

That same Wednesday afternoon Marcellus made an excursion to the public baths where he joined Titus and the other dandies. To his disgust the disappointment of the week followed him. The blues had lost at the races last Sunday, and with the defeat Marcellus lost a tidy sum. That meant he could not have covered Quintus's taxes for him if he needed to. He did not want his friends to know that his financial embarrassment was wiped away by his tenant farmer's incorrigible slave. Then there was the nagging worry that he could still lose Good Will to the state. Nor was that all. His friends did not let him forget that the Magistrate won the span of magnificent bays back from him the other day on the highway.

"That was quite a race, I hear, Marcellus," a dandy commented through the laughs of his friends.

"You said it!" Marcellus added wryly, "It was like this: my blacks came in second, and Titus's span . . . well, Titus came in next to the last!" At this he dunked the Magistrate in the tepid pool. Only it did not seem to be as much fun. Nor did he enter into the ball game of keepaway with the usual enthusiasm. A whole life of wasteful and exploitative living pressed on his mind.

"Think fast, Marcellus!" Marcellus made a half-hearted pass at the ball coming his way. It splashed in the water behind him.

"Say, old boy, what's the matter with you today! Sluggish in the head?"

That's it! Old boy. I am old. I have done everything—useless. Even if I am the best damned instructor of virgins in the state brothel. That's just it . . . damned . . . for exploiting women. Life is a perpetual circle of meaninglessness. Endless. Endless. No, it isn't as pretty as a perfect circle. Life is a distorted circle. Life is an oval race track.

Yet he experienced times when life could be straightened out into a continuum with a definite beginning and a purpose. The time he rescued Quintus and was forgiven by him was like that. A new beginning. Now see what he did with his new beginnings!

Lucan's words kept turning in his mind, Lucan, whom he had abused. Marcellus, please do not destroy yourself. Member of a family . . . do not destroy yourself . . . brother in Christ . . . do not destroy . . .

Marcellus could not shake off the light lady who kept rippling her way up to his side. Her coan bathing dress clung and revealed an exquisite bosom, but he did not take interest today.

By my indifference I desert my God . . . by my uncertainty of convictions I deny him . . . by my indecision I crucify him . . . Marcellus had overheard Marcipor in an act of contrition preparing for the Pascha. Christ is risen. Triumphant. Forgiving. In whose service is perfect freedom . . .

The only cure for cynicism is an honest look at oneself, and when Marcellus took courage to put aside all his inner cloaks and see his inner self stark naked, he was ashamed of what he saw. He searched the benches lining the pool for Marcipor. The slave was not there. He was passing his time in the reading room of the public library.

"Hey you!" Marcellus called at a public slave. "Get me Marcipor . . . at the books . . . and fast!" At this his friends poked crass fun at him.

"Oh I know, I know," cried the light lady, "you have another sweetheart, do you, or have you taken a bride?"

"Not exactly," Marcellus rejoined. "The Bridegroom is coming and here he finds me naked and unclean!"

"Bridegroom!" His friends became wild with teasing. "You haven't taken to older men! By the gods, you're not a *pathicus*?"

Marcipor appeared, who had been duly warned by the public slave that his domine was "acting queer in the head."

"My towel, Marcipor." Marcellus ascended the steps out of the water and wrapped himself immediately with unprecedented modesty. He went quickly to the locker room. He smirked at the identifying painting above his tray. It was a lascivious sex scene intended to provoke laughter that would drive evil spirits from his vulnerable nudity. It failed to lift his dark mood. He dressed, and to the disappointment of his friends and the light lady, went directly home.

"One more thing before I dismiss you tonight, Marcipor. When you go up to Good Will to worship tomorrow morning, I'm coming with you."

"Sir!"

"Yes, all these years I've looked the other way when you snuck up there. And I've been aware of the many things you endure on my account. Marcipor, I've never spoken to you in this way before. Marcipor . . . Andrew . . . I have seen things happen at Good Will and in this room that no mere men can perform. I'm going to Good Will, I'm going to-ah-follow through on Lucan."

"Yes, Domine, of course." Then Marcipor threw caution to the wind. "Certainly you will be welcome, Domine."

* * *

Early Maundy Thursday Marcellus pounded vigorously with his foot on the atrium door at Good Will. Quintus greeted him quietly. He was in no mood for Marcellus to meddle in his affairs today.

"Quintus! Titus—the Magistrate—is a mere half mile behind me. My blacks outran his bays! I have come to warn you. You must act quickly. Get Lucan out of here, if you're going to."

"Do me a favor when he comes in, Marcellus?" Quintus was evasive.

"Yes?" Marcellus's voice was edged with suspense.

"Send him to my office in the atrium, would you?"

"Count on it, friend."

"Is that why you came up here at this hour, Marcellus? To warn me?" Quintus managed a smile.

"Actually, Beans, I've come to witness you lunatics in action."

"You . . . what?"

"I came to visit your house church. But the Magistrate comes breathing fire!"

"Not so fast, my friend. I have an appointment with the Magistrate. About a-a-an unsettled matter with my slave."

"Your brother in Christ?"

"No sarcasm today, please, Marcellus."

"No sarcasm, Quintus. As you said, Lucan has come back to you! I tried to demoralize him and he pleaded with me not to destroy myself. And this same kind of forbearance has come from Marcipor. What I took to be infidelity on Marcipor's part turned out to be supreme loyalty. And you, Quintus, you—"

"Marcellus, you're gushing." Quintus was certain that his friend ridiculed him.

"Not at all! I've seen Divine Love at work and I want to—"

"Meet Titus for me, would you, Marcellus? Send him to the alcove?" Quintus interrupted tersely and limped toward the office in the alcove.

"Serves me right," Marcellus uttered. Yet he was not going to let his friend down this time. When Titus came to the door, Marcellus intercepted him.

"Now Titus, before you prosecute this household, let me talk to you. I am prepared to cover any fines for him." Marcellus gestured toward Quintus's office. "I-I'll get the money, believe me!"

"Is Quintus in there?" Titus asked curtly.

"My blacks, Titus, I'll give you my blacks!" Marcellus followed after him.

Titus only laughed.

"Gods alive, Titus, haven't these two suffered enough? Look at the two of them, on their knees together!"

Titus turned in mid-stride and stared at him full face.

"Is that what you think, Marcellus? Now if you will excuse me," Titus returned deaf ears.

"Listen, Titus," Marcellus detained him by the sleeve. "Quintus has letters from influential people strongly recommending Lucan. Including his former employer Bishop Alexander, and his senior partner in Rome. The partner has great aspirations for him. In the New Rome next year. He can save Good Will from obliteration! He can keep our heads above water here so the decurion won't have to fill our tax quota out of his shrinking purse! Or worse, sell Good Will to the state! Drop the charges! Eradicate Lucan's incorrigible status! Let him return to the city! Give him the benefit of the *Lex Aulius*; you know that they had chained him without his master's consent! That they had branded stolen goods! Quintus had to compensate the old man. Allow Lucan the loophole!"

"Are you quite finished?" Titus strode past Marcellus toward the office.

"Are you going to destroy the goose that lays the golden egg?" Marcellus called after him.

"Now you sound more like yourself, Marcellus. Jupiter!" Titus continued under his breath, "why else do you think I'm keeping him pinioned!"

Marcellus felt inconsequential. Something crucial was happening on his own property that he could not control. He moved slowly toward the kitchen.

Marcipor saw him approach and came out from the hallway to meet him. "Do you care to join us, sir?"

"Marcipor? I can't bear not knowing what's happening."

Marcipor gestured toward the kitchen. "I'll explain as we go along."

"I mean, in the office. Do you know?"

"I pray that it is less than I fear and more than I hope." Marcipor pointed out that the household was keeping a prayer vigil for Lucan and Quintus. Then he started explaining the Maundy Thursday liturgy, on which day penitents were restored to communion in anticipation of Resurrection Day. Marcellus didn't hear a thing he said.

When they saw movement from the office, Marcipor interrupted himself. They watched them emerge. Lucan walked tall. Looking self-satisfied, the Magistrate clasped arms all around, then departed immediately. With Letitia at his side, Quintus led the way across the atrium to the kitchen. It seemed to Marcellus that Quintus strode quite freely for one who had been broken on the trestle. Marcellus fell in behind Marcipor. As he entered the kitchen, Olipor was reading the Gospel for Maundy Thursday.

> "If I then, your Lord and Teacher, have washed
> your feet, you also ought to wash one another's feet.
> For I have given an example that you should do
> as I have done to you."

Finis

BIBLICAL QUOTES AND ALLUSIONS FOR PERUSAL

Revised Standard Version

NOT BY FORCE BUT BY GOOD WILL, Roman proverb

You shall not give up to his master a slave who has escaped, Deut 23:15-16
I am sending him back to you, sending my very heart, Philem 1:12

PART I: Abba, Father

Chapter I: Rescued into slavery 1

he has heard my voice and my supplications, Ps 116

Chapter II: One of us 16

light of the world, Mt. 5:14, Lk 2:32, Ac 13:47, Phil 2:15
The stone which the builders rejected, Psalm 118:22
Christ being raised from the dead dies no more, Rom 6:9-11
the promise of the Father, God's Holy Spirit, Jn 16:16
with us always, even to the end of the world, Mt 28:20
as by a man came death, 1 Cor 15:20-22
As a deer longs for the flowing streams, Ps 42
The Lord is my shepherd, Ps 23
a member of Christ, Eph 3:6, Gal 3:27
fellow heir with Christ, Rom 8:17

Chapter III: The courage to respond 45

now in a mirror dimly, then face to face, 1 Cor 13:12
the great among us must be our servant, Mt 20:25-28, Mk 10:42-44, Lk 22:24-27
my yoke is easy, Mt 11:30
I am the true vine, Jn 15:1, Rom 11:16
receive a hundredfold now, Mk 10:29-30

Chapter IV: A price on his head 66

He who has seen me has seen the Father, Jn 14:9
as by a man came death, 1Cor 15:21
as one man's trespass, Rom 5:18-19
no one knows the Father except the Son, Mt 11:27
seek not what is too difficult, Ecclus. 3:21 (Apocrypha)
The Lord created me at the beginning of his work, Prv 8:22-24
Wisdom has built her house, Prv 9:1
my witnesses to the ends of the earth, Acts 1:8-11
Slaves, be obedient, Eph 6:5-8, 1 Pt 2:18, Tit 2:9-10
be subject to the governing authorities, Rom 13:1-2
God's sun and rain fall impartially, Mt 5:45

Chapter V: Give him your heart 84

When thou sendest forth thy Spirit, Ps 104:30
How good . . . when brothers dwell in unity, Ps 133:1-4
you have led captivity captive, Ps 68:18
serve from the heart, Eph 6:5-7
by grace you have been saved through faith, Eph 2:8

Chapter VI: A very spiritual task 92

In the beginning was the Word, Jn 1:1
lord of the harvest, Mt 20:1-16
remain in the state in which he was called, 1Cor 7:20,24
a slave is a freedman of the Lord, 1 Cor 7:22

Be not like a horse or a mule, Ps 32:9
you are neither hot nor cold, Rev 3:15
I stand at the door and knock, Rev 3:20
Be angry, but sin not, Ps 4:3-4
We love because he first loved us, 1 Jn 4:10, 1 Jn 4:19
For God so loved the world, Jn 3:16-21
The Last Supper, Mt 26:26-29, Mk 14:22-24, Lk 22:17-20
I wait for the Lord, Ps 130:5
Eucharistic prayers, Hippolytus, Ap Trad 4, 10:4 (Dix)

Chapter XI: The least of my brothers 165

Love is patient and kind, 1 Cor 13:4-8
I AM WHO I AM, Ex 3:14
as you did it to one of the least of my brethren, Mt 25:40
For God so loved the world, Jn 3:16

PART II: Lord, I am not worthy

Chapter XII: Keep the possibility open 183

Wives be subject to your husbands, Eph 5:22, Col 3:18, 1 Peter 3:1
husbands love your wives as yourselves, Eph 5:25, Col 3:19, 1 Peter 3:7
the unmarried and widows remain single, 1 Cor 7:32
if a slave when called, there remain with God, 1 Cor 7:21-24
brothers baptized into the family of Christ, Gal 3:26-27, 1 Cor 12:13
no slave nor free, Jew nor Greek, male nor female, God shows no partiality, Rom 10:12, Gal 2:6, 3:28, Eph 6:9
the unmarried man, 1 Cor 7:1, 8, 25
love the lord your God . . . and your neighbor, Mt 22:37-39
the two shall become one, Eph 5:31-32
you are all one in Christ Jesus, Gal 3:28
the beloved ewe lamb, 2 Sam 12:1-4

Chapter XIII: Bonded without bondage 196

shadows lengthen, Book of Common Prayer, 1979, p 833
worldly matters not worth a Christian's pursuit, Mt 6:19-21
slave ask what is fair? Jn 21:22

Chapter XIV: The way of the world 208

done only what we ought to have done, Lk 17:7-10
forgiven a transgression, Mt 18:21-22, Jn 8:7, Col 3:12-13, Eph 4:31-32
Blessed are the peacemakers . . . persecuted, Mt 5:9-10
The subtle pressures of love, 1 Cor 13:7.

Chapter XV: A stiff-necked people 223

The Lord is my rock, Ps 18:1-2, 2 Sam 22:2-3, Ps 62:2
turn other cheek, Mt 5:39, do not seek revenge, Lev 19:18, Rom 12:19
You are the man, 2 Sam 12:7
Purge me with hyssop, Ps 51:7-10

Chapter XVI: House built on a rock 236

make disciples of all nations, Mt 28:19
house upon the rock, Mt 7:24
endure pain unjustly, 1 Peter 2:18-21

Chapter XVII: Enduring all things 254

Cast all your anxieties on him, for he cares about you, 1 Pet 5:7
avoid pagan holidays, 1 Cor 10:14, 1 Cor 10:20, 1 Cor 15:33, 2 Cor 6:16-17, 1 Jn 5:21
burden endured in the name of the Lord, 1 Peter 2:18-21, 1 Cor 13:7

Chapter XVIII: Having neither to weigh thoughts nor measure words 265

weigh thoughts, Dinah Craik, 1859, A Life for a Life, Ch 16
I do not the good that I want, Rom 7:19

Chapter XIX: Lord of my life, my heart is crushed to ashes 272

My heart is in anguish within me Ps 55:4, 12-14
My God, why hast thou forsaken me? Ps 22:1-2, Ps 88:14-18
A broken and contrite heart, Ps 51:17

Chapter XX: The world does not come to an end ....

Try to be good by yourself, Rom 7:19-25.
Better to marry than burn with passion, 1 Cor 7:9
Judge not that you be not judged, Mt 7:1-5

PART III: But thanks be to God!

Chapter XXI: Light of my life, shine on me again 297

God loves his unthankful and bad children, Rom 10:21

Chapter XXII: The penalty has already been paid 309

Greater love has no man than this, Jn 15:13
more than a slave, as a beloved brother, Philem 1:15,16
We share abundantly in Christ's sufferings, 2 Cor 1:5
God shows his love for us in that while we were yet sinners Christ died for us, Rom 5:8
apart from me you can do nothing, Jn 15:5
Rainbow, a sign of God's promise to Noah, Gen 9:13-15

Chapter XXIII: If your brother has something against you 320

Do not drink to your damnation, 1 Cor 11:27-28
If your brother has something against you, Mt 5:23
If your brother sins against you, Mt 18:15, Mk 11:25
this is my body which is broken for you, Lk 22:19, Mt 26:26, Mk 14:22

Chapter XXIV: Of One Substance, to be obeyed 327

Be obedient . . . rendering service with good will as to the Lord, Eph 6:7
I and the Father are one, Jn 10:30
He who has seen me has seen the father, Jn 14:9
He is the image of the invisible God, Col 1:15
Christ who is the likeness of God, 2 Cor 4:4
he sent his Son to be the expiation for our sins, 1 Jn 4:10
he sent me, Jn 7:29, Jn 8:42, Jn 16:28, Jn 17:18, Jn 17:23

my Father and your Father, my God . . . your God, Jn 20:17, 28
no man knows the Father but the Son, Mt 11:27
In the beginning was the Word . . . and the Word was God, Jn 1:1
Christ Jesus, who, though he was in the form of God, Phil 2:6-8
you shall love your neighbor as yourself, Mt 22:39
See also Lev 19:18, Mt 19:19, Mk 12:31, Lk 10:27, Rom 13:9, Gal 5:14, Jas 2:8
No man has ever seen God; if we love one another, God abides in us, 1 Jn 4:12
love his brother also, 1 Jn 4:21
love one another, Jn 13:34, 1 Jn 3:11
you wrestle with God, Gen 32:24-30
Christ shall be the ladder, Gen 28:11-13, Jn 1:47-51
deny himself and take up his cross and follow me, Mt 10:38, Mt 16:24
light a lamp and put it under a bushel, Mt 5:15
buried the talent, Mt 25:14-30
You shall not give up to his master a slave who has escaped, Deut 23:15-16
no longer live for themselves but for him, 2 Cor 5:15
he who finds his life will lose it, Mt 10:39, Lk 17:33, Jn 12:25
Christ . . . gave us the ministry of reconciliation, 2 Cor 5:18-20
Christ leaving you an example that you should follow in his steps, 1 Pet 2:21

You have one master, the Christ, Mt 23:10
slaves freed in the seventh year, Ex 21:2
He who did not spare his own son, Rom 8:32

good shepherd leaves flock to find the lost lamb, Mt 18:12-14
your brother has something against you, Mt 5:23-24
if your brother sins against you, Mt 18:15-18
Lazarus was raised from the dead, Jn 11:43-44
your mansion has many rooms, Jn 14:2
freedman in Christ, 1Cor 7:22, Gal 3:28, Col 3:11
as you have done to the least of my brothers, Mt 25:40
deny yourself, Mt 16:24
invest your talent, Mt 25:14-30
slave's reward is more work, Lk 17:7-10

Chapter XXX: To wash one another's feet.. 406

The Bridegroom (Christ) is coming, Jn 3:29, 2 Co 11:2
Seen things happen, the new life, Col 3:12-15
Divine love at work, Eph 5:1-2
wash another's feet . . . I have given you an example, Jn 13:13-17, Gal 5:13, Lk 22:27

BVG